PACK OF CARDS

Penelope Lively

PACK OF CARDS

STORIES 1978–1986

HEINEMANN : LONDON

William Heinemann Ltd
10 Upper Grosvenor Street, London W1X 9PA
LONDON   MELBOURNE   TORONTO
JOHANNESBURG   AUCKLAND

This collection first published 1986
Copyright © Penelope Lively 1978, 1980, 1981,
1982, 1984, 1985, 1986
ISBN 0 434 42743 8

Filmset by
Deltatype Ltd, Ellesmere Port
Printed and bound in Great Britain by
Mackays of Chatham Ltd

Contents

Acknowledgements

THE FIRST fourteen stories in this volume were originally published by William Heinemann in 1978 as *Nothing Missing but the Samovar*: 'Nothing Missing but the Samovar'; 'The Voice of God in Adelaide Terrace'; 'Interpreting the Past'; 'Servants Talk About People: Gentlefolk Discuss Things'; 'Help'; 'Miss Charlton and the Pop Concert'; 'Revenant as Typewriter'; 'Next Term, We'll Mash You'; 'At the Pitt-Rivers'; 'Nice People'; 'A World of Her Own'; 'Presents of Fish and Game'; 'A Clean Death' and 'Party'.

'Corruption' was first published in *Encounter*, 1984; 'Venice, Now and Then' was first published in *Quarto*, 1980; 'Grow Old Along With Me, the Best Is Yet To Be' was first published in *Cosmopolitan*, 1984; 'The Darkness Out There' was first published in the Bodley Head collection, *You Can't Keep out the Darkness*, 1980, and read on BBC radio and Australian radio; 'Yellow Trains' was first published in *Vogue*, 1984; ' "The Ghost of a Flea" ' was first published in *The Literary Review*, 1980; 'The Art of Biography' was first published in *Good Housekeeping*, 1981; 'What the Eye Doesn't See' was first published in *Encounter*, 1981; 'The Emasculation of Ted Roper' was first published in *Encounter*, 1982. These nine stories, together with 'The Pill-Box' and 'Customers', were published by William Heinemann in 1984 as *Corruption*.

'A Long Night at Abu Simbel' was first published in *Encounter*, 1984; 'Bus-Stop' was first published under the title 'Transport of Delight' in *Woman's Own*, 1985; 'Clara's Day' was first published in *Good Housekeeping*, 1986; 'The French Exchange' was first published in the Bodley Head collection, *Misfits*, 1984; 'The Dream Merchant' was first published in *Good Housekeeping*, 1985; 'Pack of Cards' was first published in *Cosmopolitan*, 1986; 'The Crimean Hotel' was first published in *Encounter*, 1986; 'Black Dog' was first published in *Cosmopolitan*, 1986.

Nothing Missing but
the Samovar

It was July when he went to Morswick, early autumn when he left it; in retrospect it was to seem always summer, those heavy, static days of high summer, of dingy weather and outbursts of sunshine, of blue sky and heaped clouds. Of straw and horseflies. Blackberries; jam for tea; church on Sunday. The Landers.

Dieter Helpmann was twenty-four, a tall, fair young man, serious-looking but with a smile of great sweetness; among his contemporaries he seemed older than he was, sober, reserved, the quiet member of a group, the listener. He had come from Germany to do his post-graduate degree – a thesis on nineteenth-century Anglo-Prussian relations. His father was a distinguished German journalist. Dieter intended to go into journalism himself; he was English correspondent, now, for a socio-political weekly, contributing periodic articles on aspects of contemporary Britain. His English was perfect: idiomatic, lightly accented. His manners were attractive; he held doors open for women, rose to his feet for them, was deferential to his elders. All this made him seem slightly old-fashioned, as did his worried liberalism, which looked not shrewd nor edgy enough for a journalist. His gentle, concerned pieces about education, industrial unrest, the housing problem, read more like a sympathetic academic analysis of the ills of some other time than energetic journalism.

It was 1957, and he had spent eighteen months in England. The year before – the year of Suez and Hungary – he had seen his friends send telegrams to the Prime Minister fiercely dissociating themselves from British intervention; he had agonised alongside them outraged both with and for them; he had written an article on 'the alienation of the British intellectual' that was emotional and partisan. His father commented that he seemed deeply committed – 'The climate appears to suit you, in more ways than one.' And Dieter had written back, 'You are right – and it is its variety I think that appeals the most. It is a place that so much defies analysis – just as you think you have the measure of it, you stumble across yet another confusing way in which the different layers of British life overlap, another curious anachronism. I have to admit that I have caught Anglophilia, for better or for worse.'

He had. He loved the place. He loved the sobriety of the academic world in which he mostly moved. He loved all those derided qualities of reserve and restraint, he loved the landscape. He liked English girls, while remaining faithful to his German fiancée, Erika (also engaged on post-graduate work, but in Bonn). He liked and respected what he took to be a basic cultural stability; here was a place where things changed, but changed with dignity. To note, to understand, became his deep concern.

All that, though, took second place to the thesis. That was what mattered at the moment, the patient quarrying into a small slice of time, a small area of activity. He worked hard. Most of his waking hours were spent in the agreeable hush of great libraries, or alone in his room with his card index and his notebooks.

He had been about to start writing the first draft when it happened. 'I have had the most remarkable piece of luck,' he wrote to Erika. 'Peter Sutton – he is the friend who is working on John Stuart Mill, you remember – is married to a girl who comes from Dorset and knows a family whose forebear was ambassador in Berlin in the 1840s and apparently they still have all his papers. In trunks in the attic! They are an aristocratic family – Sir Philip Lander is the present holder of the title, a baronetcy. Anyway, Felicity Sutton has known them all her life (she is rather upper-class too, but intelligent, and married Peter at Cambridge, where they both were – this is something of a feature of the young English intelligentsia, these inter-class marriages, Peter of course is of a working-class background), and mentioned that I would be interested in the papers and they said at once apparently that I would be welcome to go down there and have a look. It certainly is a stroke of luck – Felicity says she got the impression there is a vast amount of stuff, all his personal correspondence and official papers too. I go next week, I imagine it will all be rather grand . . .'

There was no car to meet him, as promised. At least, he stood at the entrance to the small country station and the only waiting cars were a taxi and a small pick-up van with open back full of agriculture sacks. He checked Sir Philip Lander's letter: date and time were right. Apprehensively he turned to go to the telephone kiosk – and at that moment the occupant of the van, who had been reading a newspaper, looked up, opened the door and stepped out, smiling.

Or rather, unfolded himself. He was immensely tall, well over six foot. He towered above Dieter, holding out a hand, saying my dear fellow, I'm so sorry, had you been there long – I didn't realise the train was in – I say, is that all the luggage you've got, let me shove it in the back . . .

Bemused, Dieter climbed into the van beside him. It smelled of petrol and, more restrainedly, of horse.

They wound through lanes and over hills. Sir Philip boomed, above the unhealthy sound of the van's engine, of topography, of recollections of Germany before the war, of the harvest. He wore corduroy trousers laced with wisps of hay, gum-boots, a tweed jacket. He was utterly affable, totally without affectation, impregnable in his confidence. Dieter, looking out of the window, saw a countryside that seemed dormant, the trees' dark drooping shapes, the cattle huddled in tranquil groups, their tails lazily twitching. The phrase of some historian about 'the long deep sleep of the English people' swam into his head; he listened to Sir Philip and talked and had the impression of travelling miles, of being swallowed up by this billowing, drowsy landscape.

Once, Sir Philip stopped at a village shop and came out with a cardboard carton of groceries; the van, after this, refused to start and Dieter got out to push. As he got back in, Sir Philip said, 'Thanks so much. Very old, I'm afraid. Needs servicing, too – awful price, nowadays, a service. Oh, well . . .' They passed a pub called the Lander Arms, beetle-browed cottages, an unkempt village green, a Victorian school, turned in at iron gates that shed curls of rusting paint, and jolted up a long, weedy, rutted drive.

It could never have been a beautiful house, Morswick: early seven-teenth century, satisfactory enough in its proportions, with a moderately ambitious flight of steps (now cracked and crumbling) to the front door, but without the gilding of any famous architectural hand. The immediate impression was of a combination of resilience and decay: the pock-marked stone, the window frames unpainted for many years, the pedestal-less urns with planting of woody geraniums, the weeds fringing the steps, the rusted guttering.

They went in. Dieter had a muddled impression of welcoming hands and faces, a big cool hallway, a wide oak staircase, perplexing passages and doors culminating in a room with window looking out on to a field in which a girl jumped a large horse to and fro over an obstacle made from old oil-drums. He changed his shirt, watching her.

Only later, over tea, did he sort them all out. And that took time and effort, so thunderstruck was he by the room in which it was eaten, that bizarre – preposterous – backdrop to brown bread and butter, Marmite, fish paste and gooseberry jam.

It was huge, stone-flagged, its exterior wall taken up with one great high window, as elaborate with stone tracery as that of a church transept. There were family portraits all round the room – a jumble of artistic good and bad – and above them jutted banners so airy with age as to be completely colourless. The table at which they sat must have been twelve feet long; the wood had the rock-hard feel of immense age; there was nothing in sight that was new except the electric kettle with which Lady Lander made the tea. ('The kitchen is such miles away, we do as much as we can in here . . .')

He stared incredulously at the banners, the pictures, at pieces of furniture such as he had only ever seen before in museums. These, though, were scarred with use, faded by sun, their upholstery in ribbons: Empire chairs and sofas, eighteenth-century cabinets, pedestal tables, writing desks, bureaux. Bemused, he smiled and thanked and spread jam on brown bread and was handed a cup of tea by his hostess.

She was French, but seemed, he thought, poles removed from any Frenchwoman he had ever known – there was nothing left but the faintest accent, the occasional misuse of a word. And then there was the mother-in-law, old Lady Lander, a small pastel figure in her special chair (so fragile-looking, how could she have perpetrated that enormous man?) and Madame Heurgon, Lady Lander's mother, and the two boys, Philip and James, and Sophie, the old French nurse, and Sally, who was sixteen (she it was who had been jumping that horse, beyond the window).

He ate his tea, and smiled and listened. Later, he wrote to his father (and forgot to post the letter): 'This is the most extraordinary family, I hardly know what to make of them as yet. The French mother-in-law has been here twenty years but speaks the most dreadful English, and yet she never stirs from the place, it seems – I asked her if she went back to France often and she said, "Oh, but of course not, it is so impossibly expensive to go abroad nowadays." The boys go away to boarding school, but the girl, Sally, went to some local school and is really barely educated at all, daughters are expendable, I suppose. And they are all there, all the time, for every meal, the old nurse too, and in the evenings they all sit in the drawing-room, listening to the wireless – comedy shows that bewilder them all, except the children, who try to explain the jokes and references, all at once, so no one can hear a word anyway. The old ladies, and the nurse, are in there all day, knitting and sewing and looking out of the window and saying how hot it is, or how cold, and how early the fruit is, or how late, day after day, just the same, there is nothing missing but the samovar . . . Sir Philip is out most of the time, in the fields, he is nothing if not a working farmer, tomorrow I shall help him with some young bullocks they have up on the hill.

I have not yet looked at the papers.'

That first day there had been no mention of the papers at all; and he had not, he realised, as he got into bed, given them so much as a thought himself. After tea he had been shown round the place by Sally and the boys: the weedy gardens where couch grass and bindweed quenched the outline of tennis court, kitchen garden, and what had once been a formal rose garden with box hedges and a goldfish pond. From time to time they met Lady Lander, hoeing a vegetable bed or snipping the dead heads from flowers; she worked with a slow deliberation that seemed appropriate to the hopeless task of controlling that large area. To go any faster would have been pointless – the forces of nature were winning hands down in any case – to give up altogether would be craven. There was no gardener, Sally said – 'The only men are Daniels and Jim, and Jim's only half really because he's on day release at the Tech and of course Daddy needs them on the farm all the time.'

They toured the stables (a graceful eighteenth-century courtyard, more architecturally distinguished than the house) and admired the Guernsey cows grazing in a paddock nearby. Sir Philip came down the drive on a tractor, and dismounted to join them and explain the finer points of raising calves to Dieter: this was a small breeding herd. 'Of course,' he said, 'it doesn't really make sense, economic sense, one never gets enough for them, but it's something I've always enjoyed doing.'

Sally broke in, 'And they *look* so nice.'

He beamed at the cows, and his daughter. 'Of course. That's half the point.'

A car was approaching slowly, taking the ruts and bumps with caution, a new model. Sir Philip said, 'Ah, here's George Nethercott, we're going to have a chat about those top fields'. He moved away from them as the car stopped, saying, 'Good evening, George, very good of you to come up – how's your hay going, I'm afraid we're making a very poor showing this year, I'm about three hundred bales short so far. I say, that's a very smart car . . .'

His voice carried in the stillness of the early evening; it seemed the only forceful element in all that peace of pigeons cooing, cows cropping the grass, hypnotically shifting trees.

Sally said, 'Mr Nethercott's land joins our farm on two sides. Daddy may be going to sell him the three hill fields because we've got to have a new tractor next year, it's a pity, you oughtn't to sell land . . .' Her voice trailed away vaguely, and then she went on with sudden enthusiasm, 'I say, do you like riding? Would you like to try Polly?'

'You will never believe it, I have been horse-riding,' he wrote to Erika. 'Not for long, I hasten to say – I fell off with much humiliation, and was made a great fuss of. They are such a charming family, and have a way of drawing you into everything they do, without ever really bothering about whether it is the kind of thing you are fitted for, or would like . . . So that I find myself leading the most extraordinary – for me – life, mending fences, herding cattle, picking fruit, hay-making.

Next week I must get down to the papers.'

Sir Philip had taken him up to the attics. 'I really don't know what we shall find,' he said. 'Things get shoved away for years, you know, and one has very little idea . . . I've not been up here for ages.'

There were pieces of furniture, grey with dust, and suitcases, and heaps of mouldering curtains and blankets; a sewing-machine that looked like the prototype of all sewing-machines; gilt-framed pictures stacked against a wall; a jumble of withered saddlery that Sir Philip picked up and examined. 'I wonder if Sally mightn't be able to make use of some of this.'

Dieter, looking at an eighteenth-century chest of drawers pushed away beneath a dormer window, and thinking also of the furniture with which the rest of the house was filled, said, 'You have some nice antique pieces.' Sir Philip, still trying to unravel a harness, said, 'Oh no, Dieter, not really, it's all just things that have always been here, you know.' He put the harness down and moved away into another, inner attic room with a single small window overlooking the stable-yard. 'I have a feeling the stuff we're looking for is in these boxes here.'

Later, Dieter sat at a small folding green baize card table he had found in a corner, and began to open the bundles of letters and papers. It was much as Felicity Sutton had predicted: there were family letters all mixed up with official correspondence both from and to the Sir Philip Lander of the 1840s. It was a research worker's gold-mine. He glanced through a few documents at random, and then began to try to sort things out into some kind of order, thinking that eventually, before he left, he must suggest tactfully that all this should be deposited in the Public Record Office or some other appropriate place. In the meantime it was just his own good luck . . .

Curiously, he could not feel as excited or interested as he should. He read, and made a few notes, and yawned, and beyond the fly-blown window small puffy clouds coasted in a sky of duck-egg blue, the garden trees sighed and heaved, and if he lifted himself slightly in his chair he could see down into the stable-yard where Sally was in attendance on that enormous horse of hers, circling its huge complacent rump with brush and comb. Presently Sir Philip drove the tractor into the yard, and, with one of the boys, began to unload bales of hay. Dieter put his pen down, tidied his notes into a pile, and went down to help.

He had never known time pass so slowly – and so fast. The days were thirty-six hours long, and yet fled by so quickly that suddenly he had been there for two and a half weeks. Much embarrassed, he went one morning to find Lady Lander in the kitchen and insist that he should pay for his keep.

She was making jam. The room was filled with the sweet fruity smell; flies buzzed drunkenly against the windows. Astonished, she said, 'Oh, but of course not, we couldn't hear of such a thing, you are a guest.'

'But I am staying so long, originally Sir Philip suggested a few days, and with one thing and another it has got longer and longer. Please, really I should prefer . . .'

She would have none of it.

He hardly knew himself how it was that his departure was always postponed. Of course, he had done no work at all, as yet, on the papers, but he could get down to that any time. And always there was something that loomed – 'You must be sure to be here for the County Show next week,' Sir Philip would say. 'You'll find it amusing if you've not seen that kind of thing before – do you have the equivalent in Germany, I wonder?' Or Sally would remember suddenly that the first cubbing meet was in ten days' time. 'You'll still be here, won't you, Dieter? Oh, you must be – honestly, if you've never seen a meet . . .'

He protested to Lady Lander – 'Please, I would be happier . . .', but could see that there was no point in going on. 'In any case,' she said, turning back to the pink-frothing pan on the stove, 'you have been most helpful to my husband, he is always short-handed at this time of year, I am afraid only that we drive you into things you would never normally dream of doing. You must say, you know, if it bores you – we tend to forget, down here, that not everyone lives this kind of life.'

And she, he wondered, had she not once been someone quite different? On Sundays, both she and her mother appeared for church in quite unfashionable but recognisably expensive clothes – silk dresses and citified hats of pre-war style. In these incongruous outfits, they walked down the lane to the village church. The family filled the whole of the front pew; Sir Philip's confident tenor led the sparse congregation; afterwards they would all stand, every week, for the same amount of time, chatting to the vicar. Then back to Morswick, stopping again from time to time to talk with village people.

He had thought, when he first came, that it was feudal, and had been amused. Now, his perceptions heightened, he saw otherwise. 'It is not that they are not respected,' he wrote to his father. 'Far from it – people are deferential to them – a title still means something, and they have always been the big family in these parts. But it is as though they are runners in a race who are being outstripped without even realising it. I think they hardly notice that their farming neighbours have new gadgets they have not – washing machines, televisions – that theirs is the shabbiest car for miles around, that the Morswick tractor is so out-of-date Nethercott (the neighbour) declined the loan of it when his broke down. And why? you will be saying, after all they have land, a house, possessions. But the land is not good, a lot of it is rough hill-grazing, I suppose that is at the root of the problem – and a mansion and a family past are not very realisable assets. I certainly can't imagine them selling the furniture. But when you come down to it – it is as though there is also some kind of perverse lack of will, as though they both didn't know, and didn't want to know.'

The children were where it most showed. Beside their contemporaries – the sons and daughters of the local farming families (many of them at private schools, their country accents fast fading), they seemed quaint, too young for their ages, innocent. Sally, talking to other adolescent girls at an agricultural show, was the only one without lipstick, a hair-do, the quick glancing self-consciousness of young womanhood. She seemed a child beside them.

At the cubbing meet – held outside the village pub – he found it almost unbearable. Standing beside Lady Lander, he watched her. Lady Lander said, 'She's not well mounted, I'm afraid, poor darling – we've only got old Polly these days.'

It was a huge horse, with a hefty muscularity that suggested carthorse ancestry. Seated on it, Sally towered above the dapper ponies of the other children. Beaming, unconscious of the vaguely comic figure she cut, she yanked the horse's head away from a tray of glasses that was being carried around, and waved at Dieter. She wore her school mack over grubby breeches and a pair of battered hunting-boots. The other girls were crisp in pale jodhpurs, tweed jackets and little velvet caps.

Dieter was wrenched by pity, and love.

He adored her. With horror he had recognised his own feelings, which smacked, it seemed to him, of paedophilia. She was sixteen; her rounded features, her plump awkward body, were raw with childishness. He was obsessed by her. He forced himself to contemplate her ignorance, her near-illiteracy. He thought of Erika, of her sharp clever face, the long hours of serious discussion, the shared concerns, and it did no good at all.

And Sally had not the slightest inkling, nor ever would, of how he felt. She jostled him in puppyish horse-play; she worked beside him in the harvest field, her breasts straining at her aertex shirt, her brown legs as shiny with health and vigour as the rump of that incongruous horse she rode; he could hardly take his eyes off her, and was appalled at himself.

In the evenings, he played board games with the two boys, held skeins of knitting wool for old Lady Lander as she wound the balls. Sometimes, he took a book from the great high cases that lined the walls of the drawing-room. They held an odd assortment: bound volumes of *Punch*, row upon row, Edwardian books about hunting and fishing, the classic Victorian novelists, books of humorous verse, Henty and Buchan and Rider Haggard. He read with perplexity novels like *The Constant Nymph*, *Precious Bane* and *Beau Geste* that seemed to fit not at all with the concept of English twentieth-century literature that he had formed after two years' carefully selective leisure reading. Scanning the titles on the shelves, he had a confusing impression of being presented with a whole shadow culture of which he had been unaware. Yet again he felt his own judgements and perceptions to be hopelessly inadequate. Sir Philip, standing beside him at the book case one evening, said, 'Glad to see you're making use of the library, Dieter – I'm afraid none of us get much time for reading.' There was hardly a single recent addition, not an untattered dust-cover to be seen.

On a day of sullen rain clouds, when the whole landscape seemed sunk in apathy, the old tractor broke down with more than usual finality. For hour after hour, Sir Philip and Daniels crawled around it, oiling and adjusting; Dieter, on edge with vicarious anxiety (it was needed for several urgent jobs), watched in frustration, cursing his lack of mechanical know-how. The worry on Sir Philip's face distressed him greatly; he longed to help. Eventually, the tractor sputtered into fitful life, and everybody stood back smiling. Sir Philip said, 'Well, Daniels, we shan't have any of these crises next year, when we've got the new one, I hope.' And Daniels said, 'That's right, sir, we'll be in clover then', and added, looking down the drive, 'Here's Mr Nethercott now.'

Nethercott had come, though, to talk not about fields but to look at the bull Sir Philip proposed selling. It was a young bull, whose performance was proving unreliable. Daniels was in favour of going over to artificial insemination. Sir Philip had reluctantly concurred, as they stood side by side at the gate, a few days before, watching the bull at work among the cows in a steeply sloping field opposite. Sir Philip said, 'You're right, Daniels, I'm not too happy about him either.'

'Silly bugger don't realise he got to do it downhill.'

Sir Philip turned away. 'Oh well, there's nothing to be done – he'll have to go. Now, George Nethercott's wanting a bull, I know – I'll give him a ring tonight.'

And now Nethercott too stood at the field gate, studying the bull. Other matters were talked of for a while, then he said, 'How much were you thinking of asking for him?'

Sir Philip named a price.

Nethercott nodded. There was a brief silence and then he said with a trace of embarrassment, 'He might well work out more satisfactory than he looks just now – but the fact is, what I'm looking for's going to cost a fair bit more than that. Thanks for letting me have a look at him, though.'

A week or so later, they heard through the postman that Nethercott had paid five hundred pounds for a bull at the Royal Show. Sir Philip said, 'Well, good heavens! Lucky fellow.' He was standing with Dieter in the front drive, the two or three brown envelopes that the postman had brought in his hand. 'I really don't know how people manage it, these days. He's a good chap, Nethercott – they're a nice family. His grandfather used to work here, you know, for mine – stable-lad he was, I think. Well, I suppose we might get on with that fencing today, eh?'

Up in the attic, the sun striking through the window had browned Dieter's single page of notes; there was a faint paler stripe where the pencil lay.

At the beginning of September, the boys went back to boarding school.

The corn was down, the blackberries ripening, the green of the trees spiced here and there with the first touch of autumn colour. Since he had come here, Dieter realised, the landscape had changed, working through its cycle so unobtrusively that only with an effort did one remember the brimming cornfields of July, the hedgerows still bright with wild flowers, the long light evenings. Now, the fields were bleached and shaven, the hedges lined with the skeletal heads of dried cow-parsley and docks, the grass white with dew in the mornings. It came as a faint shock to realise that the place was not static at all, that that impression of deep slumber was quite false, that change was continuous, that nothing stood still. That he could not stay here for ever.

There was a dance, in the local market town, in connection with some equestrian activity, to which he went with Sally and her parents. It was the first time, he realised, that he had ever been anywhere with them when the whole family had not come, grandmothers and all. Sally wore an old dress of her mother's that had been cut down for her; it did not fit and was unbecoming, but she shone with excitement and anticipation. In the hotel where the dance took place, the other young girls were waiting about in the foyer in sharp-eyed groups and he was stricken again at Sally's frumpish looks in contrast to their fashionable dresses, their knowingness. But she was quite happy – laughing, greeting acquaintances.

He danced with her once at the beginning, and then left her with a group of her contemporaries. But later, the evening under way, whenever he saw her she was dancing with friends of her parents, or sitting alone on one of a row of gilt chairs at the edge of the room, holding a glass of lemonade, but still radiant, tapping her foot in time to the music. After a while he went over and sat beside her.

'Are you having a good time, Sally?'

'Marvellous!'

'Let's dance, shall we?'

She was clumsy; he had to steer her round the room. She said, 'Sorry, I'm hopeless. We did have dancing lessons at school but it's quite different when it's a real man, and anyway I always had to take man because of being tall, so I'm no good at being the woman. I say, Mummy says perhaps I can go to the hunt ball this year – will you still be here?'

He said, 'I'm afraid not. I have to go back before the term begins in October.'

'Oh, what a pity.' They danced in silence for a minute or two and then she said suddenly, 'What are you going to do after you've finished your – your what's-it, the thing you're writing?'

'I shall go back to Germany and get a job. I expect I shall get married,' he added after a fractional pause. He had never spoken of Erika at Morswick.

'Will you?' she looked amazed. 'Gosh – how exciting. Do write and tell us, won't you, so that we can send a present.'

She beamed up at him; she smelled of toothpaste and, very faintly, of a cheap scent that she must have acquired in secrecy and tentatively used. He had seen, once, into her room; there had been a balding toy dog on the pillow, photographs of horses pinned to the walls, glass animals on the windowsill. She said, 'Do you know, they want me to go to a sort of finishing school place in Grenoble next year.'

'I should think you would like that.'

She said, 'Oh no, I couldn't possibly go. I couldn't bear to leave Morswick. No, I can't possibly.'

Dieter said, 'Sally, I think you should, I really do.'

She shook her head.

Later, back at Morswick, he sat with Sir Philip in the drawing-room; Sally and her mother had gone to bed. Sir Philip had taken a bottle of whisky from the cupboard and poured them both a glass: it was almost the first time Dieter had ever seen alcohol produced at Morswick, except for the glass of sherry offered to their rare visitors. Sir Philip said, 'Quite a successful evening, I thought. Of course, you get rather a different kind of person at this sort of do now – it's not really like before the war. I daresay my father would be a bit taken aback if he was still alive.'

He began to talk about his war-time experiences in Italy and France: he had been with the Sicily landings, and then in Normandy shortly after D-day, advancing through France and into Germany. Remembering suddenly the delicacy of the subject, he looked across at Dieter and said, 'I hope you don't . . . of course, one realised at the time how many people like yourself, like your father . . . What a wretched business it all was, so much worse in many ways for you than for us.'

Dieter said, 'I think you would be interested to see Germany now. I wish you would come to visit us – my father would be so delighted to make arrangements, if all of you could come, or perhaps at least the boys and Sally.'

'How awfully kind. We really must try to – you know, I can't think when we last had a holiday of any sort. Yes, we really must.' He swilled the whisky in his glass, peering down into it. 'Yes. Of course, one is so awfully tied up here, being pretty short-handed nowadays. I daresay things will pick up in time, though. I must admit, it is getting a bit hard to manage just at the moment – still, we keep our heads above water. Anyway, I really mustn't burden you with our problems. By the way, I hope you didn't mean what you said earlier about leaving us next week – I'd imagined we'd have you with us for some time to come. There's the harvest festival on Sunday week – I'm sure Jeanne was intending to rope you in for one thing and another.'

'I have to get back – the term begins soon, you see. My supervisor –

well, they must wonder what on earth has become of me. And in any case, you've been far too kind already, too hospitable. I don't know how to thank you enough.'

'I'm afraid what with one thing and another you've not had all that much time to put in on those papers. They've been of some interest, I hope?'

Dieter said, 'Oh yes, extremely interesting.'

The day before he was to leave he went to the attic to clear up the green baize table. His note-pad, with its single page of notes, was curled at the edges now, and dusty. Insects had died on the opened bundles of letters. Beyond the window, the landscape had slipped a notch further into autumn: there was a mist smoking up from the fields, and long curtains of old man's beard hanging down the wall beside the stable-yard. He tied up the letters again and put them away in the trunk, folded the card table, gathered up his things. He opened the window for a moment, with some vague notion of airing the place, and heard, faintly, Sally whistling as she did something out of sight in one of the loose boxes.

His departure for the station was delayed for a few minutes by the arrival of Nethercott. Sir Philip stood with him at the field gate nodding and listening. When at last he finished, and Nethercott, apologising for turning up at what was obviously an inappropriate moment, had driven away, the whole family was gathered on the steps to say goodbye to Dieter. He had shaken hands with them all, several times; everyone was smiling and interrupting. Sir Philip came across the drive to them and said, 'Sorry about that – had to have a word or two since he'd taken the trouble to come up.'

Lady Lander said, 'What was it about?'

'Oh, just the fields – you know, the hill fields. He'd like to make an offer for them but I'd got things a bit wrong, I'm afraid – they're worth rather less than I'd imagined, on the current market. Rather a lot less, I'm afraid. George was awfully apologetic – you'd have thought it was his fault. He's a good chap.'

'Oh dear, does that mean no new tractor?'

'I suppose it does. I don't know how I'm going to break that to poor Daniels. Well, anyway,' he went on cheerfully, 'we'll be able to send the old one for a thorough overhaul, we'll have to make do with that. Now, Dieter, we'd better be on our way, hadn't we, where's your case . . .'

He saw them like that, in his mind's eye, for long after – the women – standing on the front steps waving and smiling. 'It's au revoir, anyway,' Lady Lander had said, 'because we shall see you again, next time you're in our part of the world, shan't we?' And her mother-in-law, that frail old lady in her pale floppy clothes and regimental brooches, had piped up, 'Oh yes, we're always here, you know, you'll always find us here', and Sally was calling out not to forget to let them know about the wedding.

She had given him a hug and a kiss; the feel of her arms, her warm soft face, the smell of her, stayed with him all the way to the station, and beyond. And the sight of them, and of the house behind, frozen in the furry yellow light of the September morning, like an old photograph – the figures grouped around the steps, the house with its backdrop of fields and hills and trees.

At the station, Sir Philip shook him by the hand. 'We've enjoyed having you, Dieter. You must get down to us again sometime. You'll find everything goes on much as ever at Morswick. And the best of luck with your doctorate.'

In the train, Dieter began a letter to Erika, and then sat staring out of the window at that placid landscape (the landscape of Constable, he told himself, of Richard Wilson, of the English novelists) and saw only the irresistible manifestations of change: the mottled trees, the tangle of spent growth in the hedgerows.

The Voice of God
in Adelaide Terrace

Miss Avril Pemberton, in her fifty-seventh year, suffered from insomnia. She did not consider this an insupportable affliction; she would lie with her eyes open in the protective darkness of her bedroom, think her thoughts, and listen to the nocturnal London sounds. These were not many, for Adelaide Terrace was a quiet and respectable neighbourhood, its inhabitants given to early nights and not inclined to car ownership.

It was on such a night, in that static tract of time between three and five in the morning so familiar to insomniacs, that Avril first heard the voice.

She was a devout woman and a regular churchgoer. Even so, she did not regard herself as blameless; merely as a reasonably proficient Christian, given to occasional error rather than deliberate transgression. She had certainly never expected to be singled out in this way.

The voice said, 'Avril?'

She sat up, and stared into the dusky cavern beside the wardrobe from which it seemed to come; later, she recalled its curious sexlessness, the voice of neither man nor woman.

'Avril,' it said, 'are you listening carefully? There is something I want you to do.'

Avril, wide awake, more interested than awed, said, 'What would You like me to do?'

'I shall explain,' said the voice. 'Pay attention. I wish you to make a start with the attic room . . .'

Avril listened, with mounting astonishment.

It should be explained at this point that Avril Pemberton let rooms. She let rooms because her mother had done so before, ever since, indeed, Mr Pemberton had died in 1951, because the house was too large for her own needs and because the money came in very handy. Without it, she would have found it difficult to manage on her salary from the part-time secretarial work for a local firm of accountants. She let the first-floor front and back (single, with washbasins) and the large attic room (own bathroom). Cooking facilities for the tenants were provided in the small scullery on the first floor. Avril herself occupied the ground floor, using the second-floor front as her bedroom. The two small back rooms on the second floor remained empty, in use as boxrooms. Her mother had not liked the house to become overcrowded.

Mrs Pemberton had died four years before, irascible in extreme old age. To the bitter end, she had exercised her powers of discrimination over would-be tenants, vetting them, finally, from her bed. Avril had found it all extremely embarrassing; so, presumably, had the tenants. Two of the present three, Mr Harris, the bank clerk in the first-floor front, and the nursing sister in the attic had been her mother's choices. Sandra Lee, the student from the teacher training college around the corner, Avril had admitted a year or so ago, irritably aware that the pasty girl, with her total absence of personality, opinion or discernible tastes, was exactly the kind of person of whom her mother would have approved as a tenant.

There had never been any shortage of people wanting rooms. Adelaide Terrace was conveniently near bus routes and a tube station, not too far from central London, but quiet. The area was something of a buffer state; to the east, middle-class 'reclamation' had sent prices rocketing and let loose a tide of primrose and terracotta front doors, bay trees in tubs and petunia-crammed window-boxes; to the west, quite other things had been going on. There, Indian take-aways alternated with Chinese, the market stalls were piled high with garish and glittery stuffs, peculiar vegetables and cut-price carpets and pop records. The streets ran with black school children and the pubs blared forth unfamiliar music. The inhabitants of Adelaide Terrace kept their eyes turned resolutely to the east, and hoped for the best.

And, where possible, played a part. Many of the tall terrace houses, like the Pembertons', belonged to elderly people and diminished families who let out rooms; others were divided, rather inefficiently, into flats. The long-term inhabitants, such as Mrs Pemberton and her immediate neighbour, Mrs Fletcher, knew one another well and were resolute as to certain matters, though divided about methods of exercising that resolution.

Mrs Fletcher sported, for many years, a small notice stuck to the inside of a glass panel in the front door. It said 'No coloureds' and had been nicely lettered, with stencils, by her niece who had done a year at art college.

Mrs Pemberton thought this silly and unnecessary. It was a simple matter, she said, to make one's position perfectly clear without that. Occasional small unpleasantnesses might arise, but could be quickly dealt with: front doors open, but they also close again. It was with a certain satisfaction that she had pointed out to Mrs Fletcher, in 1965, that the notice would have to be removed.

'Who's to make me?' said Mrs Fletcher, bristling.

'Well, dear,' said Mrs Pemberton, 'you'll have to do as you think best, but I wouldn't like to see you get had up, and personally I've never found the need in the first place.'

Mrs Fletcher went on at some length about individual liberty and diabolical interferences therein and how you couldn't pass laws to make people think differently to what they always had done. Mrs Pemberton pointed out, smoothly, that all this was true enough but what was clear as day was that you could pass laws until you were blue in the face but there would still be ways and means.

Mrs Fletcher removed the notice and took instructions from Mrs Pemberton as to ways and means. There were seldom, if ever, mis-understandings or unpleasantnesses, and Adelaide Terrace remained much as it had been before. At the far end, where Mrs Pemberton's influence was weakest, there was a certain falling-off. An Indian family took one of the flats and were to be seen, on Sunday's immaculately dressed, pushing a pram in Adelaide Gardens. Their eldest son, in grey flannel trousers, navy blazer, spotless white shirt and puce turban, cycled down the street to school every day. Avril, watching once from the window, was misguided enough to say that they seemed quite nice people; her mother was unmanageable for a week.

And now, lying there in the dark, she listened to the voice – a little hectoring in tone – as it went on and on. Instructing. Lecturing. 'Remember the Bishop?' it said. 'Now supposing *he* had come to the door . . .'

'I know,' said Avril. 'I said as much to mother at the time.'

The Bishop of somewhere in Africa, he had been, but you couldn't tell that at once from the name. He had come as visiting preacher to St Bartholomew's, one autumn Sunday. They had been invited to the Vicar's after the service, for coffee, because Mrs Pemberton was treasurer, then, of the Mothers' Union. And he had been as black as your hat. Big and black and beaming. Avril had thought, at first, seeing him climb into the pulpit, that her mother wouldn't go to the vicarage. But she had. She had gone, and sat there, and drunk coffee and eaten biscuits. And afterwards she had said that she wouldn't have Mrs Brinton's job, not for the world. Mrs Brinton was the Vicar's wife. And Avril had said what she had said and there had been unpleasantness between them. And now here was the voice, harking back.

'I spoke my mind,' said Avril sulkily.

She had never taken up arms against her mother lightly: the cost was too high. As the years went by, she did so less and less, the instinctive resistance of her youth snuffed out by her mother's more implacable temperament. She ceased to counter Mrs Pemberton's vaunted opinions and preferences, ceased to say, from time to time, 'There are two sides to everything, mother,' and 'Well, personally, I do think . . .' She took to silence.

By and large, she conceded Adelaide Terrace as Mrs Pemberton's territory and guarded jealously the privacy of her life beyond it, what little there was – the voluntary evenings at the Scout and Guide hut, her Red Cross afternoon, and her job at Hackle and Starbuck.

Never, for instance, would she have told Mrs Pemberton about Gloria.

Gloria came to the office as a temp when the senior, and permanent, secretary, had to have several weeks' sick leave after an operation. She was seventeen, fresh from school, an indifferent typist, as noisy as a puppy, and West Indian. Her abundant, frizzy hair was worn in two huge puffs elaborately teased out at either side of her head; she had wide, flat features with large brown eyes, big lips delicately painted; there was a bloom to her skin that entranced Avril. Surreptitiously she kept glancing at Gloria; bewildered, she realised that she found the girl beautiful.

Gloria bounced and giggled her way through the days and played merry hell with the filing system. The office was torn between amusement and irritation; Mr Hackle, who had been as startled as Avril when Gloria appeared from the agency, grumbled at the mangled letters with which Gloria presented him, and enjoyed, like Avril, the throaty laughter that brightened office hours. Gloria teased the office boy, charmed clients, bungled every telephone message, and spent much time in the washroom attending to her appearance. At the typewriter, she moaned and whimpered and, every now and then, leaned back to indulge in a huge luxuriant stretch that made it seem as though her plump rubbery young body might spring apart entirely, like an over-ripe pea-pod.

One day, looking across at Avril, she said, 'Hey, that's nice.'

'What?' said Avril.

'That sweater you got on. It suits you – it's your colour, blue. You look really good today.'

Avril had flushed and muttered something and gone back to the letter she was typing. Later, tidying her hair before she left the office, she stared at herself in the mirror, turning this way and that, adjusting the collar of her jacket.

She had been sorry when Gloria left, and Maureen Davidson returned, with her migraines and her proficiency and her faint odour of Lifebuoy soap.

Guiltily, she dismissed recollections of Gloria and returned to here and now, and to the voice, which seemed to be concluding its homily.

'. . . as quickly as you can, with the normal period of notice to the present tenants.'

As she listened, the corners of Avril's mouth turned up in an incredulous smile.

'*All* black?' she said.

'Every one of them,' said the voice sternly.

*

There was not a great deal of difficulty with Mr Harris, Sandra Lee and the nursing sister. Since she gave formal notice to all three at once, it was simply assumed that she wished to reclaim the house for her own occupation. Mr Harris, who had been there for nine years, was clearly a little put out, but gave her a large box of chocolates as a parting present and made over to her the tradescantia in the scullery, which he thought might not take kindly to a move. The nursing sister asked if she wasn't going to rattle around rather, all on her own. Sandra Lee vanished, wordless, into the obscurity from which she had come.

The process, allowing for the correct periods of notice, took nearly four months. Not until the last tenant had departed did Avril place her advertisement in the *Gazette*; she had decided to deal with the attic room first, and retained her usual wording, except that she added 'Married couples not objected to'.

There was a flood of responses. Avril, turning away, with her mother's murmured formula of regret – 'So sorry . . . already taken . . . person who called last night' – first a young Irish couple, and then a Scottish nurse and another girl of indeterminate extraction, realised that covertly exercised discrimination is indeed extremely easy.

The Singhs presented themselves at the door on a Tuesday morning. By Friday they were installed in the attic.

On Saturday morning, returning from the shops, Avril was halted, key in the lock, by Mrs Fletcher, springing from her own door at the sound as though released by an elastic. 'I been wanting to have a word with you, dear,' she said. 'I must say I couldn't hardly believe my eyes, seeing them pull up in the taxi like that, with all their stuff. I said to myself what old Mrs P. would say I don't even like to think . . .'

Avril stood there, her foot inside her own door, half-listening, and it came to her with sudden welcome clarity that, in nearly thirty years of enforced congress, she had never really liked Mrs Fletcher. It was as though you might discover that tea, bread, or some other unconsidered object of routine was not really to your taste. She stared at her opening and closing mouth, the tuft of hairs that crowned a surface irregularity on her chin, the cameo brooch that puckered the neck of her blouse, and thought: silly old bag.

'. . . seen some perfectly nice people come to the door, Sunday and Monday, after you put your ad in,' concluded Mrs Fletcher, 'so I don't know what to think, I simply don't.' She stared at Avril. 'And who are they, one would like to know?'

'They're my new tenants,' said Avril coolly (she liked that: *my* new tenants). 'They've taken the attic room.'

There was a silence. In Mrs Fletcher's face, whole volumes of analysis, speculation, and adjustment to circumstances were written, revised, rewritten; granite assumptions crumbled to dust, and were reconstructed in other forms. When she spoke again, it was from twenty miles away, and ten years on. She said, 'That girl's expecting. I daresay you'll not have noticed that.'

Avril, who had not, flushed a little, and went into the house.

The Singhs were quiet tenants; they pattered up and down the stairs like well-behaved children, talking to each other in low tones if at all. Occasionally, radio music, turned low, seeped from beneath their door, and with it, culinary smells.

With complete detachment, Avril considered the smells. She had once taken a meal in an Indian restaurant with two girls from the office and had not, in fact, much cared for it. The smells, at first, raised a whisker of alarm. And then, considering over a day or two, she decided that they were no more, indeed rather less, disagreeable than the bacon (cut-price, she had always suspected) Mr Harris used to do himself for breakfast every day. In fact, they grew on you.

Over the next three weeks she filled the first-floor front and back.

The front went within three days to a bescarved and bespectacled student from Nigeria. The back was less straightforward; there was a tussle of wills with a forceful woman who refused to believe that the room had already been taken within an hour of the advertisement (the 'occasional small unpleasantness' that old Mrs Pemberton had grown accustomed to) but Avril held her own, then and for a further day and a half until the arrival of an immensely fat black dental nurse called Brenda.

In the silence and darkness of her room she said, 'All right?' There being no reply, she assumed that her arrangements had met with approval.

The house was no longer so quiet. The Nigerian student turned out to have many friends, some of whom, Avril suspected, were not entirely transitory visitors. Having always respected the privacy of her tenants (unlike her mother, who kept duplicate keys and made forays into their rooms in their absence) she made no comment. He and Brenda struck up a friendship, conducted for the most part rather noisily on the stairs. Both, though, were unfailingly genial; the Nigerian cleared a blocked sink in the kitchen and Brenda, when Avril took to her bed with a throat infection, plied her with hot drinks laced with suspect but delicious substances. She would stand at Avril's bedroom door, entirely filling it, brandishing a thermos and shouting encouragingly, as though to a slightly deaf child; she was a maturer and more strident version of Gloria.

Avril felt a greater affinity with the Singhs, their deprecating smiles and self-effacing comings and goings. Mrs Singh – Kamala, as she whispered once, in a rare moment of intimacy – was indeed swelling week by week, as Avril had now to observe and admit. Nothing was said, until one day Brenda, in raucous progress up the stairs, said casually, 'That Kamala, she goin' to have it any day now', which alarmed Avril but left her better prepared for contingencies. When, a week or so later, she heard Mr Singh come down the stairs with more than usual haste, and then his soft voice on the telephone, asking for the doctor, she was calm and indeed quite excited. Being familiar with the processes of childbirth from her reading of novels (though the kind of novel, admittedly, in which the narrative tended to shift, at the crucial moment, to the role of non-participant characters such as husbands and sisters) she amassed all the kettles and saucepans she could find and set them to boil. Only as they began to hum, did it occur to her that she really did not know for what all this boiling water was required: the novels never went into that. And when she came out into the hall to find Kamala, smiling weakly, coming down the stairs on her husband's arm, suitcase in hand, she was distinctly disappointed. The birth was to take place in hospital, apparently. She went rather glumly back into her room, and forgot the saucepans, which were boiling briskly ten minutes later, when Brenda returned, filling the house with steam and prompting much noisy comment and enquiry. Avril, who suspected that she might have been rumbled, gave some sheepish explanations about sterilising jamjars.

Kamala returned, after what Avril thought a surprisingly short period, with a tiny, fragile baby (a boy, apparently) cocooned in yards of shocking pink blanketing. The Nigerian produced a couple of bottles of wine for the household to drink the baby's health; everybody gathered in the kitchen, the Singhs silent but beaming, Brenda and the Nigerian loudly talkative, Avril, who had seldom in her life touched alcohol, feeling increasingly unstable, but stimulated. It was all rather enjoyable; afterwards, she watched television, a little restlessly, and tried not to pay attention to the curious sounds from the Nigerian's room, where he and Brenda were completing the evening on their own.

Mrs Fletcher, tight-lipped, had complained a number of times about the pitch of Brenda's transistor radio. She spoke seldom to Avril, but was frequently to be seen in the street, in eloquent discourse with one or other of the neighbours. They are talking about me, Avril would think, and found that she did not care at all.

It was curious: she was a person who had always been deeply sensitive to the opinions of others.

At night, in the privacy of her room, she checked with the voice for approval and encouragement, and received it. Her life, in every other respect, continued much as it always had done: she went to the office, on Monday and Tuesday mornings and Thursday and Friday afternoons, to the Scout and Guide hut on Monday evenings, the Red Cross on Thursdays, St Bartholomew's on Sunday for communion and again for evensong. She was not entirely surprised when the Vicar called one day. He was a man easily swayed by others (an opinion she seemed always to have had, though only now did it express itself – tacitly – with ease and conviction) and she heard in his voice the conspiratorial tones of Mrs Fletcher. He sat uneasily on the edge of a chair and asked Avril if she had been keeping well lately; afterwards, the two indentations of his behind remained for some while on the upholstery, prolonging the tension of the visit. When Avril replied, shortly, that she had, he hummed and hawed, reflected on the weather, the new block of flats springing up alongside the churchyard, and his summer holiday plans, before hoping that if she, er, ever felt at all, er, in need of a chat she must remember that she had many good friends in the neighbourhood, many good friends. There was a silence, at the end of which the Vicar made the proposition that some people find living alone a bit of a strain, especially after the sad loss of a dear relative, that sometimes possibly, er, a chat with a sympathetic friend . . .

Avril said that she did not live alone.

The Vicar, with some eagerness, said that yes, quite, and since she'd mentioned it he wondered if . . .

Avril asked what he wondered. And the Vicar's voice had trailed off, and with it the Vicar, till all that was left of him were those two dents in the chair seat.

Avril wondered if the voice had ever addressed the Vicar, in the darkness of *his* nights.

The Singh baby prospered. Mr Harris's tradescantia in the scullery died; the Nigerian presented Avril with a rather violent oil-painting attributed to his brother which she felt obliged to hang on the stairs. She did not like it and indeed had asked the voice for guidance over the matter, and the voice had suggested the darkish corner on the first-floor landing. She frequently asked the voice for guidance, these days, and was frequently given it.

When Brenda, coming in from work one evening, heard her in one of the boxrooms, she peered inquisitively through the door.

'My, you got a lot of stuff in there, Miss Pemberton. You havin' a tidy-up, then?'

'The room's going to be used,' said Avril. 'I have to clear it out.'

'You expectin' a visitor, then?'

Avril, distracted by the problem of a broken table-lamp, replied that she was making room for a further lodger. Brenda did not receive this news with the enthusiasm Avril had expected: she said it was enough hassle getting that Pius to hurry up with the bathroom in the mornings and the shelves in the scullery were cram full as it was. She implied a fit of profiteering on Avril's part. Avril ignored this, with dignity.

She got rid of the first two applicants for the room, who were unsuitable; the third threw her into a quandary. He stood before her on the doorstep, small, slight, brown, and almond-eyed. Avril had little idea from which part of the world he hailed, but knew on which side of the dividing-line her mother would have placed him. She hesitated, showed him the room, and succumbed.

In the night she was woken by the voice (she had been sleeping much better of late). It was displeased.

Avril said defensively, 'Well, mother wouldn't ever have taken him.'

The voice continued, didactic in its assertions as to what was what. Avril, lying there in the dark, felt a twinge of resentment: there was a note, a distinct note, of Mrs Pemberton's hectoring dogmatism. She pointed out, sulkily, that it was too late to do anything about it now, and Mr Lee had looked a good dark brown to her. She did not say that in any case she had rather taken to him, a nice-spoken boy who had stood aside to let her come down the stairs first.

The voice, unmollified, issued further instructions.

'*Both* the boxrooms?' said Avril. And then, thoughtfully, 'Very well, then.'

The Health Visitor sat at the kitchen table and said that she had just thought she would pop in, since she was in the house anyway to see Mrs Singh. She said the baby was coming along nicely. Avril agreed. She said you must miss your mother a lot, I gather it's three or four years since she died. Avril agreed, wondered from whom the gathering had been done, saw Mrs Fletcher pass the window, bundled against the spring wind, and shoot a quick glance sideways. Looking after yourself all right, are you? said the Health Visitor. Avril said she was, and observed the Health Visitor's quick, surreptitious professional examination of the room.

The Health Visitor believed that Avril was thinking of letting another room. Avril neither confirmed nor denied this; with a spurt of indignation she thought, nosey thing. The Health Visitor made some enquiries about toilets, and washbasins, which Avril answered with restraint. The Health Visitor left. Through the window, Avril watched Mrs Fletcher's interception of her, in Adelaide Terrace.

Mr Lee had been installed for a week when she put her second advertisement in the *Gazette*. She had cleared out and prepared the second boxroom during the daytime, in the absence of all the other tenants except Mrs Singh and the baby, who kept themselves to themselves on the top floor. Consequently, the first they knew of her new arrangements was the arrival of the new tenant.

There were comments, amounting to open hostility. The Singhs said nothing, but pattered with a little more assertion in their journeys up and down stairs. The Nigerian grumbled, outside Avril's kitchen door, about the additional strain on the resources of the scullery: he had quite a nasty temper, Avril realised. Brenda said, 'She *stayin'* here, that Chinese girl? You running some kind of United Nations in this house, Miss Pemberton?' A sour expression replaced her normal grin.

The voice, too, had its say.

'I will choose my own tenants,' said Avril, in the darkness of her bedroom. 'I will use my own discrimination.' She lay there, these nights, with the house silent around her, and contemplated the filling of it, and the nature of the filling of it, and her part therein, and experienced the most satisfactory feeling of having created. The house was a kaleidoscope, but the jugglings of its occupancy were no longer random: they had form. She ceased to pay much attention to the voice, which nagged on irritatingly from beside the wardrobe.

The atmosphere of the house was no longer harmonious, but Avril did not notice; she was preoccupied with her own plans.

She transferred her possessions from the second floor to her ground-floor sitting-room by degrees, those that she could handle on her own. The bed, which presented too great a problem, she left where it was, and ordered a new one for herself from the furniture shop in the High Street. It was its delivery that alerted Brenda; she stood, hands on massive hips, at the turn in the stairs and said, 'You not letting *another* room, Miss Pemberton? This house getting too full by half, you know, that lavatory up here's only working half-cock again, you're going to have the health people after you, you not careful.' Avril went into her room and closed the door, intent upon the phrasing of the advertisement for the *Gazette*.

After she had installed Mr Achimota in what had been her bedroom, she locked herself into her sitting-room, whenever she was in the house. She did not really feel like talking to people, and was dimly aware of unrest around her. People whispered on the stairs, and sometimes did not whisper: on one occasion she heard Brenda's raised voice saying, 'She barmy, I'm telling you, she not right in her head any more.'

The Health Visitor hammered on the door, once. She said, 'I'd like to have a chat with you, dear, just for a few minutes.' Avril ignored her.

At night, she held dialogues with the voice, but nowadays it was she who did much of the talking: the voice had grown feebler and feebler and as it whined on, asserting and instructing, its tones had become more and more like those of Mrs Pemberton, but diminished, and susceptible to counter-arguments in a way that Mrs Pemberton never had been. 'Nobody's right all the time,' said Avril, 'not even You. Not on every subject. Now in my opinion . . .'

Mrs Fletcher had avoided her for months, crossing the street when they happened to coincide in Adelaide Terrace. Now, Avril noticed, other neighbours did the same, or observed her furtively, in shops or from adjacent pews in St Bartholomew's. Hurt, though not greatly so, Avril maintained a lonely dignity. She missed, more, the convivial atmosphere that had prevailed in the house during the early months of its reorganisation. Nowadays, there were arguments on the stairs about the bathroom and the scullery, complaints about the lavatory and the telephone, noise and contention. Moreover, it seemed to her that her tenants did not like her, which distressed her more than anything: they were, after all, her chosen people, each and every one of them. Thus isolated, she was prepared even to relinquish the upper hand and mention this to the voice, to seek, maybe, its advice and guidance as in the old days; the voice, disconcertingly, was silent. She lay alone in her bedroom and brooded on what had come about.

And so, when next she heard the Health Visitor in the hall she opened her door.

The Health Visitor did not mince her words. She said there were too many people in the house, too few lavatories, and a smell of drains from out the back somewhere that must be investigated forthwith. She was brisk, but not unpleasant. Avril, less disposed to hostility than on the previous occasion, promised to summon a plumber. The Health Visitor, studying her intently across the table, said, 'And another thing, dear, it's neither here nor there but you do seem to go in for coloured people as tenants, don't you? You've got some of your neighbours properly upset, I can tell you, though as I say that's neither here nor there.'

And so it came about that Avril, because she never had anyone to talk to these days, and because the Health Visitor seemed really quite a nice little body after all, began to tell her about the voice. And as she talked, the Health Visitor, who had been gathering her belongings and indeed had got up from the chair to go, sat down again, and let her bag slither to the floor, and listened with an expression that grew more and more alert and more and more unfathomable. She said, 'Yes?' and 'I see, dear' and nodded and smiled her nice professional smile; it was quite impossible to know what she thought. 'So you see,' Avril concluded, 'it wasn't altogether my choice, though I'm not saying I wasn't perfectly willing to go along with it, more than willing.' And the Health Visitor said yes, she quite understood that, and then she patted Avril on the hand and said she'd look in again, quite soon, in a few days' time maybe.

The conversation, Avril found, had been a release. She'd been keeping herself to herself too much, she realised, no wonder people had been behaving as though she were a bit peculiar or something. And, thinking things over, and remembering the Health Visitor's sympathetic, encouraging interest, it came to her that her experience had been a singular one and, as such, should be shared, not kept from others. And the one person, she reflected (though with slight regret, for she had never really cared much for the man), with whom it should be shared, whose professional concern, after all, it was, was the Vicar. She telephoned the vicarage, and made an appointment to call that evening.

Later, she mulled over her disappointment in the privacy of her room. She had not, before her visit, speculated much if at all about what kind of response she would get: she had expected professional interest, that was

all there was to it. And what she had met with had been something quite
different.

It could most nearly be described, she thought with anger, as
embarrassment. He had sat there, that rather colourless man (even her
mother, she now recalled, used to describe him as wishy-washy), and
avoided her eye and leapt with alacrity to the phone when it rang and
eventually, it seemed to her, cut short the visit and bundled her from the
house. There had been a look on his face of alarm, no less. He had said not
one thing that had been in any way appropriate. And, Avril thought with
bitterness, which, if any, of his parishioners can ever before have come to
him and told him, in cold blood and in all humility, what I told him?

She went about her affairs, but in a state of some cynicism. The voice
remained silent, though she made tentative overtures, in the privacy of
her nights.

The Health Visitor returned, bringing with her another woman,
described as Mrs Hamilton who would like a little chat with you, dear.
Mrs Hamilton had the same quality of attentive, sympathetic and yet
non-committal interest as the Health Visitor. She wondered if Avril
would like to tell her about this voice she sometimes heard and Avril, with
the bitter taste of the Vicar's inadequacy still in her mouth, was glad to do
so. Mrs Hamilton asked if she still had conversations with the voice and
Avril explained that a coolness had arisen, but she hoped in time to put
that right. She might possibly, she realised now, have been a bit assertive
with it, a bit forceful; she would make amends for that. I like, Avril said,
talking to it, even if it was, to begin with, on the bullying side, inclined to
order people around, if you see what I mean. I don't mind telling you, she
went on confidingly, it reminded me of my mother, there was quite a
resemblance there.

Mrs Hamilton listened and nodded and smiled. She asked Avril some
questions, questions that were maybe a bit personal, Avril thought, and
that did not have anything to do with what they had been talking about,
or not in any way that she could see. But she seemed a nice enough
person, and Avril did not really mind; nor did she mind, though she was
surprised, when Mrs Hamilton asked if she would come and have a chat
(everybody seemed to want to chat . . .) with a colleague of hers, a Doctor
someone, at a place where Mrs Hamilton worked, called the Clinic.

It was nice to have people taking so much interest in you.

And at the Clinic they took even more interest. They nodded and
listened and from time to time jotted down a few words on a little white
notepad. They seemed to have nothing to do but listen, these people.
Avril began, at their suggestion, to pay regular visits to the Clinic; the
visits became part of the cycle of her week, like the Red Cross, and the
Scout and Guide hut, and evensong. And as the visits went on the voice
was heard once more, in the solitude of the nights. And Avril, pleased to

have something more substantial and up-to-date for her new friends reported everything it said, though what it had to say was sometimes embarrassing. For it evidently distrusted these people. Don't, it said. Don't go there. Don't talk to them. Don't talk to them about me.

They won't understand, it said. It spoke sulkily. It knew what it was talking about, it said. It had come across all this before. If you knew what I know, it said darkly, if you'd seen what I've seen. They're what we're up against, it said, people like that.

Avril answered conciliatingly. She placated. She tried to conceal her visits to the Clinic.

The voice, of course, knew.

She thought the voice a little uncompromising; the people at the Clinic, after all, displayed no such unswerving prejudice, where the voice was concerned. They were interested, not hostile.

The situation in the house deteriorated; the drains flooded again, Brenda and the Chinese girl, at loggerheads, had a scrap on the stairs in which blood was shed.

At the Clinic, they wondered, in their quiet friendly voices, if Avril would like to come in for a few weeks. For a rest, they said, for treatment. They used the expression in-patient, which startled Avril. She had not realised how things were, until it was put like that, and now it seemed too late to turn back.

But it's not that I . . . she wanted to say, there's no question of . . . But there, now, were the little white notebooks, and the filing cabinets and her name on a pink form, and it seemed so much easier to go along with them, be obliging, and in any case it was not all that disagreeable a place, the Clinic, and the problems of the house, its drains and its plumbing and its tenantry, hung round her neck like so many albatrosses.

She did not tell the voice. She packed her small case that very afternoon and left. Neither did she tell the tenants. With sudden detachment, she thought, well, they will have to sort things out for themselves, I have played my part, I have arranged the house, as I was told, now they must take care of themselves. I have myself to think of.

And in a different bed, that night, she waited for the voice. And presently, in the populated gloom of the ward, it manifested itself. Now look where you have got us, it complained, now look where you have landed us.

Listen, it said, craftily, listen and do as I tell you. Tell them that this is what I said to you . . . Tell them that this is what I told you to do . . .

It lectured on, with renewed confidence, so loudly that she thought it impossible that she alone could hear.

Interpreting the Past

THE TOWN of Houghcester (pronounced Hosta) was much given over, in the summer of 1977, to its antecedents; indeed, you could have called the past a growth industry. And Houghcester had, of course, plenty of it, ranging from prehistoric – not much to show of that, bar some quite nice flints, axe-heads and reconstituted burial urns in the City Museum – on through the more conveniently demonstrable layers of Roman, Saxon, medieval and so forth. It was a well-endowed place, and never had its endowments been more skilfully exploited; it had taken to tourism with magnificent effect. Since towns cannot do their book-keeping as precisely as other commercial concerns, it would not be possible to estimate even roughly how many dollars, yen, francs etc. Houghcester had earned, but if it were, the place would have been justified in claiming the Queen's Award to Industry.

All this, though, makes the town sound insensitively profit-minded. In fact, Houghcester was decently proud of its history, and concerned to make the most of it in every sense.

The excavation of the Priory was being carried out by the Houghcester City Archaeological Unit, financed by public money (with a few private contributions), and supervised by the Chief Archaeological Officer. The diggers, rank and file, were a mixture of professional archaeologists and volunteer helpers.

The volunteers ranged in age from sixteen to thirty-one and had various reasons for being there. Three were students of archaeology, one had been sent by her parents, one wished to impress her history teacher at school, with whom she was emotionally obsessed, another was unemployed and wanted to get away from home, and three liked outdoor life and were at a loose end.

Susan Price was there because she had been crossed in love.

She was nineteen and the experience was new to her; she found its effect devastating. She had never been profoundly unhappy before, but being a sensible and stoical girl she had decided to treat her condition like a debilitating illness, battle with it alone, look to the future, and seek some useful occupation. She saw the dig advertised in *The Times*, and applied.

The objectives of the dig were briefly stated: to establish, as far as possible, the ground-plan of the Saxon church which pre-dated the medieval Priory church (itself almost literally in the shadow of Hough-cester's famous cathedral) of which little now remained except the walls, and investigate the Priory burial ground which lay above the foundations of the early church. The skeletons, after removal and examination for demographic and medical purposes, were to be reinterred with Christian rites (most of them were thirteenth and fourteenth century, with a few from the Saxon Christian period), and the site tidied up and planted out as a municipal garden, preserving the ruined walls.

The diggers crouched as though in worship above their allotted squares of ground, each with paraphernalia of plastic bucket, trowel, brush, shovel and paintbrush for meticulous clearance work. It was a good summer, and they wore, for the most part, jeans or tattered shorts, T-shirts or (for the men) navvies' vests. Some of them had straw hats. The site, at this stage of its clearance, looked like the dusty section of a bee-hive – many shallow dirt pits, some with the delicate tracery of a person laid bare, dome of skull, rib-cage, hand splayed out like a fan, others with leg-bones sticking out from the dry wall of soil, or a huddle of tibia, fibula, crania and so forth that must be carefully exposed and photographed before being removed.

Maggie Spink, the director of the dig, moved all day long around the site, checking, measuring, photographing, removing finds (the detritus of sherds, fragments of china, buttons, gnarled twigs of metal, bits of clay pipe and lumps of aged glass that had accumulated at every layer) and chivvying those who knocked off periodically for a smoke in the sun. Since the site lay at the very heart of Houghcester, and on the route from the multi-storey car park to the cathedral, she had to deal also with the mild curiosity of the public, who were fenced off with wattle hurdles. When obliged to answer their questions, she was patient, but a little aloof; she would explain – briefly – the objectives and achievements of the dig, while – tacitly – making it clear that a more complex account would be above their heads. Those professionally concerned with the past, she seemed to suggest, are indeed accountable for what they are doing, but only up to a point; we are all technicians, now, and our ancestors are best approached with a proper expertise.

She was a dumpy woman in her late thirties, with short straw-coloured hair, a large bottom and brusque manner. She dressed with what seemed an aggressive disregard for femininity. Susan Price was much alarmed by her, during her first few days on the dig, and deplored particularly the ankle-socks worn with open sandals.

'You're reading what at Bristol?' she had said to Susan, and when

Susan had replied, English, she had said 'Why?'

To which Susan could find no reply at all.

The other professional archaeologists treated her with respect: she was, they informed the volunteers, first class at the job, she had a growing reputation, had dug at this place and that, been associated with a string of impressive names. The volunteers approached her with circumspection; they had all, on arrival, been a little surprised to find their presence accepted not with gratitude, but rather as though the benefit were the other way round. They were privileged, Maggie seemed to suggest, on her introductory tour of instruction and explanation, to be apprenticed in this way. It was as though they were permitted to be acolytes at the religious ceremony of some sect from which they were bound, by their nature, to be excluded. For some, this was tantalising; they picked up the technical jargon of the archaeologists and brandished it around. For a few it was irritating; one young schoolteacher left after two days, complaining that he had been patronised. For most, it was neither here nor there; they had come to pass the time, not to have opinions.

Susan Price, at the beginning, was only partly there in any case.

She squatted over Burial No. 38, brushing crumbs of soil from a battered rib-cage, and addressed someone quite different: I expect you will be in France by now, she said, you and Jane. I can see you – I only wish I couldn't – sitting by the road, waiting for the next lift. Jane is all brown by now, I daresay, looking very nice. I am brown, too, as it happens, for what that's worth which is not much since I never look at myself in a mirror, these days, there doesn't seem a lot of point.

When, exactly, did you start to go off me? I have to put it bluntly, because I suspect that only through bluntness am I going to get over this (do people?). I think, examining things, it must have been around that time we went to Bath for the day; I didn't realise it then, but looking back, I can detect a whiff of indifference. And then, there was that time you didn't turn up when we'd arranged to meet after my lecture and now I realise you must have . . .

The dig packed up, each day, at five-thirty. The plastic bags of finds were removed to the disused Victorian school nearby which had been made over to the Unit for the summer; there, Maggie Spink would begin her evening's work of sorting and classification, while the rest filled in their 'skelly charts' – the surviving bits of person coloured in on a blue-print of what there ought to be, a heap of eccentric skeleton portraits with one red leg, six ribs, half a cranium, or pelvis and right foot only. They then dispersed to their homes or to the old police station scheduled for demolition in the autumn – allotted to the rest as a billet. There, they heated baked beans on primuses, talked, read, or wandered off into the city.

Susan, for whom the process of self-distraction was a primary concern, bought guide-books and did the job properly. She studied the place as though she might be required to answer examination questions on it. She wandered in the cathedral for hours on end.

The cathedral prospered all summer long; tourists flowed through it from early morning till sunset – American, French, German, Dutch, English – a quick canter, a leisurely stroll, a protracted tour of inspection according to age, temperament and degree of interest. Not since the era of pilgrimages could the place have done such good business. Admittedly, the poor and the uncharitable slid quickly past the prominent Appeal Box at the entrance, but almost everyone bought postcards, tea-towels, leather book-marks tooled in gold with a brass-rubbing of Sir Toby and Lady Falconer (c. 1428), pottery mugs picturing the west front, transparencies of the stained glass. The chapter house, converted into a tea-room and snack bar, was also enjoying a boom. Outside, in the cloisters and on the green, itinerant young of all nationalities sprawled in the sunshine. The cathedral officials presided with benevolence and tact, discreetly hovering behind pillars and at entrances, ready with information should it be required, not intruding unless invited. Not everyone wants Perpendicular windows, late Saxon wall-paintings or fifteenth-century misericords thrust upon them, after all, they may be there for quite other reasons – to placate their relatives, for a cup of tea, a break from driving, a snooze or a cuddle on the grass. The past has no right to impose itself on people; it is there to be taken or left, as we see fit, as it suits us. It is our turn now.

Susan, her guide-books in hand, diligently sorted out styles and periods. She noted the surviving medieval street plan of the city – surviving in name and spirit only, for most of the early buildings had been torn down in the post-war zest for reconstruction. She agreed with Professor Pevsner that not all – indeed not much – of the reconstruction was successful. The shopping precinct, the public library, the new council offices, all had an aggressive immaturity, at odds with their background. They had not yet settled down, were in uneasy conflict with the old almshouses, the one remaining medieval gateway; in Sheep Street, which suggested quite other things, Boots and Mothercare confronted one another with a blaze of plate glass.

The cathedral was mature, all right. It had been quietly maturing away there since its foundation in the early eleventh century, to such effect that the west tower was now in need of a massive underpinning job, the roof would have to be completely stripped and releaded, and the external carvings were in a sorry state. The appeal target had been pushed up perforce from £750,000 to a round million. The Friends (of the cathedral, that is) were working flat out.

Susan, who had never before paid much attention to architecture, found herself not only distracted from her mourning but curiously soothed by the cathedral. There was something reassuring about this juxtaposition of period and mood, in which, eventually, what has been and what is now are reconciled and live together.

Her fellow diggers were less concerned with the place. The professional archaeologists spent much of the evenings, when they were not helping Maggie Spink in the school, discussing their career prospects; the rest – the amateurs – regretted the lack of a television and amused themselves as best they could. If they could afford cinema or pub, they went out; if not, they lounged on their camp-beds, ate, drank tea and gossiped. In the intimacy of their closed society a sense of being cronies had soon been established, a defensive solidarity as the unskilled labouring mass. The student teacher and the girl from Nottingham had begun a flirtation that looked like developing into something more; the Welsh boy taught everyone to play poker and kept intense noisy games going till late at night. They talked about themselves, about each other, about Maggie Spink.

'Hey . . .' said Gwyn, dealing the cards one evening. 'I found something out today. She's not a Miss at all, our Maggie, she's a Mrs. There's been a mister, but there ain't no more. He skipped out on her.'

Someone said, 'Wouldn't you?' There were giggles.

Maggie Spink appeared, on the dig's official documents, as Dr Spink. And yet, it was true, a married state was inconceivable, for less easily definable reasons than her ringless hands, her stridently self-sufficient manner. The girl from Nottingham said, 'How do you know?'

'John Hacker told me' – John Hacker was one of the career archaeologists – 'It was all years ago and she's dropped her married name and gone back to what she was called before and she gets hopping mad if anyone ever mentions it.'

'Lots of people don't use married names now – women – specially if they've been working before, had careers.'

'Get Ms Women's Lib there!'

'Oh, shut up,' said the girl from Nottingham. 'I was only saying. Here – it's your deal.'

Susan Price was vaguely moved by this exchange; she felt a creak of compassion for Maggie, a person who had not, hitherto, seemed in any way approachable. Even so, the feeling did not go very deep; she was still bound up in her own day-to-day survival, was only superficially present. Her internal monologues, though, she was surprised to note, were taking on a slightly different tone.

What about you? she said to Burial No. 47. Did you ever have to endure this kind of thing? Sexual jealousy, it's called, and it's just about the nastiest feeling I've ever come across. Actually, since you were probably a nun I daresay it didn't arise – I hope not, for your sake. You didn't live all that long, of course – female, aged thirty to forty, level 306,

right arm, pelvis and rib-cage, lower jaw-bone, left femur and meta-
tarsus. You had a lot of trouble with your teeth, and what was probably
arthritis, according to John Hacker, and there is evidence of malnutrition.

I'm not a lot better, not yet. Curiously, the thought of her – Jane – is the
worst; that's the one I have to squash firmest. With him it's different;
since I've got to think of him all the time, can't help it, then I might as well
accept it. Re-run things, as it were, like an old film. It hurts; the funny
thing is that each time it looks ever so slightly different.

That weekend at his parents' he was a bit off-hand with his mother; I
didn't notice at the time. It's as though, then, I saw him head-on, in one
way only (is that what's meant by love being blinkered?); now I remember
things I didn't really register then. That conversation we had once about
abstract pictures, in that art gallery, I remember every word (what I have
to avoid is the feel of his arm round me, when we were having it . . .) but I
find I'm not agreeing with him quite so much. Oh, but . . . I'd want to say,
if we were having it again, and, no I think you're wrong about that what I
think is . . .

July became August; the cathedral clocked up its first hundred
thousand of the Appeal, and celebrated by staging *son et lumière* for the
next four weeks; the diggers, scratching their way down through levels
273–401, became a small, enclosed sect, in much the same way as the
Priory whose detectable past they were so efficiently interpreting. There
was a hierarchy, alliances and enmities, in-jokes and tribal jargon. One or
two departed, a couple more came and were absorbed. The weather held.
In the school the burials were stacked in heaps of plastic bags, awaiting
collection; the skelly charts filled two walls; trestle tables were covered
with trays of finds. Unexpected dramas or reverses punctuated the
routine of the days: a conjectured drain turned out to be the entrance to an
eighteenth-century charnel house, heavily populated, which was re-
sealed after hasty investigation; the interesting depressions running
parallel to the nave of the Saxon church proved to be Victorian celery
beds, also an irrelevant intrusion. The past is a disorderly and unreliable
affair; you cannot trust it very far.

Susan, all one long, hot day, scraped with paintbrush and trowel
around the fragile, bird-like bones of a baby (level 372, male, probably
still-born, date uncertain, and what was *that* doing in a nunnery?). You'll
have got to the Mediterranean by now, she said, if you've been lucky with
lifts, or maybe you're in Spain, like you said you might, when we had that
last talk, that awful one, when I cried (which makes me hot with shame to
think of, I never cry). I slept rather well last night, you might be interested
to hear, first time for ages.

I have been going over everything we ever said to each other;
sometimes, quite frankly, you seem to me a bit opinionated. Not that that
means I *feel* any different, now; it is just rather interesting.

The thing is, am I changing you, or is that how you were? How will I ever know?

Either the heat, or the Victorian celery beds, had put Maggie Spink into an irritable state. She chivvied everybody, extended the working day by half an hour, and kept going on about how the excavation was behind schedule. 'That is the trouble about a dig with a predominantly amateur element – you simply cannot get the right sense of urgency into people.' Susan, tracing the tiny bleached splinters of the baby's foot, felt a shadow across her back and looked up into Maggie's sun-reddened face. She was agitated, on the edge of an outburst. After some discussion of the burial, and examination of a small heap of sherds, she said suddenly, 'I've had to separate those two. I really cannot stand all that whispering and pawing on the site. Tim can go and number finds in the school.'

The affair between the student teacher and the girl from Nottingham had prospered.

Susan smiled. 'Oh dear,' she said, 'I'm sure they don't really mean . . .'

Maggie said violently, 'If they want to fuck that's entirely up to them, but not on my dig, thank you very much.' Her outrage seemed quite out of proportion to the offence; Susan, embarrassed, turned back to the baby. Lately, she had found herself for some reason the object of the older woman's gruff favour; she was considered apparently more serious and responsible than the rest. Once, Maggie had said, 'It's a pity you didn't think of reading archaeology. You might have done quite well.' Susan had repeated this to one of the younger career archaeologists, who had laughed – 'Oh, Maggie doesn't recognise other branches of study. You should have told her English literature is quite well-regarded too.'

Now, Maggie had walked off along the narrow earth balk that served as a cat-walk among the burial pits, Susan, sitting back for a moment to wipe her face – the heat was exhausting – saw her ankle-socks, her stocky legs, her large loose bottom, and felt a rush of pity; there was something schoolgirlish about the woman, as though she carried an albatross adolescence with her, some fatal undevelopment of the heart.

The separation of the lovers caused general merriment. Maggie was determined to run a clean site, it was suggested, in every sense. Or maybe she wished to preserve the moral spirit of the Priory.

Susan had taken to wandering around the cathedral and its precincts for half an hour or so most evenings, before it grew dark and the place was given over to the portentous booming of the son et lumière. It was there, a few days later, that she met Maggie, who came striding through the cloister where Susan was sitting on a lower inner wall, enjoying the effects of evening sunlight on the fan-vaulting. Seeing her, Maggie stopped.

'Oh, hello, what on earth are you doing here?'

'Nothing, particularly. Just that it's specially nice at this time of day.'

'Is it? I wouldn't know. I had to see the cathedral people about this Open Day idea – endless talk, wasting half my evening. I haven't even started on the finds yet, or mapping these new walls.' She had begun to move on again, saying, 'Are you going back?' Susan, who had intended to sit for longer, found herself drawn alongside. She said, 'Open Day?'

'They want us to have an Open Day on the site,' said Maggie irritably, 'to coincide with their junketings. It's the thousandth anniversary of the reconsecration or something. Anyway, they want us to do conducted tours of the site, with explanatory talks and stuff, and a display of the finds and whatnot.'

Susan said, 'Isn't that rather a nice idea?'

'Why?'

'Well, get people interested. And they are, they're always asking us things . . .' Catching Maggie's expression she added, 'Of course, I'm afraid we're not all that good at explaining, but we do what we can.'

Maggie said, 'Oh, I suppose so. But it means losing a whole day.'

They had reached the west door of the cathedral. Susan, arrested as always by the delicacy of the carvings, the tier upon tier of saints, the lavish complexity of leaves, of beasts, of fact and fantasy, of the pious and the secular, was silent. Maggie, walking quickly through, said, 'We can do a short cut through the building, can't we? Oh, I suppose I'll have to go along with them – I did point out that it was mucking up our schedule, but I doubt if that sank in far. There was one bloke who had what I suppose was quite a valid point about attracting possible funds. You never know who may show up – local big-wigs and so forth. We need at least another season on this dig and if the Ministry grant is the same next year it quite frankly won't do.'

It was almost eight; the tourists had ebbed, leaving the cathedral in a sombre peace, except for occasional quackings over the loud-speakers outside, getting themselves into good voice for the night's event. The Gift Shop had closed, and the Chapter House Refreshment Bar. Evensong (shifted forward by an hour to accommodate the *son et lumière*) was over. It was chill, much cooler than outside, and there was that curious unanalysable ecclesiastical smell of stone, brass polish and something that could not in an Anglican cathedral be incense, and yet was oddly reminiscent. It was as though the place generated its own climate, regardless of contemporary conditions. Sunlight poured through the clerestory windows, defining quatrefoils and shafts, losing its intensity as it fell down the heights of the building to become a rainbow reflection on the hefty piers of the nave. Elsewhere, at ground level, dusk had muted all the conflicts and confusions of daylight – the material variety of marble, stone, wood, brass, iron; the shufflings of time and style; the polyglot babble of visitors. It had, for once, a unity.

Susan said, with diffidence, 'I always think it's odd you can have this part so Norman, and then all the rest later, and somehow it works. I've never really looked properly at a cathedral before.'

'Mmn,' said Maggie. 'Of course there's a lot of nonsense talked about the original plan – the official guide-book's quite wrong, Battersby did it and he's notoriously unsound.' They had reached the main entrance. Standing in a flood of multi-coloured light from the rose window, her face bathed in it, suddenly beautified, as though by some divine intervention – the miraculous staunching of a wound, the non-putrefaction of a corpse – she went on grudgingly, 'Oh well, I suppose I'll have to lay it on, this bally Open Day. You could help John and Steve with the chat bits, I won't be able to do it all and you've picked up quite a lot really.' She moved, and her face turned from rose to gold. 'By the way, why did you come on the dig? One wonders vaguely sometimes – you know, what brings people.'

It was the first time Susan had ever heard her express curiosity about another person, she realised; Maggie seemed usually quite set apart from ordinary probings and exchanges, like someone with a heavy cold, or the impediment of a language difficulty.

Susan had never told anyone on the dig of her private preoccupation. Now, she said, 'Oh, I just thought I'd like to do something different for part of the summer, learn about something new.'

Saying it, she felt shabby in the untruth, as though she had in some curious way misused the place: the beauty of the cathedral, those inaccessible people whose bones she handled every day.

But Maggie had already lost interest. She said, with a glance at her watch, 'Oh God – nearly half past eight, I'll be in the school till all hours. See you tomorrow,' and strode away over the precinct; at the far side, people were assembled on the scaffolding from which the *son et lumière* could be best appreciated; behind, the cathedral awaited its nightly bashing by searchlight and sepulchral voices.

The preparations for the Open Day drove Maggie into a frenzy of exasperated activity ('. . . though I don't know what the hell I'm thinking of, letting the schedule be set back by at least two or three days just so we can stand around answering a lot of no doubt irrelevant questions, still, I suppose public relations *do* matter . . .'): the school was cleared, in so far as possible, and a display of finds arranged on trestle tables. A large, explanatory plan of the site was drawn by Gwyn and the girl from Nottingham, the chronology clarified by the use of different coloured tempo pens. Maggie and the other professionals divided up the site between them, each to guard and explain his or her own territory. The volunteers were detailed off on to stewarding duties. Susan was in charge of the school, and had the job of explaining the finds.

They were all surprised by the success of the occasion. Admittedly, the weather helped, but even a warm sunny day could not entirely account for the file of people who shuffled through the site, tiptoeing along the

cat-walks, keeping a respectful distance from Maggie's NO VISITORS
BEYOND THIS POINT signs, listening, asking questions. In the school,
Susan was hemmed in. She felt like an overtaxed shop-assistant or
barmaid, explaining her wares for hour after hour – the Roman pottery,
the fragments of painted tile from the Priory, the coins and buttons and
broken combs, the medieval shoe, the fourteenth-century slipware dish
(almost complete), the pins and nails and pipe-bowls, the bones of the
stillborn baby arranged on cottonwool in a shoebox (the rest of the burials
were stacked away in their plastic bags in the school washroom).

It had been intended that they should close down at five o'clock.
However, this was presumably not made clear in the publicity put out by
the cathedral authorities, for at five fifteen the queue waiting for
admission still reached the length of the outer wattle barrier. There was a
hasty consultation. Maggie wanted to make a firm announcement and
have any further comers turned away; she was prevailed on to continue
till six, and grudgingly agreed. By a quarter to six she had left her own
section of the site and was patrolling, looking at her watch and frowning,
as though she would stem the flow by sheer force of will. She seemed in
an odd state of combined irritation and elation. All day, her voice had
been high-pitched in its rattle of explanation and instruction; she had
been impatient with questioners.

Coming into the school, where a couple of dozen people were still filing
past the trestle tables, she lifted her wrist, tapped her watch, mouthed at
Susan 'Time's up'. She edged past the visitors, and said sharply to a small
child whose fingers had crept towards the shoebox containing the baby's
bones, 'Don't touch, please.'

The baby had aroused interest, all day. Everybody had wanted to
speculate about how old, and why, and when. A midwife had offered
technical explanations, gleaned from something about the shape of the
skull. This particular child had been staring, fascinated, for several
minutes. Now, he said suddenly to Susan, 'Am I like that inside?'

She said, 'Yes.' His parents, over by the door, were signalling to him to
come. Slowly, he spread out his hand, staring at the fingers. Looking up
at her again, he said, 'Will I be like that when I'm deaded?'

She hesitated, glancing for a moment at the parents, still signalling, at
Maggie's expression of fretful endurance. She said, 'Yes. And me.'

The child nodded gravely; he shot out his thin arm and stared at it.
Then he turned and went after his parents. Maggie sighed and said,
'Well, I suppose we must count ourselves lucky if nothing's been
damaged or nicked. I hope nothing *has* been damaged or nicked?'

Susan said, 'I don't think so.' The last visitors were leaving now.
Maggie said, 'Well, that's it.' She drew her hand across her forehead, and
Susan saw that it was shaking. From outside, the other volunteers were
waving with glass-raising gestures: they were off to the pub. She said to

Maggie, 'I'm going now. I'll come back later and help straighten up in here, if you like.' She felt another of those small rushes of sympathy: that shaking hand – why, in what way, had the day been such a strain?

It was a couple of hours before she returned to the school, and was surprised to find Maggie alone: she had imagined that John Hacker and the others would have been there. Maggie said, 'Oh, I told them to push off, I can get on quicker on my own,' adding – not very graciously – 'I'd forgotten you said you'd come – actually you could give me a hand with these sherds, they seem to have got somewhat muddled up.'

Her voice was slightly slurred. She reached under the table and brought out a half-empty bottle of wine, 'Here, d'you want a drink? There's another glass on the windowsill, I think.'

She had done little about clearing up; the display of finds was much as it had been earlier. Instead, she seemed to have been fiddling with some bits of glazed pottery, the pieces of the slipware dish which, it was thought, could probably be reconstructed for the City Museum.

Susan said, 'It's just like stuff in trendy shops now, isn't it, that glaze?'

'Is it? I s'pose so.' Maggie began to talk about the day. '. . . Pretty well impossible to get across to people what this sort of thing is really about' – she squinted at a glazed fragment, 'That's later – how's that got in with this lot? Yes, it's from Pit 18 – I knew people would start messing things about. And all those endless irrelevant questions – like that kid you were talking to. There were kids all over the place – I was going spare at some moments, thinking they'd crash down into a burial or something.'

Susan said, 'I didn't think he *was* irrelevant – that little boy.'

'What?' Maggie slopped some more wine into her glass, waved the bottle at Susan – who saw now with a twitch of alarm that there was another bottle, empty, under the table.

Maggie talked. About past digs; about her doctorate; about the write-up of the current dig which, if things worked out right, should do her reputation '. . . no harm at all, in fact rather a lot of good – I think I may put out an interim thing even before next season.' And then, suddenly, she was talking about more personal things '. . . You didn't know I was married once, did you?' She chuckled, waving the bottle again. 'More? Come on, we might as well finish it.'

Susan, embarrassed, said, 'Well, actually, someone did once say . . .'

'That's something that simply isn't relevant either, my marriage. What's happened is over and done with. You just don't give it another thought, if you've got any sense – you move on. It's the only way to live, if you ask me.' She paused, shoving the sherds around on the table in front of her like pieces of a jigsaw puzzle. 'When Derek walked out on me I thought, right, that's that. Finished. Kaput. Take a deep breath and forget it. He wasn't an archaeologist, by the way – that was one thing that was wrong from the start. And, frankly now, it's as though he never was. Do you know, I can't really remember what he looked like.' She squinted up at Susan, her expression distinctly triumphant. 'He absolutely no longer exists.'

There was a silence. Maggie took a swig at her drink. Susan said awkwardly, 'Actually, I think – I don't know – if it was me, I think I'd want to try to work out why – try to see what it was that had happened to me, after all it's all going to be part of the person you end up being and in that case . . .'

'You're wrong,' said Maggie flatly. 'You go nuts that way, mulling things over. Take my word for it. Wipe the slate clean – wham!' She swept her arm across the table in a decisive gesture; sherds and other bits and pieces went flying; she was quite drunk now. She slumped with her head cupped in her hands, elbows on the table, as Susan scrambled on the floor, picking things up. 'Wham! Bam! Finish!'

A large piece of floor tile from the early church was shattered into several smaller pieces; the base of a glass bottle was broken, too; the shoebox had upended, scattering the baby's bones all over the place. Carefully, Susan gathered everything up. Some bones, she saw anxiously, had slipped down between two worm-eaten floorboards and would have to be retrieved tomorrow, somehow, with pincers or something, or at the worst one would have to take the boards up.

She said to Maggie, gently, 'Wouldn't you like to go back to your digs now? You look awfully tired.'

'I'm never tired. And I'll tell you another thing – celibacy's a damn sight more comfortable than people make out. Don't you be fooled.' She scowled at the sherds in front of her, roughly assembled in the form of a dish, and shunted them into confusion again with a savage gesture, spilling more on to the floor. Susan said, 'Oh please – come on, Maggie, let's go now.'

Maggie shoved her chair back from the table. She stared vacantly at the window, at the night sky, at the lurid glimmer of the cathedral, 'You take my advice, Susan, I'm a lot older than you and I know how it goes. I know the score. Don't you ever let yourself be lumbered with what's over and done with. Travel light, that's what.' Her face was red and shiny; she looked older than she was and also, in some elusive way, younger: her features had, still, the chubbiness, the expectancy, of a girl's face. She groaned suddenly. 'Oh God, what a day! I *hate* having people all around me like that, on and on . . .'

Susan took her arm. 'I'll walk back with you.'

They went out together. Maggie, staggering a little, would have left the place open; Susan found the key hanging behind the door and locked up. Walking through the empty streets, Maggie said blearily, 'Well, thanks for helping, anyway. You know, as I say, it's a pity you never thought of doing archaeology.' She tapped Susan's arm, peering sideways at her in the darkness. 'It's not half a bad career – I mean, yes, it's badly paid and all that, but there's more important things than that, aren't there? I'll tell you one thing – I've never been bored, not for fifteen years, and you can't say that in every job, can you?'

Susan walked slowly back to the police station. It was quite late; she had not been back since that morning; the others were playing poker. Someone said, 'Hey – there's a letter for you.'

She sat on the edge of her camp-bed, reading it. 'I got back a few days ago,' he wrote. 'Actually, Jane and I parted company around Rouen. It wasn't really working out all that well. I rang your mother and she said you were on this dig thing (that threw me a bit, I must say! Whatever put that idea into your head!) but probably going to finish at the end of the week. So what I've been wondering, Sue, is should I come down there and fetch you? I think I could get hold of my dad's car and maybe we could go off and have a few days somewhere . . .'

She sat there for a while, holding the letter, seeing, beyond the windows, the flare of the cathedral, hearing, behind the slam of the poker players' cards, the muffled and distorted boom of the loudspeakers, ending their nightly re-enactment of Houghcester's long and complex history. Then she got out her pad and began to write a reply: 'Actually,' she wrote, 'I think I'll stay on here a bit longer, maybe till the beginning of next term, more or less – some of the others are off soon, and I'd like to help out the woman who is in charge, I've come to feel a bit sorry for her. I suppose she's not all that nice but she means well. It has been interesting – seeing what people do who are professionally involved with history, as it were, I feel I've learned things, though I suppose nothing that's likely to be useful . . .'

Servants Talk About People:
Gentlefolk Discuss Things

'I THINK I knew his father,' said my uncle. 'Was he in India during the war?'

I said, 'I've really no idea. I don't know Mark all that well. I only mentioned him because I . . .'

'That'll be him,' said my uncle, with furrowed brow. 'He was in Calcutta in '43. Man with a limp. Played the trombone. Waiter! Could we have the menu?'

The menu, size of a wall-poster, was propped up before us by, in fact, a waitress. Even in the expensive murk of the restaurant it was difficult not to sense barely restrained passion of some kind; she stared over my uncle's head at the swing door leading to, presumably, the kitchens. My uncle, poring over the tortuously hand-written placard, said, 'I hope this place'll be all right. Neighbour of ours recommended it. They seem to go in for veal in a big way. Would you like a starter?'

The room was small – not more than half a dozen tables, only four of which were occupied – decorated in dark reds and browns with vaguely Edwardian connotations. The cuisine, from the menu, was an uncommitted mixture of continental and Sunday newspaper. My uncle said to the waitress, 'Three sherries, please, we'll order when my wife comes back.' He had to repeat himself, the girl being apparently locked in her communion of hatred with the kitchen door. 'Lucy's taking her time,' said my uncle, with irritation, looking towards the stairs.

They had arrived late and my aunt sped at once in the direction of the ladies'. She returned now with an expression of relief, freshly combed and made-up, and dabbed each cheek in turn against mine before she sat down. 'Lovely to see you, Tim. Do you know, there was a woman in there *exactly* like Aunt Christie. Do you remember Aunt Christie?'

'Not really, I was only about two when she died.'

'This woman had longer hair. Otherwise she was the spitting image. Fortyish.'

My uncle handed her the menu. 'Christie was fifty when she died.

Tummy cancer. I've ordered you a sherry, Lucy. Forty-five pence, I may say – disgraceful.'

'It's a rip-off,' said my aunt, who took pride in modernity of speech. She fished her glasses out of her handbag and studied the menu. 'I'll have veal with marsala sauce, and avocado to start. Now, we want to hear all your news, Tim.'

'Well,' I began. 'I suppose the main thing is that . . .'

My uncle interrupted, 'Does Mark Sadler live in Tunbridge Wells? That's where his father hailed from, I remember.'

'Honestly,' I said, 'I hardly know him – it was just that I went to a party of his once, when I was at college, in this street, so I knew where the restaurant was when you suggested meeting here.'

'Sadler?' said my aunt, putting her glasses away. 'Did I know him?' She was as spry as ever, her appearance nicely adjusted to the times; the glasses, at first grannyish, were up-to-the-minute fashion. Her calf and ankle, sticking out from under the dark brown linen tablecloth, were elegant. My uncle, as always, had the extremely clean, slightly over-fed look of a certain kind of upper-class Englishman. He was looking round now, with some impatience, for the waitress. 'Where's the fellow gone? We want to order?'

In fact, the sound of raised voices had been clearly audible, for the last five minutes or so, from beyond the swing door. As my uncle spoke, a longish male monologue, rising to a crescendo, was answered by something that resembled the hiss of escaping steam, followed instantly by a noise of breakage. I said, 'It was a girl, actually. There seems to be . . .' At the same moment the door opened and the waitress bounded through, her face contorted. She came to rest at my uncle's elbow, sniffing loudly.

My uncle said, 'Ah. Now we want a veal marsala, a cannelloni, and I'll have the duck. And an avocado and two pickled herrings to start with. And the wine-list, please. You wouldn't have known Sadler,' he went on, to my aunt. 'It was in the war. But he'd been at school with Jimmy Phillips.'

'I never liked Jimmy Phillips all that much. I hope they hurry up, I'm starving.'

The waitress had returned to the kitchen, and re-emerged now with two main courses for the table next to ours, at which a pair of young and spruce executives were engaged in competitive discourse. In the confidential light of the red-shaded wall lamps, tears could be seen trickling down her face. My aunt said, 'That girl's got a filthy cold – I hope she doesn't give it to us.'

'Well' – my uncle raised his glass – 'cheers. By the way, thanks very much for that thing you sent us, the er . . .'

'Article,' I said.

'That's right. I read it. Very interesting.'

'I'm going to work it up into a book eventually,' I said, 'I hope. That was just some preliminary work on sixteenth-century land tenure – what I want to do is develop it into something rather more general on pre-enclosure peasant status and the regional differences in that and in land-holding generally – there's not been a lot done on that and I think the variations, particularly between north and south, are greater than people have thought.'

'Quite,' said my uncle, 'I hadn't come across that periodical before, the er . . .'

'*English Historical Review.*'

'That's right. Who runs it?'

'I think it's someone called Henderson, at York.'

My uncle looked thoughtful, but made no comment.

My aunt said, 'I always thought it was philosophy you did – I could have sworn. Oh, we met someone from your college the other day – at least he used to be there. Peter Samuels.'

Peter Samuels was given due attention. We had been waiting for ten minutes or so, with no sign of sustenance. There had been further outbreaks of contention from beyond the swing door, but now a sinister silence. My aunt, fidgeting, said, 'I want my avocado.' A moment later, a small dark man wearing a blood-stained apron shot from the kitchens, a tray on his arm, dealt avocado and pickled herrings to our table and two lemon sorbets to the neighbouring one, and retreated once more. The door, swinging open, released a brief spasm of sobbing and the noise of a saucepan boiling over.

My uncle, dismembering his herring, said, 'How's that girl? Sarah Axbridge.'

I had hoped not to talk about Sarah. I said, 'Well, actually we don't see each other any more.' My aunt said, 'Pity. She was very pretty, I thought. I loved that dress she was wearing when we met – I don't suppose you know where she got it?' She scoured the shell of her avocado, dabbed at her lips with her napkin and went on, 'Well, anyway, it's a good thing you didn't get married, it would have been much worse breaking up then.'

There was a loud thump against the kitchen door and the waitress came bursting through, using a brown suitcase as a battering ram. She had taken off her apron and wore a coat over jeans and a T-shirt. In the other hand she carried a fistful of paper carrier bags, which banged against the tables as she stumbled through the restaurant and out of the street door. My aunt, lifting her eyes as far as the perambulant carrier bags, said, 'That reminds me, I must pop into Selfridges this afternoon. We saw Dottie last week, Tim – she sent you her love.'

We worked our way through various members of the family – their physical appearance and personal quirks; at least, my aunt and uncle did. There was, by now, a considerable restiveness apparent at the other tables; my uncle, infected, said, 'I must say this place is very slow.'

I said, 'I think there's some kind of trouble in the kitchen.'

My uncle drummed his fingers on the table irritably. In the ensuing pause I said, 'I've been getting involved in politics since I last saw you – real grass-roots politics. I'm standing for the local council, going round knocking on doors and all that. What's interesting is that local issues aren't always . . .'

'Goodness,' said my aunt. 'How frightfully energetic of you, Tim. Rupert, do yell for that waitress again.'

My uncle, thumping peremptorily on the table, said, 'Bob Chambers should never have recommended this place. I shall mention it next time I see him.'

'Bob Chambers has the most enormous wife,' said my aunt. 'She is quite the largest woman I have ever seen. Colossal.'

My uncle said with mild reproof, 'Tim hasn't actually met Bob Chambers, Lucy.'

'Oh, goodness,' said my aunt. 'Tim knows perfectly well I'm absolutely fascinated by people. I can't help that, can I?' She stared across the table at my uncle with girlish defiance.

'All right, darling,' said my uncle amiably. 'Keep your hair on. I must say if we don't get something to eat soon . . .'

There was an inrush of culinary smells, pitched to a somewhat worrying state not far short of burning, as the door swung open again and the – presumably – chef, darted through. He looked round the tables, then at the series of dishes teetering on the tray he balanced along one arm, and gave a kind of moan. Then, shooting over to our table, he said in one gasp, 'Oneduckcannellonivealmarsala?'

'What?' said my uncle. 'Oh yes, that's right. And some vegetables, I hope. Oh – and we asked for a carafe of red wine. Some time ago,' he added, severely.

The man, whose face, one now saw, was incandescent with sweat, was muttering to himself in an indecipherable language as he tipped the lid off another dish, peered into it, and glanced wildly round the room. At the neighbouring table, the executives were in a state of loud complaint.

'I daresay he's foreign,' said my aunt, inspecting her veal. 'This looks nice. Try again, Rupert – we want the wine now, not later.'

My uncle, busy at his duck, repeated the request; it was met with a *tour de force* display of suffering, resignation, despair, incredulity and exasperation. My uncle said, 'Oh, and some butter, please.' The swing doors spun twice more; the executives departed acrimoniously; somewhere out of sight a telephone rang and rang; the wine, apparently self-propelled, arrived on the table. My uncle, pouring it, said, 'Now, Tim, you're not telling us a thing about yourself – what are you doing these days?'

'Well, in fact what I was going to tell you is that I've got a job.'

'Oh, super,' said my aunt. 'What doing?'

'It's nothing very grand, but I'm very pleased about it. It's a lectureship in history at Liverpool.'

'University?' said my aunt.

My uncle, throwing her a severe glance, said, 'Liverpool. Now isn't that the place Melton is vice-chancellor of?'

'Yes.'

'You knew him, I suppose?'

'Actually, no. In any case an appointment to a junior lectureship wouldn't be . . .'

'You should have told me you were after a job at Liverpool,' said my uncle reprovingly. 'One of my co-directors is a close friend of Melton's, I happen to know.'

'Is that John Peterson?' said my aunt. 'Or Duggie?'

'Duggie.'

'Duggie's not looking well these days. Let me see now – Liverpool? I don't believe I know a soul in Liverpool. Do you think you'll like it there?'

'I really don't know. But they're going to let me do the lecturing course I'd prefer and there are some people in the department interested in the same kind of thing as I am, and I hope . . .'

My aunt put her knife and fork down and said in triumph, 'No, I'm wrong, there's those people we met years ago on holiday in Tossa – Harker, that's right – Paul and Maisie. He was something in shipping, they lived just outside, I think . . .'

The theme was developed, with occasional assistance from my uncle, until we had all finished our main course and indeed had sat in front of our empty plates for a considerable time. My uncle, looking at his watch, exclaimed, 'Good Lord, going on for two. What about a pudding?'

We were alone in the restaurant now, except for two women deep in confidences and coffee on a shadowy banquette at the far side. For at least the last ten minutes or so there had been such a silence from the kitchen that it seemed possible that we had been abandoned altogether. I said, 'Perhaps we'd better just help ourselves.'

'Not a bad idea,' said my uncle. At the same moment the street door opened and the waitress came in, still coated, carrying the same suitcase and paper bags. She was no longer weeping but wore an expression of proud endurance – the bearing of the wronged heroine of Greek drama, immeasurably experienced in suffering. She swept through the room; I found myself shifting my chair to ease her passage, with deference.

My aunt stared at her. 'I should think she's a bit late to get a meal, that girl. They'll be closing soon.'

I said, 'Actually, she's the waitress.'

'No,' said my uncle. 'She's just come in from the street, I saw. The waitress was a chap with a dirty apron, I always remember faces.'

'No, you don't,' my aunt interjected. 'Helen Simmonds said you walked straight past her in the street the other day.'

'Oh, come,' said my uncle, 'I doubt that very much. In fact, I distinctly recall . . .'

Further dissension was forestalled by staccato sounds from the kitchen into which the waitress had vanished, leaving her suitcase in front of the serving-table.

'They are foreigners.' My aunt cocked an ear. 'Italian, I'd say. What a racket. Sounds as if someone's being killed.'

One of the women from the banquette, in search of a bill, opened the serving door; through it, and over her shoulder, I glimpsed a scene of enthusiastic reconciliation – steamy, in every sense. The woman who had opened the door coughed and retreated. I said, 'No, I don't think that's what they're doing, at least not now.'

My aunt obtained a menu from the neighbouring table. 'I fancy raspberry mousse. What about you, Tim?'

'Cheese for me,' said my uncle. I said I'd have the same. My uncle looked towards the kitchen, rapped on the table, and called 'Waiter!'

Nothing happened. My aunt began to say 'Really, this is . . .' The waitress, her coat shed and an apron inadequately arranged on top of her jeans and T-shirt, came tripping through the door, radiant with promise of various kinds. Snatching up a menu, she thrust it between us, at the same time making recommendations of main course dishes, and perhaps the pâté maison for a starter.

'We've had that bit,' said my aunt crossly. 'We want a pudding.' The waitress stared at us with evident disbelief, and reluctantly accepted my uncle's order. The two women on the banquette achieved their bill, though not without also being reoffered the menu. As she returned to the kitchen I glimpsed, for an instant, the chef, arms akimbo, in beaming expectancy. My aunt said, 'Why do you keep looking through that door, Tim?'

Our puddings arrived. The waitress, now, exuded an aggressive satisfaction, clearly not related to the food, which bore signs of neglect. My aunt, mercifully, was too preoccupied with recollections of a man she had met who had once known my former girlfriend to notice. In mid-discourse, she interrupted herself for a moment to say, 'Just one thing, Tim, and you mustn't think I'm getting at you, but you're not going to get too boring and wrapped up in your work, I hope' – she laid two fingers on my arm and smiled sweetly, to sugar the pill – 'I mean, I know it's marvellous doing a think-job like that, but you mustn't forget about people, in the end it's people that are interesting. There! That's my lecture said.'

'Don't you know the saying, Lucy?' said my uncle. 'History is about chaps; geography is about maps. Chaps are Tim's business.' He repeated the tag, with satisfaction.

'*Real* people,' said my aunt loftily. 'Well, I suppose we'd better be going.'

My uncle called for the bill, and paid; there was some confusion, the waitress having apparently no record of our orders. My uncle said, 'I don't think all that much of this place – a bit run-of-the-mill. Well, Tim, it's been good to hear what you're up to. Give my regards to Melton when you get to Liverpool – we haven't actually met but he'll know my name well through Duggie Hiscocks.'

Outside, my aunt kissed me warmly. 'And don't you go shutting yourself up in an ivory tower, Tim – keep in touch with the real world. 'Bye, now.'

After they had gone, I remembered that I had left some books in the restaurant. The waitress greeted me with fervour and non-recognition, offering the menu and a table at the window; it was only with difficulty that I rescued the books and escaped.

Help

HENRY SAID, 'You'll have to get some help.' He said it in the quiet, level tone that meant there was to be no discussion, the matter was decided now. But none the less Jenny said, 'What?' She said it not because she had not heard, but, like a child, because she did not want to hear.

'You'll have to get some help. I'm tired of this mess.'

Guiltily, Jenny followed his glance across the smeared table (teak, from Heals, Aunt Mary's wedding present), the children's coats tumbled behind the sofa, the clutter of toys and newspapers in the corner; on the other side of the wall she saw, as though through a glass screen, the ravaged kitchen.

'Oh dear,' she said. 'I suppose . . .' and then, hopefully, 'I don't think we could really afford it.'

'Why ever not? You make it sound as though we were on the bread-line. We're not short of money just now.'

'You have to pay about seventy pence an hour, I think.'

'Rubbish. The cleaners at the office get sixty.'

'I would feel frightfully awkward having someone polishing my floors and things, Henry, I honestly would.' That was a real objection, but he brushed it aside with a snort.

The main objection, of course, could not be stated. It was the thought of a daily – or three-mornings-a-week or whatever it was to be – witness to her household disasters. To her failures with the children, to her panics, to her frantic sorties at inappropriate times of day because there was no milk for the baby, no bread, nothing for dinner again. To the fact that she was never quite certain how to work the washing machine, that she was capable of leaving Emma alone in the kitchen with a pan of water boiling on the stove (and had twice done so), that she dithered and forgot and neglected. That, from time to time, that old sinister feeling of fear and desolation came over her and she sat weeping for an hour or so at a time, with the children as mute, uncomprehending spectators. Henry did not know that she occasionally had these brief recurrences of the old trouble;

by the time he came home she had pulled herself together, cleaned up her face, and the children (so far . . .) were too young to tell.

Henry said, more kindly, 'She could do the worst chores. Give you time for the rest.'

And perhaps that was true. Perhaps if there were someone to wash and hoover and do nappies and all that, perhaps then she would be able to keep the shiny things polished as Henry liked, make nicer food, empty ashtrays and plump up cushions before he came home, have clean and ironed shirts ready and available. She said, 'What do I do?'

He put the paper down and said in the slow and careful voice that meant: listen because I am not going to repeat this, 'You write out a card saying that you want a domestic help, and you put on it your name, address and telephone number, and you take it along to the tobacconist on the corner and ask them to put it in the window. Or, alternatively, you telephone or visit the local newspaper offices and put an advertisement in the paper. But that might be technically beyond you – I should settle for the tobacconist's window.'

She studied the phrasing of the postcards: Woman Wanted 2–3 hrs. Mons. or Weds.; Domestic Help 2 mornings weekly, times to suit, fares paid. She copied some of them down and, at home, composed a version of her own with which she felt quite pleased, and took it to the shop. The newsagent pinned it up on the board, and she walked back down the street feeling bold and resolute, pushing the pram with one hand and trying to stop Emma dashing into the road with the other. A confidence grew; tomorrow, or the next day, the house would be swept and dusted, the meals pre-arranged and successful, Henry pleased. Henry cared a great deal about such things. It was, he had once explained, in a clipped voice, a simple matter of efficiency. Other women seemed to manage, he had said. And indeed they did – Jenny was all admiration. Henry's sister, with her four children. . . . Fiona Talbot next door . . . And how could Henry have known, in their courting days, that she would turn out like this? He had had a bit of a raw deal, she could see that, and except for the occasional sharp remark, he was very patient. Sometimes he polished things himself, or cleaned a sink or bath, and she was filled with a sense of guilt and inadequacy. Mercifully, the worst crises took place during the day, when he was at the office. Poor Henry, how could he have known . . . ? But, a small voice cried out occasionally, how could I have known either?

She waited for a response to her advertisement, vacillating between confidence and anxiety. When the front-door bell rang, and simulta- neously Emma fell down the stairs, while she was in the middle of bathing the baby, she imagined another calm, efficient presence sorting things out, and the future seemed rosy indeed. But when, half an hour before the dreaded hour of Henry's return, Emma deposited a garden trug of dirt on the hall carpet and Jenny, in her haste to clear it up, stumbled against the kitchen table and knocked over the only bottle of milk, she was glad to be alone with her panic. She could always lie, and say Emma spilled the milk. But nothing happened all day; there was no response to the advertisement.

The next day there was a phone call. It was about the job, the caller said. Were there, she enquired, any children? Jenny said yes, there were, uncertain if this was desirable or not. The caller said, regretfully, that she didn't care for a place with children, not that she had anything against them, but you never saw a job finished, did you, if there were small children around to mess the place up? They parted, with mutual apologies, and Jenny felt an unmistakable lift of relief. Later, she said to Henry, 'I'm afraid there's no luck with the help. There aren't many answers.'

He said, 'Give it a bit longer.' It was a bad evening: the dinner undercooked, and he had found all the children's toys under the sofa where she had pushed them in her efforts to tidy the room before he came home. In silence, he removed them and took them through to the playroom; she could hear the staccato sounds of his irritated sorting of bricks, beads, pieces of Lego and small wheeled objects. Later, he went next door to have a drink with the Talbots. There wouldn't be toys under Fiona's sofa.

By the next day she was again waiting hopefully for the telephone. It rang twice; the first caller decided the bus routes were not convenient. The second said she was Mrs Porch, and she would like to call this afternoon.

Mrs Porch arrived precisely at the time she had suggested. Jenny watched her from the sitting-room window, shutting the garden gate carefully behind her and walking up the path, pausing only to take an appreciative sniff at one of Henry's roses. Jenny felt a mixture of relief and apprehension. At least she was not old – one of her fears had been the embarrassment of someone middle-aged, old even, slaving away to do the work that she, Jenny, should be capable of doing herself. But this woman, though older than herself, was only in her later thirties or early forties. On the other hand, she looked disconcertingly brisk and competent, potentially critical.

Jenny opened the door. Mrs Porch said, 'Mrs Taylor? I'm Mrs Porch – about the job.'

Jenny, confused, found herself blushing and talking incoherently. She had rehearsed this moment: now, it was Mrs Porch who led the way into the sitting-room, looked round for somewhere to put her coat, sat down after a moment and said, 'They're nice, these houses, aren't they? Have you been here long, Mrs Taylor?'

They talked. She was a pleasant woman, easy. Jenny began to relax. She said, with diffidence, 'It does seem a bit silly, needing help when the house really isn't very big. But the children are so – well, they do need such a lot of looking after, you know – and my husband does like things to be nice when he gets back in the evening.'

Mrs Porch said, 'Well, they do, don't they? It stands to reason – they've had a hard day, they want things ready for them, like. It's only natural.' She didn't sound critical in any way, and leaned down to the baby, crawling around her feet, to say, 'I don't think you ought to have that in your mouth, now, my love, ought you?' She removed the button that the baby had been sucking (Henry's, the lost one from his office suit, so that was where . . .) and put it on the table, diverting the baby with a pencil from her handbag. Emma sidled through the door and Mrs Porch said, 'Hello, dear. What's your name, then? How old is she, Mrs Taylor – threeish?'

'Three next month.'

'It's a difficult age. You can't take your eyes off them for long. And the baby's into everything, I don't doubt. You've got your hands full.'

'Oh, yes,' said Jenny gratefully. 'Honestly, some days I get so tired. I know it's silly, lots of other people seem to manage so much better, but . . .'

'Oh, my goodness, you're not the only one. You can feel at the end of your tether, one way and another. When mine were this age there were times when I'd have willingly upped and walked out of the house.' It didn't seem likely, but Jenny was glad to hear her say so. She was just going to suggest showing Mrs Porch round when Emma lurched into the low coffee table and knocked over the vase of roses.

'Oh, Emma . . .' said Jenny. 'Oh, dear . . .' She began desperately stuffing the roses back, dabbing at the spilled water with a wad of Kleenex from her pocket.

'Let me,' said Mrs Porch. 'You want to be careful with those polished surfaces, they spot so easily with a drop of water. Where's the kitchen? You come along and show me, dear.' She took Emma by the hand and left the room, returning a moment later with basin and cloth. 'There we are – a wipe over with a duster and he'll never know. You pick up the flowers, now, Emma – mind the prickles, though. That's a nice table, Mrs Taylor.'

'It was a wedding present from my husband's aunt. I think it's antique. My husband's awfully fond of it.'

'I don't wonder. It's a lovely piece.' Mrs Porch wrung the cloth out with strong, freckled hands. 'There, now you run and find me the polish and a duster, Emma, there's a good girl. You've not been married all that long, then, I daresay?'

Jenny found herself telling Mrs Porch about one thing and another. About the wedding and about how frightened she'd been of doing something silly and making Henry cross, because she'd been ill on and off before (she didn't explain what kind of illness, but Mrs Porch nodded sympathetically) and about how nervous Henry's mother made her, being such a different sort of person, so busy and competent, running that enormous house and all those committees and things. Mrs Porch made reassuring remarks about everyone having their weak spots, and no one being perfect, and so forth. She seemed quite interested in Henry's parents, and indeed it turned out she'd been to the house once, one of the days the garden was open to the public. 'Must cost a lot to run, that place. I daresay they've got some lovely things there. Your husband the only son, is he?'

'Yes,' said Jenny vaguely. Mrs Porch was busy admiring the silver tea-set that had been Henry's mother's wedding-present. It badly needed polishing, Jenny saw with guilt. But all she could think of now was the need to make a favourable impression on Mrs Porch.

They toured the house. In the kitchen, Mrs Porch hung the cloth up to dry, put away the basin. At the same time she rinsed out a couple of dirty milk bottles and emptied the sink basket. Jenny said, 'Oh, please . . . You mustn't bother.' And Mrs Porch, popping the milk bottles outside the back door, said that she believed in doing things as you went along, and then you didn't have everything piling up on you, did you? Upstairs, Jenny felt her eye on the rimmed bath, Emma's unmade bed, the clouded windows, and grew confused again, hastily picking things up, trying to put clothes in piles. 'You can't expect them to clear up, can you, at that age?' said Mrs Porch. 'Bless them. And your husband's just as bad, I daresay – I've never known a man hang his own trousers up. My husband's the same – I say to Bob, if I had a pound note for every time I've folded a pair of trousers of yours, I'd be in clover by now. Here, shall I do that . . .' She put Henry's tweed jacket in the cupboard, and stood for a moment, looking. 'I can see he likes things nice, Mr Taylor.'

When she left they had arranged that she should start on Monday. Jenny could hardly believe her luck: she wandered around for a while in a daze of contented anticipation and then remembered that the delicate subject of money had not been raised. At least, Mrs Porch had said at one point, 'The usual rate will do all right, Mrs Taylor', but Jenny, too preoccupied by her relief that all was well and she had been accepted, had not followed this up by asking what the usual rate was. She would have to go next door and ask Fiona Talbot, who would be certain to know: Fiona knew about everything.

The very fact that she was able to decide to call on Fiona, and then do so without hesitation, was an indication of her mood. It wasn't that Fiona was not welcoming: far from it, she was never put out, too busy, caught in a dressing-gown, or in the bath, or washing her hair. She was always crisply dressed – jeans clean and pressed, shirts and smocks fresh and new – her hair tidy, her house spruce but comfortable-looking, her children playing happily in airy, swept rooms with good quality educational toys. They had startlingly large vocabularies for such young children, though Fiona insisted that of course she and Tim didn't believe in pushing them, they must go at their own pace. They never had runny noses, either, and did not seem to whine like Emma . . .

Jenny thought of all this as she went down her own garden path, and up Fiona's. No, it wasn't that Fiona was unwelcoming. It was just that she didn't seem to need company very much; or perhaps that she didn't much care for other women. She was polite, welcoming, and bored. She got on very well with Henry. When she and Tim came over – or when Henry and Jenny went to the Talbots – Fiona would talk a lot and make everyone laugh, or else get involved in long, serious arguments while Jenny sat silent. She had a degree and had had some rather important job in journalism before she got married. Jenny once asked her, timidly, if she did not get bored just being a housewife – she had had a couple of glasses of wine or she would never have dared.

Fiona had said, 'Good gracious, a degree isn't just a vocational training, is it? It furnishes the mind, and all that. Of course I'm not bored. I've got more time to myself than I've had for years.' Jenny had felt crushed.

She rang the bell. When Fiona came to the door, Jenny said, 'I'm awfully sorry to bother you – I hope you weren't in the middle of something – it's just that I wondered if by any chance you knew how much one ought to pay for help nowadays.'

Fiona said, 'Psychiatric, or some other kind?' Jenny was unpleasantly taken aback for a moment until she remembered that actually Fiona couldn't possibly know . . . It was a joke, obviously – one of Fiona's queer, dead-pan jokes that one didn't always follow – so Jenny laughed and said, 'Oh, domestic, I meant.'

'Never having used any I couldn't be quite certain,' said Fiona. 'But I believe the going rate is about sixty-five an hour. Scandalous, but that's the way it is.'

Jenny wasn't quite sure who it was scandalous for, but since the Talbots were said by Henry to be rather left-wing, she decided it must be for the helps.

Fiona said come in and have a cup of coffee, so she did. Emma and the baby, as usual, fell happily on the educational toys. Jenny and Fiona sat in Fiona's gay sitting-room and drank coffee made quickly and without fuss by Fiona at the same time as she smoked, talked, and sorted out the occasional squabble among the children with a quick redistribution of toys.

'What do you want help for?'

'I – well – I know it seems silly but things do get in such a mess and Henry does hate it so. It was his idea, but she seems awfully nice.'

'Why shouldn't she be?' said Fiona. 'Sorry, I didn't mean to sound sharp. Have some more coffee?' Her glance drifted to the open book on the table beside her: Jenny had the feeling that she was bored already. Presumably she had been reading the book. It was impossible to read the title upside-down, but the pages were all long chunks of text without conversation so it did not look like a novel. Most of the Talbots' books were rather new paperbacks, on politics and things like that: Henry often borrowed them.

Jenny's mood of confidence had begun to evaporate. She could not think of anything more to say to Fiona. She would have liked to comment on the very attractive shirt she was wearing, or the new curtains, but felt that it would probably be wiser not to, as she had once heard Fiona be very amusing, but scathing, about women who discussed clothes and furnishings all the time. Emma, passionately acquisitive over one of the Talbot children's brightly-coloured, unbroken toys, snatched it away and hit the other child over the head with it. Jenny smacked Emma and met Fiona's coolly disapproving gaze across the weeping children. Fiona, she remembered too late, thought that there were really no situations with children that justified physical violence: one could always deal with things rationally and calmly. Fiona went into the kitchen to fetch biscuits with which to soothe everyone's ruffled feelings and Jenny sat uncomfortably. The trouble was that Fiona always reminded her of various particularly awful crises: the Christmas she forgot half the shopping and had to trail backwards and forwards to Fiona for three days to borrow bread, tea, sugar, potatoes. The time both the children had chicken-pox together and she was reduced to such a weeping, trembly state of nervous exhaustion that Fiona came over and coped till Henry came home. She'd heard them talking in the hall, later, Henry apologising, Fiona saying, 'Good heavens, Henry, think nothing of it – some people just find it harder to manage than others, that's all there is to it.' Jenny hadn't known then that both Fiona's children had been ill at the time. Henry liked Fiona very much: he had a special tone of voice when he was talking to her, that didn't seem to crop up with anyone else.

It wasn't until she was back in her own house that Jenny remembered Mrs Porch again, and cheered up.

Mrs Porch's first weeks were positively exciting. She transformed the house within three days. Pockets of dirt that Jenny had assumed to be ineradicable vanished; the bath and basins ceased to be slimy; mounds of dirty clothes disappeared and were found later in the airing-cupboard, washed and ironed. Jenny hadn't realised that the oven was meant to be that nice grey-blue colour inside, or that you could get all those marks off the floor around the stove. Henry was delighted, and Jenny found herself getting undeserved credit. There were other advantages, too. The children loved Mrs Porch; when she was around they played more and cried less. She brought Jenny the occasional home-made pie or cake.

'Oh, Mrs Porch, you mustn't . . .'

'If you're making one you might as well make two, mightn't you?'

On these occasions Jenny left extra money out, and hoped she was doing the right thing. The business of payment had filled her with embarrassment: it seemed so awful to hand over notes, just like that, so she had taken to putting the money discreetly in an envelope which she left on the kitchen table on the appropriate days, from whence it duly disappeared, leaving their relationship untarnished.

It was such a nice relationship. There had never been any need to tell Mrs Porch what to do. She just knew – far better than Jenny had, anyway. She thought of everything. She reminded Jenny of household shortages, prompted her to have the baby's second vaccination done, told her how to get the broken window repaired and noticed, in time, that Jenny had left Henry's good secateurs (birthday present from his mother . . .) out in the rain. She answered the telephone if Jenny was in the garden, posted the letters that Jenny had forgotten, turned out the larder. When the milkman rang the door bell during the baby's bath, as he invariably did, Mrs Porch called up the stairs, 'Don't you bother coming down, dear. I'll settle up with him for you, shall I?'

'Oh, you are an angel, Mrs Porch. My purse is in the top drawer of the dresser.'

And at eleven they drank coffee together in the kitchen and Mrs Porch talked endlessly about her family, which was large, diffuse and unpredictable. It was like being plunged into a serial story: Jenny found herself looking forward to the daily episode.

'What happened about your sister-in-law in the end, Mrs Porch?'

'Well, she told Fred she wasn't having any more of that, and he knew what he could do, and she upped and off to her auntie's round the corner. And then, the next thing I knew, there was my mum coming tanking over on her bike to say . . .'

Henry's mother, on her next visit, did not fail to observe the altered state of the house. She said she gathered Jenny had this awfully good woman now, and she'd better hang on to her. The tone in which she said it made Jenny faintly defensive: it sounded as though she doubted Jenny's capacity to do so, and Jenny found this annoying, because she was such friends with Mrs Porch, really friends she felt, and actually Henry's mother wasn't all that nice to her helps, she ordered them about and checked up on what they had been doing.

Several weeks after Mrs Porch's arrival she met Fiona. Fiona had called to ask if Henry would like to come over on Saturday evening and meet this friend of theirs from Cambridge – she thought he'd be interested. She added hastily, 'And you, of course.' Jenny, knowing that Mrs Porch would be making the coffee, was able with confidence to ask her in for a cup. Mrs Porch, appearing from the kitchen, said, 'I'll bring the coffee for you and your friend into the sitting-room, Mrs Taylor', but Fiona said quickly, 'Oh heavens, no, if you usually have it in the kitchen don't start being posh for me.' So they all three sat in the kitchen. Fiona and Mrs Porch got on at once. It turned out that Fiona's eldest child was just starting at the primary school where Mrs Porch's had been, and they talked with animation about the new maths teaching, and different kinds of reading primer, and what the teachers were like. Fiona stayed for ages, and then said good heavens, she'd no idea it was that late, she really must rush. On the doorstep she said to Jenny, 'What a nice woman – awfully bright. Lucky you, Jenny – I suppose she's what used to be called a treasure, in the bad old days.'

Jenny repeated this remark to Henry, and after that he sometimes referred to Mrs Porch as the treasure, with an indulgent grin.

Henry himself did not meet Mrs Porch for some time, and when he did it was not under the most auspicious circumstances. He got flu, badly, and was in bed for over a week. Mrs Porch came in every day, because, as she said, Jenny couldn't cope with him up there needing trays and all that, and the children underfoot. Consequently the illness went off with great smoothness. Jenny was able to make enticing little meals which Mrs Porch laid on a tray covered with a starched cloth and a crisply folded napkin. Henry loved it. He became very affectionate and teasing with Jenny, like he used to be before they were married, when he had seemed to find her failings more endearing than irritating. During the convalescence, before he went back to the office, he met Mrs Porch properly: they had long conversations and once or twice Jenny had the feeling that they had talked about her. There was a faintly odd look in Mrs Porch's eye, and Jenny hadn't been able to help hearing Henry's voice through the door, on one occasion, saying something about being so grateful, made such a difference, my wife finding it hard to cope, rather prone to nerves, bit of a breakdown when she was younger, luckily quite cleared up now . . . Jenny went quickly past and into the kitchen where she sat quite still for a minute until that awful, reminiscent, shaky feeling went away.

The months passed. Everything was so much better that it became hard to remember the dark days before Mrs Porch came: life without her was unimaginable. The days when she didn't come still had their dangers and crises, but fewer of them because there was always salvation around the corner, the next day, after the weekend . . . And if catastrophe threatened when she was there she could always avert it with some deft action, a few reassuring words. Jenny was hardly ever gripped by that sense of bleak hopelessness now, as though the house, the children, Henry, were some kind of trap waiting to be sprung. Mrs Porch, even in absence, propelled her through the days, gave her reserves of strength.

Nor was she ever patronising or critical; she seemed to take the line that far too much had been expected of Jenny all along.

The only snag was that for some reason it was working out much more expensive than Jenny had anticipated. Naturally Henry had given her extra house-keeping money to cover Mrs Porch's wages, but even so there always seemed to be less money than there should be. Twice she took out her purse in shops and found she had less – quite a bit less – than she'd thought. She had to ask Henry to give her more money.

'I'm awfully sorry. It's just I never seem to have enough.'

'Well, never mind – no need to look so guilty, Jen. You don't have to go short – we can afford a bit more nowadays.'

She said to Mrs Porch that everything seemed to be terribly expensive. 'Oh, don't I know it! Shocking, that's what it is. Every time you're in the supermarket there's another penny on this and twopence on that. You can't keep track of where it goes, not like you used to.'

And then one day Jenny found that there was a pound note missing from her purse – at least she felt almost certain there was. She'd been to the corner shop for something and they'd given her change for five pounds: four notes and some silver. Now there were only three, and the loose change. She was puzzled and slightly worried.

'Emma, just come here a moment, darling. Listen, you haven't taken anything from Mummy's purse, have you? No, don't cry, just tell me. You didn't? No, I'm not cross, darling, I just wanted you to tell me . . .'

She hunted in the places where Emma often hid things, and found nothing. She began to have doubts: had they perhaps only given her three pounds in the shop by mistake? And yet she had felt so sure. Oh well, never mind . . .

A week later, it happened again. This time, she felt a little thud of shock in her stomach. She'd been trying to be more careful about money, budgeting, working out what she had spent, noting prices . . . She'd been quite sure she had fifteen pounds in her purse, and now there were thirteen. At least she *thought* she'd been quite sure . . .

In the evening, she said to Henry, slipping it in casually while she was washing up the dinner, 'You didn't by any chance borrow some money from my purse this morning, did you?'

'No, why?'

'Oh, nothing. It's just I seem to have less than I thought.'

'Well, how much did you have?'

'Fifteen pounds, I think.'

'What do you mean – you think? Either you had fifteen pounds or you didn't.'

'Well, I suppose it mightn't have been. I did count, I feel sure – perhaps I didn't.'

Henry said, 'Do you mean you don't always know how much money you've got?'

She said unhappily, 'No, I'm afraid not. I do try to.'

'You really must be more careful, Jen.'

She flushed. He didn't know some of the awful things she'd done with money, in fact. Leaving her purse in shops, or stuck on the top of her basket where anyone could take it, or dropping it in buses. Only the other day she'd left it on the wall outside the garden gate when Emma had fallen on the pavement, but mercifully Mrs Porch had spotted it and brought it in. He was right: she must be more careful.

The next morning she went out early, even before Mrs Porch came and bought a little notebook from the corner shop. With a glow of determination, she wrote down the exact sum in her purse on the first page. Then, later, she would enter any expenditures on the other side and check notebook against purse at the end of the day. That way, there wouldn't be these silly muddles, and she would be able to keep an eye on how, and where, the housekeeping money was going. She put the notebook away in satisfaction and went to open the door to Mrs Porch.

At the end of the day there was a pound less in her purse than there should have been. Shakily, she counted and recounted the notes out on to the kitchen table, added and re-added the five items of expenditure. There wasn't any doubt, absolutely no doubt at all. She sat down, still clutching the notebook and purse, overcome by a strange feeling of unreality, as though this were a dream – or a nightmare. Or, said a sinister little voice in her head, was the *other* unreal – *did* you count properly this morning, write down exactly what you spent? You make mistakes, don't you – dither, get things wrong . . ?

There had been no one in the house all day except herself and Mrs Porch. And the children. She searched again in Emma's hiding-place, under cushions, beds, chairs, carpets. Nothing.

It just isn't possible. I counted wrong, I must have done.

Forget it. Ignore it. Pretend it didn't happen. Start the notebook again – something went wrong that time. Give it another try.

For five days the opposing pages of the notebook tallied exactly. Seventeen pounds forty-nine there should be, and seventeen pounds forty-nine there were; fifteen twelve and fifteen twelve . . . It was a small private triumph – just a matter of persevering, and there was nothing to worry about after all.

On the seventh day two pounds were missing. It was a Friday, one of Mrs Porch's days.

Jenny lay awake much of the night. She tossed and turned, experiencing in manifold versions the conversation she would not, could not, have with Henry.

'Henry, I'm afraid Mrs Porch has been taking money from my purse.

Quite a lot, over quite a long time.'

'What the hell do you mean, Jenny? That's a very serious accusation to make against anyone, you know. Are you sure?'

'Yes, quite sure, really sure, Henry. I've counted and counted. I . . . either it's that or I . . .'

'Or what?'

'Or I'm imagining it all, I'm going mad . . .'

And Henry stared at her in silent assessment, joined, from time to time in that tormented night, by his mother, whose serious but resigned expression said that she had known all along, been prepared for a recurrence, that kind of problem never really . . . When at last Jenny slept it was to plunge into a frenetic dreamscape where pound notes floated like beech leaves, elusive and uncountable.

She felt rather ill and shaky the next day. She tried to avoid Mrs Porch, but she seemed to be everywhere, talking loudly and cheerfully. Once or twice she looked at Jenny with an odd sharpness. 'You feeling all right, dear? You don't look all that good – sure you're not going down with something. There's a tummy bug about.'

'I'm quite all right,' Jenny said.

Halfway through the morning the bell rang. Mrs Porch, coming into the playroom, where Jenny was giving the baby a belated breakfast (it had been a wretched morning, everything going wrong, just like the old days . . .) said, 'It's the bread man – I'll just pay him, shall I? I can't seem to lay hands on your purse, though, Mrs Taylor – it's not in the usual place.'

Jenny said in a strangled voice, 'It's all right, Mrs Porch, I'll do it.' She got up hastily, spilling the baby's milk as she did so.

'Don't you bother,' said Mrs Porch. 'Ah, there it is.' She reached forward to take the purse from the table beside Jenny, adding, 'I'll bring a cloth for that milk when I've seen to him. Coming, Mr Binns . . .'

'No!' said Jenny shrilly. 'Please leave it, Mrs Porch. I'll pay him myself.' The baby was crying now, and the bread man ringing the bell again. She left the room hastily.

When she came back Mrs Porch was soothing the baby. Jenny, her heart thumping horribly, sat down again and said, 'I'll take him back – thanks.'

Mrs Porch was looking at her intently. She said, 'I don't think you're quite yourself this morning, Mrs Taylor, I don't really.' Jenny, still holding the purse, put it on the floor beside her, self-consciously, and Mrs Porch went on, 'I'll put that back in the dresser for you, shall I, before young mischief here gets hold of it.'

Jenny said, 'No, it's all right, I'll see to it.'

There was a silence. When Jenny looked up from the baby's bowl of half-eaten cereal Mrs Porch was still standing there; her expression was hard to analyse – she might have been angry, or concerned. She reminded Jenny of firm-faced sisters in hospital wards. Jenny found herself shaking again, though she was trying to hold herself rigid. Her eyes met Mrs Porch's, and she looked away again at once.

Mrs Porch said slowly, 'Is there something wrong with the purse, Mrs Taylor? Something bothering you?'

'No,' said Jenny wildly. 'At least I don't want – I couldn't bear . . . There's some sort of mistake, I'm sure, it's just I felt certain . . .'

'I see,' said Mrs Porch. She sounded, for a moment, subdued, sad almost, but when she spoke again it was with her old briskness. 'If it was anyone else I'd be very angry, Mrs Taylor, but I've got fond of you, I really have, I like working here, we get on, I thought. And I'll tell you what I think, I think you're having a spot of that old trouble of yours, that's what I think. So I'm not going to say anything more about it, nor mention it to your husband, not that I don't feel perhaps I ought to, but it would be a worry to him, poor man. So we'll keep it between us two, Mrs Taylor, and pretend it never happened, and that's all there is to it.'

There was a pause. Jenny could not look at her. 'All right, Mrs Taylor?'

Jenny said, 'There's really nothing wrong with me. It was all ages ago, that, and ever since I've been . . .'

'Unless, of course,' said Mrs Porch, 'you'd rather I didn't come any more?'

After a moment Jenny said, 'No, honestly, I . . . I'm sorry, I expect there's been a mistake.'

'Then we'll forget about it. Right?' Mrs Porch gathered up the dirty crockery from the table. As she was leaving the room she turned and said, 'And I'd put the purse back in the dresser, if I were you, Mrs Taylor, it'll be a nuisance if I can't find it, next time the milkman's wanting his money, when you're not about, won't it?'

Jenny said, 'Yes. Yes, all right, Mrs Porch.' She sat in the empty playroom – Mrs Porch had borne the baby away with her, to wash and change him – staring at the door. She felt exhausted: there was a ringing noise in her ears. I don't know, she thought, I don't know, I don't know, I don't know . . .

That evening she said to Henry, 'I'm afraid I need more housekeeping money again.'

'Good grief, Jen, again! It's only a few weeks since last time.'

'I'm sorry.'

Henry sighed. 'All right, then. How much?'

She said dully, 'I think about another couple of pounds a week will do. For the moment, anyway.'

Miss Carlton and the
Pop Concert

It was Miss Carlton's custom to walk in Hyde Park most afternoons from three till four: up the Broad Walk, round the Pond, a short excursion to the hinterland beyond, and then home. She preferred the park in winter; then, the misty shapes of the trees receding into undefined distances gave it a spaciousness and a mystery which it quite lost in summer. Now, in late June, it was at its worst, the dusty growth of trees and bushes only a pale reflection of the real summer going on elsewhere, the poor grass worn quite down to the roots by the tramp of feet. Even the sunlight had a tawdry quality. In the country, Miss Carlton thought, it would not be like this. But her regret was perfunctory: Miss Carlton was a townswoman at heart, and she knew well that a country field, however delectable, could never provide her with the spectacle, the interest, the endless variety of the park.

She studied her fellow walkers with avid attention. Each visit provided some new entertainment, some small incident. She delighted in novelty: eccentricities of dress, perplexing snatches of conversation. She moved up and down the wide paths, across the grass, between the neat flower beds, alert and expectant – an inquisitive ghost foraging among the walkers. Few people spare a second glance for trim, elderly ladies.

Today the park was more than usually crowded. Miss Carlton, crossing the Broad Walk and heading for the Round Pond, had a busy time absorbing the many people who surrounded her. Indeed, it was some while before she became aware of a uniformity not only in their persons, but in their movement. They were all young, all were bizarrely dressed, and all were drifting, in an unhurried but purposeful manner, towards the centre of the park, somewhere east of the pond. Miss Carlton, deeply interested, began to drift with them.

There were men and girls; somewhat similarly clad in garments that were often long and flowing in a way that pleased Miss Carlton. She liked the style, the colours. Nearly all had long hair; many of the men were bearded and whiskered. There was an overwhelming impression of profusion, of abundance. Some of the girls wore trailing skirts, many were barefooted. There were trousered girls, and men wearing feminine shirts of lace or velvet; everything seemed interchangeable. Miss Carlton was not especially surprised: one frequently saw people thus dressed nowadays. These were the Young, and she secretly enjoyed their variety, and admired their self-absorption. When her friends complained about them and deplored their dress, their manners and their attitudes, she was silent; she was of a gentle disposition and did not relish dispute. Moreover, she suspected that we often attack that which we envy. The old have always criticised the young; sometimes the criticisms may be just, but the violence with which they are made betrays a deeper resentment. Miss Carlton, having herself come to terms with age, felt none of this. She was an observer, detached and uninvolved.

This strange crowd became thicker and thicker. Miss Carlton, moving over the grass with them, found herself touched by the hem of a skirt, brushed by a bare arm, forced to change direction for a motionless or slow-moving group. And now she saw that they did, in fact, have an objective. In the distance was a large, raised platform, and before and all around this was a vast crowd, sitting, squatting and lying on the grass. As the drifters reached the edge of this crowd they too would sink down on the grass so that the dense mass expanded gently all the time, amoeba-like, spreading over the park and engulfing trees and bushes. On the platform, figures moved about, and from time to time a loudspeaker crackled, blaring a short burst of music or garbled language.

Miss Carlton increased her pace a little to draw level with a couple of girls just ahead of her.

'Excuse me,' she said, 'I wonder if you could tell me what is going on?'

They turned to look at her, still walking. They both wore brightly-patterned trailing clothes, and bands around their hair that gave them a faintly oriental appearance, though their round, pink and white faces were unmistakably Anglo-Saxon. Miss Carlton thought they looked very nice: she had always liked the eastern influence. Many of her own clothes came from Liberty's.

One of the girls said, 'It's a pop concert. The Applejacks and a whole lot of other groups.'

'Oh, dear,' said Miss Carlton. 'I have no ticket.' She looked at them in dismay: suddenly she wanted very much to remain with these young people.

'It's free,' said the girl. They both stared at her for a moment, and then turned away.

How very pleasant, thought Miss Carlton, like a brass band. Full of anticipation, she approached the crowd. Already people around her were beginning to sit down on the grass and the mass ahead was so dense that it was becoming difficult to move but she felt a strong desire to achieve the very centre of this event and struggled along, murmuring, 'I'm sorry . . . please excuse me . . . thank you so much.'

The crowd of young people was like a gently waving sea-anemone. Their hair lifted in the wind, their clothes made a kaleidoscopic pattern of colour so that the whole mass, shifting, rippling, ebbing and flowing at the edges, was like some primitive sea-creature and Miss Carlton, advancing, felt herself, like a shrimp, most pleasantly digested. She continued until at last she reached a point where the crowd was so closely packed that further advance would be anti-social. People were sitting and lying all around, except for isolated figures who stood swaying in a trance-like way. Miss Carlton took her small folding stool from her bag, sat on it, and looked around her with interest.

The platform was some way away, but she could see it more clearly now, and from the considerable activity going on there guessed that the concert must be about to begin. Musical instruments were being assembled. She began to study her immediate neighbours. Next to her was a young man with the bearded, long and tragic face of a Renaissance Christ. Miss Carlton observed him, fascinated. He wore a flowered shirt, gaping open to the waist to reveal a thin, hairless chest. Below that were very tight trousers, faded in patches that had a curious symmetry, and bare feet. He looked every inch the religious ascetic. In front of Miss Carlton, and facing her, was a girl. Indeed, they were so close that Miss Carlton could feel the stuff of her dress shiver delicately under the girl's breath. She was very young, with a pale face and long thick wavy hair, hanging over either shoulder almost to her waist. She too had associations with some other age; she was, Miss Carlton thought, the very image of a Rossetti painting. Her clothes, too, suited the part – thin and floaty, in the muted colours of which Miss Carlton herself was fond; plum, russet and heavy greens. As Miss Carlton watched her she leaned forward suddenly and touched the ropes of beads around Miss Carlton's neck.

'Hey,' she said, 'that's nice.'

Miss Carlton looked down. She was wearing her amber necklace, as she usually did, and her mother's pearls – the long rope that came nearly to her waist – and several strings of jet.

'Fantastic,' said the girl, in an appreciative tone. Miss Carlton realised that she, too, wore several strings of beads, and indeed, looking around, she saw that most of the girls and some of the men were decked out with necklaces much like her own. There was, she now saw, a conformity about their dress, and her own appearance matched it in many ways. The style, the colours, and the materials they favoured were much like the things she wore herself. Miss Carlton, who knew that she stood somewhat apart in taste from many of her own generation, felt for the first time in her life a member of a group. Only her age distinguished her from her companions.

The girl had turned aside to talk to a friend, and Miss Carlton looked around her again. What she saw filled her more and more with a strange nostalgia. These people, she knew – had known for some time – were ghosts from her own past. They were the students she had watched go in and out of the art school her father would never allow her to attend; in their brave, flamboyant clothes, their huge-brimmed hats, their beards, they were the people of *Trilby*, of William Morris, of the Pre-Raphaelites, of all that culture she had secretly admired in her own youth. They were the bohemians against whom her father had railed – the disrupters of society, the profligates, the fiddling grasshoppers. How she had admired and envied them! Not that she had borne her father any ill will, but by the time he died she had been over forty – far too old to do any of those things for which she had yearned so deeply. She had always kept up her interest in art, of course, visiting the Summer Academy every year, and after her father's death she had allowed herself certain indulgences of dress and behaviour that would never have been permissible in his lifetime. What would he have thought of these young people? Miss Carlton gave a sudden little laugh.

The girl who had admired her necklaces stared at Miss Carlton, a faint look of enquiry on her rather impassive face. She was a nice girl; Miss Carlton had seen that at once, before she spoke. She reminded her slightly of her great-niece in Dorset, though she was prettier.

'I was thinking of my father,' said Miss Carlton apologetically. 'He so disliked what they called aesthetes in his day, you know. Very intolerant, I'm afraid. My brother too – he used to tell me how he and his friends would go round de-bagging them when he was up at Oxford. I must say I always found the story distasteful.'

'What?' said the girl.

'Taking their trousers off,' said Miss Carlton, 'to indicate disapproval.'

'I think that's disgusting,' said the girl. 'Hey, did you hear that?' She leaned over and nudged the Christ-like young man, who shrugged.

'I quite agree,' said Miss Carlton with enthusiasm. 'It was barbaric. Anti-aestheticism was something of a cult, of course. I always felt *Patience* was responsible for a lot of it.' Seeing that the girl again looked bewildered, she added, 'Gilbert and Sullivan, you know. There was that song – "A greenery-yallery, Grosvenor Gallery, foot-in-the-grave young man".'

The man and the girl gazed at her and after a moment the girl said, 'I never heard of that.'

The conversation flagged and indeed it was becoming difficult to talk above the increasing noise from the platform. The loudspeaker crackled almost non-stop now; people, in their appearance much like the members of the crowd who stared up expectantly, scurried on and off with microphones and coils of wire. And then, suddenly, four young men came on to the platform and the crowd began to scream and yell; even the Rossetti-girl opened her mouth and shrieked, but any sound she made was quite lost in the noise all around. Miss Carlton shrank a little, assaulted by the din.

The music, when it began, was no better. To begin with, it was far too loud: the very ground seemed to throb with it. Miss Carlton decided that something must be wrong with the microphones, but then, looking at the unconcerned faces around her, changed her mind. However, she soon discovered that by the simple expedient of turning down her deaf-aid she could reduce the sound to a distant murmur, in no way offensive. Thus insulated, she was able to appreciate the spectacle and the company without any aural discomfort.

She gave herself up to enjoyment. Just to sit among these people was to experience a sense of release. Here she was, at last – too late, but at last – surrounded by people who were as she had longed, once, to be. Young people free to follow the direction of their own creative urges, unfettered by social conventions, released from the restraints of conformity. They were the heirs, half a century later, of those little pioneer groups, the brave and the fortunate, who had escaped the Edwardian world to feed in the lush pastures of Art and Literature. And there were so many of them. They reached as far as the eye could see: it was amazing. Miss Carlton, aged seventy-five, had a sudden dizzying sensation that the society in which she lived was totally alien to her, that she knew nothing of it. There she was, passing quietly from one day to another in the Campden Hill house left her by her father, and there outside, all around but unknown to her, was this great new England, vibrant with sensitivity and awareness. Of course, she had always tried to keep abreast of the times. She read the newspapers, listened to the wireless, was a member of an art appreciation group, an amateur dramatic society, and a book club. But she had thought herself one of a minority – few of her friends, even, shared her tastes. Now, she realised, with a surge of excitement, things had changed beyond all possible belief. The world was simply not as it had been; here, in Hyde Park on a Saturday afternoon, was the stuff of which it was made now, the new generation. It was a heady moment; just to look at her companions, to project herself into what their lives must be, gave her a thrill. She studied their faces, tried to penetrate for herself the wide-ranging thoughts in their heads, longed to eavesdrop their conversations. She noted girls with the delicate features of Botticelli angels and madonnas, appropriately clad in dresses that floated and swam around their thin bodies. She slanted cautious stares (sideways, not to be too obvious) at young men plumed like tropical birds, hung about with velvet and satin, their faces whiskered and bearded, the faces of artists, poets and playwrights. It was as though she had strayed, all accidentally, into the cultural nub of England, the very nerve-centre of the nation, and she felt appropriately awed. She did not want to participate, but she wanted most desperately to absorb all that there was to be absorbed. That, at least, she was owed by the grudging Fate that had cheated her of experience. These fortunate people, born into a more generous age, could allow her at least a vicarious taste of their more expansive lives.

The song finished and the performers left the platform. It seemed that there was to be a short interval. Miss Carlton edged herself closer to the pair of young men behind her, velvet-jacketed youths with the faces of desperate Chekhov heroes, all sideboards and silky whiskers, and listened unashamedly to their conversation.

'You get fantastic suspension, on a BMW.'

'Yeah.'

'Great acceleration, too.'

'What about the m.p.g.?'

'Thirty or so. 'Course, you got to remember there's a higher premium on a sports job.'

'Yeah.'

Miss Carlton was disappointed. It was inevitable, though, that the conversation of people closely attuned to one another's patterns of thought should have an allusive, excluding quality. She abandoned the young men and turned her attention to the group of girls on either side, exquisite creatures, all long hair and pale, oval faces, like Primaveras dumped down on the dry London grass. Their exchanges were equally baffling.

'Thirty-eight fifty, with lunch vouchers. And no Saturdays.'

'That's fantastic. Commission?'

'Ten per cent.'

'Great.'

Frustrated, Miss Carlton decided that there was nothing for it but a direct approach. She would resume contact with the young man and the girl in front of her. She had been thinking about them in particular during the song, and was filled with a deep curiosity. The young man, for instance: what did he do when he was not listening to music in Hyde Park? It was hard to envisage him in other, more mundane, situations, but presumably he had to support himself in some way, unless, of course, he had private means.

She leaned towards him and tapped his knee. 'Please forgive me – I hope you won't think me impertinent – but I should so very much like to know more about you. Do you have a job – or are you some kind of student?' She hoped she had not offended him by her curiosity.

He turned his saint-like face towards her and contemplated her. 'I'm with the Thames Gas Board,' he said.

Miss Carlton was thunderstruck. For a moment she thought it was a joke, and was about to laugh, and then she caught sight of the dead-pan face of the girl, dead-pan not in collusion but acquiescence, and choked back the laugh.

'He's a fitter,' said the girl. 'When your cooker busts it's him comes along to fix it. Eh, Len?' She nudged her companion and he said, 'Yeah. That's about it.'

Shaken, Miss Carlton looked again at the man's thin, ascetic face. It was a face she knew well: it looked at you, almond-eyed, tilted at unnatural angles, from Russian icons; it stared through encrustations of brown varnish from the walls of the National Gallery; gilt-haloed, it watched you from triptychs in Italian churches.

And there was, after all, no reason why it should not also be the face of a young man who repaired gas cookers. Miss Carlton decided to probe further. Her first question had been met not with resentment, but indifference.

She said, 'Are you enjoying the music?'

'It's all right.'

'Are the performers especially talented, or merely average?'

'They're all right.'

The lack of commitment was disturbing. Miss Carlton, studying the faces of the young couple, had to admit to herself that they had a quality of flatness. The features were beautiful, but flat. There was no animation. Miss Carlton had always believed that feelings showed. Inner qualities were displayed in a face. This belief had brought her much pleasure – in buses, on trains, in shops. She turned to the girl. 'And what do you do, my dear?'

'I'm still at school, aren't I?' said the girl. 'Roll on July, that's what I say.'

Miss Carlton was surprised: she had not realised the child was so young. 'And what are your plans after that?' she asked hopefully. She had – a few minutes ago – had an interesting future mapped out for her: art school, the Royal College of Music, a university.

'I dunno,' said the girl. 'I'm not bothered. I may go on the gift counter at Boots. My sister's there.'

Miss Carlton was silent. After a moment she said, 'You hadn't thought of any – well, further training?'

'Training for what?'

Miss Carlton plunged. 'I was thinking,' she said, 'that with your – well, with your nice taste in clothes, that dress is really quite charming – that perhaps you might be artistic. Are you at all interested in painting?'

She had their attention. The young man, in the act of lighting a cigarette, lowered his hand and turned brown eyes upon her. Surprise and self-consciousness lent a new depth to the girl's features; she smoothed down her dress, patted a strand of hair.

'They had one of my drawings up in the art room at school.'

'Hey!' said the young man. 'What's all this, then?'

Miss Carlton beamed encouragement.

'My friend Eileen,' said the girl, 'she got a job as a window-dresser with the Co-op.'

'That the one with the frizzy hair?' said the young man.

'Yeah. Anyway,' the girl went on decidedly, 'I'm not staying on at school, am I? I'm leaving, July.'

The conversation withered. Miss Carlton was beginning to feel dispirited. Her folding chair was uncomfortable, the place was hot and dusty. The music had started up again and battered the whole city, it seemed, for the duration of the next song. Miss Carlton's deaf-aid had revealed some fundamental deficiency and no longer filtered the sound as it had before. She was obliged to listen to the singer, a manic creature who sang of love in tones of strangled loathing. It was a relief to see him subside, at last, in a Laocoön tangle of wires and microphones. Miss Carlton took out her handkerchief and wiped her forehead. She was perspiring most unpleasantly, and would have liked a cup of tea. The young man was slumped with his head in his hands, apparently dozing, and the girl was studying her own hair with minute attention. She prodded her companion and said, 'Eh, you! I've got split ends.' He made no reply.

Fragmented talk reached Miss Carlton. A man and a girl picked their way through the crowd, brushing past without apology, and their conversation floated down to her: they had loud, educated voices and spoke of car racing. 'Fantastic!' they said. 'Really great!' The young men she had listened to before were dicussing the money earned by the singer who had just been heard. 'A thousand quid a week, easily, and he'll dodge the tax somehow.' 'The Dead Beats get five for a concert.' The girl, abandoning the investigation of her hair, said, 'My mum's going into hospital, Monday.' The young man lifted his head for a moment and said, 'Do you mind? Who wants to hear about Monday on a Saturday afternoon?' And she said, 'Sorry, Len.' Somewhere a baby cried; two girls were dancing together; skeins of midges hung in the sunlight; on the platform instruments were being assembled for the next song. Miss Carlton got to her feet with difficulty. She folded the stool and stowed it away in her bag. She looked down at the young man and the girl and said, 'Goodbye. It was so nice to talk to you,' and they nodded. There was a momentary distortion of the girl's features that was not a smile but might have been some kind of acknowledgement.

Miss Carlton extracted herself from the crowd. It took some time; bodies protruded wherever she tried to put her feet. She saw things she would have preferred not to see. Nobody looked at her or responded to her apologies, though she felt as alien and conspicuous now as a clothed person among sunbathers. A faint smell lifted from the crowd, of sweat, hair and cheap scent. There were flies and discarded cigarette packets and little piles of dog mess. Miss Carlton battled on, and reached the point at last where the crowd began to diminish, like a nebula disintegrating at the rim. She was able to walk without interruption; behind her, the music crashed again, but with reduced volume. And behind her, also, sat and sprawled the young people in their floating dresses, their silks and velvets, their wide-brimmed hats and their strange, misleading faces.

Miss Carlton walked to the Round Pond. She sat down on a bench and saw small, white-winged yachts skim to and fro. Gulls rode above her head on translucent wings. The water was delicately pleated by the wind; squadrons of ducks moved to and fro. Under the water, Miss Carlton knew, was a disagreeable deposit of old Coke bottles and rusty tins, but it was pointless to dwell on that. All around the edge of the pond were small children, skipping, playing with balls, doing things with boats. Miss Carlton had never much cared for children, but she found herself looking at them intently, noticing, for the first time, it seemed, their small unformed features across which emotion and involvement flitted like the shadows of the birds on the water.

Revenant as Typewriter

MURIEL RACKHAM, reaching the penultimate page of her talk, spoke with one eye upon the public library clock. The paper ('Ghosts: an analysis of their fictional and historic function') lasted precisely fifty-one minutes, as she well knew, but the stamina of the Ilmington Literary and Philosophical Society was problematic; an elderly man in the back row had been asleep since page seven, and there was a certain amount of shuffle and fidget in the middle reaches of the thirty-odd seats occupied by the society's membership. Muriel skipped two paragraphs and moved into the concluding phase; it had perhaps been rash (not to say wasteful) to use on this occasion a paper that had had a considerable success at the English Studies Conference and with her colleagues at the College Senior Seminar, but she had nothing much else written up at the moment and had felt disinclined to produce a piece especially for the occasion. She paused (nothing like silence to induce attention) and went on: 'So, leaving aside for the moment its literary role as vehicle for authorial comment in characters as diverse as Hamlet's father and Peter Quint, let us in conclusion try to summarise the historic function of the ghost – define as far as we can its social purpose, try to see why people needed ghosts and what they used them for. We've already paid tribute to that great source book for the student of the folkloric ghost – Dr Katharine Briggs' *Dictionary of British Folk-Tales* – of which I think it was Bernard Levin who remarked in a review that a glance down its list of Tale-Types and Motifs disposes once and for all of the notion that the British are a phlegmatic and unfanciful people.' (She paused at this point for the ripple of appreciative amusement that should run through the audience, but the Ilmington Lit. and Phil. sat unmoved; there were two sleepers now in the back row.) '. . . We've looked already at the repetitious nature of Motifs – Ghost follows its own corpse, reading the funeral service silently; Ghost laid when treasure is unearthed; Revenant as hare; Revenant in human form; Wraith appears to person in bedroom; Ghost haunts scene of former crime; Ghost exercises power through possessions of its lifetime –

and so on and so forth. The subject-matter of ghostly folklore, in fact, perfectly supports the thesis of Keith Thomas in his book *Religion and the Decline of Magic* that the historic ghost is no random or frivolous character but fulfils a particular social need – in a society where the arm of the law is short it serves to draw attention to the unpunished crime, to seek the rectification of wrongs, to act as a reminder of the past, to . . .'

She read on, the text familiar enough for the thoughts to wander: Bill Freeman, the chairman, had introduced her appallingly, neglecting to mention her publications and reducing her Senior Lectureship at Ilmington College of Education to a Lectureship – she felt again a flush of irritation, and wondered if it had been deliberate or merely obtuse. They were an undistinguished lot, the audience; surely that woman at the end of the third row was an assistant in W. H. Smith's? Muriel observed them with distaste, as she turned over to the last page; schoolteachers and librarians, for the most part, one was talking right above their heads, in all probability. A somewhat wasted evening – which could have usefully been spent doing things about the house, or going through students' essays, or looking at that article Paul had given her, in order to have some well-thought-out comments for the morning.

She concluded, and sat, with a wintry smile towards Bill Freeman, at her side, who, as one might have expected, rose to thank her with a sequence of remarks as inept as his introduction: '. . . our appreciation to Dr Rackham for her fascinating talk and throw the meeting open to discussion.'

Discussion could not have been said to flow. There was a man who had been to a production of *Macbeth* in which you actually saw Banquo and did the speaker think that was right or was it better if you just kind of guessed he was there . . . and a woman who thought *The Turn of the Screw* wasn't awfully good when they made it into an opera, and another who had been interested in the bit about people in historical times believing in ghosts and had the speaker ever visited Hampton Court because if you go there the guide tells you that . . .

Muriel dealt politely but briefly with the questioners. She glanced again at the clock, and then at Bill Freeman, who would do well to wind things up. There was a pause. Bill Freeman scanned the audience and said, 'Well, if no one has anything more to ask Dr Rackham I think perhaps . . .'

The small dark woman at the end of the front row leaned forward, looking at Muriel. 'I thought what you said was quite interesting and I'd like to tell you about this thing that happened to a friend of mine. She was staying in this house, you see, where apparently . . .'

It went on for several minutes. It was very tedious, a long rigmarole about inexplicable creakings in the night, objects appearing and disappearing, ghostly footsteps and sounds and so on and so forth, all classifiable according to Tale-Type and Motif if one felt so inclined and hadn't in fact lost interest in the whole subject some time ago, now that one was doing this work on the metaphysical poets with Paul . . . Muriel sat back and sighed. She eyed the woman with distaste; the face was vaguely familiar, someone local, presumably. An absurd little person with black, straight, short hair (dyed, by the look of it) fringing her face, those now unfashionable spectacles upswept at the corners and tinted a disagreeable mauve, long ear-rings of some cheap shiny stone. Ear-rings, Muriel noted, more suitable for a younger woman; this creature was her own age, at least. Her skirt was too short, also, and her shirt patterned with what looked like lotus flowers in a discordant pink.

'. . . and my friend felt that it had come back to see about something, the ghost, something that had annoyed it. I just wondered what the speaker had to say about that, if she'd ever had any experiences of that kind.' The woman stared at Muriel, almost aggressively.

Muriel gathered herself. 'Well,' she said briskly, 'of course we've really been concerned this evening with the fictional and historical persona of the ghost, haven't we? As far as I'm concerned I would subscribe to what has been called the intellectual impossibility of ghosts – and of course experiences such as your friend's, if one stops to think about it, are open to all kinds of explanation, aren't they?' – she flashed a quick, placating smile – 'And now, I feel perhaps that . . .' – she half-turned towards the chairman – 'if there are no more questions . . .'

Going home (after coffee and sandwiches in someone's house; the black-haired person, mercifully, had not been there) she shook off the dispiriting atmosphere of the evening with relief: the dingy room, the unresponsive audience. The paper had been far too academic for them, of course. She felt glad that Paul had not come. He had offered to, but she had insisted that he shouldn't. Turning the Mini out of the High Street and past the corner of his road, she allowed herself a glance at the lighted window of his house. The curtains were drawn; Sheila would be watching television, of course, Paul reading (the new Joyce book, probably, or maybe this week's *TLS*). Poor Paul. Poor, dear Paul. It was tragic, such a marriage. That dull, insensitive woman.

'Your friendship is of the greatest value to me, Muriel,' he had said, one week ago exactly. He had said it looking out of the window, rather than at her – and she had understood at once. Understood the depth of his feeling, the necessity for understatement, for the avoidance of emotional display. Their position was of extreme delicacy – Paul's position. Head of Department, Vice-Principal of the College. She had nodded and murmured something, and they had gone on to discuss a student, some problems about the syllabus . . .

At night, she had lain awake, thinking with complacency of their relationship, of its restraint and depth, in such contrast to the stridency of the times. Muriel considered herself – knew herself to be – a tolerant woman, but occasionally she observed her students with disgust; their behaviour was coarse and vulgar, not to put too fine a point upon it. They brandished what should be kept private.

Occasionally, lying there, she was visited by other feelings, which she recognised and suppressed; a mature, balanced person is able to exercise self-control. The satisfaction of love takes more than one form.

She put the car in the garage and let herself into the house, experiencing the usual pleasure. It was delightful; white walls, bare boards sanded and polished, her choice and tasteful possessions – rugs, pictures, the few antique pieces, the comfortable sofa and armchairs, the William Morris curtains. It was so unlike, now, the dirty, cluttered, scruffy place she had bought five months ago as to be almost unrecognisable. Only its early Victorian exterior remembered – and that too was now bright and trim under new paint, with a front door carefully reconstructed in keeping, to replace the appalling twenties porch some previous occupant had built on. The clearing-out process had been gruelling – Muriel blenched even now at the thought of it: cupboards stacked with junk and rubbish that nobody had bothered to remove (there had been an executors' sale, the elderly owner having died some months before), the whole place filthy and in a state of horrid disrepair. She had done the bulk of the work herself, with the help of a local decorator and carpenter for the jobs she felt were beyond her. But alone she had emptied all those cavernous cupboards, carting the stuff down to a skip hired from a local firm. It had been a disagreeable job – not just because of the dirt and physical effort, but because of the nature of the junk, which hinted at an alien and unpleasing way of life. She felt that she wanted to scour the house of its past, make it truly hers, as she heaved bundle after bundle of musty rubbish down the stairs. There had been boxes of old clothes – too old and sour to interest either the salerooms or Oxfam – brash vulgar female clothes, shrill of colour and pattern, in materials like sateen, chenille and rayon, the feel of which made Muriel shudder. They slithered from her hands, smelling of mould and mouse droppings, their touch so repellent that she took to wearing rubber gloves. And then there were shelves of old magazines and books – not the engrossing treasure-trove that such a hoard ought to be (secondhand bookshops, after all, were an addiction of hers) but dreary and dispiriting in what they suggested of whoever had owned them: pulp romantic fiction, stacks of the cheaper, shriller women's magazines (all sex and crime, not even that limited but wholesome stuff about cooking, children and health), some tattered booklets with pictures that made Muriel flush – she shovelled the beastly things into a supermarket carton and dumped the lot into the skip. This house had seen little or no literature that could even be called decent during its recent past, that was clear enough; with pleasure she had arranged her own books on the newly-painted shelves at either side of the fireplace. They seemed to clinch her conquest of the place.

There had been other things, too. A dressmaker's dummy that she had found prone at the back of a cupboard (its murky shape had given her a hideous shock); she had scrubbed and kept it, occasionally she made herself a dress or skirt and it might conceivably be useful, though its torso was dumpier than her own. A tangle of hairnets and curlers in a drawer of the kitchen dresser, horribly scented of violets. Bits and pieces of broken and garish jewellery – all fake – that kept appearing from under floorboards or down crevices. Even now she came across things; it was as though the house would never have done with spewing out its tawdry memories. And of course the redecorating had been a major job – stripping away those fearful wallpapers that plastered every room, every conceivable misrepresentation of nature, loud and unnatural roses, poppies and less identifiable flowers that crawled and clustered up and down the walls. Sometimes two or three different ones had fought for survival in the same room; grimly, Muriel, aided by the decorator, tore and soaked and peeled. At last, every wall was crisply white, a background to her prints and lithographs, her Georgian mirror, the Khelim rug.

Now, she felt at last that she had taken possession. There were one or two small things still that jarred – a cupboard in her bedroom from which, scrub as she might, she could not eradicate the sickly smell of some cheap perfume, a hideous art nouveau window (she gathered such things were once again in fashion – *chacun à son goût*) in the hall which she would eventually get around to replacing. Otherwise, all was hers; her quiet but distinctive taste in harmony with the house's original architectural grace.

It was just past nine; time for a look at that article before bed. Muriel went to her desk (which, by day, had a view of the small garden prettily framed in William Morris's 'Honeysuckle') and sat reading and taking notes for an hour or so. She remembered that Paul would be away all day tomorrow, at a meeting in London, and she would not be able to see him, so when she had finished reading she pulled her typewriter in front of her and made a résumé of her reflections on the article, to leave in his pigeon-hole. She read them through, satisfied with what she felt to be some neatly put points. Then she got up, locked the back and front doors, checked the windows, and went to bed.

In the night, she woke; the room felt appallingly stuffy – she could even, from her bed, smell that disagreeable cupboard – and she assumed that she must have forgotten to open the window. Getting up to do so, she found the sash raised a couple of inches as usual. She returned to bed, and was visited by unwelcome yearnings which she drove out by a stern concentration on her second-year Shakespeare option.

She had left her page of notes on the article in the typewriter, and almost forgot it in the morning, remembering at the last moment as she was about to leave the house, and going back to twitch it hastily out and put it in her handbag. The day was busy with classes and a lecture, so that it was not until the afternoon that she had time to write a short note for Paul ('I entirely agree with you about the weaknesses in his argument; however, there are one or two points we might discuss, some thoughts on which I enclose. I do hope London was not too exhausting – MCR'), and glance again at the page of typescript.

It was not as satisfactory as Muriel remembered; in fact it was not satisfactory at all. She must have been a great deal more tired than she had realised last night – only in a stupor (and not even, one would have hoped, then) could she have written such muddled sentences, such hideous syntax, such illiteracies of style and spelling. 'What I think is that he developped what he said about the character of Tess all wrong so what you ended up feeling was that . . .' she read in horror '. . . if Hardy's descriptive passages are not always relivant then personally what I don't see is why . . .' And what was this note at the bottom – apparently added in haste? 'What about meeting for a natter tomorrow – I was thinking about you last night – ssh! you aren't supposed to know that!' I must have been half-asleep, she thought, how could I write such things?

Hot with discomfort (and relief – heavens! she might not have looked again at the thing), she crumpled the paper and threw it into the wastepaper basket. She wrote a second note to Paul saying that she had read the article but unfortunately had not the time now to say more, and hoped to discuss it with him at some point; she then cancelled her late-afternoon class and went home early. I have been overdoing things, she thought – my work, the house – I need rest, a quiet evening.

She settled down to read, but could not concentrate; for almost the first time, she found herself wishing for the anodyne distraction of television. She polished and dusted the sitting-room (finding, in the process, a disgusting matted hank of hairnets and ribbon that had got, quite inexplicably, into her Worcester teapot) and cleaned the windows. Then she did some washing, which led to an inspection of her wardrobe; it seemed sparse. A new dress, perhaps, would lift her spirits. On Saturday, she would buy one, and in the meantime, there was that nice length of tweed her sister had given her and which had lain untouched for months. Perhaps with the aid of the dressmaker's dummy it could be made into a useful skirt. She fetched the dummy and spent an hour or two with scissors and pins – a soothing activity, though the results were not quite as satisfactory as she could have wished. Eventually she left the roughly-fashioned skirt pinned to the dummy and put it away in the spare-room cupboard before going to bed.

A few days later, to her pleasure, Paul accepted an invitation to call in at the house on his way home to pick up a book and have a drink. He had hesitated before accepting, and she understood his difficulties at once; such meetings were rare for them, and the reasons clear enough to her: the pressures of his busy life, Sheila . . . 'Well, yes, how kind, Muriel,' he had said. 'Yes, fine, then. I'll give Sheila a ring and tell her I'll be a little late.'

Poor Paul; the strains of such a marriage did not bear contemplation. Of course, they always appeared harmonious enough in public, a further tribute to his wonderful patience and restraint. Nor did he ever hint or complain; one had to be perceptive to realise the tensions that must rise – a man of his intellectual stature fettered to someone without, so far as Muriel understood, so much as an A-level. His tolerance was amazing; Muriel had even heard him, once, join with well-simulated enthusiasm in a discussion of some trashy television series prompted by Sheila at a Staff Club party.

She was delayed at the College and only managed to arrive back at the house a few minutes before he arrived. Pouring the sherry, she heard him say, 'What's this, then, Muriel – making a study of popular culture?' and turned round to see him smiling and holding up one of those scabrous women's magazines that – she thought – she had committed to the skip. Disconcerted, she found herself flushing, embarking on a defensive explanation of the rubbish that had been in the house . . . (But she had cleared all that stuff out, every bit, how could that thing have been, apparently, lying on the little Victorian sewing-table, from which Paul had taken it?)

The incident unnerved her, spoiled what should have been an idyllic hour.

Muriel woke the next day – Saturday – discontented and twitchy. She had slept badly, disturbed by the muffled sound of a woman's shrill laugh, coming presumably from the next house in the terrace; she had not realised before that noise could penetrate the walls.

Remembering her resolution of a few days before, she went shopping for a new dress. The facilities of Ilmington were hardly metropolitan, but adequate for a woman of her restrained tastes; she found, after some searching, a pleasant enough garment innocent of any of the nastier excesses of modern fashion, in a wholesome colour and fabric, and took it home in a rather calmer frame of mind.

In the evening, there was the Principal's sherry party (Paul would be there; with any luck there would be the opportunity for a few quiet words). She went to take the dress from the wardrobe and indeed was about to put it on before the feel of it in her hands brought her up short; surely there was something wrong? She took it to the window, staring – this was never the dress she had chosen so carefully this morning? The remembered eau-de-nil was now, looked at again, in the light from the street, a harsh and unflattering apple-green; the coarse linen, so pleasant to the touch, a slimy artificial stuff. She had made the most disastrous mistake; tears of frustration and annoyance pricked her eyes. She threw the thing back in the cupboard and put on her old Jaeger print.

Sunday was a day that, normally, she enjoyed. This one got off to a bad start with the discovery of the *Sunday Mirror* sticking through the front door instead of the *Sunday Times*; after breakfast she rang the shop, knowing that they would be open till eleven, only to be told by a bewildered voice that surely that was what she had asked for, change it, you said on the phone, Thursday it was, for the *Sunday Mirror*, spicier, you said, good for a laugh. 'There's been some mistake,' said Muriel curtly. 'I don't know what you can be thinking of.' She slammed down the receiver and set about a massive cleaning of the house; it seemed the proper therapeutic thing to do.

After lunch she sat down at her desk to do some work; her article for *English Today* was coming along nicely. Soon it would be time to show a first draft to Paul. She took the lid off the typewriter and prepared to reread the page she had left in on Friday.

Two minutes later, her heart thumping, she was ripping out the paper, crumpling it into a ball . . . I never wrote such stuff, she thought, it's impossible, words like that, expressions like – I don't even *know* such expressions.

She sat in horror, staring into the basilisk eye of a thrush on her garden wall. There is something wrong, she thought, I am not myself, am I going mad?

She took a sleeping pill, but even so woke in the depths of the night (again, those muffled peals of laughter), too hot, the room heavy around her so that she had to get up and open the window further; the house creaked. There must be a fault in the heating system, she thought, I'll have to get the man round. She lay in discomfort, her head aching.

In the days that followed it seemed to her that she suffered from continuous headaches. Headaches, and a kind of lightheadedness that made her feel sometimes that she had only a tenuous grip on reality; in the house, after work, she heard noises, saw things. There was that laughter again, which must be from next door but when she enquired delicately of the milkman as to who her neighbours were (one didn't want actually to get involved with them) she learned that an elderly man lived there, alone, a retired doctor. And there were things that seemed hallucinatory, there was no other explanation; going to the cupboard where she had put the dummy, to have another go at that skirt, she had found the thing swathed not in her nice herring-bone tweed but a revolting purple chenille. She slammed the cupboard closed (again, the lurking shape of the dummy had startled her, although she had expected to see it), and sat down on the bed, her chest pounding. I am not well, she thought, I am doing things and then forgetting that I have done them, there is something seriously wrong.

And then there was the wallpaper. She had come into the sitting-room, one bright sunny morning – her spruce, white sitting-room – and, glancing at her Dufy prints, had seen suddenly the shadowy presence of the old, hideous wallpaper behind them, those entwined violets and roses that she and the decorator had so laboriously scraped away. Two walls, she now saw, were scarred all over, behind the new emulsion paint, with the shadowy presence of the old paper; how can we have missed them, she thought angrily – that decorator, I should have kept a sharper eye on him – but surely, I *remember*, we did this room together, every bit was stripped, surely?

Her head spun.

She went to the doctor, unwillingly, disliking her list of neurotic symptoms, envying the bronchitic coughs and bandaged legs in the waiting-room. Stiffly, she submitted to the questions, wanting to say: I am not this kind of person at all, I am balanced, well-adjusted, known for my good sense. With distaste, she listened to the diagnosis: yes, she wanted to say, impatiently, I have heard of menopausal problems but I am not the kind of woman to whom they happen, I keep things under better control than that, overwork is much more likely. She took his prescription and went away, feeling humiliated.

It was the examination season. She was faced, every evening, on returning home, with a stack of scripts and would sit up late marking, grateful for the distraction, though she was even more tired and prone to headaches. The tiredness was leading to confusion, also, she realised. On one occasion, giving a class, she had been aware of covert glances and giggles among her students, apparently prompted by her own appearance; later, in the staff cloakroom, she had looked in a mirror and been appalled to discover herself wearing a frightful low-cut pink blouse with some kind of flower-pattern. It was vaguely familiar – I've seen it before, she thought, and realised it must be a relic of the rubbish in the house, left in the back of her cupboard and put on accidentally this morning, in her bleary awakening from a disturbed night. Condemned to wear it for the rest of the day, she felt taken over by its garishness, as though compelled to behave in character; she found herself joining a group of people at lunch-time with whom she would not normally have associated, the brash set among her colleagues, sharing jokes and a conversation that she found distasteful. In Paul's office, later, going over some application forms, she laid her hand on his sleeve, and felt him withdraw his arm; later, the memory of this made her shrivel. It was as though she had betrayed the delicacy of their relationship; never before had they made physical contact.

She decided to take a couple of days off from the College, and mark scripts at home.

The first day passed tranquilly enough; she worked throughout the morning and early afternoon. At around five she felt suddenly moved, against her better judgement, to telephone Paul with what she knew to be a trumped-up query about an exam problem. Talking to him, she was aware of her own voice, with a curious detachment; its tone surprised her, and the shrillness of her laugh. Do I always sound like that? she thought, have I always laughed in that way? It seemed to her that Paul was abrupt, that he deliberately ended the conversation.

She got up the next morning in a curious frame of mind. The scripts she had to mark filled her with irritation; not the irritation stemming from inadequacy in the candidates, but a petulant resentment of the whole thing. Sometimes, she did not seem able to follow the answers to questions. 'Don't get you,' she scribbled in the margin. 'What are you on about?' At the bottom of one script she scrawled a series of doodles: indeterminate flowers, a face wearing upswept spectacles, a buxom female figure. At last, with the pile of scripts barely eroded, she abandoned her desk and wandered restlessly around the house.

Somehow, it displeased her. It was too stark, too bare, an unlived-in place. I like a bit of life, she thought, a bit of colour, something to pep things up; rummaging in the scullery she found under the sink some gaily patterned curtaining that must have got overlooked when she cleared out those particular shelves. That's nice, she thought, nice and striking, I like that; as she hung it in place of the linen weave in the hall that now seemed so dowdy, it seemed to her that from somewhere in the house came a peal of laughter.

That day merged, somehow, into the next. She did not go to the College. Several times the telephone rang: mostly she ignored it. Once, answering, she heard the departmental secretary's voice, blathering on: 'Dr Rackham?' she kept saying, 'Dr Rackham? Professor Simons has been a bit worried, we wondered if . . .' Muriel laughed and hung up. The night, the intermediate night (or nights, it might have been, time was a bit confusing, not that it mattered at all) had been most extraordinary. She had had company of some kind; throughout the night, whenever she woke, she had been aware of a low murmuring. A voice. A voice of compulsive intimacy, coarse and insistent; it had repelled but at the same time fascinated her. She had lain there, silent and unresisting.

The house displeased her more and more. It's got no style, she thought, full of dreary old stuff. She took down the Dufy prints, and the Piper cathedral etchings, thinking: I don't like that kind of thing, I like a proper picture, where you can see what's what, don't know where I ever picked up these. She made a brief sortie to Boots round the corner and bought a couple of really nice things, not expensive either – a Chinese girl and a lovely painting of horses galloping by the sea. As she hung them in the sitting-room, it seemed to her that someone clutched her arm, and for an instant she shuddered uncontrollably, but the sensation passed, though it left her feeling light-headed, a little hysterical.

Her own appearance dissatisfied her, too. She sat looking at herself in her bedroom mirror and thought: 'I've never made the best of myself, a woman's got to make use of what she's got, hasn't she? Where's that nice blouse I found the other day, it's flattering – a bit of décolleté, I'm not past that kind of thing yet. She put it on, and felt pleased. Downstairs, the telephone was ringing again, but she could not be bothered to answer it. Don't want to see anyone, she thought, fed up with people, if it's Paul he can come and find me, can't he? Play hard to get, that's what you should do with men, string them along a bit.

Anyway, she was not alone. She could feel, again, that presence in the room, though when she swung round suddenly – with a resurgence of that chill sensation – there was nothing but the dressmaker's dummy, standing in the corner. She must have brought it from the cupboard, and forgotten.

She wandered about the house, muttering to herself; from time to time, a person walked with her, not someone you could see, just a presence, its arm slipped through Muriel's, whispering intimacies, suggestions. All those old books of yours, it said, you don't want those, ring the newsagent, have them send round some mags, a good read, that's what we want. Muriel nodded.

Once, people hammered on the door. She could hear their voices; colleagues from the department. 'Muriel?' they called. 'Are you there, Muriel?' She went into the kitchen and shut herself in till they had gone. For a moment, sitting there, she felt clearer in her head, free of the confusion that had been dragging her down; something is happening, she thought wildly, something I cannot cope with, can't control . . .

And then there came again that presence, with its insistent voice, and this time the voice was quite real, and she knew, too, that she had heard it before, somewhere, quite recently, not long ago. Where, where?

. . . I thought what you said was quite interesting, and I'd like to tell you about this thing that happened to a friend of mine . . .

Muriel held the banisters, to steady herself (she was on her way upstairs again, in her perpetual edgy drifting up and down the house): the Lit. and Phil., I remember now, that woman.

And it came to her too, with a horrid jolt, that she knew now, remembered suddenly, why, at the time, that evening, the face had been familiar, why she'd felt she'd seen it before.

It had been the face in a yellowed photograph that had tumbled from a tatty book when she had been clearing out the house; Violet Hanson, 1934, in faded ink on the back.

Sale by auction, by order of the Executors of Mrs Violet Hanson, deceased, No. 27 Clarendon Terrace, a four-bedroomed house with scope for . . .

Someone was laughing, peals of shrill laughter that rang through the house, and as she reached the top floor, and turned into her bedroom, she knew that it was herself. She went into her bedroom and sat down at her dressing-table and looked in the mirror. The face that looked back at her was haggard. I've got to do something about myself, she thought, I'm turning into an old frump. She groped on the table and found a pair of ear-rings, long, shiny ones that she had forgotten she had. She held them up against her face; yes, that's nice, stylish, and I'll dye my hair, have it cut short and dye it black, take years off me, that would . . .

There was laughter again, but she no longer knew if it was hers or someone else's.

Next Term, We'll Mash You

INSIDE THE car it was quiet, the noise of the engine even and subdued, the air just the right temperature, the windows tight-fitting. The boy sat on the back seat, a box of chocolates, unopened, beside him, and a comic, folded. The trim Sussex landscape flowed past the windows: cows, white-fenced fields, highly-priced period houses. The sunlight was glassy, remote as a coloured photograph. The backs of the two heads in front of him swayed with the motion of the car.

His mother half-turned to speak to him. 'Nearly there now, darling.'

The father glanced downwards at his wife's wrist. 'Are we all right for time?'

'Just right. Nearly twelve.'

'I could do with a drink. Hope they lay something on.'

'I'm sure they will. The Wilcoxes say they're awfully nice people. Not really the schoolmaster-type at all, Sally says.'

The man said, 'He's an Oxford chap.'

'Is he? You didn't say.'

'Mmn.'

'Of course, the fees are that much higher than the Seaford place.'

'Fifty quid or so. We'll have to see.'

The car turned right, between white gates and high, dark, tight-clipped hedges. The whisper of the road under the tyres changed to the crunch of gravel. The child, staring sideways, read black lettering on a white board: 'St Edward's Preparatory School. Please Drive Slowly'. He shifted on the seat, and the leather sucked at the bare skin under his knees, stinging.

The mother said, 'It's a lovely place. Those must be the playing-fields. Look, darling, there are some of the boys.' She clicked open her handbag, and the sun caught her mirror and flashed in the child's eyes; the comb went through her hair and he saw the grooves it left, neat as distant ploughing.

'Come on, then, Charles, out you get.'

The building was red brick, early nineteenth century, spreading out long arms in which windows glittered blackly. Flowers, trapped in neat beds, were alternate red and white. They went up the steps, the man, the woman, and the child two paces behind.

The woman, the mother, smoothing down a skirt that would be ridged from sitting, thought: I like the way they've got the maid all done up properly. The little white apron and all that. She's foreign, I suppose. Au pair. Very nice. If he comes here there'll be Speech Days and that kind of thing. Sally Wilcox says it's quite dressy – she got that cream linen coat for coming down here. You can see why it costs a bomb. Great big grounds and only an hour and a half from London.

They went into a room looking out into a terrace. Beyond, dappled lawns, gently shifting trees, black and white cows grazing behind iron railings. Books, leather chairs, a table with magazines – *Country Life, The Field, The Economist*. 'Please, if you would wait here. The Headmaster won't be long.'

Alone, they sat, inspected. 'I like the atmosphere, don't you, John?'

'Very pleasant, yes.' Four hundred a term, near enough. You can tell it's a cut above the Seaford place, though, or the one at St Albans. Bob Wilcox says quite a few City people send their boys here. One or two of the merchant bankers, those kind of people. It's the sort of contact that would do no harm at all. You meet someone, get talking at a cricket match or what have you . . . Not at all a bad thing.

'All right, Charles? You didn't get sick in the car, did you?'

The child had black hair, slicked down smooth to his head. His ears, too large, jutted out, transparent in the light from the window, laced with tiny, delicate veins. His clothes had the shine and crease of newness. He looked at the books, the dark brown pictures, his parents, said nothing.

'Come here, let me tidy your hair.'

The door opened. The child hesitated, stood up, sat, then rose again with his father.

'Mr and Mrs Manders? How very nice to meet you – I'm Margaret Spokes, and will you please forgive my husband who is tied up with some wretch who broke the cricket pavilion window and will be just a few more minutes. We try to be organised but a schoolmaster's day is always just that bit unpredictable. Do please sit down and what will you have to revive you after that beastly drive? You live in Finchley, is that right?'

'Hampstead, really,' said the mother. 'Sherry would be lovely.' She worked over the headmaster's wife from shoes to hairstyle, pricing and assessing. Shoes old but expensive – Russell and Bromley. Good skirt. Blouse could be Marks and Sparks – not sure. Real pearls. Super Victorian ring. She's not gone to any particular trouble – that's just what she'd wear anyway. You can be confident, with a voice like that, of course. Sally Wilcox says she knows all sorts of people.

The headmaster's wife said, 'I don't know how much you know about us. Prospectuses don't tell you a thing, do they? We'll look round everything in a minute, when you've had a chat with my husband. I gather you're friends of the Wilcoxes, by the way. I'm awfully fond of Simon – he's down for Winchester, of course, but I expect you know that.'

The mother smiled over her sherry. Oh, I know that all right. Sally Wilcox doesn't let you forget that.

'And this is Charles? My dear, we've been forgetting all about you! In a minute I'm going to borrow Charles and take him off to meet some of the boys because after all you're choosing a school for him, aren't you, and not for you, so he ought to know what he might be letting himself in for and it shows we've got nothing to hide.'

The parents laughed. The father, sherry warming his guts, thought that this was an amusing woman. Not attractive, of course, a bit homespun, but impressive all the same. Partly the voice, of course; it takes a bloody expensive education to produce a voice like that. And other things, of course. Background and all that stuff.

'I think I can hear the thud of the Fourth Form coming in from games, which means my husband is on the way, and then I shall leave you with him while I take Charles off to the common-room.'

For a moment the three adults centred on the child, looking, judging. The mother said, 'He looks so hideously pale, compared to those boys we saw outside.'

'My dear, that's London, isn't it? You just have to get them out, to get some colour into them. Ah, here's James. James – Mr and Mrs Manders. You remember, Bob Wilcox was mentioning at Sports Day . . .'

The headmaster reflected his wife's style, like paired cards in Happy Families. His clothes were mature rather than old, his skin well-scrubbed, his shoes clean, his geniality untainted by the least condescension. He was genuinely sorry to have kept them waiting, but in this business one lurches from one minor crisis to the next . . . And this is Charles? Hello, there, Charles. His large hand rested for a moment on the child's head, quite extinguishing the thin, dark hair. It was as though he had but to clench his fingers to crush the skull. But he took his hand away and moved the parents to the window, to observe the mutilated cricket pavilion, with indulgent laughter.

And the child is borne away by the headmaster's wife. She never touches him or tells him to come, but simply bears him away like some relentless tide, down corridors and through swinging glass doors, towing him like a frail craft, not bothering to look back to see if he is following, confident in the strength of magnetism, or obedience.

And delivers him to a room where boys are scattered among inky tables and rungless chairs and sprawled on a mangy carpet. There is a scampering, and a rising, and a silence falling, as she opens the door.

'Now this is the Lower Third, Charles, who you'd be with if you come to us in September. Boys, this is Charles Manders, and I want you to tell him all about things and answer any questions he wants to ask. You can believe about half of what they say, Charles, and they will tell you the most fearful lies about the food, which is excellent.'

The boys laugh and groan; amiable, exaggerated groans. They must like the headmaster's wife: there is licensed repartee. They look at her with bright eyes in open, eager faces. Someone leaps to hold the door for her, and close it behind her. She is gone.

The child stands in the centre of the room, and it draws in around him. The circle of children contracts, faces are only a yard or so from him; strange faces, looking, assessing.

Asking questions. They help themselves to his name, his age, his school. Over their heads he sees beyond the window an inaccessible world of shivering trees and high racing clouds and his voice which has floated like a feather in the dusty schoolroom air dies altogether and he becomes mute, and he stands in the middle of them with shoulders humped, staring down at feet: grubby plimsolls and kicked brown sandals. There is a noise in his ears like rushing water, a torrential din out of which voices boom, blotting each other out so that he cannot always hear the words. Do you? they say, and Have you? and What's your? and the faces, if he looks up, swing into one another in kaleidoscopic patterns and the floor under his feet is unsteady, lifting and falling.

And out of the noises comes one voice that is complete, that he can hear. 'Next term, we'll mash you,' it says. 'We always mash new boys.'

And a bell goes, somewhere beyond doors and down corridors, and suddenly the children are all gone, clattering away and leaving him there with the heaving floor and the walls that shift and swing, and the headmaster's wife comes back and tows him away, and he is with his parents again, and they are getting into the car, and the high hedges skim past the car windows once more, in the other direction, and the gravel under the tyres changes to black tarmac.

'Well?'

'I liked it, didn't you?' The mother adjusted the car around her, closing windows, shrugging into her seat.

'Very pleasant, really. Nice chap.'

'I liked him. Not quite so sure about her.'

'It's pricey, of course.'

'All the same . . .'

'Money well spent, though. One way and another.'

'Shall we settle it, then?'

'I think so. I'll drop him a line.'

The mother pitched her voice a notch higher to speak to the child in the back of the car. 'Would you like to go there, Charles? Like Simon Wilcox. Did you see that lovely gym, and the swimming-pool? And did the other boys tell you all about it?'

The child does not answer. He looks straight ahead of him, at the road coiling beneath the bonnet of the car. His face is haggard with anticipation.

At the Pitt-Rivers

THEY'VE GOT this museum in Oxford, called the Pitt-Rivers; I spend a lot of time there. It's a weird place, really weird, stuff from all over the world crammed into glass cases like some kind of mad junk-shop – native things from New Guinea and Mexico and Sumatra and wherever you like to think of. Spears and stone axes and masks and a thousand different kinds of fish-hook. And bead jewellery and peculiar musical instruments. And a great totem from Canada. You can learn a lot there about what people get up to: it makes you think. Mostly it's pretty depressing – umpteen different nasty ways of killing each other.

I didn't start going there to learn anything; just because it was a nice quiet place to mooch around and be on my own, Saturdays, or after school. It got to be a kind of habit. There aren't often people there – the odd art student, a few kids gawping at the shrunken heads, one or two serious-looking blokes wandering around. The porter's usually reading the *Sun* or having a snooze; there's not a lot of custom. The Natural History Museum is a bigger draw; you have to go through that to get into the Pitt-Rivers. You'll always get an audience for a dinosaur and a few nasty-looking jellyfish in formalin. Actually I'm partial to the Natural History Museum myself; that makes you think, too. All those fossils, and then in the end you and me. I had a go at reading *The Origin of Species* last term, not that I got very far. There's a room upstairs in the museum where Darwin's friend – Huxley – had this great argument with that bishop and the rest of them. It says so on the door. I like that, it seems kind of respectful. Putting up a plaque to an argument, instead of just JOE SOAP WAS BORN HERE or whatever. It should be done more often.

It was in the Natural History Museum – underneath the central whale – that I first saw her, and since my mind was on natural selection I thought she wasn't all that good an example of it. I remember thinking that it was funny it doesn't seem to operate with girls, so you got them getting prettier and prettier, because good-looking girls have a better deal than bad-looking ones, you've only got to observe a bit to see that. I always notice girls, to see if they're pretty or not, and she wasn't. She wasn't specially ugly; just very ordinary – you wouldn't look at her twice. She was sitting on a bench, watching the entrance.

All the girls I know – at school or round where I live – are either attractive or they're not. If they're attractive they have lots of blokes after them and if they're not they don't. It's as simple as that. If they're attractive just looking at them makes you think of all sorts of things, imagine what it would be like and so forth, and if they're not then it doesn't really occur to you, except in so far as it occurs to you a good deal of the time, actually. This girl was definitely not attractive. In the first place she was in fact quite old, not far off thirty, I should think, and in the second she hadn't got a nice figure; her legs were kind of dumpy and she didn't have pretty hair or anything like that. I gave her a look, just automatically, to check, and then didn't bother with her.

Until I came alongside, where I could see her face clearly, and then I looked again. And again. She still wasn't pretty, but she had the most beautiful expression I've ever seen in my life. She glowed; that's the only way I can put it. She sat there with her hands in her lap, watching the door, and radiating away so that in a peculiar fashion it made you feel good just to look at her, a bit like you were joining in how she felt. Stupid, I daresay, but that's how it was.

And I thought to myself: oh ho . . . I mean, I've seen films and I've read books and I know a bit about things.

As a matter of fact I've been in love myself twice. The first time was with a girl in my class at school and I suppose it was a bit of a trial run, really, I mean I'm not altogether sure how much I was feeling it but it seemed quite important when it was going on. The second time was last year, when I was fifteen. She came to stay with her married sister who lives round the corner from us and though it's months and months ago now I still feel quite faint and weak when I go past the house.

Oh ho, I thought. I felt kindly – sort of benign – and a bit curious to see what the bloke would be like. I thought he couldn't be much because of her not being pretty. I mean, in films you can always tell who's going to fall for who because they'll be the two good-lookers and while I'm not saying real life's like that there is a way people match each other, isn't there, you've only got to look round at married people. Let me hasten to say that I'm not all that good-looking myself, only about B+. Not too bad, but not all that marvellous either.

But he didn't show up and I wanted to get on into the Pitt-Rivers, so I left her there, waiting. What I haven't said is that one of the things I go to the Pitt-Rivers for is to write poetry. I write quite a lot of poetry. I could do it at home – I often do – and it's not that I'm coy or anything, my parents know about it and they're quite interested, but I just like the idea of having a special place to go to. It's quiet there, and a bit odd like I've said, and nobody takes any notice of me.

Sometimes I feel I'm getting somewhere with this poetry, and other times it looks to me pretty awful. I showed a few poems to our English master and he was very helpful: he said what was good and pointed out where I'd used words badly, or not worked out what I was thinking very well, so that was quite encouraging. He's a nice bloke. I like his lessons. He's very good at explaining poetry. I mean, I think poetry's amazingly difficult: sometimes you read a thing again and again and you just can't see what the hell the person's getting at. He reads all sorts of poetry to us, our English master, and you really get the hang of it after a bit – hard stuff like Hopkins and *The Hound of Heaven*, and Donne. He read us some of those Donne poems about love the other day which are all very explicit and I must say first time round I hadn't quite got the point – 'Licence my roving hands . . .' and so forth – but he wasn't embarrassed or anything, our English master, and when you realise that it's not geography he's talking about, the poet, then as a matter of fact I think that poem's lovely. I got a bit fed up with the way some of my mates were sniggering about it, being all-knowing; truth to tell I doubt if they know any more than I do, it's all just show. And that's a beautiful poem: I mean, if anything makes it clear that there's nothing wrong about sex, that poem does, they ought to make it compulsory reading for some people.

Anyway, I went on into the Pitt-Rivers and I was up on the first floor, in a favourite corner of mine among the arrow-heads, when I saw her again, and I must say I got quite a shock. Because the man with her was an old bloke: he was older than my father, fiftyish and more, he must have been at least twenty years older than her. So I reckoned I must have made a mistake. Not that at all.

They were talking, though I couldn't hear what they were saying because they were on the far side of the gallery. They stopped in front of a case and I could see their faces quite clearly. They stood there looking at each other, not talking any more, and I realised I hadn't made a mistake after all. Absolutely not. They didn't touch each other, they just stood and looked; it seemed like ages. I don't imagine they knew I was there.

And that time I was shocked. Really shocked. I don't mind telling you, I thought it was disgusting. He was an ordinary-looking person – he might have been a schoolmaster or something, he wore those kind of clothes, old trousers and sweater, and he had greyish hair, a bit long. And there was she, and as I've said she wasn't pretty, not at all, but she had this marvellous look about her, and she was years and years younger.

It was because of him, I realised, that she had that look.

I didn't like it at all. I got up, from where I was sitting, with quite a clatter to make sure they heard me and I went stumping off out of the museum. I wasn't going to write any more poetry that day, I could see. I went off home and truth to tell I didn't really think much more about them, that man and the girl, mainly because of being rather disgusted, like I said.

A couple of weeks later they were there again. They were on the ground floor, at the back, by the rush matting and ceremonial gear for with-it tribesmen, leaning up against a glass case that they weren't looking into, and talking. At least he was talking, quiet and serious, and she was listening, and nodding from time to time. I was busy with some thinking I wanted to do, and I tried not to take any notice of them; I mean, they were neither here nor there as far as I was concerned, none of my business, though I still thought it was a bit creepy. I couldn't see *why*, frankly. You fancy people your own age, and that's all there is to it, is what I thought. What I'd always thought.

So I ignored them, except that I couldn't quite. I kept sneaking a look, every now and then, and the more I did the more I felt kind of friendly towards them; I liked them. Which was a bit weird considering they didn't know I even existed – they certainly weren't interested in *me* – so it was a pretty one-sided kind of relationship. I thought he seemed like a nice bloke, whatever you thought about him and her and all that. It was something about the way he smiled, and the way he told her things (not that I ever heard a word they said, I wasn't eavesdropping, not ever, let's be quite clear about that) that made her look interested and say things back and so on. I thought it was obvious they liked talking to each other, quite apart from anything else. I thought that was nice.

I only took out that girl I mentioned – the one who came to stay with her sister – once, and as a matter of fact we couldn't find much to talk about. I was still in love with her – no doubt about that – but it was a bit sticky, I don't mind admitting. In fact I was quite glad when it was time to take her back to her sister's. In many ways the best part was just thinking about her.

Every time I looked at the girl – the Pitt-Rivers one, that is – I found myself imagining what it must be like being able to feel that you've made someone look like that. Radiant, like she was. Which is what that bloke must have been able to feel. I found myself putting myself in his place, as it were, and wondering. I've done a lot of wondering about things like that – everybody does, I suppose – but mostly it's been more kind of basic. Now, I began to think I didn't really know anything. Looking at those two – watching them, if you like – was a bit like seeing something go on behind a thick glass window, so it was half removed from you. You could see but not hear, hear but not touch, or whatever. I could see, but I didn't know.

I suppose you could say I was envious, in a funny kind of way. I don't mean jealous in that I fancied the girl, or anything like that. As I've said already, she wasn't pretty, or even attractive. And I wasn't envious like you might be envious of someone for being happier than you are, because I'm not specially unhappy, as it happens. I think I was envious of them for being what they were – as though one fossil creature might be envious of a more evolved kind of fossil creature, which of course is a stupid idea.

When I was in the Pitt-Rivers again I looked for them, quite deliberately, but they weren't there. I was disappointed, though I pretended to myself it really didn't matter. I wondered about why they went there in the first place; I mean, people have to meet each other somewhere but why *there*? It doesn't exactly spring to mind as a romantic spot. I supposed there were reasons they didn't want to meet somewhere obvious and public: maybe he was married, I thought, or maybe she was, even. I wondered if that was the only place they met, or did they have others. Once walking through the botanical gardens, I found myself looking for them in the big glasshouses there.

I know the inside of the Pitt-Rivers pretty well by now. Considering it's not anthropology or ethnology or whatever I went there for in the first place, it's quite surprising what a lot I could tell you about the things people believe and do. Primitive people, that is – what the Pitt-Rivers calls primitive people. And I think it's all very sad, actually: sad because it's like children, not understanding how things work and getting it all wrong, and carving each other up because of it a lot of the time. It does actually make you feel things get better – wars and bombs and everything notwithstanding. Nobody wants to go on being a child all their lives.

I was thinking about this – looking at a case full of particularly loony stuff to do with witchcraft – when I saw them again. At least I saw her first, standing by the totem with her hands in her coat pockets, and I didn't have to look at the door to know he'd arrived: her face told you that. He came up to her and gave her a kind of hug – arm round her shoulders and then quickly off again – and they wandered away up the stairs, heads together, talking.

I didn't follow them; it had been nice to see them again, and know they were there, and that was it. I was busy on a poem I'd been writing and unpicking and rewriting for some time. It was a poem about an old man sitting on a bench in a park and getting into conversation with a boy – someone around my age – and they swap opinions and observations (it's all dialogue, this poem, like a long conversation) and it's not till the end you realise they're the same person. It sounds either corny, or pretentious, I know; and what I could never decide was whether to have it as though the old man's looking back, or the boy's kind of projecting forward – imagining himself, as it were. So I went on fiddling about with this, and didn't really think much about the man and the girl, until I saw it was latish and there was no one else in the museum except me and some feet on the wooden floor of the gallery overhead, walking round and round, round and round. Two pairs of feet. They'd been doing that for ages, I realised; I'd been hearing them without registering.

I saw them go past – just their heads, above the glass cases – and something wasn't right. They weren't talking. She had her arm through his, and she was looking straight in front of her, and when I saw her face I had a nasty kind of twinge in my stomach. Because she was miserable. Once, she looked at him, and they both managed a bleak sort of smile. And then they walked on, round the gallery again, and next time past they still weren't talking, just holding on to each other like that, like people who're ill, or very old. And then the attendant rang the bell, and I heard them come down the stairs, and they came past me and went out into the Natural History Museum.

I went after them. I saw them stop – under the central whale, just where I first saw her – and then they did say something to each other. I couldn't see her face; she had her back to me. He went off then, on his own, out through the main entrance, quickly, and she sat down on a bench. For a moment or two she just sat staring at that wretched whale, and then she felt in her bag and got out a comb and did her hair, as though that might help. And then she dropped the comb and didn't seem to have noticed, even, because she just sat; she didn't bother to pick it up or anything. I could see her face then, and I hope I don't ever see anyone look so unhappy again. I truly hope that.

I don't know what had happened. I never will. Somehow, I don't think they were ever going to see each other again, but why . . . well, that's their concern, just like the rest of it was, except that in this peculiar way I'd come to feel it was mine too. I didn't think there was anything disgusting about them any more, or creepy – I hadn't for a long time. I suppose you could say I'd learned something else in the Pitt-Rivers, by accident. I never did go on with that poem. I tore it up, as far as it had got; I wasn't so sure any more about that conversation, that there could even be one, or not like I'd been imagining, anyway.

Nice People

JAMES WINTON, in faded drill trousers and flowered shirt, his bathing towel and trunks in a roll under his arm, a large, battered straw hat on his head, walked slowly up the path from the beach. He took it easily, in stages, a fifty-yard leg at a time, and then a pause to look back at the sea, which glittered in the late afternoon light, quilted by the wind, roving through all the blues from pale turquoise to the darkest midnight. He sat, breathing a little heavily, on a slab of rock, and saw that he was accompanied by the children and the goats. They moved up the hillside parallel to him, not using the path, flitting through the scrub, the prickly pears and small thorny bushes and striped green and yellow cacti that furnished the island's landscape.

The children came down to the beach every day at this time, as he did. He was never clear why. While he swam and sunbathed, they squatted at the back of the beach, in the scruffy hinterland of rusty tins, seaweed and snatches of torn plastic – chattering, throwing stones, and occasionally chivvying the goats. They paid no attention to James. Once, they had watched and commented, giggling behind their small brown hands, fleeing in simulated panic if he approached them. They would never respond much to his attempts at conversation, refusing to be drawn on the subject of names and ages, glancing shyly at each other and shaking their heads though he guessed that they knew quite enough English to understand. But nowadays they hardly seemed to notice him; the goats swarmed up the hillside, sharply black and brown, surprisingly clean, their udders huge and swinging, and the children swarmed with them, calling to each other, ignoring the more slowly moving James. This pleased him: he felt accepted.

Though, heaven knows, one should be accepted now. Two years it would be, this summer. He sat in the sun, relishing the heat, the rasp of grasshoppers around him, the whiff of some aromatic plant, the sight of his own body, burnt as dark as the children. One had made absolutely the right decision, no question about it, the island was (except for a few small things) an earthly paradise, hot, cheap, the people so nice, and oneself quite amazingly fit for one's age.

A plane flew low overhead (packed with holiday people, their fortnight done, bound for Heathrow, poor things) – the six o'clock one presumably, which reminded him that he must pick up a bottle of gin at Mary Vella's on the way home, so he got up and set off again, his heart thumping a little uncomfortably. The hill was steep, of course, which accounted for that, but it might be wise all the same to lose a bit of weight.

He reached the car, and sat for a moment to rest before starting the engine. Heat quivered off the seats, although he had left all the windows open (quite all right to do that here, not like Spain or Italy, the islanders were quite staggeringly honest). The children were all around, foraging in the litter that accumulated everywhere (their honesty, unfortunately, was not matched by tidiness). James watched them for a moment, thinking that some were undoubtedly old Mary's progeny, Lucia's brothers and sisters. He searched for a family likeness, but truth to tell they all looked much the same, thin and dark with boot-button black eyes. 'Lucia?' he said encouragingly, 'Lucia Vella?' and they scattered with smiling, backward glances, clambering over the stone walls that divided the neatly terraced fields. The sight of their bodies, their graceful brown limbs, never failed to give them a sense of well-being; they were most attractive in youth, the islanders, less so, alas, as adults. That boy in particular – the thin, very dark lad perched on the wall now, looking back – sad to think that he would mature into someone like old Joe Vella in the bar. Starting the car, James waved a friendly hand, but the boy, staring, did not wave back.

He drove to the village, noticing with distaste that a great ugly board on the outskirts heralded yet another burst of new buildings. There was always the nagging fear that this place might be spoiled within a few years, like the Spanish coast after the war, like some of the Greek islands. Of course, there was no airport, nor any possibility of one, people would always have to come by ferry from the main island, which was a help, but even so, the danger was there. Oh, he thought, it'll last my time, with any luck.

They were obviously going to be hideous, too, the new houses, from the garish illustration on the agent's board: cheap, vulgar little boxes. That, of course, was what was a pity about the island, that almost everything – except, of course, its natural assets of sun and sea and rock – was aesthetically unpleasing. The islanders, somehow, had never been blessed with that lightness of touch of most Mediterranean peoples; they had, one was bound to admit, unswervingly bad taste. Their houses were ugly, plonked down without regard for the natural contours of the landscape, uncompromisingly squat and dumpy – a little like the people themselves, who were also without the physical grace of Greeks, Italians,

Spaniards, stout and temperamentally a little dour. A bit, James sometimes felt in irritation, like displaced English. That was one of the minor snags tempering the island's paradisial quality: it was always slightly mortifying to see one's visitors' expressions as they surveyed, on their first day, the scene, noting the banal villages, the unappetising little bars plastered with Coke and beer advertisements (no gay pavement cafés), the ubiquitous photographs of the Queen and the Duke of Edinburgh. He had then to point out the older farmhouses, like his own, with their pleasantly pink-washed walls and more graceful arched windows, stress the quality of the light (which one's painter friends, of course, were always quick to appreciate), the variety of vegetation and amusing local quirks like the ripening pumpkins that decorated the rooftops, the roadside shrines (garish, but fun) the marvellously pagan and atavistic bull-horns above the doors. And, of course, the cheapness of everything: wine, cigarettes, labour.

The restoration of the farmhouse had cost considerably less than he had expected; it was always pleasing to detect the gleam of incredulous envy as he detailed the cost of the new flooring, electricity, plumbing, pretty wrought-iron balconies, terrace overlooking the valley, construction and paving of the garden. Really, James? they would say, but it's amazing, in England you'd have paid three times as much. I know, he'd say, I know, the thing is, you see, that they are quite unspoilt, as yet, these people, they are *not* grasping, not ambitious, they are simple people leading simple lives and satisfied with what they have. The great thing, he would say, is that they should stay like that, not be spoiled, I do so pray this place doesn't go the way of so much of the Med. They are such nice people. And his visitors, watching Lucia wash the chequered black and white stone floor or potter in the kitchen, would say yes, they do seem to be, I must say I envy you, James.

Lucia was Mary Vella's daughter. James, crossing the village square towards the Union Jack Bar outside which Mary sat, her enormous bottom quite engulfing the three-legged stool, reflected that she could not be much more than forty. She looked sixty. They aged so young, the island women. A brief slim girlhood, then fifteen years of child-bearing, and a precipitate middle age. The Church, James thought severely, has a lot to answer for.

Mary was conducting a conversation at the shout with a neighbour on the other side of the square. What the islanders lacked in Latin gaiety they fully made up for in stridency of voice; the women screamed to one another all day long. James had had to be firm with Lucia about that, right at the beginning. No bawling to the neighbours or passers-by, and when you have something you want to ask me, Lucia, you come to me and say it quietly, do you see, not shout from the other side of the house. And Lucia, in the first flush of submission and anxiety to please, had nodded and smiled and remembered for at least two days.

It was not that they were stupid; child-like, more. Not childish, but child-like – which was what, of course, made them so attractive, in many ways. If somewhat exasperating. You had to tell them everything two, three times. The training of Lucia had been a long, laborious affair of many recessions, many defeats. Now, at last, one was beginning to reap the fruits.

Mary Vella had seen him, and was heaving herself to her feet, yelling to Joe her husband back in the dark gorge of the bar that Mr Winton was here, and where are the crates? and get a beer from the fridge, Mr Winton is tired, will want a drink.

'Not now, Mary,' he said – Tom Harley was coming in for supper, and the Pierces – 'I haven't time. Just the crates, please, and a bottle of gin.'

She bustled about him as they went together through the bead curtains and into the stuffy gloom of the bar, children attendant at her heels. 'Lucia is good, yes, you are pleased? She do her work well?'

Lucia, of course, was the eldest. 'Yes, fine, fine,' said James abstractedly. He was trying to remember if he had some whisky for Tom Harley, or not. 'And a bottle of Scotch, Mary, and twenty Embassy. Perhaps I will have a beer after all, while Joe puts the stuff in the car.'

He sat outside, on Mary's stool; that, of course, was one of the pleasant little things about the island, people being so willing and helpful, Joe taking the stuff to the car, not those wretched impersonal supermarkets that were everywhere in England now. Mary was standing beside him – at a level with his eyes, the varicose veins coiled like vines around her legs, poor old dear, now the Health Service is something they really *could* do with out here – wanting to know about groceries for next week: the bar's function extended beyond that of an English pub, dealing in foodstuffs as well as drink. He remembered the time Mary had brought Lucia for interview, toiling up the hill to the house with Father Grech in tow, like, he had thought in amusement, some kind of chaperon. As though one might pounce on one or the other of them, though heaven knows the choice was not really to one's taste, either way . . .

It would have been a relief to her – and a local scoop – to get a daughter placed in a secure, well-paid job. The island was overpopulated; there was widespread unemployment; the young left for Italy, Australia, England. The airport on the main island teemed, day and night, with excited, distraught relatives, entire families seeing off departing members, welcoming returning ones home on a visit. Mary Vella, standing foursquare in the middle of the terrace, Lucia at her elbow, Father Grech lurking in the background, had depicted Lucia as the domestic paragon of all time (not, of course, that one had been in the least taken in, having observed the islanders' home habits), in ferocious pursuit of a job that scores of local girls would jump at. And the deal had been struck, the priest nodding approvingly, assuring James of the wisdom of his choice. ('Very nice people, Mr Winton, a very good family, good mother, a good girl, she will work hard.') James had been quite firm and sensible, not offering more money than was proper, the girl must not be spoilt – 'Five pounds a week to start with, and in a year's time, when she's learned what to do, we'll think about it again.'

And he would, he thought, put it up to six, in all probability. She had turned out well. She cleaned assiduously, washed and ironed exquisitely, cooked – well, cooking was the main stumbling-block (their own cuisine, of course, was non-existent) but even that, with constant guidance and instruction, she was picking up. You had to keep on at her all the time, but she could do a few dishes quite passably now, salads and pizzas could be left to her, her cold soups were not bad at all.

Oh yes, she was worth six pounds a week, well worth it.

Six? – friends from England would say – Nan Chalmers, Roger Bates, *Six*, James, you must be joking. Goodness, you are pampered out here.

He finished his beer and drove home. Things seemed to be under control. Lucia was laying the table – on occasions when people were coming in for supper she had a few hours off in the afternoon and came in for the evening instead – and appeared not to have made too much of a hash of it. She was wearing one of the striped cotton frocks he had got Roger to bring out from Marks and Spencer for her and looked reasonably neat. Her appearance had been a problem, at the beginning. She had arrived in her own tawdry 'best' clothes, which were of distressing vulgarity – shrill and cheap of texture and design. He had toyed with the idea of putting her into a simple little uniform, but had thought that might seem a bit affected. Finally he had solved the problem with plain, inoffensive cotton frocks from England. Lucia, he knew, did not like them; she thought them dowdy, and changed into her own clothes to go home. She was not a pretty girl, but there was a certain attractive oddity to her face, something to do with an unevenness about her large dark eyes. Lopsided, Roger had said, she looks like a Picasso, charming – and for a while they had called her La Demoiselle d'Avignon. How is La Demoiselle? Roger would say, in his letters, still trying to polish the silver with Windolene? It was Roger who had set what had become the accepted tone of visitors towards Lucia – quietly teasing, making a bit of fuss of her, even, sometimes, James feared, spoiling her rather with little presents. One would have to watch that; Lucia, of course, loved it. Her eyes would light up at the sight of air-mail envelopes – 'Mr Bates, he is coming to stay, yes? Mrs Fletcher – here is a letter from Mrs Fletcher, perhaps she is saying she will come back soon . . .'

There was a letter from Roger now, and one from Nan Chalmers. He sat on the terrace reading them, while Lucia hovered, anxious to share the contents. 'What? Yes, I'll get the wine out in a minute, see that there are glasses at every place, the green ones, not the plain. No, Mr Bates didn't send any message and no, he isn't coming for his holidays.'

Good luck to him, James thought, with a spurt of malice, with his film friend who has this villa on Spetsae, and yes of course I understand, only too well, as it happens. He put Roger's letter aside and turned to Nan Chalmers's, perking up as he read that Nan would adore to come out in June, for a good fortnight if he could bear her for that long, she couldn't wait to see the house and . . .

One did feel just a tiny bit cut off, sometimes, on the island. Of course, with everything being so cheap it was possible to be extravagant with subscriptions to papers and periodicals, so that really one had all the advantages of London life – of English life – without having to live there. No, it was just that when the summer visitors had gone, the island could seem just a bit restricted, despite all its advantages. But things were bound to improve; the English community was growing all the time, with one or two live wires who were really getting things off the ground a bit – a Dramatic Society that might be rather fun, and a literary group with visiting speakers from time to time, and so on. And the mechanics of life were looking up, too, the little things that had seemed, initially, part of the island's appeal – the bad roads and uncertain services – but which had begun to pall after a few months. Most of the roads were being surfaced now, and the telephone exchange no longer remained incommunicado for half the day, which had been so infuriating when one was trying to arrange a little dinner or something.

So Nan would be here in June. And then in July there would be the Fletchers. Restored, in pleasant anticipation of the evening, the next few weeks, he set about the necessary briefing of Lucia. 'And you hand the dishes from the left, remember, Lucia, the left side of people – which is the left? Oh, Lucia, how many times have I told you? The side they wear their watch, the side ladies have their wedding ring.'

Mary Vella sat outside the bar and continued the shouted conversation with her neighbour; the conversation distracted her in no way from her own anxieties, which were several, or the pain in her legs, which was habitual. She was pregnant, though she did not count that among her anxieties, and indeed had hardly registered the fact; fertility was something to be proud of, especially a fertility as proven as hers. The anxieties were matters of money, spiritual offences, a discrepancy between the number of crates of Double Diamond there ought to be in the store and the number there actually were (and the part that her husband Joe might have played in this), and her daughter Lucia.

Lucia would be twenty-two next birthday. Mary herself had been married and a mother by that age. Lucia was no prettier than the next girl – indeed rather less so; there were fewer marriageable men on the island every year. A Lucia with a small nest-egg accumulated by the judicious saving of several years' wages, or the best part of them, on the other hand, was a marketable proposition. Mary Vella, totting up figures in her head, shifting her weight from one ham to the other, screaming tit-bits of information across the dust and the parked cars and the playing children, considered all this and balanced it against the risks, the imponderables, the unknown quantities.

She did not like Mr Winton. She did not like his clothes (shabby, for a man so evidently rich, and more suitable for a woman, often, and a young woman at that, flowered shirt, bright colours . . .) or his way of talking or, most particularly, his friends. It was his friends who worried her where Lucia was concerned. There were young men whose winning smiles and overfriendliness made her uncomfortable; one, once, had brought Lucia home in Mr Winton's car, late at night, after she had helped at a party. Appalled, Mary had screamed at the girl for half the next day; a Lucia whose morals were open to doubt would not be a marriageable prospect at all. And there were women as distasteful as the men – women as old as herself and older who would stroll into the bar with blouses unbuttoned over bathing-costumes, with bare legs, with skirts as short as a child's. One of them, once, had given Lucia a discarded dress; it was indecent and Mary had thrown it angrily into the dustbin.

But it was a good job, well-paid. And almost certainly less risky, less imponderable, than a job in one of the hotels or bars on the main island, even had such a job been obtainable. Mary Vella calculated and assessed and worried, discussed the price of a plastic-covered kitchen table, cuffed a straying child, beamed and bobbed at Father Grech, performing his evening tour of the parish.

James made careful plans for Nan's visit. One wanted her to get the best possible impression of the place; she had been just a bit derogatory (as had one or two other friends) when he had announced his intentions. 'There, James? But isn't it awfully English – why not Greece or Italy? Yes, I daresay prices are lower . . .' Nan, of course, had been a great traveller all her life; whatever obscure French village you mentioned, whatever remote Greek island, she had been there, probably years ago, before it got so spoilt, when it was really lovely and untouched. It could be irritating, even in as old and dear a friend as Nan. The house, he knew, could not fail to impress – to inspire envy (pretty as one had to concede was Nan's Georgian Cheltenham house) – it was the island's shortcomings that were a nuisance. But there was nothing to be done about it except make a joke of the worst eyesores and exploit all that was most exploitable – sea, climate, the abundance and cheapness of all those fruits and vegetables that would be most expensive or unavailable in England.

And Nan was gratifyingly appreciative. She arrived wan and tired (the winter had been appalling, life not easy with everything so dear now, what a wise decision you did make, James . . .) and unfurled within the first week, becoming tanned and gay, her old amusing self. She must be pushing sixty now, one would hardly believe it. She had a great way with people, of course, Nan. Within days she was much in demand, socially – invitations galore for them both. And she had nice things to say about the quality of the social life the island offered, such interesting people, people who painted and wrote and that kind of thing, really, it wouldn't be hard to settle down here, you'd hardly miss London theatres and exhibitions at all. They swam and sunned themselves, ate and drank, explored and talked.

She was sweet to Lucia (and very good with Mary Vella, whenever they were in the bar, a graceful mixture of jokiness and charm). She gave Lucia some bits and pieces (but nothing too lavish – just a simple little blouse, oddments of junk jewellery), taught her how to make a really delicious gazpacho, was able, with amazing tact, to achieve what James had never managed and persuade the girl to use a deodorant.

All in all, it was a most agreeable fortnight. Nan was a pleasant and stimulating companion (if, occasionally, just a tiny bit inclined to go on about plays one hadn't seen, or books one hadn't come across) – always eager and interested, sympathetic and understanding about things like the way people let you down – Roger, the French boy. Nan, of course, was a very intelligent and sensitive person; broad-minded, perceptive. James, in an appreciative mood, told her so. Nan laid a hand on his arm in graceful acknowledgement of the compliment.

'I do think, you know,' she said, 'I do think that honestly our generation had the best of things' – an elegant return, this, Nan must be ten or twelve years younger than he was. 'It was so much easier to get about in our day, travel, see something of what life is like for other people. And I do believe,' she went on, 'I really do believe, James, that that has done so much for us. I mean, we mustn't be smug, and I know it's a cliché, but travel *does* broaden the mind, we *don't* have quite the same outlook on things as if we'd just lived in one little pond, but now, of course, it's so difficult for people, the young, how can they move around?' She sighed, leaning back in the new cane garden chair that looked so well on the terrace, against the background of vine and pergola. 'What an eye-opener it's all been. I am just so thankful that we had the opportunity.'

James nodded. Peacefully, gratefully, they watched the sun set over the island while in the background Lucia hummed pop songs in the kitchen, pattered out from time to time to replenish glasses, fill the ice-bucket.

He would have been pleased enough for Nan to extend her fortnight, but at the end of it she seemed quite eager to get back to Cheltenham – incomprehensibly so, James felt. Oh well yes, I know, she said, no doubt it'll be pouring with rain and one blanches at the thought of all that grind of housework and shopping again – it has been the most wonderful break, James – but there are things coming up, the Festival and then all the London things, so one way and another, and it's sweet of you to suggest it, I think I'll get back.

He felt a bit flat, after she had gone. There would be the Fletchers next month, and in the meantime Tom Harley had some very amusing people in television staying, making a documentary about the island for the BBC, so that there were diversions, and others to look forward to, but even so a bleakness crept over him from time to time. He was wheezing a bit, for no apparent reason, and toyed with the idea of going over to the main island to see one of the English doctors at the hospital (the local man was quite all right for run-of-the-mill things but for a proper check-up he wouldn't really do, of course). It could no doubt be left for a month or two, though. And in the meantime he could cheer himself up by deciding to have a new car in the autumn (and that was something he could never have afforded in England), and getting Lucia's second cousin to redecorate the bathroom a very successful terracotta colour at a quite ridiculously low price.

When the blow fell he could hardly believe what he was hearing, at first. He had to make the girl repeat what she had said before he could be quite clear what it was she was on about. Lucia was incoherent to begin with, and then truculent, defensive even, in the face of James's indignation. Finally he ordered her out of the house. It took a good stiff drink to restore him sufficiently to get on to the telephone and relieve his feelings slightly by telling the whole story to Tom Harley and the Pierces, who, he reflected bitterly, were among those who had been most taken with Nan and her little ways.

To think that they must have worked all this out behind his back, the pair of them. All those little chats in the kitchen; so this was what they had been about. No wonder Lucia had seemed moody and restless since Nan's departure.

'Your friend say if I like to come to England she give me good job, and at first I say no, because of my family, you see, and then after she go I think and think about it and I think maybe yes. I would much like to see London . . .'

'She doesn't live in London,' said James savagely, 'and how precisely do you imagine you're going to pay for the air fare?'

Lucia delved in her pocket. Out of an air-mail envelope she produced a single BEA ticket to London, and a lot of instructions in Nan's neat handwriting.

'When she go she say all right, my dear, you think it over and let me know. So when I have think, I write where she tell me, and she send me these.' Lucia folded the documents with care, and returned them to her

pocket. Not a word of regret, of apology; the ingratitude was unbelievable, absolutely unbelievable, the lack of any sense of obligation.

'Get out,' said James, near to tears.

Mary Vella had not much idea where London was; she knew only that it
was further away than Rome, since the aeroplane reputedly took longer
to get there, but nearer than Australia. That was neither here nor there;
Rome would have been preferable, in any case. She sat outside the bar,
not, for once, talking to anyone, and her head churned and ached. She
had a sense of things slipping from her grasp, of an erosion – by
incalculable forces – of her matriarchal position. Lucia had been a good
girl, always – docile, biddable, reasonably industrious. What had
happened was as though some dependable aspect of the physical world
had revealed itself to be quite otherwise – as though a stone had talked.
And stones do not talk without provocation. Bitterly, Mary Vella's
thoughts centred on James Winton. She cobbled, with large, inept
stitches, a child's shirt, muttered to herself, wept a little, schemed, and
knew that what had happened could not be undone by any scheming,
that it was part of the order of things, part of that lurking retribution for
sins and inadequacies, part of the wilful world that could be manipulated
only so far. She could not picture London, nor England, and did not wish
to do so. What she could picture was the reduction of her daughter – or
rather her daughter's familiar presence – to a series of blue, red and white
air-mail envelopes. She fretted, and sewed, and sought, presently, the
dark, cool, reassuring womb of the church. There, on her knees, she
recited her anxieties, for herself, for Lucia, for Lucia's immortal soul, for
Lucia's prospects of marriage and maternity.

James got a girl through Paul at the garage and set about the wearisome
task of training her. She was worse than Lucia had been. Irritably, he
instructed and instructed again and chivvied and snapped when patience
had been exhausted and nothing else would do. There was little prospect
of Carmen knowing what was what by the time the Fletchers came out,
that was clear enough.

He did not feel all that good, either. The business had brought back his
headaches; he got tired easily; some days it seemed almost too much of an
effort to go down to the beach. He slopped about the house and garden
through the long, hot days. The heat did not worry him at all, he had
always liked it – that, after all was what one was here for. But he felt
oppressed, all the same, and the island's landscape, encircling his garden
– the cluttered little fields and squat villages and dry scrubby vegetation –
seemed alien in a way they never had before. He would lie on the terrace
with his eyes closed, between the hard blue sky and the hot dry earth that
rasped all day long with grasshoppers, and experience a sense of

displacement, of unease. It annoyed him. One was, after all, a person accustomed to moving around – had lived, at one time or another, in four different countries, had never really been settled anywhere in particular, called nowhere home, was not bound by restrictions of place or culture. He tried to divert himself by replanning the garden, and planted roses ('Iceberg', for coolness and sparkle) all along the pergola, but the plants withered and sulked, water them as he might.

Mary Vella came up with Father Grech.

'Oh, so she went, did she?' snapped James. 'Well, I really don't know what it's got to do with me now. It wasn't any of my doing, you know.'

It was Father Grech who did the talking this time, with Mary standing a few yards back, silent but omnipresent, for all the world like the black governessy I-told-you-so figure in a Greek chorus.

He launched forth, Father Grech, into a long, faintly accusatory monologue, about how worried the girl's mother was, and his own doubts about the girl's welfare, and so forth and so on, to which James listened with mounting exasperation. Good heavens, with a brood like that you'd think the old girl would be glad enough to get one of them off her hands, anyone would think she'd been whipped off into the brothels of Soho or somewhere. Neither of them, clearly, had given a moment's thought to him, left in the lurch like this. He felt like pointing out that it was entirely thanks to his efforts that Lucia was now a desirable commodity as a servant. She hadn't known a thing, when she came to him in the first place.

'What?' he said crossly. 'No, I really can't imagine how she'll get the fare home again if she's not happy, she should have thought of that in the first place, shouldn't she? She'll have to save up for it, presumably. Teach her not to be so silly.' My God, they weren't surely going to have the nerve to suggest that one stump up for the price of an air ticket? 'And no, I don't know if there's a Catholic church there. I should think Cheltenham's jolly Protestant, as a matter of fact.' His temples throbbed; there was a filthy headache coming on.

Finally they went. James, standing on the terrace with thumping head, watched them walk slowly down the dusty road, a few yards apart, as though they had nothing left to say to each other. Mary had been sullen and remarkably silent, standing there with her eyes fixed on James and a kind of blaze to them that had been disconcerting; he had wondered if possibly the woman had gone a bit funny in the head. In any case, he thought, turning to go into the house, it is all quite ridiculous, they are making an absurd fuss about nothing, what on earth do they think can happen to the girl in Cheltenham, of all places? It's not exactly a den of iniquity. Come to that, it might do her good to get away from that family for a bit. They're smothered in family, these people. Family and priests.

He spent a week or so quietly at the house, hardly going out at all, and felt considerably better by the end of it. The nasty little pains in his chest seemed to have gone away, and he was not getting so breathless. He went for one or two short walks in the evenings, and was none the worse. He was longing for a swim, and decided to risk a trip to the beach.

The children were down there, the children and the goats. The sight of them was a tonic; he felt quite a rejuvenating little rush of something as he sat down on the sand, stripping off shirt and trousers, and stretched himself out in his bathing-trunks, lying on his stomach so that he could watch them – the boys' neat brown bodies and their lovely agility as they played football with a tin can picked from the rubbish at the water's edge. When he had swum, and dried himself, he walked up to them and tried, yet again, to make contact. One of the boys, he saw now, was older than he had thought – fifteen or sixteen at least. James stood there for a few minutes, fastening his trousers, rubbing the towel across his salted, sticky skin, and chatted encouragingly. Name? School? Interests? But the boy shook his head and shuffled, his eyes darting to James's trouser pocket: money, cigarettes, was that what he was after? No, thought James severely, one is not going to corrupt these people, and when all his chat had fallen upon stony ground, and the boy was retreating, edging backwards to join the others, he went back to sit for a while and rest before the upward climb to the car.

It was early evening, and hot still, though he had tried to time his bathe so that it would be cooler for his walk up the hill. There was a slight breeze; small waves frilled up the beach, leaving the sand laced with white foam. The sea was marbled with different blues; far out on the horizon there was a wispy layer of cloud. Not, of course, that that indicated anything but the inevitable sunshine tomorrow; one could be absolutely confident of the weather, that was one thing. Oh, he thought, really everything is quite all right, this little upset over Lucia is over and done with now, no point in harping on it. As for Nan Chalmers . . . Bitterness and resentment welled up, clouding the perfection of the evening. For the umpteenth time he went over the scathing, unanswerable, things that should (but never would, for Nan would take good care to see there was no opportunity) be said to her, and gained some little satisfaction. The emotion, though, made his heart race, and at last, with a deliberate effort, he forced himself to clear his head, lie in the sun, and relax.

He must have dozed off for a while. When he came to he could not for a moment think where he was; it was like one of those times of perplexity and faint panic when one wakes in a strange bedroom and cannot think, for a few seconds, where or why . . . He sat bolt upright, staring round, and he was quite alone on the golden crescent of the beach, quite quite alone, with nothing but the noise of the sea, and a long way away someone shouting. And he had the horrid sensation of having been left behind, abandoned, by whom or what he could not say. He scrambled to his feet, awkwardly, stumbling and panting, and then all of a sudden things fell into place, he knew where he was, on the familiar beach, on the island, the car not far away, out of sight at the top of the hill.

The children had gone (that, perhaps, accounted for the sense of abandonment, of loneliness). He gathered up his things and set off up the path, and as he climbed he saw them not far ahead, picking a leisurely way over the stones and through the bushes, twittering like a flock of migrating birds. He took the hill very slowly – it was hotter than he had anticipated, and the breeze had dropped – but even so it was an effort and seemed steeper, longer, than ever it had before. He trudged on, and there was a nagging pain in his chest, and a mistiness before his eyes; I am not well, he thought, I am really not too well, it was rash to come down here, I must get back and take things easy, have an early night.

He climbed, and paused for a while, and then climbed again because he felt unaccountably exposed here, unsafe – the place had lost, for the moment, its appeal and seemed hostile, alien, unfamiliar. He tripped on a stone and almost fell, and the slight shock set his heart pounding, and that pain came again, hard, a sickening jolt to the chest.

Just ahead, the children's voices were shrill; it came to him, as it had never done before, that he could not understand a word they were saying.

And then something strange began to happen. His whole body was going numb, and everything had become blurred and distant. He had fallen, he realised, though he had hardly felt himself hit the ground. He was lying there, and knew that things were not right, not right at all, that he must get help. He tried to shout, and some sound must have come out, because he was aware of the children drawing near out of the darkness, the almost total darkness, at the periphery of his vision. And then the darkness swallowed him, and it had all gone – the island, the children, everything.

The children stood a few yards off and looked at the old man. They chattered excitedly. They asked each other if he was dead. Presently one of the older girls, Maria, crept closer to make an inspection. The boys, the two big boys, had gone on ahead, missing this drama, and she was now the eldest present so that on her devolved the responsibility of action, if action was to be taken.

She squatted down in the dust beside him, and stared. She thought that he was breathing still. His face, though, was a very strange colour. Her uncle Tony, she remembered, had looked like that when he was so ill last winter, and the doctor had come, quickly, in the middle of the night, and they had taken him away to the hospital in an ambulance, there had been much commotion and haste and rushing about in the dark. It seemed to her that there was the same urgency needed here. She discussed this with the other children (one of them, a very young one, poked James's inert leg, gingerly, and then skittered back into the bushes in panic) and then they all scampered away up the hillside, taking the goats with them.

The village was a mile and a half away. When they came to the road, Maria hurried on ahead; the young ones were already forgetting about the old man and had reverted to their usual dawdling, scavenging pace, comfortably in step with the goats. She walked and ran, walked and ran, and arrived at the bar quite breathless, so that she had to stop and swing on the bead curtains, panting, for a moment or two, before she could explain to her mother what had happened.

Mary Vella listened. She went on counting the crates of 7-Up empties, and occasionally interrupted with a question. She was not excited or interested as might have been expected, though this did not altogether surprise Maria; her mother had been excited and interested by very little since Lucia had gone away. Maria concluded her account of what had happened and asked if she should go to Father Grech and get him to telephone for the doctor.

Mary Vella wrote down the total of the empties on the slate. She did not answer for a moment or two, staring out through the bead curtains, as though her mind were on something entirely different. Finally, she said, 'No. It may not be necessary; you should not waste the time of doctors. I will go myself and see if Mr Winton is all right now.'

Maria was a little taken aback by this; she pointed out that Mr Winton had not seemed, in her opinion, likely to be all right; she referred to her uncle; she reminded her mother of the distance, on foot, to the beach path. Mary Vella, in response to this, produced some of her old vigour and authority; she gave her daughter a shake, and demanded to know who decided how things were to be done, around here? Then she instructed another child to mind the bar until she came back, put a shawl around her shoulders, and set off through the square, at her usual deliberate pace, with Maria pattering along in attendance, sometimes behind, sometimes a yard or two ahead.

It took them nearly three-quarters of an hour to get to the spot. The old man was still lying there; nothing had changed, except one thing, which Maria, who, in her short life, had seen death several times, recognised at once. They stood, the woman and the child, at either side of him, and crossed themselves. An ant was crawling on James's bare stomach which Maria, with a quick apologetic gesture, flicked aside. Mary muttered a prayer, and crossed herself again. She took James's towel, and with a business-like movement, spread it across his face. Then she turned and began to walk up the hillside, Maria once more trotting behind.

At the road, she stopped for a moment, and said to the child, 'Father Grech's telephone does not always work, and in any case Mr Winton was very bad, it would not have made any difference.' Maria nodded sagely, and as the sun sank behind the island, and the heat was tempered with the freshness of evening, they set off back to the village, to arrange, now, for whatever should be done.

A World of Her Own

MY SISTER Lisa is an artist: she is not like other people.

Lisa is two years younger than I am, and we knew quite early on that she was artistic, partly because she could always draw so nicely, but also because of the way she behaved. She lives in a world of her own, our mother used to say. She was always the difficult one, always having tempers and tantrums and getting upset about one thing and another, but once mother realised about her being artistic she made allowances. We all did. She's got real talent, the art master at school said, you'll have to take care of that, Mrs Harris, she's going to need all the help she can get. And mother was thrilled to bits, she's always admired creative people, she'd have loved to be able to write or paint herself but having Lisa turn out that way was the next best thing, or better, even, perhaps. When Lisa was fifteen mother went to work at Luigi's, behind the counter, to save up so there'd be a bit extra in hand for Lisa, when she went to art school. Father had died three years before. It worried me rather, mother going out to work like that; she's had asthma on and off for years now, and besides she felt awkward, serving in a shop. But the trouble is, she's not qualified at anything, and in any case, as she said, a delicatessen isn't quite like an ordinary grocer or a supermarket.

I was at college, by then, doing my teaching diploma. Lisa went to one of the London art schools, and came back at the end of her first term looking as weird as anything, you'd hardly have known her, her hair dyed red and wearing black clothes with pop art cut-outs stuck on and I don't know what. It was just as well mother *had* saved up, because it all turned out much more expensive than we'd thought, even with Lisa's grant. There was so much she had to do, like going to plays and things, and of course she needed smarter clothes, down there, and more of them, and then the next year she had to travel on the continent all the summer, to see great paintings and architecture. She was away for months, we hardly saw anything of her, and when she came back she'd changed completely all over again – her hair was blonde and frizzed out, and she was wearing a lot of leather things, very expensive, boots up to her thighs and long suede coats. She came home for Christmas and sometimes she was gay and chatty and made everybody laugh and other times she was bad-tempered and moody, but as mother said, she'd always been like that, from a little girl, and of course you had to expect it, with her temperament.

Mother had left Luigi's by then, some time before, because of her leg (she got this trouble with her veins, which meant she mustn't stand much) but she started doing a bit of work at home, for pin-money, making cushions and curtains for people: she's always been good at needlework, she sometimes says she wonders if possibly that's where Lisa's creativity came from, if maybe there's something in the family . . .

It missed me out, if there is. Still, I got my diploma (I did rather well, as it happens, one of the best in my year) and started teaching and not long after that I married Jim, whom I'd known at college, and we had the children quite soon, because I thought I'd go back to work later, when they were at school.

Lisa finished at her art college, and got whatever it is they get, and then she couldn't find a job. At least she didn't want any of the jobs she could have got, like window-dressing or jobs on magazines or for publishers or that kind of thing. And can you blame her, said mother, I mean, what a waste of her talents, it's ridiculous, all that time she's spent developing herself, and then they expect her to be tied down to some nine-to-five job like anyone else!

Lisa was fed up. She had to come and live at home. Mother turned out of her bedroom and had the builders put a skylight in and made it into a studio for Lisa, really very nice, with a bare polished floor and a big new easel mother got by selling that silver tea-set that was a wedding present (she says she never really liked it anyway). But then it turned out Lisa didn't do that kind of painting, but funny things to do with bits of material all sort of glued together, and coloured paper cut out and stuck on to other sheets of paper. And when she did paint or draw it would be squatting on the floor, or lying on her stomach on the sofa.

I can't make head nor tail of the kind of art Lisa does. I mean, I just don't *know* if it's any good or not. But then, I wouldn't, would I? Nor Jim, nor mother, nor any of us. We're not experienced in things like that; it's not up to us to say.

Lisa mooched about at home for months. She said she wouldn't have minded a job designing materials for some good firm – Liberty's or something like that – provided there was just her doing it because she's got this very individual style and it wouldn't mix with other people's, or maybe she might arrange the exhibitions at the Victoria and Albert or the Tate or somewhere. She never seemed to get jobs like that, though, and anyway mother felt it would be unwise for her to commit herself because what she really ought to be doing was her own work, that's all any artist should do, it's as simple as that.

Actually Lisa did less and less painting, which mother said was tragic, her getting so disillusioned and discouraged, such a waste of talent. Mother would explain to people who asked what Lisa was doing nowadays about how disgraceful it was that the government didn't see that people like her were given the opportunities and encouragement they need. Goodness knows, she'd say with a sigh, it's rare enough – creative ability – and Mrs Watkins next door, or the vicar, or whoever it was, would nod doubtfully and say yes, they supposed so.

And then Bella Sims arrived and opened up this new gallery in the town. The Art Centre. Before, there'd only been the Craft Shop, which does have some quite odd-looking pictures but goes in for glass animals and corn dollies and all that too; Lisa was vicious about the Craft Shop. But Bella Sims's place was real art, you could see that at once – lots of bare floor and pictures hung very far apart and pottery vases and bowls so expensive they didn't even have a price on them. And Lisa took along some of her things one day and believe it or not Bella Sims said she liked them, and she'd put three of them in her next exhibition which was specially for local artists. Mother was so thrilled she cried when Lisa first told her.

Lisa was a bit off-hand about it all; she seemed to take the attitude that it was only to be expected. She got very thick with Bella Sims.

Bella Sims was fiftyish, one of those people with a loud, posh voice and hair that's just been done at the hairdresser and lots of clunky expensive-looking jewellery. She scared the wits out of me, and mother too, actually, though mother kept saying what a marvellous person she was, and what an asset for the town. I didn't enjoy the preview party for the exhibition, and nor did Jim; I was expecting Judy then, and Clive was eighteen months, so I was a bit done in and nobody talked to us much. But Lisa was having a good time, you could see; she was wearing all peasanty things then, and had her hair very long and shiny, she did look really very attractive. She met Melvyn at that party.

Melvyn was Bella's son. He taught design at the Poly. That meant he was sort of creative too, though of course not a real artist like Lisa. He fell for her, heavily, and who could blame him I suppose, and they started going round together, and then quite soon they said they were getting married. We were all pleased, because Melvyn's nice – you'd never know he was Bella's son – and we didn't realise till later that it was because of Francesca being on the way. Mother was rather upset about that, and felt she might have been a bit to blame, maybe she should have talked to Lisa about things more, but frankly I don't think that would have made any difference. Actually she worried more about Lisa not being able to paint once the baby was born. She was pleased, of course, about Francesca, but she did feel it might be a pity for Lisa to tie herself down so soon.

Actually it didn't work out that way. Lisa got into a habit almost at once of leaving Francesca with mother or with me whenever she wanted some time to herself – she was having to go up and down to London quite a lot by then to keep in touch with her old friends from college, and to try to find openings for her work. I had my two, of course, so, as she said, an extra one didn't make much difference. It did get a bit more of a strain, though, the next year, after she'd had Jason and there was him too. Four children is quite a lot to keep an eye on, but of course mother helped out a lot, whenever her leg wasn't too bad. Bella Sims, I need hardly say, didn't go much for the granny bit.

Lisa had Alex the year after that. I've never understood, I must say, why Lisa has babies so much; I mean, she must *know*. Of course, she is vague and casual, but all the same . . . I've had my two, and that's that, barring accidents, and I'm planning to go back to work when I can, eventually. I daresay Lisa would think that all very cold and calculating, but that's the way I am. Lisa says she doesn't believe in planning life, you just let things happen to you, you see what comes next.

Alex had this funny Chinese look from a tiny baby and it took us ages to cotton on, in fact I suppose he was eleven months or so before the penny finally dropped and we realised that, to put it frankly, Melvyn wasn't the father.

It came as a bit of a blow, especially to poor mother. She went all quiet for days, and I must admit she's never really liked Alex ever since, not like she dotes on the others.

The father was someone Lisa knew in London. He was from Thailand, not Chinese, actually. But in fact it was all over apparently sometime before Alex was born and she didn't see him again.

Melvyn took it very well. I suppose he must have known before we did. In fact, Melvyn has been very good to Lisa from the start, nothing of what's happened has been his fault in any way. Not many men would have coped with the children like he has, right from the beginning, which he had to because of Lisa being away quite a bit, or involved in her own things. Truth to tell, he was better with them, too. It's not that Lisa's a bad mother – I mean she doesn't get cross or impatient, specially, she just doesn't bother about them much. She says the worst thing you can do is to be over-protective; she says mother was a bit over-protective with her.

Bella Sims had some fairly nasty things to say; but then soon after that she sold the gallery and moved back to London and we never saw any more of her. This was the wrong kind of provincial town, apparently; art was never going to be a viable proposition.

Things got worse after Alex was born. Lisa went off more and more. Sometimes I'd find we had the children for days on end, or Melvyn would come round, pretty well at the end of his tether, saying could we lend a hand, Lisa was down in London seeing about some gallery which might show her stuff, or she'd gone off to Wales to see a woman who was doing the most fantastic ceramics.

It was after the time Francesca wandered off and got lost for a whole day, and the police found her in the end and then it turned out Lisa had been somewhere with Ravi, this Indian friend of hers, that things rather came to a head. Lisa and Melvyn had a row and Lisa brought all the children round to me, late one night, in their pyjamas, and said she was so upset about everything she'd have to go off on her own for a few days to try to think things over. Jim had flu and I'd just got over it myself so I was a bit sharp with her: I said couldn't Melvyn have them, and she said no, Melvyn had to teach all next day, which was probably true enough. And anyway, she said, they're my children, I'm responsible for them, I've got to work out what to do. She was wearing a long red and blue thing of some hand-blocked stuff, and lots of silver bracelets, and she looked exhausted and very dashing both at the same time, somehow; the children were all crying.

So I took them, of course, and she was gone for a week or so. We talked things over while she was gone. Jim and I talked, and Jim said (which he never had before) that he thought Lisa ought to pull herself together a bit, and I had to agree. It was easier with her not being there; somehow when Lisa's with you, you always end up feeling that she really can't be expected to do what other people do, I actually feel bad if I see Lisa washing a floor or doing nappies or any of the things I do myself every day. It does seem different for her, somehow.

And mother talked to Melvyn, who'd been round to find out where the children were. Mother was very sympathetic; she knows what living with Lisa is like; we all do. She said to Melvyn that of course Lisa had been silly and irresponsible, nobody could deny that. She told Melvyn, with a little laugh to try to cheer things up a bit, that there'd been occasions when Lisa was a small girl and was being particularly wilful and tiresome that she'd been on the verge of giving her a good smack. And then, she said, one used to remember just in time that there is a point beyond which she – people like her – simply cannot help themselves. One just can't expect the same things you can from other people.

I don't know what Melvyn thought about that; he didn't say. After the divorce came through he married Sylvie Fletcher who works in the library; I was at school with her and she's very nice but quite ordinary. Mother always says it must seem such a come down after Lisa. They've got a little boy now, and Melvyn takes a lot of trouble to see Francesca and Jason (and Alex too, in fact) as much as he can – and it *is* trouble because he has to trail down to London and try to find where Lisa's moved to now, unless it's one of the times Jim and I are having the children, or mother.

Mother and I had to talk, too. I'd gone round there and found her up in

Lisa's old studio, just standing looking at a great thing Lisa had done that was partly oil paint slapped on very thick and partly bits of material stuck on and then painted over; in the top corner there was a picture of the Duke of Edinburgh from a magazine, sideways on and varnished over. I think it must have been meant to be funny, or sarcastic or something. We both stood in front of it for a bit and mother said, 'Of course, it is very good, isn't it?'

I said I honestly didn't know.

We both felt a bit awkward in there; Lisa has always been very fussy about her privacy. She says the one thing people absolutely have no right to do is push themselves into other people's lives; she is very strong for people being independent and having individual rights. So mother and I just had a quick tidy because the dust was bothering mother, and then we went downstairs and drank a cup of tea and chatted. Mother talked about this book she'd been reading about Augustus John; she's very interested in biographies of famous poets and artists and people like that. She was saying what a fascinating person he must have been but of course he did behave very badly to people, his wife and all those other women, but all the same it must have been terribly exhilarating, life with someone like that. You could see she was half thinking of Lisa. I was feeling snappish, the children were getting me down rather, and I said Lisa wasn't Augustus John, was she? We don't really know, do we – if she's any good or not.

There was a silence. We looked at each other. And then mother looked away and said, 'No. I know we don't. But she just might be, mightn't she? And it would be so awful if she was and nobody had been understanding and helpful.'

Lisa came back for the children once she'd found a flat. She'd had her hair cut off and what was left was like a little boy's, all smoothed into the back of her neck; it made her look about sixteen. Lisa is very small and thin, I should say; people always offer to carry suitcases for her, if you see her doing anything involving effort you automatically find yourself offering to do it for her because you feel she won't be able to manage and anyway it makes you feel guilty watching her.

She said the hair was symbolic; she was making a fresh start and getting rid of the atmosphere that had been holding her back (I suppose she meant poor Melvyn) and actually everything was going to be good because Ravi's father who was an Indian businessman and quite rich was going to buy a little gallery in Islington that Ravi was going to run and she was frantically busy getting enough stuff together for an exhibition.

The gallery didn't last long because it kept losing money and after a bit Ravi's father, who turned out to be quite an ordinary businessman after all and not as sensitive and interested in art as Lisa had thought, said he was cutting his losses and selling up. In fact Ravi and Lisa weren't living together by then anyway because Lisa had realised that the reason her work wasn't really right was that she'd always been in cities and in fact what she needed to fulfil herself properly was to get away somewhere remote and live a very simple, hard-working life. Actually, she thought, pottery was the right medium for her, once she could scrape up enough for a wheel and everything.

Mother helped out with that, financially, and Lisa took the children down to this place in Somerset where a man she knew, someone quite rich, had this big old house that was a sort of commune for artists, and for parties of young people to come and study nature and the environment. We went down there, once when Lisa wanted us to take Alex for a bit, because he'd not been well and she was finding it a bit of a strain coping with him. There was certainly a lot of environment there, it was miles from anywhere, except the village, and there wasn't much of that, so that there seemed to be more artists than ordinary village people. It was a hot summer and Lisa and the rest were going round with just about no clothes on, more like the south of France than west Somerset and I rather got the impression that some of the older village people didn't like it all that much, and there was an outdoor pop festival one weekend that went on to all hours, and this man who owned the place had made the church into an exhibition room for the artists. It was one of those little grey stone churches with old carvings and so on and it looked queer, all done out inside with huge violent-coloured paintings and peculiar sculptures. Lisa said actually it was frightfully good for these people, to be exposed to a today kind of life, they were so cut off down there, and to be given the sort of visual shock that might get them really looking and thinking.

Eventually Lisa began to feel a bit cut off herself, and there'd been some trouble with the county child care people which Lisa said was a lot of ridiculous fuss, it was just that Francesca had got this funny habit of wandering off sometimes and actually it was good that she felt so free and uninhibited, most people *stifle* their children so. Francesca was six by then, and Jason five. Jason had this bad stammer; he still has, sometimes he can't seem to get a word out for hours.

Lisa came home to mother's for a bit then, because rents in London were sky-high and it would have meant her getting a job, which of course was out of the question, if she was going to keep up her potting, and the weaving she had got very keen on now. And at mother's she had the studio, so it might work out quite well, she thought, provided she kept in touch with people and didn't feel too much out on a limb.

Jim and I had Alex more or less permanently by then; we are very fond of him, he seems almost like ours now which is just as well, I suppose. It is just as well too that Jim is the kind of person he is; Lisa thinks he is dull, I know, but that is just her opinion, and as I have got older I have got less and less certain that she gets things right. In fact, around this time I did have a kind of outburst, with mother, which I suppose was about Lisa, indirectly. She had gone down to London to keep in touch with people, and there had been a business with Francesca at school (sometimes she steals things, it is very awkward, they are going to have the educational psychologist people look at her) and I had had to see to it all. I was feeling a bit fed up too because what with Alex, and having so much to do, I'd realised it wasn't going to be any good trying to go back to work at the end of the year as I'd planned. Maybe you should be like Lisa, and not plan. Anyway, mother was telling me about this biography of Dylan Thomas she'd been reading, and what an extraordinary eccentric person he was and how fascinating to know. Actually I'd read the book too and personally I don't see why you shouldn't write just as good poetry without borrowing money off people all the time and telling lies.

Once, when I was at college, one of the tutors got this well-known poet to come and give a talk to the second-year English. He had glasses with thick rims and a rather old-fashioned-looking suit and frankly he might have been somebody's father, or your bank manager. He was very friendly and he talked to us in the common-room afterwards and he wasn't rude to anyone. I told mother about it, later, and she said she wondered if he was all that good – as a poet, that is.

And I suddenly blew up when she was going on like this about Dylan Thomas. I said – shouted – 'T. S. Eliot worked in an office. Gustav Holst was a bloody schoolteacher.'

Mother looked startled. She said, 'Who?' She's less interested in musicians.

I said crossly, 'Oh, never mind. Just there's more than one way of going about things.' And then the children started squabbling and we were distracted and the subject never came up again, not quite like that.

Lisa got a part-share of a flat in London with a friend; she had to be down there because there was this person who was talking of setting up a craft workshop for potters and weavers and that, a fantastic new scheme, and she needed to be on the spot for when it came off. It was difficult for her to have the children there, so Francesca stayed with mother and the two little ones with us. Francesca settled down well at school and began to behave a lot better, and Jason's stammer was improving, and then all of a sudden Lisa turned up, as brown as a conker, with her hair long again, and henna-dyed now, and said she'd met these incredible Americans in Morocco, who had this atelier, and she was going to work there and learn this amazing new enamelling technique. That was what she ought to have been doing all along, she said, if only she'd realised, not messing about with pots and fabrics. She was taking the children with her, she said, because growing up in an English provincial town was so stultifying for them, and it was nice and cheap out there.

She took Alex too, but after six months she suddenly sent him back again with a peculiar German friend of hers; we had to collect him at Heathrow. He kept wetting the bed apparently and although Lisa isn't particularly fussy about that kind of thing she said she had the feeling he wasn't very adaptable.

And so it goes on. She came back from Morocco after a couple of years, and there was a spell in London when a rather well-off Dutch person that we thought she was going to marry bought her a house in Fulham. For six months Francesca went to a very expensive school where all the teaching was done in French, and then the Dutch person went off and Lisa found the house was rented, not paid for like she'd thought, so she came home again for a bit to sort things out, and Francesca went to the comprehensive.

And then there was Wales with the Polish sculptor, and then the Dordogne with the tapestry people, and London again, and back here for a bit, and the cottage in Sussex that someone lent her . . .

The last time she was here she had a curious creased look about her, like a dress that had been put away in a drawer and not properly hung out, and I suddenly realised that she is nearly forty now, Lisa. It doesn't seem right; she is a person that things have always been in front of, somehow, not behind.

Mother and I cleaned out her old studio, the other day. Mother has this feeling that Francesca may be talented, in which case she will need to use it. We dusted and polished and sorted out the cupboard with Lisa's old paintings and collages and whatnot. They all looked rather shabby, and somehow withered – not quite as large or bright as one had remembered. Mother said doubtfully, 'I wonder if she would like any of these sent down to London?' And then, 'Of course it is a pity she has had such an unsettled sort of life.'

That 'had' did not strike either of us for a moment or two. After a bit mother began to put the things away in the cupboard again, very carefully; mother is past seventy now and the stooping was awkward for her. I persuaded her to sit down and I finished off. There was one portfolio of things Lisa did at school, really nice drawings of flowers and leaves and a pencil portrait of another girl whose name neither mother nor I could remember. Mother put these aside; she thought she might have them framed and hang them in the hall. Holding them, she said, 'Though with her temperament I suppose you could not expect that she would settle and at least she has always been free to express herself, which is the important thing.' When I did not answer she said, 'Isn't it, dear?' and I said, 'Yes. Yes, I think so, mother.'

Presents of Fish and Game

'WELL,' SAID the Fellow in Philosophy and Senior Tutor, 'this is a sad task. And an impossible one, too, as I see it.' He looked round at the other members of the Committee to appoint a Fellow and Tutor in Modern History. 'We won't find a man of Bob's standing, and that's for sure.'

The Fellow in French said plaintively, 'I must say he has rather left us in the lurch, taking up this appointment for January. Can we get someone else by then? Of course it's a tragedy he's leaving us.'

'Quite,' said the Bursar. He added, after a moment, 'How much does Berkeley pay?'

A figure was suggested.

The Bursar whistled.

'Wouldn't we all?' said the Fellow in Politics.

'Personally,' said the Senior Tutor, a little stiffly, 'I would find the attractions resistible. However, to our muttons . . .'

Muttons, thought the Fellow in Economics, who was twenty-four, and impressionable in several ways. Muttons. Hams. Thighs. He thought lovingly of a girl he knew, and addressed himself sternly to the problem of the appointment of a new Fellow in Modern History. He listened with attention to the Senior Tutor, an older and wiser man.

'We have to go all out for the best chap we can get,' the Senior Tutor was saying. 'And no two ways about it. Put out feelers of our own – see if we can't attract some applications the advertisement may not pull in. Sound people out – you never know who may be ripe for a move.'

The Fellow in Politics said, 'I must say myself I'd like to see if John Herbert would be interested.'

'Hasn't he got a Chair somewhere?' said the Bursar sharply.

'Yes, of course.'

'He'd want a stipend a bit over and above what Bob was getting, then.'

'Oh come,' said the Senior Tutor with a laugh, 'we're not counting pennies – we're trying – in so far as it's possible – to replace one of the most distinguished scholars the College has.'

The Fellow in Economics, who believed profoundly in the sanctity of scholarship, nodded with vehemence.

'Quite,' said the Bursar, 'we're all with you there.' He was scanning some sheets of figures. 'Anyway, I'm not absolutely clear that even *with* economies we could give ourselves a rise this year – or possibly next either. Or get the new squash courts off the drawing-board.'

There was a brief silence. The Fellow in Politics looked reflective. 'I doubt if John Herbert would want to move, in fact, when it came to the point.'

'I thought,' said the Tutor in French plaintively, 'there was no question about an increase in October. I must say it would be awfully inconvenient if . . .'

The Senior Tutor cleared his throat. 'So the usual advertisement, of course. But we look around, too. I don't think there's any doubt that we want an older man – someone with plenty of teaching experience, quite apart from the academic distinction we're looking for. The Governing Body has been getting younger over the last few years, very nice too' – with a benign glance at the Fellow in Economics – 'but in this instance I do feel that in replacing Bob, we must have a person of his seniority.'

'Definitely,' said the Fellow in Economics, who was sometimes taken for an undergraduate, which unnerved him.

'Of course,' said the Bursar thoughtfully, 'wage for age . . .' He did not complete the sentence, appearing distracted by some figures he was totting up.

Today I am twenty-four, thought the Fellow in Economics, and this time last year I was twenty-three, and this time next year I shall be twenty-five and when I am thirty-five I shall get six thousand a year, or is it seven? And my FSSU contributions will be of incalculable value to the widow I do not at the moment have. He thought again of the girl he knew; the thought threatened to become improper so he pushed it firmly aside, since he was a serious young man who believed in a time and a place for everything, and this was the time and place for the administration of a distinguished academic institution. He said, with diffidence, 'Are we going for a social historian again? Or should we possibly be thinking more of someone in the political field, since George Templer's interests . . .'

'Of course the University will want to stick their oar in,' said the Bursar with a yawn.

'The University, I'm sure, will accept our recommendation,' said the Senior Tutor.

The Fellow in Politics sighed, 'It's a pity George is on sabbatical – we could do with his advice. You know the thought does cross my mind that given we can't *replace* Bob, as Peter so rightly says, then I wonder if we *are* right in setting our sights on a very senior chap – academic distinction, yes, of course, that goes without saying, but I wonder if age is necessarily . . .'

'I never really see the need for all this stress on publications,' said the Fellow in French, who had none to his name.

The Fellow in Economics, who knew himself to be undistinguished but promising, looked out of the window and observed the Bursar's secretary, who had nice legs, crossing the quad. He resolved to work very hard and write a great many books in order never to become like the Fellow in French. There were times, he had sadly to admit, when academic life was a disappointment to him. The cut and thrust of intellectual debate was not all it was held to be; some of his colleagues could spend an entire meal discussing the merits of a particular make of car. He sighed, and looked hopefully at the Senior Tutor, in whom he had faith.

The Senior Tutor was attending to his pipe. He frowned. 'Y – es . . . Possibly. Of course you don't want to feel you're getting someone whose important work is behind them, as it were.'

'Quite,' said the Fellow in French, for whom this was not a problem.

The Fellow in Politics held his hand out across the table to the Bursar. 'Could I just have a look at those stipend scales?'

The Fellow in Economics said, 'From a teaching point of view, I do think the greatest need is for someone whose interests are on the political side, then he could help out with the . . .'

'We want someone who'll teach the whole range,' said the Fellow in French. 'Bob used to farm out no end of people. Cost the College a lot. I can't understand this passion for specialisation,' he added disapprovingly, having none himself.

'Good Lord,' said the Fellow in Politics, in reflective tones. 'As much as that . . .' He was doing sums on the back of the agenda.

The Bursar leaned forward and murmured, 'And you've got to take the housing allowance into consideration, Tony, it works out rather more like this . . .' More figures were scribbled.

The Fellow in Economics, despite his trade, had been surprised to discover how much of academic life was a matter of house-keeping. He said, a little anxiously, 'Surely there's no question – I mean, Peter's absolutely right, we've got to get someone as good as Bob and . . .'

The Fellow in Politics sat back in his chair looking meditative. 'We could save, at my estimate around three or four thousand, which in terms of a capital sum . . .'

'Would that mean . . . ?' said the Fellow in French, to the Bursar.

'Should be O.K.,' said the Bursar.

The Senior Tutor said, 'That's interesting, Tony, not of course that it's a consideration that would sway us in any way. What's really at issue is, what does the College most need – an established figure, or someone on the way up who possibly . . .'

'I must say I think there's a lot to be said for a younger man,' said the Fellow in French.

'Under thirty,' said the Bursar, 'would keep us below the fifth increment on the . . .'

'Yes,' said the Senior Tutor hastily, with a quick glance at the Fellow in Economics, whose face perhaps betrayed a sudden wild surmise about the circumstances of his own appointment. 'And it's not as though the College hasn't a fine reputation in History as it is, with George, and the goodwill, as it were, of Bob's fifteen years here. It's not exactly that we *need* a big name, in fact . . .'

'In fact,' put in the Fellow in Politics, 'there is a sense in which it might be held to be incumbent on us to offer a helping hand, as it were . . .'

'To a chap on the way up,' said the Bursar. 'Under thirty.'

'Quite,' said the Senior Tutor, avoiding the eye of the Fellow in Economics. 'Or, another thought occurs, which is that perhaps' – he frowned at the Fellow in French, who was asking the Bursar if by any chance he had that latest tender for the squash court handy – 'perhaps we might consider the idea of a lectureship, and not appoint to a fellowship at all.'

'Ah,' said the Fellow in Politics thoughtfully. 'That's an interesting idea, Peter. Or course it's perfectly true that if George agreed to increase his teaching load a little – which I'm sure in the interests of the College he'd be happy to do – and we sent out the second-year people, and possibly some of the prelim. lot, then . . .'

'Bob was always off on sabbaticals or leave of absence anyway,' the Fellow in French remarked. 'Hardly ever seemed to be here.'

'A scholar of his standing . . .' said the Senior Tutor severely. 'Naturally he was much in demand. But it's true that possibly from the point of view of run-of-the-mill teaching . . .'

'No point in being overstaffed,' said the Bursar.

'Quite,' the Senior Tutor went on. 'Not of course that there would be any question of cutting back, merely that we ought to look carefully at the . . .'

The Fellow in Economics, who was given to reading outside his subject, said with a slightly frantic laugh, 'Oh come, this is beginning to sound like an exercise in self-deception. We shall end up with some presents of fish and game.'

'What?' snapped the Fellow in French. 'I don't take your point, Nick.'

The Senior Tutor said in tones of gentle reproof, 'Not really, Nick – it's just that we need to review the situation in terms of the College as a whole, rather than the immediate demands of the subject, of the teaching situation. Tragic as Bob's loss is, it does give us the chance to look carefully, to think about . . .'

'A Research Fellowship?' offered the Fellow in Politics. 'Two years. Non-renewable.'

'Without dining rights,' said the Bursar.

'They always manage to hang on after their time's up, Research Fellows,' said the Fellow in French. 'Why bring someone in specially?'

There was a moment's silence, tampered with only by the Fellow in Economics, who seemed to be having difficulty with something he would have liked to say. The Senior Tutor, who knew him to be a bright young man, but diffident and perhaps a little inexperienced, gave him an avuncular smile and said, 'Why bring someone in? Now that's an angle I hadn't thought of.'

'There's Ken Lambert,' suggested the Fellow in Politics.

'Lambert?' said the Fellow in French.

'Research student,' said the Bursar.

'Ah,' said the Senior Tutor thoughtfully.

'He'd be glad of a bit of teaching,' the Fellow in Politics went on. 'Good practice for him.'

'Cheaper than sending them out,' said the Bursar.

'If he needs teaching practice,' said the Fellow in French, 'I should have thought he'd be grateful enough for the chance without us feeling we need . . .'

'Well, that's something we can look into another time.' The Senior Tutor spoke firmly, gathering up his papers. 'There are bound to be a few loose ends to tie up, but I think we've had a very useful session, and a valuable discussion of the broader aims of College policy. Perhaps, Tim' – to the Bursar – 'I could look in this afternoon and run through some figures with you?'

The Committee to appoint a Fellow and Tutor in Modern History broke up. The Senior Tutor laid a friendly hand on the arm of the Fellow in Economics, thinking that the lad was looking a trifle peaky, and suggested a glass of sherry before lunch.

A Clean Death

THE TRAIN windows were still painted midnight blue for the black-out. Here and there, people had scraped at the paint, making channels and circles of bare glass behind which fled the darkening landscape. They had left King's Cross at four, in twilight, would be home, Aunt Frances said, by seven at the latest. Do, she had announced at the ticket office, assembling her welter of Christmas shopping – parcels and boxes from Harrods, Fortnum's, Marshall and Snelgrove – do call me Frances, just, I don't really like aunt, and Clive would like to be Clive, I'm sure. And Carol, smiling sideways, not looking at her, had known she could not, would have to say 'you' now, for always, be for ever picking her way round the problem. She huddled into her school coat, stiff with cold, her knees raw red between the top of her socks and hem of her skirt, and fingered again the ticket in her pocket, checked the brown suitcase in the rack, in which were her holiday clothes, her good tweed skirt and her two jerseys and the tartan wool dress bought today by Aunt Frances – Frances – with money sent by her father from India. The money had meant complicated arrangements of cheques and deposit accounts and Frances, irritated, queueing at the bank, glancing at her watch. Money from the bank in Calcutta, hot and crowded, rupees not pounds and shillings. Don't think of it, she told herself, the tears pressing again behind her eyelids, don't think of India. But it came, as it never ceased to do, clamorous with smells and sounds and what-used-to-be, and she sat, miserable with longing, watching the lights of Suffolk villages twinkle through the tattered black-out paint.

Frances, in her corner, was wedged beside a young soldier with hair so short his head seemed almost shaven, and battledress that smelled of damp and sweat; she had flinched away from him, Carol could see, turning to the window, reading her London Library book. She looked up, caught Carol's eye, and said, 'Ipswich in another few minutes now – lovely thought!'

I've put you in the spare room, she had said earlier, not in with Marian,

I thought you might rather be on your own, and Carol, who had feared to be classified with her cousins, as child, had been relieved. She did not know how to be with children, what to say, they made her feel awkward, inadequate. But I don't know how to be with grown-ups either, she thought, there is no one I talk to, I am quite by myself, it is as though I was some kind of thing there is only one of. At school she was not unpopular, but had no friends; she never walked with her arm round someone else's waist, or gathered over the tepid radiator in the form room, warming her hands and whispering. The other girls alarmed her; they were so worldly-wise, so cushioned by their confidence in how things were done, how to talk and act and respond. The school bewildered her, with the jungle of its customs and taboos. She remained uninitiated, an outsider, doing her best to use the right language, show the right interests, have the right emotions. She collected, as the others did, photographs of the royal family cut from newspapers; she stared at the battered fashion magazines passed from hand to hand, exhaustively discussed and analysed. At night, she lay silent in bed, hearing their whispers of cinemas and London musicals, and India created and re-created itself in the darkness, and she could hardly bear it. It set her apart from them, she knew; it was not quite the thing, to have been born in another country. It was not good to be different. She knew it, and felt inadequate; there was nothing she could do about it, nothing could make her one of them. Sometimes, not often, they asked her about India, but their curiosity was brief, it would evaporate within minutes. She would be talking – of the house, the garden, the heat, the people – and they would be gone, their attention switched, back with their own concerns. The other thing they never mentioned. The girl who had shown her round, her first day – one of the prefects – had said, 'Bad luck about your mother, Carol,' and she had known that it was unmentionable, death you did not talk about, like God, or love.

She had learned how she ought to be, what was expected, and was quietly pleased that she had learned so much. She made fewer mistakes now, was more acceptable. She was managing.

The train slid to a stop. Frances opened the door, and steam oozed up between carriage and platform, cold air gushing in, and country voices, voices all related to one another, Carol could hear. Accents. There was a girl at school who had an accent; that was not good either, she too was apart. Her parents did not pay, it was said, she had the Scholarship. Listening, in streets, on buses, Carol felt dizzied, sometimes, by voices: different, the same, connected. Like the babel of tongues in an Indian bazaar. You have to know who you are, she thought, who other people are, or it is impossible, you do everything wrong. Often I do not know who I am.

They got out, festooned with parcels. If you could take the children's stocking presents, Frances said, and Nigel's train-set, I can manage the Fortnum's bag and the curtain stuff. And Clive will get the cases, no hope of a porter of course, not these days.

Clive had come up almost at once, out of the darkness, and Carol thought wildly: do I kiss him or not, I can't remember, is it all relations, or not men ones? But he solved the problem himself by holding out a hand, and they shook awkwardly, and yes, she said, I had a good term, and yes, it is lovely to think it's nearly Christmas.

In the car, bumping through the East Anglian night, Frances recounted the day. London was awful, she said, I can't tell you, the shops so crowded, such a struggle on the buses, but I got everything, nearly everything, there was a problem with John's school things, they hadn't the games socks in yet . . . She sounded tired, but triumphant, like a huntsman at the end of the day, the job done. The road shone wet black in the car headlights and the fields that slid by were ribbed with snow; it was bitterly cold. A frost tonight, Clive said, Marian's cold seems a bit better – oh, and Mrs Binns left a pie in the oven for supper, she said give it another half hour or so, after you get back.

They were close, easy, in their concerns, the running of their lives. Once or twice, remembering, they passed questions to her, or comments, over the back of their seats. Is it this summer you do School Cert., Carol, or next? This village is called Kersey, the church is so pretty, you'll have to walk over one day and have a look.

They arrived, and the house seemed to burst, spilling out into the night like a ripe fruit; light, voices, the small shapes of children running and leaping beside the car. Dogs barking. Wireless music. The country night lay black and still and freezing all around, and here was this confident, unassailable place, waiting. The children bounced and shrieked. Did you find the balloons? they cried, and have you got my ribbon, and are there any sweets? Mummy! they shrieked, Mummy! And Frances was hugging and recounting and saying, oh, and here's Carol, say hello to Carol.

Hello, they said, and then their voices were back on that note of excitement and demand, and everyone was going into the house, shutting out the darkness – the endless snowy fields, the black roads.

She woke early in the morning, perished with cold. She had got up in the night to put on her underclothes beneath her pyjamas, and then her jersey on top, and still had lain frozen in the bed, curled knees to chest, the rest of the bed an icy pond. She listened to the noises of the house expand around her: the children's scampering feet, their voices crooning to cats or dogs, the rattle of a boiler being filled, Frances and Clive talking in the bedroom. It was an old, wooden house; it rang and echoed. Presently she got up and went to the bathroom that Frances had said she should share with the children. It smelled of flannels and damp and toothpaste; there was a full pottie in the corner. She stripped to the waist, as you had to do at school, and washed under her arms, up her neck, over the growing breasts that she felt must be so obvious, that slopped and bounced under her jerseys.

She dressed and went downstairs. On the bottom step there was a dog, a great golden lion-headed thing, lying right across it. She stood there, not knowing what to do, and it did not move, but looked at her and away again. And then one of the children – Nigel, the youngest – came from some room and saw her and said, 'Are you frightened of her?' And before she could answer he had gone running into the kitchen and she could hear him shout, 'Daddy! She's frightened of Tosca – Carol's frightened of Tosca.'

She could hear them laughing. Frances said, 'I expect she's not used to dogs, darling.' She came out and tugged at the dog's collar, still laughing, saying what a stupid, soft old thing she was, wouldn't hurt a fly, you mustn't mind her. And Carol could think of no reply: she was not afraid of dogs, liked them, but in India a dog may be rabid, you do not go near a strange dog, never. It was instinctive, now, the hesitation, a conditioned response, just as at night, always, she thought, for the rest of her life, she would feel unsafe without the shrouding security of a mosquito net.

Clive was in the kitchen, nursing a cat. He stroked and tickled it, talking baby-language to it so that Carol was both embarrassed and fascinated. There was something wrong, apparently, it was ill. 'Poor Mr Patch,' crooned Clive. 'Poor pussy. Poor patchums,' and the children gathered round soft with sympathy, offering it tit-bits. 'We are a terrible animal family, I'm afraid, Carol,' said Frances, frying bacon. 'Everybody is mad about animals. The children will show you the pony after breakfast.'

She trailed with the children, in a wind that cut through her mack, clutched her bare knees, was shown the garden and its secret places, the hens, the rabbit hutches, the pony, the orchard. And then they became involved in some game of their own and she came back into the house alone and stood at a loss in the kitchen, where Frances mixed things and talked to a woman washing up at the sink.

'This is Carol, Mrs Binns,' she said. 'My niece, you know.' And Carol felt herself appraised, not unkindly, not critically, just with the shrewdness of a person who liked to see what was what, how things were.

'You'll be much of an age with my Tom, I should imagine,' said Mrs Binns. 'Fourteen he was, in October. We'll have to get you together. He's at a loose end, in the holidays, Tom, there's no one much his age, not nearer than the village.'

At school there were girls who had, or who were rumoured to have, boyfriends. The reputation gave them an aura, of daring but also of distinction; they too were set apart, but in a desirable way. They had moved on a little, on and up. Carol knew no boys, had not, she thought, spoken to one since long ago, since nursery days on another continent.

She stared at Mrs Binns in alarm.

'Mmmn,' said Frances. 'What a good idea,' and Carol, puzzled now, saw that for some reason it was not. But Mrs Binns, saying, 'Well, you must look in at the cottage, dear, your auntie'll tell you where it is,' had turned now to the table and taken up the pink and pimpled carcase of a chicken. 'I'll do this for you, Mrs Seaton, shall I?'

Frances looked at the chicken with distaste. 'Yes, please, if you would. A beastly job. I'd be sunk without you, I really would.'

Mrs Binns laughed. She stood at the sink, rummaging with deft, knowledgeable hands in the chicken's insides. 'It's a matter of what you're used to. I did my first bird when I was – oh, younger than Carol here.' Appalling things slid from within the chicken and lay on the draining-board. Frances, Carol saw, had turned firmly away, busy with her pie-dish. Carol said, 'In India you buy chickens live. They hang them up by their feet in the bazaar, in bunches.'

'How absolutely horrid!' Frances exclaimed; her voice was tense with emotion. Mrs Binns, halted in her work, looked up. Frances went on, vehemently, 'That is what is so awful about those places – they are so foul to animals. One really cannot stand it. I remember going to Morocco, before the war, and it simply spoiled the holiday, the way they treat the donkeys and things. You had to walk about trying not to notice – it was wretched, we were so glad to come home.'

Mrs Binns said in neutral tones, 'It's not nice to see, cruelty to animals.' She swilled the chicken out under the tap and put it on a plate. 'His dad give Tom a gun for his birthday, for rabbiting, but he told him he's to use it properly, no maiming things, he's to see there's a clean death.'

Frances's face was set in disapproval. 'Mmmn. Isn't fourteen a bit young for a gun?'

Mrs Binns was packing the chicken with stuffing now. Crumbs of it fell from her fingers and lay on the table, smelling of herbs, of summer. 'Rabbits are terrible round us now – had all my cabbage. He's the makings of a good steady hand, Bob says – Tom has. Three he got, last week.'

'Mmmn,' said Frances again. She got up, putting away flour and fat. 'Could you do the bedrooms next, Mrs Binns, and then I think the dining-room windows need a going over.'

At lunch, Frances and Clive talked of Mrs Binns. Clive said that she was a card, quite a character, and tales were recounted, remarks that Mrs Binns had made, her opinions, her responses. They were told with affection, with indulgence – much, Carol noted, as the children were spoken of in their absence. 'But,' said Frances, 'I cannot approve of that boy being given a gun. They *will* start them off slaughtering things so early, people like that, I hate it.'

Marian said in stricken tones, 'Does he kill rabbits, Tom? Oh, *poor* rabbits . . . Mummy, can't you tell him not to?'

'No, I can't, darling, it's not up to me. There, don't think about it – I don't expect he does it much. Finish up your sausage and then you can get down.'

One girl at school got letters from her boyfriend. It was known, and envied. She took them away and read them alone, in the cloakroom, and later could be seen, pink-faced and giggling, poring over selected passages with her best friend. Carol said, staring at the bowl of frost-nipped chrysanthemums in the middle of the table, 'Mrs Binns said I could go over to her cottage sometime.'

There was a silence. Clive picked up the cat and blew softly into its fur, murmuring to it. 'Poor Mr Patch,' he mumbled. 'How are your insides today – how's your poor tummy?'

'Yes,' said Frances. 'Well, just as you like, Carol.' She began to clear the table. 'I think a walk this afternoon, to the village and back, I need some things from the post office, anyway.'

The landscape was black and white under huge white skies – black ploughlands striped with white runnels of snow, criss-crossed with the dark lines of hedges, trimmed with the stiff shapes of trees. They walked along a road bordered by fawn-coloured rushes and grasses, each one starred and bearded with frost; icy wind poured through the skeletal hedges; there was a chain of crisp puddles along the uneven surface. The children skittered ahead, sliding on the ice, darting off into the fields on brief excursions. Clive and Frances walked arm in arm, Carol a few paces behind. Their talk and occasional laughter came back to her in irrelevant, incomprehensible snatches. I am so cold, she thought, colder than I have ever been, colder even than I am at school, will I ever be warm, how do people get warm, ever, in their lives? In India, in childhood, she had been too hot; always, one was sticky with sweat, looking for a place out of the sun. I cannot remember that now, she thought, I have no idea, really, how it was, it is like something in a book, something that happened to someone else. The gap had lengthened between her and the others; Frances, looking back over her shoulder, called, 'Not far now – we shall have to get you used to walking, Carol.'

At the house, in Frances's sitting-room, on the desk, there was a photograph of her and her brother, Carol's father, in youth. Around seventeen or eighteen. It was a bad photograph, muzzy, and Carol had not at first recognised the faces. Then, her father's familiar features had somehow emerged, but displaced and distorted; the boy in the photograph was him, and yet not him. She thought of this, and of herself; her hands, thrust into the pockets of her school coat, were rigid with cold; it was three o'clock in the afternoon, there was no reason, it seemed to her, why this day should not go on for ever. She stumped behind Frances and Clive, through the sphere of that silent, suspended landscape; it is so lovely here in summer, Frances had said, quite perfect, you must come in August, in the holidays.

At nights, at school, the other girls planned and recalled; the long thin room in which she slept with eight others was filled with disembodied voices, whispering in the dark of holidays past and holidays to come, of what they had done and what they would do. The limbo of the term was put away; they roamed into other times, other places. And Carol lay silent; to roam, for her, had too many dangers. Recollection must be checked; that way lay disaster. And the other way? She had nothing there, either, to offer; no plans nor expectations.

The children came running from a field, solemn-faced and important, with a dead bird they had found, a lapwing, bright-plumaged and uncorrupt, its eyes closed by filmy lids. Marian was on the brink of tears. Her father took the bird and they huddled round him, quiet and comforted, as he dug a grave, lined it with leaves, buried the body, marked the place with a ring of berries collected from the hedges. 'I don't expect it *felt* anything, Mummy, did it?' begged Marian. 'It didn't *hurt* it, did it?' And Frances said, 'No, darling, it would be just like going to sleep, it would hardly know anything about it.'

In the village, Frances bought things in the warm, cluttered post office that smelled of soap, matches and bacon; the children fingered and fidgeted, their voices shrill and confident. 'This is my niece Carol,' Frances explained, 'who is here for the Christmas holidays.' And the shop lady, petting the children, giving them each a toffee from a personal store behind the till, hesitated, the open tin in her hand, as also did Carol hesitate; we neither of us know, she thought in despair, what I am, if I am a child or not. The shop lady reached a decision, good or bad, and put the tin back on its shelf, unproffered.

On the way back, Marian pointed suddenly over the fields and said to Carol, 'That's Mrs Binns's cottage, down that track: they've got chickens, and a dog called Toby.'

Carol stared over a grass field, patched with unmelted snow; smoke filtered from a chimney, barely darker than the sky; washing hung limp on a line in stiff geometric shapes of sheets, towels, shirts with outstretched arms.

On Christmas morning she lay in bed hearing the children open their stockings in their parents' room across the corridor; their high-pitched voices alternated with their parents' deeper ones like a series of musical responses, statement and commentary. She heard their feet pattering on the bare boards, the dogs barking in excitement; the animals too had Christmas presents – bones wrapped in scarlet crêpe paper, beribboned rubber mice. The day proceeded through a series of ceremonies and rituals: after breakfast we have presents under the tree, before church we telephone grandmother, in the afternoon we walk to Clee Hill. Frances said, 'I forgot to tell you, Carol – tomorrow our old friends the Laidlaws are coming. Mark is fifteen so he will be someone for you, I thought – it is dull for you, being always with the younger ones.'

The children did not like her, she knew. At first they had been shy, the small boys arch, trying to appeal as they would appeal to a grown-up. But they saw her now for what she was, neither fish nor fowl, not exempt like them from adult obligations, but without adult privileges either. Sharp-eyed, they noted her position as a classless person, without position, and exploited their own the more; if she would not join in their games when they wanted her to they complained to Frances, and Carol felt her aunt's resentment, unstated but none the less evident. I have a hundred things to do, her silent back said, the least you could do is help to amuse them for a while. They danced around Carol, more agile in every way; they made her feel lumpish of mind and in body.

The prospect of Mark filled her with apprehension. He is at Marl-borough, said Frances, he is awfully clever, he has such nice manners, we have always liked him so much.

They came, the Laidlaws; there were kisses and handshakes and the house was filled with talk, with people at ease with one another. Mark, Carol furtively noted, had longish hair that flopped over one eye and was dressed as a man – tweed jacket, grey flannels, grown-up tie. He sat next to Frances at lunch and talked with what Carol saw to be charming attention, listening when listening should be done, taking the initiative when that was appropriate. After lunch he played with the children – an absurd game of crawling on the floor, romping, and he was in no way diminished by it, it made him seem more grown-up, not less so. And Frances beamed upon him.

He had said to Carol, 'Where do you go to school?' She had replied to this. He had asked her how many School Cert. subjects she was doing and she replied to that too. And then there had been a silence, she had searched wildly for something to fill it, and seen that he wanted to get away from her, to get back to the others, that she did not interest him. 'It must have been awfully exciting, growing up in India,' he said. 'What was it like?' and India swirled in her head, a kaleidoscope of sights and sounds and responses, and there was nothing she could say. 'Yes,' she stammered. 'It was . . . I mean . . . Yes, I . . .', and felt Frances's gaze upon her, observing, regretting. 'Have you ever seen Gandhi?' he asked, and she shook her head.

Later, in the evening, Frances said, 'The Laidlaws are having a small party for Mark, at the New Year, but of course you will be gone by then, Carol – they were so sorry.'

It snowed in the night. She drew her curtains and saw the landscape powdered over, not deeply, but shrouded as it were, in a state of suspension once again, motionless. The children, outside, were rushing about trying to scoop up enough for snowballs or snowmen; they came in wet and querulous, their hands scarlet with cold. Their exhilaration disintegrated into tears and fretfulness; Frances was irritable. Later, she had letters to write, and the children wanted to go to the village, to buy sweets. Carol can take us, they cried, and Frances, relieved, said yes, of course, Carol can take you – wrap up well; don't let them run on the road, Carol.

They met him on the way back. She was walking behind the children, who were quiet now, amiable, tamed by chocolate. He came down the track from the cottage, the gun crooked over his arm, and they arrived together precisely at the gate. Marian said, 'Hello, Tom.'

He nodded, 'Hello.' And then he looked at Carol and smiled, and quite easily, without her eyes sliding away to left or right, without a problem, she smiled back, He said, 'Mum told me you were stopping with your auntie.'

The children wanted to see the gun. But their curiosity was tinged, even at this remove, with Frances's disapproval. In silence they watched him demonstrate its workings; his thin fingers clicked this and pressed that, ran over the sleek metal, caressed the polished butt. He was immensely proud of it; in his light voice, not yet broken, a boy's voice, but with its sudden odd lurches into manhood, he described the make and model. It was not a toy, it was real, serious, it marked him. It told him what he was. 'My dad gave it me for my birthday. My fourteenth. He reckoned you can learn to use a gun, then, when you're fourteen, it's time.'

The children were restive, moving away. Come on, they said, let's go, it's cold, let's go home.

Tom turned to Carol. 'I'll be going out tomorrow morning, shooting. Early, when it's getting light. Sevenish. You could come if you like.'

She said, 'Yes, please', before she could stop to think. 'Right,' he said. 'Come by the cottage then, and we'll go.'

She walked back to the house amazed; things like this did not happen, it was astonishing, she could hardly believe it.

It was in the cold, wakeful reaches of the night that it struck her she should have told Frances, asked Frances. But now it was too late. Frances was asleep: at seven – before seven – she would not be about. And suppose she said no, or even just implied no? I have to go, Carol thought, I must go, it is the only thing that has ever happened to me.

She woke again long before dawn and lay looking at her watch every few minutes. When it said half past six she got up, making as little noise as possible, and dressed in all her warmest things. But she was warm already, for the first time in days, weeks, it seemed, and when she crept down the stairs, and opened the back door the air outside was tinged with mildness, she thought. The wind that met her face was not so keen, and the snow, in the drive, had melted. Only in the lee of the hedges it lay still in thickish drifts.

It was almost dark. The sky was streaked with light in the east; dark clouds lay like great fish along the horizon. She walked down the road and there was no one else in the world, except her; she was alone, and it was quite all right, she felt confident, at ease with things, she walked briskly with her hands in her pockets and there was beauty in the landscape that wheeled around her, she could see that. It was still and quiet, clenched in its winter state, but there was a flush of reddish brown on the plough, where the snow had melted, and the bare shapes of the trees on the skyline were of amazing delicacy, they held the suggestion of other times, the ripeness to come, summer.

She hesitated outside the cottage door; there was an easy murmuring of voices from inside, and the chink of crockery, and smells of toast and something frying. And then a man came out, at that moment, in old jacket and muffler, his trousers clipped ready for a bicycle – Tom's father, presumably – and told her to go on in, Tom wouldn't be a moment.

Mrs Binns gave her a cup of tea, but she could not eat the food offered; she felt in her stomach all the instability of before a journey, before an event. But it was good, it was the best thing she had known, beyond things which must not be remembered, things from other times. Tom said little; he attended to the gun with oil and a rag and a stick, and when he had done he got up and said, 'We'll be off now, Mum,' and Carol rose too, in a state still of amazement. She felt quite comfortable, quite in place. I have a friend, she thought, and could hardly believe it.

He led her over the fields, up a shallow hillside. Out of the cottage, he became talkative. He told her about the ways of rabbits, and how you must go after them downwind, towards their burrows, towards the slope where he knew they would come out to graze around now. He had shot two, he said, the week before, and Carol said, no, three your mother said, and he corrected her, carefully – two it was, one I missed, I told Mum, she got it wrong. I'm not good with sighting, he said, seriously, not yet, and I've got a shake in my wrist, I'll have to work on that, and she nodded, intent, and stared at his wrists. They were bony wrists, white-knobbed, sticking out from the frayed sleeve of his too-short jersey. His hair was cut short, almost cropped, like the soldier in the London train. He spoke with the accent of the place, this place to which he belonged, where he had been born, where his parents had been born; sometimes she could not quite follow what he said. She thought confusedly of this, as they climbed the hill, the ground wet and springy under their feet: of her own speech, which was quite different, and of the place where she had been born, none of whose many tongues she spoke. Once, climbing a gate, he gave her the gun to hold for a moment; she felt the sting of the cold metal on her hands, and cradled it gingerly, with reverence.

They reached the side of the field where, he said, the rabbits would come. It ran downhill from a small copse, and she could see the brown markings of burrows at the top. He edged cautiously along the ditch until he came to a place in long grass where they could lie and wait. 'They might have heard us,' he said. 'We'll have to sit tight a bit, and they'll come out again.'

They lay flank to flank on the wet grass. She could feel its damp and cold creep through to her skin, and the faint warmth of his body beside hers. Their breath steamed. Occasionally they whispered a little; it was better, though, he said, to stay quiet. He seemed to expect nothing of her; if she had not complied, if she had infringed the rules in any way, he did not let her know. He let her hold the gun again, and she peered down the long barrel into the field and saw, suspended cinematically beyond it, the cropped turf with its dark enigmatic holes and scrapings of rich earth and pockets of snow. He said, 'They're a long time about it, usually they come out quicker than this, once you've sat quiet a bit,' and she could feel the tension in him; the rabbits mattered, they were the most important thing in his life just now. She said suddenly, amazed at her own temerity, 'What is it like, killing something, do you like it?' And turning to look at him, saw with shock that a slow tide of colour had crept up his face.

'I don't like them dying,' he said, mumbling with his head to the ground, so that she could hardly hear. 'I hate that. The first time I came out with my dad, I felt sick, I didn't want to do it. I couldn't say, not to him. He gave me the gun, see, for my own. Now it's all right. They die quick, it's over just like that.' He looked at her, his face still red. 'It's not for the killing, it's not for that.'

She nodded. There wasn't anything to say. And then suddenly he touched her arm, pressed his fingers down on her coat, and she looked out towards the field and there was movement on the turf, something brown shifting against the green – two, three of them. One sat up, nosing the wind, and she saw its pricked ears, and, as it turned, the white scut.

He lifted the gun, aimed; she was clenched in excitement, breathless. And then he pressed the trigger, and the noise was startling, louder than ever she had imagined, but in the second before, in a fraction of a second, something had happened out there and the rabbits had bolted, homed back on their burrows, gone. The field was empty.

She said, 'Oh . . .' He sat up, breaking the gun apart angrily, unloading. 'Won't they come out again?'

He shook his head. 'Not for hours, maybe. That's done it, that has. Something scared them.' His hands were shaking, she could see that, they had been shaking earlier too, when he lay still on the grass, aiming. Now he seemed almost relieved. 'Come on,' he said. 'Have to get back. Mum'll be wondering.'

They ran down the field; there was no longer any need to be quiet. At

the gate he showed her how he could vault over it, and she, who was
unathletic, who lumbered hopelessly around the games pitch at school,
found that she could do it also; there was no end, it seemed, to the
surprises this day held. There are bits of me I know nothing about, she
thought, I am not so clumsy after all, I can talk to people, I can feel part of
something. The sky was crossed and recrossed by ragged flights of birds.
'What are they?' she asked. 'What kind of bird is that?' and he told her
that those were rooks, and these on the plough, in the field, were
lapwings, surprised at her ignorance but uncritical. 'Mum said you grew
up somewhere else,' he said, 'somewhere foreign,' and she talked about
India; she brought heat and dust and the sound of the place on to this
wintry Suffolk field and it was painless, or almost so.

At the corner of the track to the cottage he asked her if she would like to
come out again the next morning; she had half-expected this and yet not
dared to hope. Such coincidence, in the normal way of things, of what
you would like and what was available, did not happen. She said, 'Yes
please,' and thought it sounded childish, and blushed.

Back at the house, she was amazed to find it past breakfast-time,
Frances clearing the table, the children staring as she came in at the
kitchen door, Clive reading a letter. Frances sounded annoyed. '*There* you
are, Carol, we were beginning to wonder, where have you been?'

She had prepared nothing, given no thought to this moment. She
stood, silent with confusion, and then one of the children said, 'She's
been shooting rabbits with Mrs Binns's Tom. We heard him ask her
yesterday.'

Frances swept things off the table on to a tray. 'Oh, really. I can't
imagine why you should want to, Carol, I must say.'

'Did he kill any rabbits?' said Marian.

Carol muttered, 'No.' She could feel her face scarlet; the day, and all
that it had held, died on Frances's kitchen floor; she felt dirty.

'Goody,' said Marian. 'Can I go out now?'

Clive had not spoken; he had put down his letter and was playing with
the dog, gently pulling its ears, mumbling to it; Carol, catching his eye by
accident, saw it go cold, excluding her. 'Well,' he said to the dog,
'walkies, is it? Walkies for a good girl?' The dog beamed and fawned and
swished its feathered tail.

All that day was sourly flavoured with Frances's disapproval; nothing
was said, but it hung in the air at lunchtime, in the afternoon, over tea.
Mrs Binns did not come, for which Carol was grateful; there would have
been references, Tom would have been mentioned, and that she could
not endure.

In the afternoon there was a letter from her father, enclosed in one to
Frances. She read it by the drawing-room fire, and it seemed to come not
from another country but from another time; his familiar handwriting,

speaking of the house, the garden, neighbours, referred to things that no longer were, they had perished long ago. 'Poor Tim,' said Frances, reading her own letter. 'He is so anxious to get home, pack things up out there. It must be trying for him, but it is not long now, he has booked his passage.' Carol read that the bulbuls had nested again in the bush outside the laundry, that the cannas were a lovely show this year, that the rains had come early; it was as though he were frozen in another age, her father, in an imagined world. She asked, in sudden panic, 'Will he really be here this summer, here in England?' And Frances, preoccupied now with the demands of the children, of the hour, said that of course he would, he was bound to, the house was sold, the furniture to be packed and shipped. If you are writing to him, she went on, you had better put it in with mine, and save the stamp.

Lying awake, after everyone else had gone to bed, Carol knew that she would go with Tom in the morning. She had thought about it, on and off, all day; she felt grubby, condemned by Clive's cold eye, by the children's indignation. '*Poor* rabbits,' Marian said once. 'I think it's beastly. Horrid Tom,' and she had answered nothing, being without defence. Now, staring at the dim square of the window, she knew that she would go, had to go, whatever they thought, whatever happened. Guilt clutched her; she lay sleepless for most of the night.

He was waiting for her at the bottom of the track. 'Hello,' he said, 'I thought you weren't coming,' and his innocence compounded her guilt. She carried now the burden not only of what she was doing, but of the fact that he did not know what they were doing, did not know that what they did was wrong, despised by decent people.

They climbed the hill again. It was raining; the wind blew wet sheets into their faces and they walked with heads down, not talking much. At the gate Tom did not vault but climbed over; Carol noticed how thin his legs were, childishly thin, like his bony wrists. Walking behind him, she observed that his hair made a ducktail at the nape and that the cleft had the softness, the look of vulnerability that the back of a small boy's neck has. She saw, for a moment, the ghost of the child that he had recently been; Mark Laidlaw's stocky frame had suggested the man from whom he stood at one remove. She thought of her own body, which seemed always to scream out in conflict – the alien, uncontrollable breasts, the pudgy hands and face, the scar on her knee that remembered a fall when she was ten. Her body held her back; at the same time it dragged her inexorably onwards.

At the place where they had waited before, he gestured her down into the grass. They lay again side by side, staring through rain-studded greenery at the point in the field where something might happen. The time passed slowly; it stopped raining and a weak sun shone opalescent behind the clouds. Occasionally, they murmured to each other. 'Taking their time again,' he said. 'Hope I'll have better luck today.' And she nodded and murmured yes, hope so, and ssh! look, isn't that one? no, it's just a thistle, sorry. Something had lifted, things had eased once more, guilt had been put to flight; Frances, Clive and the children no longer hovered behind her shoulder. The crystal globes of water on the grass blades shivered with a thousand colours; the dried head of a summer flower held between delicate stalks a miniature of the landscape beyond – skyline trees, clouds; the sun on the back of her hand was a breath, a promise, of warmth.

And then, together, they saw it on the grass beside the burrow; a moment ago it had not been there and now suddenly there it was, quietly munching grass, bobbing away a yard or so, sitting up to sniff the wind.

He raised the gun, hesitated for what seemed far too long, fired.

The rabbit bucked into the air. Bucked, and at the same time screamed. The sound was hideous; it rang over the field, obscene in the quietness of the morning. She cried, 'You got it! You hit it!' and they jumped up together and ran across the grass.

And saw, together, at the same moment, that the rabbit was not dead. It lay threshing and writhing and as they came near it screamed again, humanly, like a hurt child, and they pulled up short and stood there in horror, a few yards off, staring. Blood welled from its ear; it writhed and twitched.

Tom was shaking. His voice was high-pitched, out of control, 'I got to do something. You got to kill them, when that happens, you got to finish them off.'

She said, 'Oh, I don't want to see!' and turned away, her hands over her eyes, but then turned back, moments later, and he was standing above the rabbit, white-faced, and the rabbit bleated again, and arched its back, and kicked. He said, 'I don't know what to do. I've seen my dad do it – you have to break their necks. I don't know how to do it.' He was distraught.

She covered her eyes again.

When she looked back he had the rabbit in his hands, and the rabbit was limp. Blood dripped from it. He put it on the ground and it lay still. He was shaking violently. He moved away a few paces and sat on the grass, turned from her, and she could see his whole body tremble. She felt sorry for him, and yet at the same time exasperated. She could not help him; they were quite separate now, it was as though they did not know each other; the whole fragile structure of confidence, the sense of being at ease with the world, had been destroyed with the rabbit. She saw Tom, wretched, and could think only: I am wretched, too, I hate myself, and what we have done, and what people must think of us for it.

He got up, without a word, and began to walk away down the field, and wordlessly she followed him. He carried the gun all anyhow, not with pride, cradled over his arm; it looked, now, disproportionately large, as though it had grown and he had shrunk.

At the road he turned to her. 'Don't say anything about what happened – not to my mum.'

She shook her head.

'Cheerio, then.'

'Goodbye.'

It was raining once more. She trudged towards the house; she was shrivelled with guilt. They did not know what had happened, could not know, but she felt that the very look of her announced the incident; she carried still, in her head, the rabbit's scream.

They were having breakfast. As she came into the kitchen silence fell and the children looked expectantly towards Frances.

Frances said, 'You'd better have something to eat, Carol'; her voice was not friendly. When Carol was sitting at the table she went on, 'It would have been a good idea, you know, to mention that you were going out with Tom Binns again. Clive and I are responsible for you, while you are here.'

Carol stared at the table. 'I'm sorry,' she said.

Clive had not looked once at her. He kept his back half-turned. Now, he busied himself giving milk to the cat. He poured the creamy top from a bottle into a saucer and put it by the stove. 'There, Mr Patch,' he murmured. 'There. Come on then, puss.' The kitchen was filled with well-loved, well-tended animals.

'Did Tom kill a rabbit?' said Marian in her small, clear voice.

Scarlet-faced, Carol noted the bordered tablecloth: red flower, cluster of leaves, spray of berries, red flower again. 'Yes,' she muttered.

'Children,' said Frances, 'you can get down now and go up and do your teeth. Oh, and tidy your bedroom, please, Marian darling.'

They went. Clive said he thought he would just go now and do the hens and the pony before he went into Ipswich. He went.

Frances began to clear the table. The room was charged with feeling; once, she dropped a cup, and swore. Carol sat, the rabbit's scream still in her ears, behind and above the sounds of the children upstairs, of Frances running water at the sink, of the cat lapping milk.

Frances slapped plates on to the draining-board and spoke again, her voice assured and tinged with indignation, 'What I cannot understand – what Clive and I cannot understand – is why you should *want* to. I daresay it has been a bit dull here for you given that the children are a good deal younger and I am frightfully busy what with little or no help these days, not like it was for people before the war, but we've tried to find things for you to do and had Mark Laidlaw over who I thought would be just right for you, so I simply cannot understand why . . .'

The room spun; Frances's voice roared. Carol wrung the tablecloth between her shaking fingers and burst out, 'He didn't mean to. Tom didn't mean to – he meant to do it like his father said, a clean death, not hurting it, and something went wrong, it wasn't. He felt awful about it. I don't think he'll go shooting again. *I* don't want to, not ever. I hated it. It was beastly, the rabbit being hurt like that.' She fought back tears.

Frances turned from the sink; she was staring now, in surprise, across the kitchen table. She said, 'What rabbit? What do you mean? I'm not talking about shooting rabbits, Carol, which is really neither here nor there, lots of people round here shoot rabbits and of course one wishes they wouldn't but there it is. I'm talking about why you should want to go off doing things with someone like Tom Binns, as though he were a friend or something, when surely you must realise that it really won't do. I don't know what Mrs Binns was thinking of, suggesting it, she is normally such a sensible woman.' She paused, and then went on, 'I know it has made things difficult for you, growing up out there in India, sometimes it is a bit confusing for you here, I daresay, but surely you must see that a boy like Tom Binns . . . well, it really doesn't do, you should know that, Carol.'

The rabbit's scream died away; in its place there came, all innocent and unaware, Tom's voice of yesterday, explaining the workings of the gun. She stared at her aunt in bewilderment and thought: I don't know what you are talking about, I knew I had done one thing and now you are saying I have done another. It came to her suddenly that there was no way, ever, that she could oblige everyone, could do both what was expected of her, and what her own discoveries of what she was would drive her to do; she would have to learn to endure the conflict, as her body endured the conflict of what she had been and what she was bound to be, like it or not.

Party

She gets out of the taxi, Ellen Greaves, the grandmother, and pays with the change that she has assembled, carefully, on the way from Paddington. Then she picks up her suitcase once more and climbs the short flight of steps to the front door of the house, her daughter's house. It is a tall, thin terrace house, nineteenth century, in the middle of a street of similar houses. Aircraft lumber overhead. She rings the bell.

The door is opened, by an adolescent she does not recognise, who explains that they are all in the kitchen. From down below, in the basement, her daughter's voice calls up, 'Halloo . . . Mum? Down here . . . It's a shambles – be warned.' And Ellen dumps her case in the hall and goes with caution down the steep stairs to the basement kitchen which is full of people and certainly most untidy. There are bottles everywhere, and food, both cooked and uncooked, and many loaves of bread. She kisses, and is kissed. Her grandchildren are there: Toby who is seventeen and Sophie who is eighteen and Paul, the little one, who is only eleven. And there are others, a dark girl and two boys and yet another she does not at first see, who is apparently mending the back of the fridge. They smile and greet; they have nice manners. Ellen smiles and greets too, and notes their appearance: all are shabbily, not to say scruffily, dressed, but their voices suggest a reasonable prosperity. Ellen finds this interesting.

Her daughter, Louise (who has got very thin again – indeed everyone is thin, they all have a lean and hungry look, despite the plenitude of things to eat) is furiously applied to something at the stove. She chops and stirs and flies to cupboards and despatches someone to the freezer and explains that *she* is doing the food for *their* party, for the grown-up dinner, and *they* are coping absolutely on their own with *their* stuff (and indeed, as Ellen now sees, Sophie is also chopping and stirring, though with what seems to be a less refined approach). The two parties, Louise explains, will coexist but there will be no mixing, in all probability – we shall be upstairs and they will do their own thing down here, and nobody will get

in anyone else's hair that way. But, she adds, doing it like this means that
we are here to keep an eye, Michael and I, there will be no hanky-panky,
no nonsense. And she casts a look at the young, who grin.

Ellen sits down at the kitchen table and wonders if, amid all this, there
will be a cup of tea going. She decides (rightly, as it turns out) that there
probably will not. Someone goes out and comes back in with a crate of
bottles which is put on the dresser; Louise shrieks no, no! not there, for
heaven's sake! The crate is removed to the floor beside the fridge. There is
a brief, whispered consultation among the young, two of whom leave;
they move with slouching purposefulness. Louise, on the other hand,
darts from point to point. Her mother observes her thoughtfully.

We, Louise explains, are having a salmon trout and a rather lavish pud
that I haven't tried before. They – and there are to be absolutely no more
than thirty, do you hear, as agreed, no last-minute additions (Sophie and
Toby nod emphatically) – are having plonk and some goo that Sophie is
fixing.

Chilli con carne, murmurs Sophie, stirring. She peers through her hair
into the saucepan; the kitchen is very hot and close. Ellen looks at the
window and at the same moment Louise dashes to it, throws up the sash,
and returns to her chopping-board.

Ellen, who is really here for her annual visit to the dentist, says that she
hopes she won't be in the way. If she had known, she says, she could
quite easily have made it another day . . . But before she can finish Louise
is saying that there is absolutely no question of her being in the way, her
usual room is empty because no one is staying the night, that's for sure
(another sharp look at the young), and this is an absolutely inter-
generational night so in fact it is very appropriate that she should be here.
Louise, in mid-chop and mid-stir, pauses to smile fondly at her mother.
Not everyone's mum, she says, would fit in, as it happens, but you will be
all right, I can count on you, I know, and actually you may rather like
some of the people who are coming. There is Tony Hatch who . . . But
Tony Hatch remains undeveloped, because at this moment the two
departed young return bearing cardboard boxes full of glasses and there
is an altercation over the disposal of these, which must not be put there,
nor there, nor above all on the dresser . . . Indeed, the kitchen is silting up
rapidly, there is not an uncluttered surface nor much uncluttered floor.
Louise and the rest dart and shuffle amid the confusion with remarkable
adroitness; Ellen decides that she is safest where she is. She sits there at
the table, and looks at Paul, who is perched on a stool, intent on some
map or plan he is studying; he seems quite impervious to what is going on
around. Once, he says, 'Mum, have you got any glue, my tube's almost
used up?' and Louise says, 'What?' and goes to the stairs to deal with
Toby, who, with a friend, is trying to bring a table-tennis table down;
there are accusations and denials concerning scraped paint. Louise comes

back into the kitchen scowling (she is also sweating profusely, her mother observes, which is odd for someone so thin); Paul sighs, slithers from the stool, and goes out.

Ellen surreptitiously rewashes some crockery stacked on the draining-board, having noted its condition with disquiet.

Louise says, 'Oh, Christ, the man never came about the stereo,' and rushes out. She can be heard upstairs, vehemently telephoning.

Ellen, who has been able to do some prospecting from her seat at the table, and has established the whereabouts of cups, tea, sugar etc., makes herself a cup of tea. She sits drinking it and listens to the conversation of two people at her feet. They are not so much exchanging observations or opinions as making statements, separate and unrelated. The girl says that she simply cannot stand anything fried nowadays, she doesn't know why, she thinks perhaps it is psychological, and the boy says there is this master at school, this bloke who has really got it in for him, it's a hassle. They are joined by another girl, who is concerned about the state of her fingernails. She sits peering at them and saying there are these little white spots, look, I'm worried, what should I do; then for a few moments these assorted themes come together in a united objection to honey (however did they get on to that?) before each is off again on a saga of personal revelation. Ellen, one of whose feet is being sat on, shifts, as un-obtrusively as possible, and pours herself a cup of tea.

Louise returns, followed by Paul, who says again, 'Is there any glue anywhere, mum?' Louise says, 'Why?' and darts with exclamations of dismay to her saucepan. Paul begins, 'Because I haven't . . .', but now Louise remembers that no one has counted and allocated cutlery, so the group under the kitchen table are jolted into action, or rather into a state of gentle drift.

It is five o'clock.

At six o'clock Louise has the most ghastly headache. Further, she is seized with some compulsion that sends her on frequent brief and furtive excursions into the large room next to the kitchen, Toby's room, in which the youthful party is to take place. She seems to be hunting for something. During these hunts the young, in the kitchen, exchange glances and roll their eyes. Once or twice, Ellen cannot help hearing whispered snatches on the stairs, unspecified threats about what Louise will do if there is the slightest suspicion of, if anyone is so damn stupid as to bring, if anything other than absolutely straightforward . . . During one of these fraught exchanges, Paul reappears, sliding past his mother and siblings without paying them any attention. He delves in the bread-bin, helps himself to bread, butter and jam, and sits once more upon the stool, lost in perusal of yet another printed sheet. Ellen says, 'What is that, dear?'

It is, Paul explains, the instructions for the assembly of the model aircraft on which he is currently working. He is stuck, he says, because he has run out of glue, almost, but also because there is a bit that he simply cannot get the hang of. It doesn't, he says, seem to make sense. The aeroplane is a De Havilland Mosquito, he explains, and the problem is that . . .

Ellen asks if she can have a look. She reads, frowns, puts her glasses on and reads again. After a few moments everything falls into place; the problem, as it turns out, is a semantic one. The model aircraft kit has been made in Japan, and the translation of the instructions, while for the most part admirable, has fallen down just at the end here, where in fact 'right' should read 'left', and 'front', 'back'. Paul is gravely grateful, and goes off again.

Michael arrives home. He kisses his mother-in-law, and immediately busies himself stowing bottles in the fridge, placing others by the stove; he says it is amazingly brave of Ellen to let herself in for all this, and Ellen, who is now repairing the zip on Toby's jeans (they have not been washed for some time, which makes the job a mite disagreeable), says not at all, a bit of gaiety will be a nice change, she leads a quiet enough life in the normal way of things. Louise, whose voice has become peculiarly shrill, interrupts to point out that the table needs laying; Sophie comes in and has an argument with Toby about some gramophone records; the telephone rings. Michael and Louise exchange clipped words about some gin, of which, it seems, there is not enough. Subdued accusations are made about responsibility.

Ellen goes up to her room, which is on the top floor. On the way, she passes the open door of Sophie's room. Sophie, within, can be seen seated at a dressing-table with tears pouring down her cheeks, a staggering sight, the incarnation of tragedy. Her grandmother, disturbed, ventures to ask if there is anything she can do, to be told, in tones of choked stoicism, that there is nothing, nothing, no one can help, it would be impossible to explain to anyone, it is to do with her friend, or rather ex-friend, Mike, and furthermore there is this dress she was to wear which is stained all down the front, ruined . . . Her grandmother nods understandingly and withdraws.

In her own room, Ellen unpacks her overnight case, hangs up a dress, and goes to the bathroom for a wash. She pats the hot-water tank in exploratory fashion; a hot-water bottle, she suspects, might be a comfort later on, but the water is not very hot. She will have to see about a kettle.

Downstairs, there are sudden bursts of loud music, as from a fairground. Louise is to be heard, also.

Ellen changes into her tidy dress and does her hair. Then she sits for a while on the edge of her bed, apparently looking out of the window over the ranges of grey London roof-tops. She was sixty-three last birthday, a small, neat person, a little fatter than in youth, her hands brown-mottled, her teeth not all her own. She sits so still, is so relaxed, that to an observer the room might appear to be empty. She watches the slow progress of an aeroplane along the line of a roof and thinks, in utter tranquillity, of her husband, ten years dead. She tells him, as is her habit, what has been happening to her today, and with the telling there is a faint, fragrant gust of sexual memory. Come now, she tells herself, this won't do, I am not here to be unsociable, and she gathers herself to go downstairs.

The house is strung up now, like a bow, any minute something might snap. As Ellen progresses downwards, people slip past her, dash from room to room, drop things. Louise comes from her bedroom, in a long dress, screwing on ear-rings, and says oh, there you are, mum, I say you do look smart, come down and Michael will find you a glass of sherry, would you believe it, the fridge has decided to play up again, now of all times. And she is gone down the stairs at a gallop, her skirt looped over her arm, her neat muscular calves visible beneath. Her mother remembers that at school she was good at games. It is not wise to mention this, though; for some reason that recollection is ill-received nowadays. Louise has a partnership in a small art gallery.

At eight, the guests begin to arrive. They arrive simultaneously on both floors – the young presenting themselves at the basement door, in twos and threes, furtive of manner, being admitted in silence, without greeting; Louise and Michael's friends climbing the steps to the front door, shedding coats in the hall, loud in greeting and comment. They are presented to Ellen: this tall thin man who is a psychiatrist, Tony Hatch, and his dark, shrieking wife; the small round unattached man who works at Sotheby's; two more couples whose allegiances she cannot for a while get straight, since they all arrive together and treat one another with indiscriminate familiarity. We are all such *old* friends tonight, declares Louise, flying from drinks cupboard to guests, it is lovely, everyone knows everyone else, I don't have to do any of that tiresome sorting people out. Except of course you, mum, she adds – and you are such a splendid adaptable lady, aren't you? She beams upon her mother and the other guests smile kindly. Ellen, who is not deaf, though it is apparently expected of her, has already heard Louise in the hall explaining that her mum is here for the night which actually is not the snag you'd think because she is really marvellous for that generation, nothing bothers her, she is amazingly well-adjusted, you'll love her.

Drinks are drunk. Ellen sits on the sofa beside the psychiatrist who tells her with boyish candour that he and Josie are recently married, just this year. He is in his early forties, and wears jeans and a jacket that reminds Ellen of her husband's old tropical bush-shirt. He is a little stout for the jeans and during the course of the evening the zip of the fly is to descend, which worries Ellen, not for herself but because embarrassment in others distresses her. As it turns out, though, there is no cause for distress; he is never aware of his plight. He talks to Ellen with nostalgia of his first wife, his divorced wife, who was the most super person; across the room, the new wife bites her fingernails and occasionally shouts out some personal comment; the niceties of social intercourse do not seem to interest her.

The volume of noise from the basement is increasing; several times Louise, or Michael, go to the stairs and remonstrate.

Dinner is had in the dining-room, which glows agreeably with candlelight and furniture polish and silver. Louise and Michael have some nice things. Ellen sits between the man from Sotheby's and one of the other husbands (she has sorted out now who is attached to whom, for what that is worth). The man from Sotheby's turns to her and says (in pursuit of the tail-end of a subject that had been bandied around earlier, upstairs) what does she think about the Mentmore sale, and does she feel that the government should or shouldn't have stepped in earlier, but while she is giving proper consideration to what she thinks (and she does, in fact, have a number of thoughts on the matter) it turns out that what he really intended was to tell her what he thinks, which he proceeds to do. Ellen listens with attention; he is telling her, in fact, a great deal more than he realises. I . . . he says . . . my opinion is that . . . personally, I feel . . . consulted me earlier . . . Ellen nods thoughtfully. Down at the other end of the table, the second wife of the psychiatrist screams that Tony is getting a bald pate, just look at him, look at his pate! Everybody laughs; the psychiatrist blows his wife a kiss; the husband on Ellen's right says that Josie is a riot, she is such a direct person, she says just what comes into her head.

By now, everybody has had a good deal to drink, except Ellen, for whom a glass of sherry has always been quite enough.

There is a muffled crash, from below; Louise, who is listening to an anecdote told by the psychiatrist, leaves the room, sharply, a frozen smile on her lips. She returns and serves the salmon trout with what seems an unnecessary amount of clatter. Everybody says what a lovely treat.

Ellen, who has got up to help Louise pass the vegetables, asks if Paul has had something earlier, or what, and is told that he is absolutely fine, he is up in his room with a plate of bangers and beans, of course he is rather out on a limb tonight, poor love, neither one thing nor t'other. Michael, who is circulating more wine, says it is a tiresome time for him, poor chap, he longs to be out in the great wide world like the others.

The psychiatrist has finished his anecdote, and the man from Sotheby's is now having his turn; people are very given to interruption, Ellen notes, they do not so much listen as interject. She watches the young woman opposite her, who has been trying for the past hour to make various points about herself, without success, chiefly because she has to compete, at the end of the table, with Louise and the psychiatrist's wife, both of whom have louder voices. The psychiatrist's wife, at this moment, bawls to Michael that Tony gets awfully randy in hot weather, it's a real sweat. Ellen, interested, is trying to define her origins (Ellen likes to know where she is about people). She thinks she can detect, beneath that stridency, a residual hint of the west country, and would like to know if she is right – in a momentary lull she leans forward and asks the girl where her home is, but she is busy now picking her teeth with a fingernail and does not hear, or does not care to.

Downstairs, there is a steady thump of music, with intermittent louder bursts; Louise occasionally frowns, but her reactions are becoming slower. A sound of splintering glass escapes her altogether, engaged as she is in banter with the man from Sotheby's. She forgets to pass the biscuits with the pudding; Ellen rescues them from the sideboard and puts them on the table.

They move back to the sitting-room, for coffee. Ellen, following Louise down to the kitchen to give a hand, peeks through the half-open door of Toby's room at a scene of semi-darkness, peopled with murky, shifting presences like an aquarium. Louise, juggling a trifle unsteadily with hot water, coffee and a strainer, is muttering darkly about having a good mind to go in there and just have a thorough check . . . Sophie comes in, hand in hand with a boy, wreathed in smiles; she says 'Hello, gran' warmly, and her grandmother says, 'Good, so everything's all right now'; Sophie beams uncomprehendingly.

They take the coffee upstairs. In the sitting-room, there is an impression of dishevelment, as though everyone had slumped a notch or two, in every sense. Michael has been handing out brandy; the psychiatrist's wife has her shoes off and is sprawled over the arm of the sofa; the man from Sotheby's is reading a book; there is talk, a little incoherent, Ellen thinks. She picks up, without anyone noticing, a couple of glasses that are threatened by people's feet.

Coffee is dispensed. Ellen takes the opportunity to go upstairs to the bathroom for a minute; on the way, she looks in at Paul's room. He sits cross-legged on the floor, in a dressing-gown, the dismembered De Havilland Mosquito around him. He says, 'You were quite right, gran – I've got the tail on now, all but.' Together they examine his achievement; he points out a further technical hitch; Ellen, who is steady-fingered, is able to complete a tricky matter of inserting a door. Regretfully, she goes downstairs again.

The telephone rings. The neighbours, it appears, are less than happy about the noise emanating from the basement. Louise makes soothing remarks and assurances of action; putting the receiver down she says that really it is a bit thick, I mean, it's only once in a blue moon. She goes to the stairs and bawls, 'Turn that thing *down*, do you hear, Toby . . .' The noise is reduced by a decibel or two.

Ellen goes down to see if there is any more coffee; she has been inspecting one of the male guests, unobtrusively, and thinks it would be a good idea if he had some, at least if he is intending to drive home. She glances again into Toby's room; there are many more than thirty people there, it seems to her. She makes coffee, humming to herself; she straightens a picture that has gone awry; she peeks into the freezer and is surprised by the orderly array of bags and parcels within, labelled and classified. 'For Xmas dinner,' she reads, '6 helps'. A boy, unfamiliar to her, slinks into the room, takes something from the fridge and slinks out again, with a deprecating smile.

Upstairs, there is further deterioration. The man from Sotheby's talks, but no one listens. Michael, on the sofa, has his arm round one of the girls. Louise, on the floor, talks intently to the psychiatrist. Someone else says something about Dorchester; the psychiatrist's wife looks up suddenly and shouts, 'Dorchester? I know Dorchester – Tony and I first copulated at Dorchester, in the back of a car.'

Ellen thinks, you poor dear, what a time you do have. She pours coffee for the man she feels could do with it; he is effusively grateful, but forgets to drink it.

The neighbours complain again.

At midnight, Ellen gets up and goes quietly from the room. To those who register her departure, she says a polite goodnight.

The light is still on in Paul's room. She goes in. They get to work. The De Havilland Mosquito is almost finished. A quarter of an hour later, it is complete. They contemplate it with pleasure. Almost casually, Paul produces the box containing the Heinkel 447 which he has not yet opened. They look at it; it presents, they agree, an interesting challenge. After a minute or two they open the box. They spread the pieces out and study the instructions. They look at one another: it is half past twelve.

Conspiratorially, Ellen says that if they are going to do it a cup of cocoa might be nice; also, she would like to get into something comfortable.

She goes up to her room and puts on her housecoat and a pair of slippers. On her way down again she is joined by Paul and the two of them pad down the stairs. They pass the sitting-room, from which, now, there is the sound of music (quieter, though, and different in style from the music below). Ellen remembers her glasses, which are on the mantelpiece; she slips in to get them, with a murmur of apology, but in fact no one pays her any attention. The psychiatrist's wife would seem to be weeping; someone else is asleep; there is a kind of heaving on the sofa which Ellen does not stop to investigate.

In the hall, they are passed by Louise, who is saying something sourly about someone being stoned out of their mind. She must be talking to herself, though, for the sight of her mother and younger son does nothing for her, in any sense. She lurches back into the sitting-room.

It is a good deal quieter now, in Toby's room. The door is closed.

Ellen and Paul make a large jug of cocoa, which they load on to a tray, along with mugs, and a plate of cheese and biscuits. They open up the freezer, because Paul fancies there is probably an ice-cream; others appear to have been here first, though – there is a certain dishevelment, and depletion of the bags and parcels. 'For Xmas dinner' has gone, Ellen notices, and so, to Paul's annoyance, has the ice-cream. He stands for a moment in the middle of the kitchen, hitching his dressing-gown (which has lost its cord) around him; he sighs; he says, with a toss of the head that includes both the room next door and the sitting-room above, 'They are all being a bit silly tonight, aren't they?' After a moment he adds, 'I suppose they can't help it.'

Ellen says she doesn't think they can, poor dears. She suggests a mousse that she has found in the fridge as an alternative to ice-cream.

They take the tray upstairs, comfortable with anticipation. There are fifty-three people in the house now. Ellen and Paul alone are in a state of unsullied consciousness.

At ten past two in the morning they are well into the Heinkel, but they have quite run out of glue, as feared. Separately, they scour the house. Paul goes through the drawers of his mother's desk (which involves shifting the man from Sotheby's, who is asleep in front of it, no mean feat for an eleven year old). Louise does not seem to be around, nor yet the psychiatrist; nor, indeed, Michael, or the psychiatrist's wife. Paul draws a blank, so far as the desk is concerned, and turns to the drawers of the sofa table; he ignores the goings-on on the sofa, which do not interest him.

Downstairs, Ellen is systematically searching the kitchen. She comes across a girl, deeply asleep (or something) between the dresser and the sink, and covers her with a rug that she fetches from the cloakroom; the child is inadequately clad as it is. She rummages in drawers, and on the shelves of the dresser, and at last, in triumph, turns up a nearly full tube of something that will certainly do. She sets off up the stairs, and then becomes aware that the gramophone in Toby's room is most irritatingly stuck; no one seems to be doing anything about it. She goes into the darkening room, and gropes her way across, to where in the muted light of a table-lamp, the record is hiccuping away; on the way she stumbles several times on recumbent forms. 'Sorry, dear,' she says. 'Excuse me just a minute . . .' She adjusts the instrument, and goes out again.

She meets Paul on the stairs and they go up together.

At three-thirty a policeman, who has been tipped off by a disgruntled would-be gatecrasher, knocks on the front door. He has reason to believe that there is consumption of . . . But when the door is opened to him by an elderly woman, wearing her dressing-gown and holding, for some reason, the superstructure of a model aeroplane, he loses his nerve, apologises, and says there has probably been a mistake.

As the dawn seeps upwards into the sky, extinguishing the street lights and redefining the London roof-tops, they finish the Heinkel. It has gone almost without a hitch; it is a triumph. They sit back, weary but aglow with satisfaction, and contemplate their craftsmanship. The house is quite quiet now; they must be the only ones still capable of celebration. Paul goes down to the kitchen and fetches a bottle of cider, the sole survivor of the night. He pours them a helping each, in tooth-mugs, and in silence and in mutual appreciation they drink to one another.

Corruption

THE JUDGE and his wife, driving to Aldeburgh for the weekend, carried with them in the back of the car a Wine Society carton filled with pornographic magazines. The judge, closing the hatchback, stared for a moment through the window; he reopened the door and put a copy of *The Times* on top of the pile, extinguishing the garish covers. He then got into the driving seat and picked up the road atlas. 'The usual route, dear?'

'The usual route, I think. Unless we spot anything enticing on the way.'

'We have plenty of time to be enticed, if we feel so inclined.'

The judge, Richard Braine, was sixty-two; his wife Marjorie, a magistrate, was two years younger. The weekend ahead was their annual and cherished early summer break at the Music Festival; the pornographic magazines were the impounded consignment of an importer currently on trial and formed the contents of the judge's weekend briefcase, so to speak. 'Chores?' his wife had said, and he had replied, 'Chores, I'm afraid.'

At lunch-time, they pulled off the main road into a carefully selected lane and found a gate-way in which to park the car. They carried the rug and picnic basket into a nearby field and ate their lunch under the spacious East Anglian sky, in a state of almost flamboyant contentment. Both had noted how the satisfactions of life have a tendency to gain intensity with advancing years. 'The world gets more beautiful,' Marjorie had once said, 'not less so. Fun is even more fun. Music is more musical, if you see what I mean. One hadn't reckoned with that.' Now, consuming the thoughtfully constructed sandwiches and the coffee from the thermos, they glowed at one another amid the long thick grass that teemed with buttercup and clover; before them, the landscape retreated into blue distances satisfactorily broken here and there by a line of trees, the tower of a church or a rising contour. From time to time they exchanged remarks of pleasure or anticipation: about the surroundings, the weather, the meal they would eat tonight at the little restaurant along the coast road, tomorrow evening's concert. Richard Braine, who was a man responsive to the moment, took his wife's hand; they sat in the sun, shirt-sleeved, and agreed conspiratorially and without too much guilt that they were quite glad that the eldest married daughter who sometimes accompanied them on this trip had not this year been able to. The daughter was loved, but would just now have been superfluous.

When they arrived at the small hotel it was early evening. The judge carried their suitcase and the Wine Society carton in and set them down by the reception desk. The proprietor, bearing the carton, showed them to their usual room. As she was unpacking, Marjorie said, 'I think you should have left that stuff in the car. Chambermaids, you know . . .' The judge frowned. 'That's a point.' He tipped the contents of the box into the emptied suitcase and locked it. 'I think I'll have a bath before we go out.'

He lay in the steamy cubicle, a sponge resting upon his stomach. Marjorie, stripped to a pair of pants, came in to wash. 'The dear old avocado suite again. One day we must have an avocado bathroom suite at home.' The judge, contemplating the rise of his belly, nodded; he was making a resolution about reduction of the flesh, a resolution which he sadly knew would be broken. He was a man who enjoyed food. His wife's flesh, in the process now of being briskly soaped and scrubbed, was firmer and less copious, as he was fully prepared to concede. He turned his head to watch her and thought for a while in a vague and melancholy way about bodies, about how we inhabit them and are dragged to the grave by them and are conditioned by them. In the course of his professional life he had frequently had occasion to reflect upon the last point: it had seemed to him, observing the faces that passed before him in courtrooms, that confronted him from docks and witness boxes, that not many of us are able to rise above physical appearance. The life of an ugly woman is different from that of a beautiful one; you cannot infer character from appearance, but you can suspect a good deal about the circumstances to which it will have given rise. Abandoning this interesting but sombre theme, he observed his wife's breasts and muscular but not unshapely thighs and the folds of skin upon her neck and remembered the first time he had seen her with no clothes on. She turned to look at him; 'If you're jeering at my knickers, they're a pair of Alison's I grabbed out of the laundry basket by mistake.' Alison was their youngest, unmarried daughter. 'I hadn't really noticed them,' said the judge politely. 'I was thinking about something quite different.' He smiled. 'And don't leer,' said his wife, flicking him with her flannel. 'It's unbecoming in a man of your age.' 'It's a tribute to your charms, my dear,' said the judge. He sat up and began to wash his neck, thinking still about the first time; they had both been embarrassed. Embarrassment had been a part of the pleasure, he reflected. How odd, and interesting.

It was still daylight when they drove to the restaurant, a violet summer twilight in which birds sang with jungle stridency. Marjorie, getting out of the car, said, 'That veal and mushroom in cream sauce thing for me, I think. A small salad for you, without dressing.'

'No way,' said the judge.

'I admire your command of contemporary speech.' She went ahead into the restaurant, inspecting the room with bright, observant eyes. When they were sitting at the table she whispered, 'There's that same woman we met last year. Remember? The classy type who kept putting you right about Britten.'

The judge, cautiously, turned his head. 'So it is. Keep a low profile.'

'Will do, squire,' said Marjorie applying herself to the menu. 'Fifteen all?' she added. 'Right?'

'Right,' said her husband.

Their acquaintance, leaving before them, stopped to exchange greetings. The judge, mildly resenting the interruption to his meal, left the work to Marjorie. The woman, turning to go, said, 'So nice to see you again. And have a lovely break from juries and things.' She gleamed upon the judge.

He watched her retreating silk-clad back. 'Rather a gushing creature. How the hell does she know what I do?'

'Chatting up the hotel people, I don't doubt. It gives you cachet, you note, your job. Me, on the other hand, she considers a drab little woman. I could see her wondering how I came by you.'

'Shall we enlighten her? Sheer unbridled lust . . .'

'Talking of which,' said Marjorie. 'Just how unprincipled would it be to finish off with some of that cheese-cake?'

Back at the hotel, they climbed into bed in a state of enjoyable repletion. The judge put on his spectacles and reached out for the suitcase. 'You're not going to start going through that stuff *now* . . .' said Marjorie. 'At least have one whole day off work.'

'You're right,' he said. 'Tomorrow will do. I'll have that Barbara Pym novel instead.'

The judge, waking early the next morning, lay thinking about the current trial. He thought, in fact, not about obscenity or pornography but about the profit motive. He did not, he realised, understand the profit motive; he did not understand it in the same way in which he did not understand what induced people to be cruel. He had never coveted the possessions of others or wished himself richer than he was. He held no stocks or shares; Marjorie, once, had been left a small capital sum by an aunt; neither he nor she had ever been able to take the slightest interest in the financial health of her investments. Indeed, both had now forgotten what exactly the money was in. All this, he realised, was the position of a man with a substantial earned income; were he not paid what he was he might well feel otherwise. But he had not, in fact, felt very much otherwise as an impecunicus young barrister. And importers of pornography tend, he understood, to be in an upper income bracket. No – the obstacle, the barrier requiring that leap of the imagination, was this extra dimension of need in some men that sought to turn money into yet more money, that required wealth for wealth's sake, the spawning of figures. The judge himself enjoyed growing vegetables; he considered, now, the satisfaction he got from harvesting a good crop of french beans and tried to translate this into a manifestation of the profit motive. The analogy did not quite seem to work.

The profit motive in itself, of course, is innocuous enough. Indeed, without it societies would founder. This was not the point that was bothering the judge; he was interested in those gulfs of inclination that divide person from person. As a young man he had wondered if this restriction makes us incapable of passing judgement on our fellows, but had come to realise at last that it does not. He remembered being involved in an impassioned argument about apartheid with another law student, an Afrikaner; 'You cannot make pronouncements on our policies,' the man had said, 'when you have never been to our country. You cannot understand the situation.' Richard Braine had known, with the accuracy of a physical response, that the man was wrong. Not misguided; simply wrong. A murderer is doing wrong, whatever the circumstances that drive him to his crime.

The profit motive is not wrong; the circumstances of its application may well be. The judge – with a certain irritation – found himself recalling the features of the importer of pornography: a nondescript, bespectacled man memorable only for a pair of rather bushy eyebrows and a habit of pulling an ear-lobe when under cross-examination. He pushed the fellow from his mind, determinedly, and got out of bed. Outside the window, strands of neatly corrugated cloud coasted in a milky-blue sky; it looked as though it would be a nice day.

The Braines spent the morning at Minsmere bird sanctuary; in the afternoon they went for a walk. The evening found them, scoured by fresh air and slightly somnolent, listening to Mozart, Bartok and Mendelssohn. The judge, who had never played an instrument and regarded himself as relatively unmusical, nevertheless responded to music with considerable intensity. It aroused him in various ways; in such different ways, indeed, that, being a thorough and methodical man, he often felt bemused, caught up by the onward rush of events before he had time to sort them out. Stop, he wanted to say to the surging orchestra, just let me have a think about that bit . . . But already he would have been swept onwards, into other moods, other themes, other passions. Marjorie, who played the piano in an unspectacular but competent way, had often suggested that the problem might be solved at least in part if he learned to read music.

She was no doubt right, he thought, wrestling now with a tortuous passage. When I retire; just the thing for a man reduced to inactivity. The judge did not look forward to retirement. But a few moments of inattention had been fatal – now the music had got away from him entirely, as though he had turned over two pages of a book. Frowning, he concentrated on the conductor.

Standing at the bar in the interval, he found himself beside their acquaintance from the restaurant, also waiting to order a drink. Gallantry or even basic good manners required that he intervene. 'Oh,' she said. 'How terribly sweet of you. A gin and tonic would be gorgeous.' With resignation, he led her back to where Marjorie awaited him.

'Your husband was so sweet and insistent – I'm all on my own this evening, my sister had a splitting headache and decided not to come.' She was a tall woman in her early fifties, too youthfully packaged in a flounced skirt and high-heeled boots, her manner towards the judge both sycophantic and faintly roguish. 'I was reading about you in *The Times* last month, some case about people had up for embezzling, of course I didn't understand most of it, all terribly technical, but I said to Laura, I *know* him, we had such a lovely talk about Britten at the Festival.'

'Ah,' said the judge, studying his programme: the Tippett next.

'I'm Moira Lukes, by the way – if you're anything like me names just *evaporate*, but of course I remembered yours from seeing it in the paper.' She turned to Marjorie. 'Aren't you loving the concert?'; patronage discreetly flowed, the patronage of a woman with a sexual history towards one who probably had none, of a lavishly clad woman towards a dowdy one. The judge's antennae slightly quivered, though he was not himself sure why. Marjorie blandly agreed that the concert was superb. 'Excuse me,' she said. 'I'm going to make a dash to the loo while there's time.'

The judge and Moira Lukes, left alone, made private adjustments to each other's company: the judge cleared his throat and commented on the architecture of the concert hall; Moira moved a fraction closer to him and altered the pitch of her voice, probably without being aware that she did either. 'You must lead such a fascinating life,' she said. 'I mean, you must come across such extraordinary people. Dickensian types. I don't think I've ever set eyes on a criminal.'

The judge thought again of the importer of pornography. 'Most of them are rather mundane, when it comes to the point.'

'But you must get to know so much about people.' She was looking very directly at him, with large eyes; a handsome woman, the judge conceded, rather a knock-out as a girl, no doubt. He agreed that yes, one did get a few insights into the ways in which people carry on.

'Fascinating,' said Moira Lukes again. 'I expect you have the most marvellous stories to tell. I envy your wife no end.' The large eyes creased humorously at the corners; a practised device, though the judge did not recognise this. 'In fact I think she's a lucky woman – I still remember that interesting chat you and I had last year.' And she laid on his arm a hand, which was almost instantly removed – come and gone as briefly as though a bird had alighted for a fleeting second. The judge, startled in several ways, tried to recall this chat: something about when *Peter Grimes* was first performed, or was it *The Turn of the Screw?* The interest of it, now, escaped him. He cast a quick glance across the foyer in search of Marjorie, who seemed to be taking an awfully long time. Moira Lukes was talking now about the area of Sussex in which she lived. Do, she was saying, look in and have lunch, both of you, if you're ever in that part of the world. The judge murmured that yes, of course if ever they were . . . He noticed the rings on her hand and wondered vaguely what had become of Mr Lukes; somehow one knew that he was no longer around, one way or the other.

'The only time,' she said, 'I've ever personally had anything to do with the law was over my rather wretched divorce.' The judge took a swig of his drink. 'And then actually the lawyer was most awfully sweet, in fact he kept my head above water through it all.' She sighed, a whiff of a sigh, almost imperceptible; thereby, she implied most delicately, hung a tale. 'So I've got rather a soft spot for legal people.'

'Good,' said the judge heartily. 'I'm glad to hear you've been well treated by the profession.'

'Oh, *very* well treated.'

No sign of Marjorie, still. Actually, the judge was thinking, this Moira Whatshername wasn't perhaps quite so bad after all, behind that rather tiresome manner; appearances, inevitably, deceive. One got the impression, too, of someone who'd maybe had a bit of a rough time. 'Well, it's a world that includes all sorts, like most. And it brings you up against life, I suppose, with all that that implies.'

The respect with which these banalities were received made him feel a little cheap. In compensation, he told her an anecdote about a case in which he had once been involved; a *crime passionnel* involving an apparently wronged husband who had turned out in fact to be the villain of the piece. 'A mealy-mouthed fellow, and as plausible as you like, but apparently he'd been systematically persecuting her for years.' Moira Lukes nodded sagely. 'People absolutely are not what they seem to be.'

'Well,' said the judge. 'Yes and no. On the other hand, plenty of people give themselves away as soon as they open their mouths.'

'Oh, goodness,' said Moira Lukes. 'Now I'll feel I daren't utter a word ever again.'

'I had in mind those I come across professionally rather than in private life.'

'Ah, then you think I'm safe?'

'Now, whatever could you have to conceal?' said the judge amiably. A bell went. 'I wonder where Marjorie's got to. I suppose we'd better start going back in.'

Moira Lukes sighed. She turned those large eyes upon him and creased them once again at the corners. 'Well, this has been so nice. I'm sure we'll run into each other again over the weekend. But do bear in mind that I'm in the East Sussex phone book. I remember that case I read about was in Brighton – if you're ever judging there again and want a few hours' retreat on your own, do pop over and have a drink.' She smiled once more, and walked quickly away into the crowd.

The judge stood for a moment, looking after her. He realised with surprise that he had been on the receiving end of what is generally known as a pass. He realised also that he was finding it difficult to sort out exactly what he felt about this; a rational response and his natural judgement of people (he didn't in fact all that much care for the woman) fought with more reprehensible feelings and a certain complacency (so one wasn't a total old buffer just yet). In this state of internal conflict he made his way back into the concert hall, where he found Marjorie already in her seat.

'What on earth happened to you?'

'Sorry,' she said cheerfully. 'There was an awful queue in the ladies' and by the time I got out it wasn't worth coming to find you. How did you make out with our friend?'

The judge grunted, and applied himself to the programme. The lights went down, the conductor reappeared, the audience sank into silence . . . But the music, somehow, had lost its compulsion; he was aware now of too much that was external – that he could achieve no satisfactory position for his legs, that he had slight indigestion, that the chap in front of him kept moving his head. Beside him, he could see Marjorie's face, rapt. The evening, somehow, had been corrupted.

The next morning was even more seraphic than the one before. 'Today,' said Marjorie, 'we are going to sit on the beach and bask. We may even venture into the sea.'

'That sounds a nice idea.' The judge had thought during the night of the little episode with that woman and, in the process, a normal balance of mind had returned; he felt irritated – though more with himself than with her – that it had interfered with his enjoyment of the concert. It was with some annoyance, therefore, that he spotted her now across the hotel dining-room, with the sister, lifting her hand in a little finger-waggling wave of greeting.

'What's the matter?' said Marjorie, with marital insight. 'Oh . . . Her. Well, I'll leave you to hide behind the paper. I'm going upstairs to get sorted out for the beach.'

He was half-way through the Home News page when he felt her standing over him. Alone. The sister, evidently, had been disposed of.

'Another heavenly day. Aren't we lucky! All on your own? I saw your wife bustling off . . .' She continued to stand, her glance drifting now towards the coffee pot at the judge's elbow.

I am supposed, he thought, to say sit down and join me – have a cup of coffee. And he felt again that quiver of the antennae and knew now the reason. Marjorie does indeed bustle, her walk is rather inelegant, but it is not for you to say so, or to subtly denigrate a person I happen to love. He rattled, slightly, his newspaper. 'We're off to the beach shortly.'

'Oh, lovely. I daresay we'll go down there later. I wonder . . . Goodness, I don't know if I ought to ask you this or not . . .' She hesitated, prettily, seized, it seemed, with sudden diffidence. 'Oh, I'll be brave. The thing is, I have this tiresome problem about a flat in London I'm buying, something to do with the leasehold that I simply do not follow, and I just do not have absolute faith in the man who's dealing with it for me – the solicitor, you know – could I pick your brains about it at some point?'

The judge, impassive, gazed up at her.

'I don't mean now – not in the middle of your holiday weekend. My sister was noticing your address in the hotel register and believe it or not my present flat is only a few minutes away. What would be lovely would be if you could spare an hour or so to look in for a drink on your way home one evening – and your wife too of course, only it might be awfully boring for her if you're going to brief me. Is that the right word? Would it be an imposition? When you're on your own like I am you are so very much at the mercy of . . .' she sighed – 'people, the system, I don't know what . . . Sometimes I get quite panic-stricken.'

I doubt that, thought the judge. He put the newspaper down. 'Mrs Lukes . . .'

'Oh, Moira . . . please.'

He cleared his throat. 'Conveyancing, as it happens, is not my field. Anything I said might quite possibly be misleading. The only sensible advice I can give is to change your solicitor if you feel lack of confidence in him.'

Her eyes flickered; that look of honest appeal dimmed suddenly. 'Oh . . . I see. Well, I daresay you're right. I must do that, then. I shouldn't have asked. But of course the invitation stands, whenever you're free.'

'How kind,' said the judge coolly. He picked up his paper again and looked at her over the top of it; their eyes met in understanding. And he flinched a little at her expression; it was the look of hatred he had seen from time to time, over the years, across a courtroom, on the face in the dock.

'Have a lovely day,' said Moira Lukes. Composure had returned; she gleamed, and wrinkled her eyes, and was gone. Well, thought the judge, there's no love lost there, now. But it had to be done, once and for all. He folded the paper and went in search of Marjorie.

She was packing a beach-bag with costumes and towels. The judge, unlocking the suitcase, took out a stack of the pornographic magazines and pushed them into the bottom of the bag. 'Oh, lor,' said Marjorie, 'I'd forgotten about them. Must you?'

' 'Fraid so. The case resumes tomorrow. It's the usual business of going through them for degrees of obscenity. There are some books too.'

'I'll help you,' said Marjorie. 'There – greater love hath no woman . . .'

The beach was agreeably uncrowded. Family parties were dotted in clumps about the sand; children and dogs skittered in and out of the surf; gulls floated above the water and a party of small wading birds scurried back and forth before the advancing waves like blown leaves. The judge, who enjoyed a bit of unstrenuous bird-watching, sat observing them with affection. The weather, this particularly delectable manifestation of the physical world and the uncomplicated relish of the people and animals around him had induced a state of general benignity. Marjorie, organising the rug and wind-screen, said, 'All right?' 'All right,' he replied. They smiled at each other, appreciating the understatement.

Marjorie, after a while, resolutely swam. The judge, more craven, followed her to the water's edge and observed. As they walked back up the beach together he saw suddenly that Moira Lukes and her sister were encamped not far off. She glanced at him and then immediately away. Now, at midday, the beach was becoming more occupied, though not disturbingly so. A family had established itself close to the Braines' pitch: young parents with a baby in a pram and a couple of older children now deeply engaged in the initial stages of sandcastle construction. The judge, who had also made a sandcastle or two in his time, felt an absurd urge to lend a hand; the basic design, he could see, was awry and would give trouble before long. The mother, a fresh-faced young woman, came padding across the sand to ask Marjorie for the loan of a tin-opener. They chatted for a moment; the young woman carried the baby on her hip. 'That sort of thing,' said Marjorie, sitting down again, 'can still make me broody, even at my time of life.' She too watched the sandcastle-building; presently she rummaged in the picnic basket and withdrew a plastic beaker. 'Turrets,' she explained to the judge, a little guiltily. 'You can never do a good job with a bucket . . .' The children received her offering with rewarding glee; the parents gratefully smiling; the sandcastle rose, more stylish.

The judge sighed, and delved in the beach-bag. 'To work, I suppose,' he said. Around them, the life of the beach had settled into a frieze, as though the day were eternal: little sprawled groups of people, the great arc of the horizon against which stood the grey shapes of two far-away ships, like cut-outs, the surface animation of running dogs and children and someone's straw hat, tossed hither and thither by the breeze that had sprung up.

The judge and his wife sat with a pile of magazines each. Marjorie said, 'This is a pretty gruesome collection. Can I borrow your hankie, my glasses keep getting salted over.'

The judge turned over pages, and occasionally made some notes. Nothing he saw surprised him; from time to time he found himself examining the faces that belonged to the bodies displayed, as though in search of explanations. But they seemed much like any other faces; so presumably were the bodies.

Marjorie said, 'Cup of tea? Tell me, why are words capable of so much greater obscenity than pictures?' She was glancing through a book, or something that passed as such.

'That, I imagine, is why people have always gone in for burning them, though usually for quite other reasons.'

It was as the judge was reaching out to take the mug of tea from her that the wind came. It came in a great wholesome gust, flinging itself along the beach with a cloud of blown sand and flying plastic bags. It sent newspapers into the air like great flapping birds and spun a spotted football along the water's edge as though it were a top. It lifted rugs and pushed over deckchairs. It snatched the magazines from the judge's lap and from Marjorie's and bore them away across the sand in a helter-skelter whirl of colourful pages, dropping them down only to grab them again and fling them here and there: at the feet of a stout lady snoozing in a deckchair, into the pram of the neighbouring family's baby, on to people's towels and Sunday papers.

Marjorie said, 'Oh, lor . . .'

They got up. They began, separately, to tour the beach in pursuit of what the wind had taken. The judge found himself, absurdly, feeling foolish because he had left his jacket on his chair and was plodding along the sand in shirt-sleeves (no tie, either) and tweed trousers. The lady in the deckchair woke and put out a hand to quell the magazine that was wrapping itself around her leg. 'Yours?' she said amiably, looking up at the judge, and as she handed him the thing it fell open and for a moment her eyes rested on the central spread, the *pièce de resistance*; her expression changed, rubbed out as it were by amazement, and she looked again at the judge for an instant, and became busy with the knitting on her lap.

Marjorie, stumping methodically along, picked up one magazine and then another, tucking them under her arm. She turned and saw that the children had observed the crisis, abandoned their sandcastle and were scurrying here and there, collecting as though involved in a treasure hunt. The mother, too, had risen and was shaking the sand from a magazine that had come to rest against the wheels of the pram. As Marjorie reached her the little girl ran up with an armful. 'Good girl, Sharon,' said the mother, and the child – six, perhaps, or seven – virtuously beamed and held out to Marjorie the opened pages of the magazine she held. She looked at it and the mother looked at it and Marjorie looked and the child said, 'Are those flowers?' 'No, my dear,' said Marjorie sadly. 'They aren't flowers,' and she turned away before she could meet the eyes of the young mother.

The judge collected a couple from a man who handed them over with a wink, and another from a boy who stared at him expressionless, and then he could not find any more. He walked back to their pitch. Marjorie was shoving things into the beach-bag. 'Shall we go?' she said, and the judge nodded.

It was as they were folding the rug that Moira Lukes came up. She wore neatly creased cotton trousers and walked with a spring. 'Yours, apparently,' she said; she held the magazine out between a finger and thumb, as though with tongs, and dropped it on to the sand. She looked straight at the judge. 'How awfully true,' she said, 'that people are not what they seem to be.' Satisfaction flowed from her; she glanced for an instant at Marjorie, as though checking that she had heard, and walked away.

The Braines, in silence, completed the assembly of their possessions. Marjorie carried the rug and the picnic basket and the judge bore the beach-bag and the wind-screen. They trudged the long expanse of the beach, watched, now, with furtive interest by various eyes.

Venice, Now and Then

'VENICE!' SHE said, getting up, crossing the room. 'Of course! The Doge's Palace and the Campanile. It's nice. Where did you get it?'

'I saw it in a junk shop.'

London traffic rumbled beyond the window. 'Yes,' she went on. 'Doesn't it take you back! We went over to that church once, the picture must have been done from that side. San – San . . .'

'Santa Maria della Salute.'

'That's it.' She stabbed a finger on the glass. 'That's where I bought the fluorescent necklace. There – under that arch.'

He peered, as though the past should be made manifest. 'Really? I thought it was in the square. How things get distorted. What I remember is the heat at night. Like being in warm soup.'

There are long quivering ribbons of light on the water. A tanker passes, huge black bulk eclipsing churches and palaces, bigger than any of this, sending ridge after ridge of waves to slosh against the quay, against the tethered boats. To and fro the people go, hundreds of them, to and fro, walking and talking, us with them: Liz and I and Belinda and Alan. Here today, gone tomorrow – well, next week. Has everyone in the world passed this way, at some time or another? A place is a receptacle; perhaps only places exist, not people.

I should like to eat. I catch the others up. Liz is buying something from a man with a tray of postcards, scarves, ties. Alan holds Belinda's hand. Liz says, 'Look, I couldn't resist it! Fix it for me, James.'

They curl round people's necks like glow-worms. I say, 'I must have one!' Alan and Belinda watch, smiling; Alan wears a blue shirt, his hair is crimped by sea and salt. James fastens the necklace, he fastens it to the hairs at the back of my neck and I complain. 'Il faut souffrir,' says Alan, 'pour être belle.' We sit down at a pavement restaurant, laughing. There are live fish in a tank, and shafts of light furry with insects.

'How much?' she said. 'Twenty-five – that's not bad, I suppose, for nowadays. Actually I'd have hung it over the desk. If I was consulted. By the way you haven't said what you think of the new hair-do.' She turned her head from side to side, displaying.

'There's less of it,' he observed at last, cautiously.

'Of course there's less of it, you nit, that's the idea.'

'Where was it,' he said, 'that those Carpaccios were?'

'O Carpaccios, where art thou?' sings Belinda. 'Wherever art thee – thou – they?' She leans over a parapet. 'Two plastic bottles, seventeen lettuce leaves, something horrible I don't want to know about, someone's T-shirt, yesterday's paper . . .'

James stands with the map in his hand, scowling. He turns the map this way and that; he aligns map and street; he squints to right and left; he tries to marry print and the real world. We hang about.

'Perhaps,' suggests Alan, 'we should give them a miss. We're back where we were ten minutes ago, I rather think, James.'

And James fusses that no, no, we can't possibly miss them, they are one of the things, the book says, and just a sec he's got it now, if we go up there and then right . . .

We follow him. 'Carpaccio, Carpaccio,' sings Belinda. 'Wherefore art thou, Carpaccio?'

We wander through a trompe-l'œil *landscape in which streets run slap into buildings and canals, in which people vanish into walls, in which a square has no visible exit. We pick our way from here to there, from there to here. I shunt my dark glasses off and on, on and off; we plunge from heat to cool murky interiors. We stand in attentive observation; we switch back over bridges. I shell out money into the hands of a grumpy custodian; we file into the hot dim room. Outside, men are drilling the street. The man closes the door and the noise is quenched. 'Aren't they small?' says Liz. 'I imagined enormous, somehow.'*

'Oh, goodness,' she said. 'San something or other. Do I get a drink, James dear, I'm whacked.'

He stood beside her, fiddling with bottles. 'Do you ever, in fact, see anything of Alan?'

'I work in the same organisation as Alan. Now, as then. Of course I see Alan. From time to time. Alan has got a bit stout. Alan has moved to Fulham.'

'I just wondered.'

'Actually,' she said, 'I like Alan, still. Ah well.'

Alan, who has nice manners, hands me into the boat. He holds my elbow, steadying. He says, 'Here, give me the bag. O.K.?' We have been dropped out of the sky into an apricot evening. The sky is apricot and the amazing horizon and the quivering molten air. Belinda says, 'Oh dear, I should have been to the ladies' at the airport, I wonder how long it takes?' Alan sits beside her. 'Control yourself, my girl,' he says, and he smiles across at me. 'Well, far cry from Whitehall now, eh?' I look round for James, but James has gone to sit at the end, the prow, the whatever it is. He stares all round; he is trying to get his bearings; James likes to know where he is, always.

We dash through a world that is manifestly circular, leaving a carven white wake; we fly across this disc of water rimmed with land, an indeterminate ring of substance that resolves itself here and there into a scribble of cranes and chimneys, a sequence of domes and towers. Pewter clouds lie all around the horizon, with bellies of lemon and gold and silver. Liz shouts into the throbbing air; I cannot hear a word. I lean forward. She bawls, 'Isn't it fun! I'm so glad we didn't take the bus.' I nod.

'Hmn . . .' he said, 'I don't know about time clarifying things. What it does do is add something.'

'Years?' she suggested. 'Grey hairs?'

'I can't see any. Or did they cut them all off?'

'Beast. Belinda, now, is just the same.'

'I can't,' he said, 'remember Belinda any more. Belinda then. Odd, that.'

'Oh, I can. That bag she was always leaving behind in cafés. Some special sunburn stuff. Graham Greene.'

Belinda is reading Brighton Rock. *'It's ages since I read that,' I say. 'He dies in the end, doesn't he? The boy. Pinky. He has this bottle of acid and . . .'*

'You wretch!' cries Belinda. 'Now you've told me what happens. Now you've spoilt it.' 'Not spoilt it,' corrects Alan. 'You can still enjoy it, it's the same book.' 'No it isn't,' says Belinda. 'I know how it ends now. Everything is changed when you know what's coming.' 'Sorry,' I say. 'Tiresome girl,' complains Belinda. She puts her glasses back on; she reads.

I pick my way past tables to where Belinda sits, reading. She looks up. 'Oh,' she says. 'James. Alan's just checking on those ferry times. Wretched Liz has told me how my book ends so she's gone to buy the Sunday papers, as a penance. Tea or coffee?' And she gazes at me, eyes screwed up against the brightness in a face I can no longer see, because it no longer exists, the face of Belinda then, the face of Alan's wife Belinda. I sit opposite her on an uncomfortable metal chair with patterned seat; I can feel metal and absence of metal through the cotton of my trousers; I sit there wondering how it is possible to feel a pattern. Belinda talks about a film at the Notting Hill Classic.

'It could do,' she said, 'with a nicer frame.'

'Ah. Possibly.'

'And a bit of a clean-up. Shall I do the glass? Or would that be considered forward?'

He reflected. 'I should wait, maybe.'

'Scuola di something. Where the Carpaccios were. Scuola di . . . di . . .'

The ceiling is all red and gold. My sandal hurts where the strap has rubbed. There is this fearful drilling noise and then snap! it is cut off, turned down to a mumble, and instead there is a voice in German, level, instructive, impassive. We move, James and Belinda and Alan and I, around the room keeping as far as we can from the guided German party, superior in our unconducted independence. We are absorbed; we forget, perhaps, about each other.

I look up and see James stand beside Belinda. I can see them still: my tall stooping brother James and Belinda in a flowered cotton skirt and a pink top, people who do not know each other very well, staring at a painting.

I stand beside Belinda, who is the friend of my sister, whose husband Alan is also the friend of my sister, and I look at the picture. I can see it now; the man's face turned to the light, the little white dog, the book fallen to the floor. Belinda says, 'St Augustine in his study.' And then, 'The dog is just like our neighbour's dog.' I smile politely at Belinda; I look down at her: I see a pleasant woman, plumpish. As though through a glass, darkly.

'I can't stay long, but I'll have a top up if you're pressing me. Is it for something special – the picture?'

'Something special?'

'Birthday?'

'Oh no.' He looked again at it, in surprise, as though it were unexpectedly there. 'Nothing special, no. Just that it caught my eye. You know . . . Struck one as pleasant. Familiar. Did I pay too much?'

'Familiar? Well, yes, I suppose. Familiar, I mean – not paying too much. And yet you know I could have sworn *that* was *there.*' She tapped, again, the glass. 'Remember the thunderstorm?'

Lightning flares. Wild, operatic lightning. The buildings are projected against sculptural cloudshapes from which surely must ride forth Valkyrie or seraphim or a trio singing Mozart. It is quite unreal, as unreal as the cathedral, the palace, the campanile, all of which must have been erected yesterday in mockery of what is claimed. All is a stage-set, as are the people extras, a great Hollywood army of extras that ebbs and flows around the square, up and down, to and fro, this way and that. Should one applaud? Or is the climax yet to come?

James suddenly claps his hands. He stands there in shirt-sleeves clapping his hands. 'Your brother,' says Alan, 'is determined to be the original eccentric Englishman.' He smiles, benignly; he is older than we are, sometimes there creeps in a licensed avuncular note. And now there is fork lightning against sheet lightning, a stunning effect, a metallic sizzle against the great white flare, and far away the landscape growls, off-stage. 'It isn't,' says Alan, 'happening here at all. Over the Dolomites, I reckon. Miles away.' And Belinda is uneasy; it's going to pour, she claims, any minute now, it's going to come chucking down and anyway lightning always makes me queasy, suppose it hit one of those pinnacles, we'd all be . . . She scuttles round us, like a sheepdog, chivvying. She chivvies James, who stands now with arms folded, intently appreciative, and James gives one last clap or two and smiles, amiable, detached, and we all move away, back to the hotel.

'Things,' he said, 'are so inconstant. That's the trouble.'

'Buildings don't move. If it isn't where I think it was then it isn't. Places stay the same.'

'True,' he agreed. 'It's nice there's something to rely on.'

'Where are the children? There's the most unearthly hush.'

He stared at her over the rim of the glass. 'Let me see now . . . I was told. Out. Out at . . . a music lesson?'

'I do envy you,' she said, 'that capacity for insulation.'

'It's been put to the test these last few years, I must admit.'

'They are perfectly delightful, as children go.'

'So I'm told.'

'How odd it is,' she said, 'to think that then, in Venice, they simply didn't exist.'

'Inconceivable,' he said, 'or unconceived?'

'Both. If anyone had suggested then . . .'

'Oh, quite. Astonishment would have laid us flat. It would have spoiled,' he went on, 'a rather nice little holiday.'

Beneath the gleaming ceilings shuffles the crowd, necks askance, speaking with tongues. A river of people, self-perpetuating, surely, there cannot be so many different people passing this way. In at one end, out at the other, drifting through. I find a point where I can sit before a tumultuous canvas; the painted people too are legion, saints and Christs and Marys and those who weep and those who watch. I consult the book. I look up again and Liz is there, plumping herself down beside me. 'Do you like them?' she says, and I consider the great spread before me, the great complex glittering spread. 'Not that, silly,' she says. 'Them. Alan and Belinda.' I reply that it is too hot for judgements and in any case I am hungry.

'Your brother,' says Belinda, 'is terribly earnest about looking at things. Not,' she adds hastily, 'that he isn't sweet. He puts us all to shame. Dare we, do you think, move him on?' And we look across the room at James, screened from us by people, an ebb and flow of bodies through which we glimpse James sitting with his book, his now battered book, relating this to that and that to this. I go and sit by James and James tells me about annunciations and crucifixions and resurrections

'Spoiled? It might have made it more interesting. It would have added a certain something, you must admit.'

'Spoiled,' he said firmly.

'There's the front door.'

He took a third glass. 'Let's hope I shan't be thought to have been extravagant.'

'Oh – the picture. Of course not. She'll love it, I should think. Scuolo di San Giorgio – there, I've got it! Now I'm happy. It's maddening when you can't remember something right.'

'Was it?' he said. 'I daresay. I'm never good on names. There was a dragon, wasn't there, and St Jerome with his lion.'

A most humane lion. And fleeing affronted figures and greens and reds overlaid with a hazy gold, the sunshine of another century, it seems to be. I stand in a pleasant trance of observation, thinking of nothing, a pair of eyes, no more. I feel space occupied beside me; I glance; Belinda is sharing St Augustine – his window, his dog, his fallen book.

We are linked by the permanence of the painting, standing for ever in a hot dim room; the painting is still there, in the mind's eye, but Belinda has gone, Belinda then, rubbed out by what has come since, Belinda cannot be retrieved.

Well, I think, it's as well we did find it, James was right, or James's blessed book, they aren't to be missed. And I wander round the room, homing on this one and then that. I sit down on a bench and try to do something about my sandal strap, about my foot with its red itching groove. I stuff a tissue in and go back to the dragon painting. I look round for the others and see Alan buying postcards, waiting patiently in a cluster of people, his hands in his pockets.

Belinda is standing beside James at the other side of the room. James stoops a little to hear what she says; she tilts her head up at him. I can see them still, but they are overlaid with the wisdoms of now; James looks down at Belinda, he smiles, he smiles at his wife.

Grow Old Along With Me,
the Best Is Yet To Be

'Oh, I DON'T know . . .' said Sarah. 'Decisions, decisions. I hate them. I mean, one of the things that bothers me is – would I stop being *me*? Would I change. If we did.'

She wore dungarees in pale turquoise, and a white T-shirt. She drove the Fiat hunched forward over the steering wheel. Her face was engulfed by large reflecting sun-glasses across which flew hedges, trees, a passing car. 'It's rather gorgeous round here, isn't it? Half-asleep, as though nothing happens in a hundred years.'

Tony said, 'We both might. It's a significant step in a relationship – that's the point of it, I suppose.'

'And the point of waiting. Thinking about it. Not rushing.'

'Not that we have.'

'Quite. Shall we stop and eat soon?'

'Yes – when there's a reasonable pub.'

Gloucestershire unreeled at either side: dark green, straw-coloured, unpopulated. Trees drooped in the fields; a village was still and silent except for a lorry throbbing outside a shop. High summer gripped the landscape; birds twitched from hedge to hedge.

'Half the time,' said Sarah, 'it doesn't crop up. One sort of puts it out of one's mind – there are too many other things to think of. And then it begins to nag. We've got to either do it or not do it.'

'We've been not doing it for three years, darling.'

'I know, I know. But all the same, it looms.'

'We are actually,' he said, 'better off, from a tax point of view, unmarried. Since your rise. We went into that in the winter – remember?'

'What about this – Free House, Bar Snacks. How much better off, exactly?'

'Oh, Lord, I don't know. Hundreds, anyway.'

She turned the car into the pub yard. 'It's a point, then. Ma keeps saying, what happens if there's a baby? And I say well that would of course put a different complexion on things but *until* we are absolutely free to choose. The trouble is that dear ma thinks I'm on the shelf at twenty-six. I keep saying, there aren't shelves now.'

The woman behind the bar watched them come in, a good-looking young couple, in the pink of health, not short of money, the kind of people who know their way around. She served them lagers and chicken salad, and noted Sarah's neat figure, not an ounce in the wrong place, which induced vague discontent. I'm dieting, she thought, as from Monday I am, I swear to God. She observed also Tony's tanned forearms, below the rolled sleeves of an indefinably modish shirt, like blokes in colour supp. ads. Thirtyish, nice voice. He didn't look at her, pocketing the change, turning away with the plates. She watched them settle in the corner by the window, sitting close, talking. In love, presumably, lucky so-and-so's.

'Tax is certainly a point,' said Sarah. 'Getting dependent on each other is another. Look at Tom and Alison. But one still feels that eventually we're going to have to make some kind of decision. You can have my pickled onion.'

'Lots of people don't. Decide. I mean. Look at Blake and Susan.'

'I don't want to look at Blake and Susan. Blake's forty-two, did you know that? And anyway he's *been* married. Oh, isn't it all difficult? We decided no baby, barring accidents, at least not yet, and that was one decision. Thank God for the pill, I suppose. I mean, imagine when they just *happened*.'

'They still do sometimes. Look at Maggie.'

'Oh, Maggie meant to, for goodness sake. That baby was no accident. It was psychological.'

They ate, for a while, in silence. At the bar middle-aged men, locals, sporadically conversed, out of kilter like clocks ticking at different speeds. The woman wiped glasses. A commercial traveller came in and ordered steak and kidney with chips. On the wall, hand-written posters advertised a Bring and Buy, a Darby and Joan Outing. Tony stacked their empty plates. 'Not exactly the hub of the universe, this.'

'It's rather sweet. Laurie Lee country. I used to adore that book – what's-it-called? – we did it for O-levels. Sex in the hedges and all that. O.K. – I'll find the loo and we'll get moving. Where are we, by the way, I've lost track?'

When she came back he had the map book open on his knee. 'Let's have a look, there might be something to go and see. Oh, goodness, there is – we're not far from Deerhurst. Oh, we must see Deerhurst. You know – Saxon church, very special.'

'Right you are. Do we have Pevsner?'

'On the back shelf of the car. What luck – I never realised Deerhurst was hereabouts.'

'Aren't you a clever girl?' he said, patting her knee. 'Knowing about Saxon churches.'

The woman behind the bar, watching them, thought, yes, that's how it is when you're like that. Can't keep your hands off each other. Ah well. 'How's the back, John?' she said. 'That stuff I told you about do any good?' The young couple were getting up now, slinging sweaters about their shoulders, leaving without a backward glance. People passing through, going off into other lives. Young intense lives. 'What? Oh, thanks very much – I'll have a lager and lime. Cheers, John.'

'Drive or navigate?' said Sarah, in the car park. 'You're better with the map than I am, and it's all side roads to this church. I'll tell you one thing – if we do get married it's not going to be any flipping church business. That's what ma's got her eye on, you realise.'

'There'd have to be some sort of do.'

'We could have it at the flat. Cheaper. The do, I mean. And registry office. But it's all a bit academic, until we actually decide something. Do I go left or right?'

Signposts fingered towards slothful hinterlands. Cars glittered between the hedges, sparks of colour in a world of green and fawn. On the edge of a village, washing-lines held up stiff shapes of clothes, slumping pink and yellow sheets, a rank of nappies. A man scraped around young cabbages with a hoe.

'Corfu,' said Tony, 'was livelier.'

'I thought we agreed never again a package holiday. Anyway, it's the new car this year instead.'

'This is our fourth holiday together, Sarah.'

'Cor . . . Hey – you're not directing me. That sign said Deerhurst.'

'Sorry. My mind was on other things. Incidentally, what started us off on this marriage discussion? Today, I mean.'

'I can't remember. Oh yes I can – it was you talking about this aunt of yours. Will you have to go to the wedding, by the way?'

'I hope not. I'd be the only person there under fifty, I should imagine. No – hearty good wishes over the phone and that kind of thing.'

'It's nice for her,' said Sarah charitably. 'At that age. If a bit kind of fake, if you see what I mean.'

'Yes. But for that generation there wouldn't be any alternative.'

They nodded, sombrely.

'Here we are,' said Sarah. 'And this must be where you leave cars. Good – there's no one else there. I hate looking at churches when there's anyone else. Where's Pevsner? We're going to do this place properly – it's supposed to be important.'

They advanced into the churchyard. The church, squatting amid yews, seemed almost derisive in its antiquity, tethered to something dark and incomprehensible, uncaring, too far away to be understood. Its stone was blurred, its shapes strange and unlovely. Gravestones drowned in grass. An aeroplane, unseen, rumbled across the milky sky.

' ". . . tall narrow nave of the C8" ' Tony read. 'Seven hundred and something. Jesus! That makes you think, doesn't it?'

'There's this famous sculpture thing over the door. An animal head. That's it, I suppose. Goodness, isn't it all sinister?'

They stood in silence. 'Things that are so incredibly old,' Sarah went on, 'just leave you feeling respectful. I mean, that they're there at all.'

They went into the church. Tony took a few steps down the nave. 'Yes. I know what you mean. Even more so inside. All this stone standing for so long' – he gestured at piers, crossing arch, narrow uncompromising windows. 'Read Pevsner,' instructed Sarah. 'I like to understand what I'm looking at.' They toured the building, side by side, heads cocked from book to architectural feature, understanding.

The church door, which they had closed behind them, burst open. The sound made them both jump. Turning, they saw a man who stood framed in the gush of light from without: a tall man in tweed jacket and baggy-kneed trousers, an odd prophetic-looking figure with a mane of white hair, like a more robust version of the aged Bertrand Russell. A memorable person, who stood for a moment staring wildly round the church, at Sarah and Tony for one dismissive instant, and who then strode down the aisle searching, apparently, the pillars, and then back to the entrance and out, slamming the door.

'The vicar?' said Tony, after a moment.

'No. Frankly. That was no vicar. Funny to storm out like that, though. This place *vaut le détour*, as *Michelin* says.'

'P'raps he's seen it already.'

'Presumably.' Sarah turned back to Pevsner. 'Apparently there's this other carving outside, round at the back, we'd better go and find it. We've done the rest, I think.'

She led the way out of the church and round the side, through the long grass and the leaning gravestones. And came, thus, upon them first.

In the angle of a buttress, up against the wall of the church. The man, the white-haired tall man, his back now turned. Turned because he was locked in an embrace, a succulent sexual embrace (the sound, just, of mouths – the impression of loins pushed together) with a woman, little of whom could be seen as, eyes averted, Sarah scurried past, followed a few paces behind by Tony. Both of them at once seeing, and quickly looking away. Seeing of the man, his tweed back and his mane of yellow-white hair, and of the woman – well, little except an impression of blue denim skirt and plimsolls. And more white hair: crisp curly grey-white hair.

They achieved the back of the church and stood peering up at the wall. 'I can't see this sculpture,' said Sarah (voice firm, ordinary, not lowered, rather loud indeed). 'It's supposed to be a Virgin – ah, that must be it. Right up just under the window there.'

When they came back past the buttress the couple were gone. The churchyard was quite empty. The whole place, which had briefly rocked, had sunk back into its lethargy. That crackling startling charge of passion had dissipated into the stagnant air of the summer afternoon. It was three o'clock, and felt as if it for ever would be. Somewhere beyond the hedge a tractor ground across a field.

'Let's go,' said Sarah brightly. 'I think I've had Deerhurst.'

The car was no longer alone. Two others, now, were parked alongside. Sarah whipped the key into the lock and opened the door. She plumped down into the driving-seat. 'You know what? That was an assignation we stumbled into.'

'So it would seem.'

'Where are they now, do you imagine?'

Tony shrugged.

Sarah started the engine. She said with sudden violence, 'You know, it was a bit revolting. They were seventy if they were a day.'

Tony nodded. Embarrassment filled the car.

The Darkness Out There

SHE WALKED through flowers, the girl, oxeye daisies and vetch and cow parsley, keeping to the track at the edge of the field. She could see the cottage in the distance, shrugged down into the dip beyond the next hedge. Mrs Rutter, Pat had said, Mrs Rutter at Nether Cottage, you don't know her, Sandra? She's a dear old thing, all on her own, of course, we try to keep an eye. A wonky leg after her op and the home help's off with a bad back this week. So could you make that your Saturday afternoon session, dear? Lovely. There'll be one of the others, I'm not sure who.

Pat had a funny eye, a squint, so that her glance swerved away from you as she talked. And a big chest jutting under washed-out jerseys. Are people who help other people always not very nice-looking? Very busy being busy; always in a rush. You didn't get people like Mrs Carpenter at the King's Arms running the Good Neighbours' Club. People with platinum highlights and spike heel suede boots.

She looked down at her own legs, the girl, bare brown legs brushing through the grass, polleny summer grass that glinted in the sun.

She hoped it would be Susie, the other person. Or Liz. They could have a good giggle, doing the floors and that. Doing her washing, this old Mrs Rutter.

They were all in the Good Neighbours' Club, her set at school. Quite a few of the boys, too. It had become a sort of craze, the thing to do. They were really nice, some of the old people. The old folks, Pat called them. Pat had done the notice in the Library: *Come and have fun giving a helping hand to the old folks. Adopt a granny.* And the jokey cartoon drawing of a dear old bod with specs on the end of her nose and a shawl. One or two of the old people had been a bit sharp about that.

The track followed the hedge round the field to the gate and the plank bridge over the stream. The dark reach of the spinney came right to the gate there so that she would have to walk by the edge of it with the light suddenly shutting off, the bare wide sky of the field. Packer's End.

You didn't go by yourself through Packer's End if you could help it, not after tea-time, anyway. A German plane came down in the war and the aircrew were killed and there were people who'd heard them talking still, chattering in German on their radios, voices coming out of the trees, nasty, creepy. People said.

She kept to the track, walking in the flowers with corn running in the wind between her and the spinney. She thought suddenly of blank-eyed helmeted heads, looking at you from among branches. She wouldn't go in there for a thousand pounds, not even in bright day like now, with nothing coming out of the dark slab of trees but birdsong – blackbirds and thrushes and robins and that. It was a rank place, all whippy saplings and brambles and a gully with a dumped mattress and bedstead and an old fridge. And, somewhere, presumably, the crumbling rusty scraps of metal and cloth and . . . Bones?

It was all right out here in the sunshine. Fine. She stopped to pick grass stems out of her sandal; she saw the neat print of the strap-marks against her sunburn, pink-white on brown. Somebody had said she had pretty feet, once; she looked at them, clean and plump and neat on the grass. A ladybird crawled across a toe.

When they were small, six and seven and eight, they'd been scared stiff of Packer's End. Then, they hadn't known about the German plane. It was different things then; witches and wolves and tigers. Sometimes they'd go there for a dare, several of them, skittering over the field and into the edge of the trees, giggling and shrieking, not too far in, just far enough for it to be scary, for the branch shapes to look like faces and clawed hands, for the wolves to rustle and creep in the greyness you couldn't quite see into, the clotted shifting depths of the place.

But after, lying on your stomach at home on the hearthrug watching telly with the curtains drawn and the dark shut out it was cosy to think of Packer's End, where you weren't.

After they were twelve or so the witches and wolves went away. Then it was the German plane. And other things too. You didn't know who there might be around, in woods and places. Like stories in the papers. Girl attacked on lonely road. Police hunt rapist. There was this girl, people at school said, this girl some time back, who'd been biking along the field path and these two blokes had come out of Packer's End. They'd had a knife, they'd threatened to carve her up, there wasn't anything she could do, she was at their mercy. People couldn't remember what her name was, exactly, she didn't live round here any more. Two enormous blokes, sort of gypsy types.

She put her sandal back on. She walked through the thicker grass by the hedge and felt it drag at her legs and thought of swimming in warm seas. She put her hand on the top of her head and her hair was hot from the sun, a dry burning cap. One day, this year, next year sometime, she would go to places like on travel brochures and run into a blue sea. She would fall in love and she would get a good job and she would have one of those new Singers that do zig-zag stitch and make an embroidered silk coat.

One day.

Now, she would go to this old Mrs Rutter's and have a bit of a giggle with Susie and come home for tea and wash her hair. She would walk like this through the silken grass with the wind seething the corn and the secret invisible life of birds beside her in the hedge. She would pick a blue flower and examine its complexity of pattern and petal and wonder what it was called and drop it. She would plunge her face into the powdery plate of an elderflower and smell cat, tom-cat, and sneeze and scrub her nose with the back of her hand. She would hurry through the gate and over the stream because that was a bit too close to Packer's End for comfort and she would . . .

He rose from the plough beyond the hedge.

She screamed.

'Christ!' she said. 'Kerry Stevens you stupid so-and-so, what d'you want to go and do that for you give me the fright of my life.'

He grinned. 'I seen you coming. Thought I might as well wait.'

Not Susie. Not Liz either. Kerry Stevens from Richmond Way. Kerry Stevens that none of her lot reckoned much on, with his black licked-down hair and slitty eyes. Some people you only have to look at to know they're not up to much.

'Didn't know you were in the Good Neighbours.'

He shrugged. They walked in silence. He took out an Aero bar, broke off a bit, offered it. She said oh, thanks. They went chewing towards the cottage, the cottage where old Mrs Rutter with her wonky leg would be ever so pleased to see them because they were really sweet, lots of the old people. Ever so grateful, the old poppets, was what Pat said, not that you'd put it quite like that yourself.

'Just give it a push, the door. It sticks, see. That's it.'

She seemed composed of circles, a cottage-loaf of a woman, with a face below which chins collapsed one into another, a creamy smiling pool of a face in which her eyes snapped and darted.

'Tea, my duck?' she said. 'Tea for the both of you? I'll put us a kettle on.'

The room was stuffy. It had a gaudy lino floor with the pattern rubbed away in front of the sink and round the table; the walls were cluttered with old calendars and pictures torn from magazines; there was a smell of cabbage. The alcove by the fireplace was filled with china ornaments: big-eyed flop-eared rabbits and beribboned kittens and flowery milk-maids and a pair of naked chubby children wearing daisy chains.

The woman hauled herself from a sagging armchair. She glittered at them from the stove, manoeuvring cups, propping herself against the draining-board. 'What's your names, then? Sandra and Kerry. Well,

you're a pretty girl, Sandra, aren't you. Pretty as they come. There was –
let me see, who was it? – Susie, last week. That's right, Susie.' Her eyes
investigated, quick as mice. 'Put your jacket on the back of the door, dear,
you won't want to get that messy. Still at school, are you?'

The boy said, 'I'm leaving, July. They're taking me on at the garage, the
Blue Star. I been helping out there on and off, before.'

Mrs Rutter's smiles folded into one another. Above them, her eyes
examined him. 'Well, I expect that's good steady money if you'd nothing
special in mind. Sugar?'

There was a view from the window out over a bedraggled garden with
the stumps of spent vegetables and a matted flowerbed and a square of
shaggy grass. Beyond, the spinney reached up to the fence, a no-man's
land of willowherb and thistle and small trees, growing thicker and
higher into the full density of woodland. Mrs Rutter said, 'Yes, you have a
look out, aren't I lucky – right up beside the wood. Lovely it is in the
spring, the primroses and that. Mind, there's not as many as there used to
be.'

The girl said, 'Have you lived here for a long time?'

'Most of my life, dear. I came here as a young married woman, and
that's a long way back, I can tell you. You'll be courting before long
yourself, I don't doubt. Like bees round the honeypot, they'll be.'

The girl blushed. She looked at the floor, at her own feet, neat and slim
and brown. She touched, secretly, the soft skin of her thigh; she felt her
breasts poke up and out at the thin stuff of her top; she licked the inside of
her teeth, that had only the one filling, a speck like a pin-head. She
wished there was Susie to have a giggle with, not just Kerry Stevens.

The boy said, 'What'd you like us to do?'

His chin was explosive with acne; at his middle, his jeans yawned from
his T-shirt, showing pale chilly flesh. Mrs Rutter said, 'I expect you're a
nice strong boy, aren't you? I daresay you'd like to have a go at the grass
with the old mower. Sandra can give this room a do, that would be nice,
it's as much as I can manage to have a dust of the ornaments just now, I
can't get down to the floor.'

When he had gone outside the girl fetched broom and mop and
dustpan from a cupboard under the narrow stair. The cupboard, stacked
with yellowing newspapers, smelt of damp and mouse. When she
returned the old woman was back in the armchair, a composite chintzy
mass from which cushions oozed and her voice flowed softly on. 'That's
it, dear, you just work round, give the corners a brush, if you don't mind,
that's where the dust settles. Mind your pretty skirt, pull it up a bit,
there's only me to see if you're showing a bit of bum. That's ever such a
nice style, I expect your mum made it, did she?'

The girl said, 'Actually I did.'

'Well now, fancy! You're a little dressmaker, too, are you? I was good with my needle when I was younger, my eyesight's past it now, of course. I made my own wedding dress, ivory silk with lace insets. A *Vogue* pattern it was, with a sweetheart neckline.'

The door opened. Kerry said. 'Where'll I put the clippings?'

'There's the compost heap down the bottom, by the fence. And while you're down there could you get some sticks from the wood for kindling, there's a good lad.'

When he had gone she went on, 'That's a nice boy. It's a pity they put that stuff on their hair these days, sticky-looking. I expect you've got lots of boyfriends, though, haven't you?'

The girl poked in a crack at a clump of fluff. 'I don't really know Kerry that much.'

'Don't you, dear? Well, I expect you get all sorts, in your club thing, the club that Miss Hammond runs.'

'The Good Neighbours. Pat, we call her.'

'She was down here last week. Ever such a nice person. Kind. It's sad she never married.'

The girl said, 'Is that your husband in the photo, Mrs Rutter?'

'That's right, dear. In his uniform. The Ox and Bucks. After he got his stripes. He was a lovely man.'

She sat back on her heels, the dustpan on her lap. The photo was yellowish, in a silver frame. 'Did he . . .?'

'Killed in the war, dear. Right at the start. He was in one of the first campaigns, in Belgium, and he never came back.'

The girl saw a man with a toothbrush moustache, his army cap slicing his forehead. 'That's terrible.'

'Tragic. There was a lot of tragedies in the war. It's nice it won't be like that for you young people nowadays. Touch wood, cross fingers. I like young people, I never had any children, it's been a loss, that, I've got a sympathy with young people.'

The girl emptied the dustpan into the bin outside the back door. Beyond the fence, she could see the bushes thrash and Kerry's head bob among them. She thought, rather him than me, but it's different for boys, for him anyway, he's not a nervy type, it's if you're nervy you get bothered about things like Packer's End.

She was nervy, she knew. Mum always said so.

Mrs Rutter was rummaging in a cupboard by her chair. 'Chocky? I always keep a few chockies by for visitors.' She brought out a flowered tin. 'There. Do you know, I've had this twenty years, all but. Look at the little cornflowers. And the daisies. They're almost real, aren't they?'

'Sweet,' said the girl

'Take them out and see if what's-'is-name would like one.'

There was a cindery path down the garden, ending at a compost heap where eggshells gleamed among leaves and grassclippings. Rags of plastic fluttered from sticks in a bed of cabbages. The girl picked her way daintily, her toes wincing against the cinders. A place in the country. One day she would have a place in the country, but not like this. Sometime. A little white house peeping over a hill, with a stream at the bottom of a crisp green lawn and an orchard with old apple trees and a brown pony. And she would walk in the long grass in this orchard in a straw hat with these two children, a boy and a girl, children with fair shiny hair like hers, and there'd be this man.

She leaned over the fence and shouted, 'Hey . . .'

'What?'

She brandished the box.

He came up, dumping an armful of sticks. 'What's this for, then?'

'She said. Help yourself.'

He fished among the sweets, his fingers etched with dirt. 'I did a job on your dad's car last week. That blue Escort's his, isn't it?'

'Mmn.'

'July, I'll be starting full-time. When old Bill retires. With day-release at the tech.'

She thought of oily workshop floors, of the fetid undersides of cars. She couldn't stand the feel of dirt, if her hands were the least bit grubby she had to go and wash, a rim of grime under her nails could make her shudder. She said, 'I don't know how you can, all that muck.'

He fished for another chocolate. 'Nothing wrong with a bit of dirt. What you going to do, then?'

'Secretarial.'

Men didn't mind so much. At home, her dad did things like unblocking the sink and cleaning the stove; mum was the same as her, just the feel of grease and stuff made her squirm. They couldn't either of them wear anything that had a stain or a spot.

He said, 'I don't go much on her.'

'Who?'

He waved towards the cottage.

'She's all right. What's wrong with her, then?'

He shrugged. 'I dunno. The way she talks and that.'

'She lost her husband,' said the girl. 'In the war.' She considered him, across the fence, over a chasm. Mum said boys matured later, in many ways.

'There's lots of people done that.'

She looked beyond him, into distances. 'Tragic, actually. Well, I'll go back and get on. She says can you see to her bins when you've got the sticks. She wants them carried down for the dustmen.'

Mrs Rutter watched her come in, glinting from the cushions. 'That's a good girl. Put the tin back in the cupboard, dear.'

'What would you like me to do now?'

'There's my little bit of washing by the sink. Just the personal things to rinse through. That would be ever so kind.'

The girl ran water into the basin. She measured in the soapflakes. She squeezed the pastel nylons, the floating sinuous tights. 'It's a lovely colour, that turquoise.'

'My niece got me that last Christmas. Nightie and a little jacket to go. I was telling you about my wedding dress. The material came from Macy's, eight yards. I cut it on the cross, for the hang. Of course, I had a figure then.' She heaved herself round in the chair. 'You're a lovely shape, Sandra. You take care you stay that way.'

'I can get a spare tyre,' the girl said. 'If I'm not careful.'

Outside, the bin lids rattled.

'I hope he's minding my edging. I've got lobelia planted out along that path.'

'I love blue flowers.'

'You should see the wood in the spring, with the bluebells. There's a place right far in where you get lots coming up still. I used to go in there picking every year before my leg started playing me up. Jugs and jugs of them, for the scent. Haven't you ever seen them?'

The girl shook her head. She wrung out the clothes, gathered up the damp skein. 'I'll put these on the line, shall I?'

When she returned the boy was bringing in the filled coal-scuttle and a bundle of sticks.

'That's it,' said Mrs Rutter. 'Under the sink, that's where they go. You'll want to have a wash after that, won't you? Put the kettle on, Sandra, and we'll top up the pot.'

The boy ran his hands under the tap. His shirt clung to his shoulder-blades, damp with sweat. He looked over the bottles of detergent, the jug of parsley, the handful of flowers tucked into a coronation mug. He said, 'Is that the wood where there was that German plane came down in the war?'

'Don't start on that,' said the girl. 'It gives me the willies.'

'What for?'

'Scary.'

The old woman reached forward and prodded the fire. 'Put a bit of coal on for me, there's a good boy. What's to be scared of? It's over and done with, good riddance to bad rubbish.'

'It was there, then?'

'Shut up,' said the girl.

'Were you here?'

'Fill my cup up, dear, would you. I was here. Me and my sister. My sister Dot. She's dead now, two years. Heart. That was before she was married, of course, nineteen forty-two, it was.'

'Did you see it come down?'

She chuckled. 'I saw it come down all right.'

'What was it?' said the boy, 'Messerschmitt?'

'How would I know that, dear? I don't know anything about aeroplanes. Anyway, it was all smashed up by the time I saw it, you couldn't have told t'other from which.'

The girl's hand hovered, the tea-cup halfway to her mouth. She sipped, put it down. 'You *saw* it? Ooh, I wouldn't have gone anywhere near.'

'It would have been burning,' said the boy. 'It'd have gone up in flames.'

'There weren't any flames, it was just stuck there in the ground, end up, with mess everywhere. Drop more milk, dear, if you don't mind.'

The girl shuddered. 'I s'pose they'd taken the bodies away by then.'

Mrs Rutter picked out a tea-leaf with the tip of the spoon. She drank, patted the corner of her mouth delicately with a tissue. 'No, no, 'course not. There was no one else seen it come down. We'd heard the engine and you could tell there was trouble, the noise wasn't right, and we looked out and saw it come down smack in the trees. 'Course we hadn't the telephone so there was no ringing the police or the Warden at Clapton. Dot said we should maybe bike to the village but it was a filthy wet night, pouring cats and dogs, and fog too, and we didn't know if it was one of ours or one of theirs, did we? So Dot said better go and have a look first.'

'But either way . . .' the boy began.

'We got our wellies on, and Dot had the big lantern, and we went off. It wasn't very far in. We found it quite quick and Dot grabbed hold of me and pointed and we saw one of the wings sticking up with the markings on and we knew it was one of theirs. We cheered, I can tell you.'

The boy stared at her over the rim of the cup, blank-faced.

'Dot said bang goes some more of the bastards, come on let's get back into the warm and we just started back when we heard this noise.'

'Noise?'

'Sort of moaning.'

'Oh,' cried the girl. 'How awful, weren't they . . .'

'So we got up closer and Dot held the lantern so we could see and there was three of them, two in the front and they were dead, you could see that all right, one of them had his . . .'

The girl grimaced. 'Don't.'

Mrs Rutter's chins shook, the pink and creamy chins. 'Good job you weren't there, then, my duck. Not that we were laughing at the time, I can tell you, rain teeming down and a raw November night, and that sight under our noses. It wasn't pretty but I've never been squeamish, nor Dot neither. And then we saw the other one.'

'The other one?' said the boy warily.

'The one at the back. He was trapped, see, the way the plane had broken up. There wasn't any way he could get out.'

The girl stiffened. 'Oh, lor, you mean he . . .'

'He was hurt pretty bad. He was kind of talking to himself. Something about mutter, mutter . . . Dot said he's not going to last long, and a good job too, three of them that'll be. She'd been a VAD so she knew a bit about casualties, see.' Mrs Rutter licked her lips; she looked across at them, her eyes darting. 'Then we went back to the cottage.'

There was silence. The fire gave a heave and a sigh. 'You what?' said the boy.

'Went back inside. It was bucketing down, cats and dogs.'

The boy and girl sat quite still, on the far side of the table.

'That was eighteen months or so after my hubby didn't come back from Belgium.' Her eyes were on the girl; the girl looked away. 'Tit for tat, I said to Dot.'

After a moment she went on. 'Next morning it was still raining and blow me if the bike hadn't got a puncture. I said to Dot, I'm not walking to the village in this, and that's flat, and Dot was running a bit of a temp, she had the 'flu or something coming on. I tucked her up warm and when I'd done the chores I went back in the wood, to have another look. He must have been a tough so-and-so, that Jerry, he was still mumbling away. It gave me a turn, I can tell you, I'd never imagined he'd last the night. I could see him better, in the day-time; he was bashed up pretty nasty. I'd thought he was an old bloke, too, but he wasn't. He'd have been twentyish, that sort of age.'

The boy's spoon clattered to the floor; he did not move.

'I reckon he may have seen me, not that he was in a state to take much in. He called out something. I thought, oh no, you had this coming to you, mate, there's a war on. You won't know that expression – it was what everybody said in those days. I thought, why should I do anything for you? Nobody did anything for my Bill, did they? I was a widow at thirty-nine. I've been on my own ever since.'

The boy shoved his chair back from the table.

'He must have been a tough bastard, like I said. He was still there that evening, but the next morning he was dead. The weather'd perked up by then and I walked to the village and got a message to the people at Clapton. They were ever so surprised; they didn't know there'd been a Jerry plane come down in the area at all. There were lots of people came to take bits for souvenirs, I had a bit myself but it's got mislaid, you tend to mislay things when you get to my age.'

The boy had got up. He glanced down at the girl. 'I'm going,' he said. 'Dunno about you, but I'm going.'

She stared at the lacy cloth on the table, the fluted china cup. 'I'll come too.'

'Eh?' said the old woman. 'You're off, are you? That was nice of you to see to my little jobs for me. Tell what's-'er-name to send someone next week if she can, I like having someone young about the place, once in a while, I've got a sympathy with young people. Here – you're forgetting your pretty jacket, Sandra, what's the hurry? 'Bye then, my ducks, see you close my gate, won't you?'

The boy walked ahead, fast; the girl pattered behind him, sliding on the dry grass. At the gateway into the cornfield he stopped. He said, not looking at her, looking towards the furzy edge of the wood. 'Christ!'

The wood sat there in the afternoon sun. Wind stirred the trees. Birds sang. There were not, the girl realised, wolves or witches or tigers. Nor were there prowling blokes, gypsy-type blokes. And there were not chattering ghostly voices. Somewhere there were some scraps of metal overlooked by people hunting for souvenirs.

The boy said, 'I'm not going near that old bitch again.' He leaned against the gate, clenching his fists on an iron rung; he shook slightly. 'I won't ever forget him, that poor sod.'

She nodded.

'Two bloody nights. Christ!'

And she would hear, she thought, always, for a long time anyway, that voice trickling on, that soft old woman's voice; would see a tin painted with cornflowers, pretty china ornaments.

'It makes you want to throw up,' he said. 'Someone like that.'

She couldn't think of anything to say. He had grown; he had got older and larger. His anger eclipsed his acne, the patches of grease on his jeans, and lardy midriff. You could get people all wrong, she realised with alarm. You could get people wrong and there was a darkness that was not the darkness of tree shadows and murky undergrowth and you could not draw the curtains and keep it out because it was in your head, once known, in your head for ever like lines from a song. One moment you were walking in long grass with the sun on your hair and birds singing and the next you glimpsed darkness, an inescapable darkness. The darkness was out there and it was a part of you and you would never be without it, ever.

She walked behind him, through a world grown unreliable, in which flowers sparkle and birds sing but everything is not as it appears, oh no.

The Pill-Box

THE WRITER of a story has an infinity of choices. An infinity of narratives; an infinity of endings. The process of choosing, of picking this set of events rather than that, of ending up here rather than there – well, call it what you like: craft, art, accident, intuition.

Call it what you like, it's a curious process.

I teach Eng. Lit. Consequently I try to point this sort of thing out to the young. Life and literature – all that. Parallels; illuminations. I'm no mystic, but there's one thing that never ceases to astonish me: the fixity of things. That we live with it, accept it as we do. That we do not question that the course of events is thus, and never could be other. When you think of how nearly, at every moment, it is not.

Think of it. Stare it in the face and think of it.

I come out of my front gate, I bump into old Sanders next door, we have a chat . . . Shift the point at which I emerge by ever so little, and I do not meet Sanders, we do not have a word about the cricket club dinner, he does not offer to drop over later with his Black & Decker and fix that shelf for me.

I cross the street, looking first to right and left, a lorry passes, I alight upon the pavement opposite.

I cross the street, not looking first to right and left; the lorry driver's concentration lapses for a second, I am so much meat under his wheels.

Some bloke is gunned down in Sarajevo. In another country, evil is bred. And then and then and then . . . A tired voice comes from a crackling wireless: there is war. 'May God bless you all,' he says.

A trigger jams. Elsewhere, a mad house-painter dies young of polio. And then, and then, and then . . . 3rd September 1939 is a fine day, sunshine with a hint of showers.

Oh well *of course* you say, any fool can play those games. Intriguing but unproductive. We inhabit, after all, a definite world; facts are facts. The sequence of my life, of your life, of the public life.

Listen, then. I went up to the pill-box this evening – the wartime pill-box on the top.

The pill-box is on the brow of the hill and faces square down the lane. I take my time getting up there; it's a steep pull up and the outlook's half the point of the walk. I have a rest at the first gate, and then at the end by the oak, and again at the gate to Clapper's field. You get the view from there: the village down below you and the fields reaching away to the coast and the sea hanging at the edge of the green, a long grey smear with maybe a ship or two and on clear days the white glimmer of the steelworks over on the Welsh coast.

It was sited to cover anything coming up and heading on over the hill. Heading for the main road – that would have been the idea, I suppose. It would have had the village covered, too, and a good part of the valley. Very small it looks now, stuck there at the edge of the field: barely room for a couple of blokes inside. I never know why it's not been taken away – much longer and it'll be a historical monument I daresay and they'll slap a protection order on it. The field is rough grazing and always has been so I suppose no one's felt any great call to get rid of it. Dalton's field, it is; from time to time you find he's stashed some cattle feed away in the pill-box, or a few bags of lime. It comes in handy for the village lads, too, always has done: get your girl up there, nice bit of shelter . . . I've made use of it that way myself in my time. Back in – oh, forty-seven or thereabouts. Yes, forty-seven, that spring it rained cats and dogs and there was flooding right left and centre. Rosie Parks, black curly hair and an answer to everything. Lying in there with the rain coming down in spears outside; 'You lay off, Keith Harrison, I'm telling you . . .' 'Ah, come on, Rosie . . .' Giggle giggle.

The rain started this evening when I was at the oak, just a sprinkle, and by the time I got to the top it was coming down hard and looked set in for a while so I ducked down into the pill-box to sit it out.

I was thinking about the past, in a vague kind of way – the war, being young. Looking out from inside the pill-box you see the countryside as a bright green rectangle, very clear, lots of detail, like a photo. And I've got good eyesight anyway, even at fifty-seven, just about a hundred per cent vision. I could see the new houses they've put up on the edge of the village and I was thinking that the place has changed a lot since I was a boy, and yet in other ways it hasn't. The new estate, the shop, cars at every door, telly aerials, main drainage; but the same names, by and large, same families, same taste to the beer, same stink from Clapper's silage in hot weather.

I can see the house where I was born, from the pill-box. And the one I live in now. The churchyard, where my parents are, God bless 'em. The recreation ground beside the church hall where we used to drill in 1941; those of us left behind, too old like Jim Blockley at sixty-odd, too young like me at seventeen-and-a-half, too wonky like the postmaster with his bronchitis, too valuable like the farmers and the doctor.

I can see the road, too – the road that takes me daily to work. Ten miles to Scarhead to try to drum a bit of sense and a bit of knowledge into forty fifteen-year-old heads. Full cycle. Back then, mine was the empty head, the bloke at the blackboard was . . . was old Jenkins, Jenks. It's not been a mistake, coming back. I'd always thought I'd like to. The day I saw the advert in the *Times Ed. Supp.* I knew at once I'd apply. Yes, I thought, that's it, that's for me, end up back at home, why not? I've always thought of it as home, down here, wherever I've been – Nottingham, up on the north-east, London. Not that it's local boy made good, exactly. Teaching's a tidy enough occupation, they reckon down here, but not high-flying. Farmers do a sight better. I don't drive a Jag, like Tim Matlock who was in my class at the grammar and farms up on the county border now. Not that I care tuppence.

I lit a pipe to keep the midges off; the rain was coming down harder than ever. It looked as though I might have to pack in the rest of my walk. I opened the newspaper: usual stuff, miners reject pay offer, Middle East talks, rail fares up.

When I heard the first voice I thought there was someone outside in the field – some trick of the acoustics, making it sound as though it were in the pill-box.

'They're bloody coming!' he said.

And then another bloke, a young one, a boy, gave a sort of grunt. You knew, somehow, he was on edge. His voice had that crack to it, that pitch of someone who's keyed up, holding himself in. Shit-scared.

'Can I have a look, Mr Barnes? Oh God – I see them. Heading straight up.'

How can I put it? Describe how it was. The words that come to mind are banal, clichés: eerie, unearthly, uncanny.

They were there, but they were not. They were in the head, but yet were outside it. There were two men, an old and a younger, who spoke from some other dimension; who were there with me in the pill-box and yet also were not, could not be, had never been.

Listen again.

'Give me them field-glasses . . . They've set Clapper's barn on fire. There's more tanks on the Scarhead road – six, seven . . . They'll be at the corner in a few minutes now, son.'

And the young chap speaks again. 'O.K.,' he says. 'O.K., I'm ready.'

The voices, you understand, are overlaid by other noises, ordinary noises: the rain on the roof of the pill-box, sheep, a tractor in the lane. The tractor goes past but the voices don't take a blind bit of notice. The old bloke tells the other one to pass him another clip of ammo. 'You all right, son?' he says, the boy answers that is he all right? There is that high sharp note in his voice, in both their voices.

There is a silence.

And then they come back.

'I can see him now. Armoured car. Two.'

'O.K. Yes. I've got them.'

'Hold it. Hold it, son . . .'

'Yes. Right . . .'

'Hold it. Steady. When they get to the oak.'

'O.K., Mr Barnes.'

And everything is quiet again. A quiet you could cut with a knife. The inside of the pill-box is tight-strung, waiting; it is both a moment in time and a time that is going on for ever, will go on for ever. I drop my tobacco tin and it clatters on the concrete floor but the sound does not break that other quiet, which, I now realise, is somewhere else, is something else.

The old bloke says, 'Fire!'

And then they are both talking together. There is no other sound, nothing, just their voices. And the rain.

The boy says, 'I got him, my God, I got him!' and the other one says, 'Steady. Re-load now. Steady. Wait till the second one's moving again. Right. Fire!'

'We hit him!'

'He's coming on . . .'

'Christ, there's another behind!'

'Bastards! Jerry bastards!'

And the boy cries, 'That's for my dad! And that's for my mum! Come on then, bloody come on then . . .'

'Steady, son. Hold it a minute, there's a . . .'

'What's he doing, Christ he's . . .'

'He's got a grenade. Keep on firing, for God's sake. Keep him covered.'

And suddenly they go quiet. Quite quiet. Except that just once the old bloke says something. He says, 'Don't move, Keith, keep still, I'm coming over, I . . .'

He says, 'Keith?'

And there is nothing more.

I went on sitting there. The quietness left the inside of the pill-box, that other quietness. The tractor came back down the lane again. The rain stopped. A blackbird started up on the roof of the pill-box. Down in the valley there was a patch of sunlight slap on the village; the church very bright, a car windscreen flashing, pale green of the chestnuts in the pub car park.

I knew, now, that from the first moment there'd been something about that young chap's voice. The boy.

Mr Barnes. Joe Barnes worked the manor farm in the war. He left here some time ago, retired to Ilfracombe; he died a year or two back.

I was in his platoon, in 1941. I've not thought of him in years. Couldn't put a face to him, now. He died of cancer in a nursing-home in Ilfracombe. Didn't he?

Or.

Or he died in a pill-box up on the hill above the village, long ago. Him and a boy called Keith. In which case the pill-box is no longer there nor I take it the village nor the whole bloody place, at least not in any way you or I could know it.

No young fellow called Keith ever put his hand up the skirt of Rosie Parks in that pill-box, nor did another bloke, a fifty-seven-year-old teacher of English, walk up that way of an evening for a smoke and a look at the view.

I came out, filled my pipe, looked down at the village. All right, yes, I thought to myself – interesting, the imaginative process. The mind churning away, putting pictures to a line of thought. I dozed off in there.

Later I knew I did not imagine it. I heard it. Heard them. So what do you make of that? Eh? What can anyone make of it? How, having glimpsed the possibility of the impossible, can the world remain as steady as you had supposed?

Suppose that the writer of a story were haunted, in the mind, for ever, by all those discarded alternatives, by the voices of all those assorted characters. Forced to preserve them always as the price of creative choice.

Then suppose, by the same token, that just once in a while it is given to any one of us to experience the inconceivable. To push through the barrier of what we know into the heady breathtaking unbearable ozone of what we cannot contemplate. Did that happen to me? In the pill-box on the hill on a summer Monday evening, with the world steady under my feet and the newspaper in my hand, telling me what's what, how the world is, where we are?

Customers

MAJOR ANGLESEY and Mrs Yardley-Peters worked slowly up and down the aisles of the chain store. They picked up garments and held them against each other. Mrs Yardley-Peters undid her coat, and Major Anglesey tried blouses around the broad slope of her bosom, measuring them carefully armpit to armpit. Mrs Yardley-Peters pondered over a red paisley dressing-gown, chest forty, looking from the pattern to the Major's rather ruddy complexion and gingery toothbrush moustache. Rejecting the blouses and the dressing-gown, they paused at the hosiery counter, where Mrs Yardley-Peters selected three pairs of tights (Brown Haze, Large) and paid for them at the nearest cash desk. They hesitated for a long while over ladies' v-neck lambswool sweaters, eventually deciding on a light grey size sixteen which Mrs Yardley-Peters popped into her shopping bag.

At Men's Accessories, Major Anglesey held various ties under his chin and decided on a red and navy stripe, which he folded tidily and put in his pocket. From there they wandered to the shoe section. Major Anglesey tried on a pair of brown brogues, took a step or two and shook his head, returning them to the rack. Mrs Yardley-Peters, meanwhile, had put on some black pumps – size four since, although a stout woman and not short, she had surprisingly small feet. The Major nodded approval and Mrs Yardley-Peters slipped her own shoes into the shopping bag, keeping on the pumps. Major Anglesey, at this point, glanced at his watch, said something, and the two of them moved rather more quickly to the food department where they filled a wire basket with a carton of coleslaw, two portions of cooked chicken, a packet of jam fancies and a jar of powdered coffee, lining up with those at the checkout.

The store detective, having joined them at the time of the red and navy striped tie, stood discreetly to one side. She was an unexceptional-looking woman, wearing a brown crimplene dress and fawn anorak, with a basket over one arm. The basket held, today, a bunch of bananas and a packet of Kleenex. She tended to vary the contents; meat, of course, would not do, being inclined to go bad in the heat of the store, over a long day.

Major Anglesey and Mrs Yardley-Peters passed through the checkout and back into the main part of the shop. At the entrance, they stopped for a moment, Mrs Yardley-Peters being evidently fussed in case she had lost her gloves; a search of her handbag, however, apparently put things right, and they proceeded under the blast of tropical wind issuing from somewhere in the ceiling and out into the street.

The store detective caught up with them at the zebra crossing, as they stood waiting for a lull in the traffic. She asked if they would please come back to the manager's office. The Major and Mrs Yardley-Peters received this request with considerable surprise but made no objection, except that the Major looked again at his watch and said he hoped it wouldn't take too long, as it was getting on for lunch-time.

Several sales assistants, watching the detective walk through the store a step or two behind Major Anglesey and Mrs Yardley-Peters, exchanged glances and grinned. One girl stuck her chest out and mimicked the store detective's slightly military gait; it was a standing joke that Madge, having made a capture, went all official. At that point, the crimplene dress and the anorak took on, if you knew what you were looking at, the authority of the uniform she would herself have much preferred and that she had so regretted when giving up the traffic-warden job. In most other respects, of course, her present position was far preferable. Her friends occasionally said that they didn't know how she could do a job like that, going on to add, uncertainly, that of course they supposed someone had to . . . Personally, she never found it a problem; people could be a lot more unpleasant when you handed them a parking ticket. Aggressive. Your average shop-lifter tended to crumple; she'd hardly ever – bar a gang of French schoolchildren once – had any trouble. And it was a sight warmer, on a winter afternoon, than patrolling the windy lengths of the High Street.

The manager, seated behind his desk, listened in silence to the store detective's account of the events of the last half hour. So, at first, did Mrs Yardley-Peters and Major Anglesey, until the Major began to shake his head, more in sorrow than distress, it seemed, and Mrs Yardley-Peters exclaimed, 'Oh, gracious me, no,' and then, 'No, no, it wasn't like that at all, you see we . . .' The store detective continued her account, as unemphasised as recitative.

The manager said to Mrs Yardley-Peters, 'Would you open your shopping bag, please?'

At first Mrs Yardley-Peters did not appear to take this in. She was rummaging again in her handbag. After a moment she said, 'Ah *there* it is.' And then, 'Oh no, I'd rather not, really, you see I've got it all sorted out, with the squashy things on top.'

The manager turned to Major Anglesey. 'It would really be much better if your wife . . .'

The Major made a small gesture. 'The lady,' he said with dignity, 'is my mistress.'

Mrs Yardley-Peters patted her hair, which was greying and set in neat ridges, a style that somehow disturbed the manager – it reminded him of something and he could not think what. 'That's right. Until my divorce comes through, you understand. Which should be before Christmas, all being well but you know what lawyers are. They drag their feet so. Have you ever had dealings with lawyers, Mr er . . . ?'

The manager swallowed. The store detective, who was standing beside the desk as though at attention, shifted position and drew in breath with a little hiss.

Mrs Yardley-Peters glanced round the room and located a chair. 'I must sit down for a minute. I've got this trouble with swollen ankles, and in any case . . .' – she looked down at the black pumps, frowning – 'you know, I've a horrid feeling I should have had a half size larger. These are pinching.'

The manager said, 'Can you show me a receipt for those shoes, madam?'

'Receipt?' Mrs Yardley-Peters appeared bewildered. 'Oh, from the place where you pay . . . Well, no, in fact I don't remember . . . I expect the Major paid, did you, dear? But you know I think I'll have to change them.' She turned to the store detective. 'Do you do half sizes? – I didn't notice. A four-and-a-half, it would need to be.'

The manager remembered suddenly that Mrs Yardley-Peters's hair-style reminded him of the actress who played the Duchess of Windsor in that TV series, though of course she was dark and much younger. This small satisfaction went some way to halt his mounting sense of disorientation. He said, 'I must ask you again to open your shopping bag, madam.'

'Oh, I say,' said Major Anglesey.

Mrs Yardley-Peters looked at the manager in bewilderment. 'I do think . . .' she began, and then, 'Oh well, I suppose if I'm careful.' She lifted out the packaged jam fancies and the chicken pieces. The store detective swayed forward, peering into the bag; 'That's the sweater, and that's her own shoes.'

'That's right,' said Mrs Yardley-Peters. 'You know, I wonder if I won't put them back on.' She was stacking things on the manager's desk.

The store detective straightened. She had gone quite red in the face. Her stomach rumbled.

The manager turned to Major Anglesey. 'May I please see the tie that you put in your pocket.'

The Major blinked. 'Tie? Oh, yes – rather.' He took out the tie and laid it on the desk.

'I'm not sure about that red, after all,' said Mrs Yardley-Peters. The store detective's stomach rumbled again. Mrs Yardley-Peters opened her handbag. 'I should have a magnesia tablet somewhere. Yes, here we are.' The store detective took a step backwards, violently, and landed against the wall of the office, as though at bay. 'No?' said Mrs Yardley-Peters. 'I always find they do the trick. It's getting near your lunch-time, I expect.' She eased off the black shoes, grimacing.

The manager realised he was losing his grip; tears he could cope with, protestations of innocence, truculence. He said, 'You understand that unless you can provide some proof that you paid for these goods I shall have to call the police?'

'Oh, I say,' said Major Anglesey again. Mrs Yardley-Peters, now in stockinged feet, flexed her toes; 'Oh, my goodness, I shouldn't do that, specially since it's all a silly mistake. You get into the most frightfully deep waters once you're involved with the police. My husband and I – my ex-husband, that is, all but – had an awful business once after we were the only people who saw this road accident. Witnesses, you see. Oh no – I don't think you should involve the police, not that they can't be awfully efficient sometimes, I will say that.'

The manager lined up the papers on his desk, for something to occupy the hands, and looked steadily at Major Anglesey; it was better, he found, though better wasn't really the word under the circumstances, if he simply tried to pretend the woman wasn't there. The store detective made a strangled noise. The manager said, rather sharply, 'Yes, all *right*, Mrs Hebden. Now, sir, did you pay for that tie, and did your – did the lady pay for the sweater and the shoes?'

'Oh, I don't think so,' said Major Anglesey. 'No, I don't think she would have. You see, it was a question of whether she'd left her cheque book in the car or whether . . .'

'I've got it, Rupert,' said Mrs Yardley-Peters. 'It's quite all right – it was in my bag all along, isn't that silly?'

The Major patted her shoulder. 'But at the time there was this bother about whether it was lost or not, so if anyone paid it would have been me. No doubt about that.'

'He didn't,' said the store detective.

'Really?' said Major Anglesey. 'Well, that's an extraordinary thing.' He looked at the tie. 'One wouldn't have bothered with a cheque for that, of course, it can't have cost more than a pound or two.'

'You should have had the blue one,' said Mrs Yardley-Peters. 'That's not going to be any good with your dark suit, you know.'

The manager made a convulsive movement and shot a black plastic pen container on to the floor. Major Anglesey, with cries of concern, got down and scrabbled for the pens – 'Here we are, all intact, I think.'

'So silly,' said Mrs Yardley-Peters, 'about the cheque book. Shall I pay you back while it's in my head, Rupert? I'll write *you* a cheque.'

'Look,' said the manager, with a sort of gasp, 'I simply want to . . .'

'Consider them a present, my dear,' said the Major gallantly.

'You didn't pay for them,' said the store detective. The words came out as a hoarse cry and both the Major and Mrs Yardley-Peters turned to look at her in surprise. Mrs Yardley-Peters shook her head and frowned, evidently put out, 'No, no, that's absurd. You've just heard the Major say they're to be counted as a present and that's sweet of you, Rupert, though I do think we ought to keep our finances separate at least for the time being. You know, I'm wondering if the shoes may not be all right once one's worn them in a bit. Do you usually reckon,' she went on, addressing the store detective, 'on them giving a bit as you wear them?'

'Mrs Hebden is not a member of the sales staff,' said the manager. 'And in any case it is hardly a question of . . .'

The Major interrupted. 'I remember now, it all comes back – that tie was one pound ninety-five. I thought at the time good grief in real money that's all of two quid and I've got ties in my cupboard I paid four-and-six for, in the old days. Two quid for a tie, I ask you! Not,' he went on quickly, 'that it's not good value for nowadays.'

The manager rose. His collar clung to his neck and sweat trickled down inside his shirt. He went to the window and opened it.

'Yes, I was feeling it was a wee bit stuffy too,' said Mrs Yardley-Peters. 'You'd think they'd give you a bigger office, wouldn't you? But I suppose you're out and about quite a lot, looking after the shop. I always say, the thing about this sort of place is, you can see exactly what you're getting, and there's never a bit of argument about changing anything.'

Once, the manager had had to deal with an Arab lady and her three daughters, not a word of English between them, all weeping, and twenty-eight pairs of bikini briefs stuffed inside their coats. At this moment, he looked back on that occasion almost with nostalgia. He sat down again and addressed the Major. 'Now, sir, if there is any explanation you feel you'd like to give, naturally I . . .'

The note of hysteria in his voice did not escape Mrs Yardley-Peters. She said kindly, 'You know, you look to me a bit under the weather, I should think you might be coming down with something. If I were you I'd . . .'

The Major tapped her reprovingly. 'Mona, I'm sure our friend here's well able to take care of himself. All he wants is to get this bit of bother sorted out so we can all be off for our dins.'

Madge Hebden, all her life, had had strong feelings about legality. She'd never, herself, stepped out of line, not once. And she believed in plain speaking. At this point she exploded.

'It's theft, that's what it is! Honest to goodness theft. Thieves! Bit of bother, indeed! I saw them with my own eyes and in all the ten months I've been in the store I've never . . .'

The manager got to his feet in one violent movement. His hands, as though acting independently of the rest of him, twitched about the surface of the desk, apparently seeking a hold on something. 'Thank you, Mrs Hebden, you've done a grand job. In this case I feel though that there may be extenuating circumstances to be taken into consideration' – he was gabbling now, looking through and beyond rather than at Major Anglesey and Mrs Yardley-Peters – 'and naturally one prefers rather than perpetrate possibly an injustice to exercise in some cases and I believe this to be one such discretion as is at one's disposal our policy in such instances being always to . . .'

'Oh dear,' said Mrs Yardley-Peters, 'I'm afraid I'm not following this very well. Could you begin again?'

The manager wiped his forehead. He said, 'Go away.'

'Eh?' said the Major.

'Please go. Just go.'

Mrs Yardley-Peters stared at him. 'Well, I must say. I think that's a bit abrupt. After all, you invited us in here, it wasn't us who wanted to come. Very well, then.' She bent down and put her shoes on. The manager, leaning across the desk, pushed towards her the contents of the shopping bag. Mrs Yardley-Peters put them carefully into it, slowly, removing things once or twice to re-arrange them. As she picked up the shoes, the lambswool sweater and the tie the store detective gave a kind of croak; the manager was silent, nerves twitching all over one side of his face.

'There,' said Mrs Yardley-Peters. She rose. 'Have you got the car-keys, Rupert, or have I?' At the door she paused and looked back. 'You know one doesn't like to interfere but I do have the most distinct impression that they overwork you people, the powers that be. You both look done in.'

Major Anglesey and Mrs Yardley-Peters walked slowly through the shop. Mid-way they paused and Major Anglesey took over the shopping bag. They stopped once to cast an eye over the shirt counter but evidently decided against any further acquisitions. At the entrance Major Anglesey held the door open for a woman with a push-chair and was then trapped for a couple of minutes by his own solicitude, as a procession of people entered from the street; at last he was able to join Mrs Yardley-Peters outside and the two of them moved away towards the multi-storey car park.

Major Anglesey drove. Mrs Yardley-Peters remarked that that poor man had seemed awfully neurotic, and the assistant rather bad-tempered. Detective, Mona, corrected the Major, they call them detective. Whatever they are, said Mrs Yardley-Peters, anyway, it's not a job I'd care for. The Major agreed. They recalled one or two previous experiences. When they reached the bungalow the Major put the car in the garage and carried the shopping bag inside. Mrs Yardley-Peters, humming to herself, removed the food items; the Major took the bag into the spare bedroom. He put the lambswool sweater, still in its plastic wrapping, into a big cupboard whose shelves were filled with many other sweaters, cardigans, shirts and pyjamas, also still in their wrappings. The tie he added to a rail already piled with ties, in a wardrobe pressed tight with suits and coats and ladies' dresses, from which dangled price tickets and labels giving washing instructions. Mrs Yardley-Peters came in and said playfully, 'Have I been a clever girl?'; the Major, without speaking, patted her bottom. 'Din-dins,' said Mrs Yardley-Peters, and the Major followed her through into the sitting-room, where the chicken pieces and the coleslaw were set out on Beatrix Potter plates. 'My turn for Jemima Puddleduck,' said Mrs Yardley-Peters. The Major poured light ale from a can into glasses decorated with cartoon mice; 'Cheers.' Mrs Yardley-Peters looked at him roguishly over the top of her glass. 'Cheers, Rupie. We've been naughty again, haven't we!' The Major, in reply, waggled his moustache, an accomplishment which had been one of his initial attractions.

Yellow Trains

'I AM UNHAPPY,' said the girl to her friend. She looked out of the window through the shimmering folds of the net curtains to the parked cars in the street; their windscreens snapped in the sunshine and a small dog rummaged in the gutter. 'I am so unhappy,' she repeated, and across the city the friend sighed and murmured.

'Yesterday,' she said, 'I was so happy I could have cried. Listen, I rode in a train with blue seats, bright bright blue, and there was this factory chimney smoking white against the sky and the sky was grey like velvet. Do you know what I mean? And clouds like carvings. I tell you, I sat there looking and I could have cried.'

'He isn't,' asked the friend delicately, 'coming?'

'He isn't coming. There is this business with the office and his mother that he must go to on Saturday come what may and something about someone for whom he has to hold keys to a flat. He isn't coming.'

'People,' said the friend, after a pause, 'get so involved.'

The girl watched the small dog nose an empty tin. She looked at the sky above the rooftops and at the thread of vapour from an aeroplane. 'I sat in that train and I wasn't thinking of anything in particular. I wasn't thinking: tomorrow, tomorrow, tomorrow. It was just a state of mind. And today . . . Listen, I'm looking at the sky now, and it's nothing. Nothing at all. And yesterday there were these clouds like sculptures. I don't understand how what you see is a question of what you feel.'

The friend, across streets and parks and rooftops, sighed again. 'Did he phone, or what?'

'He phoned.'

'Excuse me a minute,' said the friend. 'I've got something on the stove.'

The girl saw a pigeon with pink twiggy legs walk round and round, round and round. She saw a child go past chanting incantations. She saw an old woman put down a carrier bag and stand for a moment, hunched up.

The friend came back. 'Sorry. I expect he just couldn't get out of it.'

'Possibly. Probably. I made pizza. And got that beer he likes. He phoned very late last night. I feel as though I've put on pounds and pounds.'

'Sorry?' said the friend.

'Weight. Yesterday I felt as though I was floating slightly. Walking along the platform at Clapham Junction. Like bubbles going up through you. And these yellow trains dashing all over the place, yellow like daffodils. I thought, I'm always going to remember feeling like this.'

'Mmn.'

'And the funny thing is I do now. Remember. I'm miserable, I'm pissed off, I feel as heavy as a rock. But it's all there still, underneath. The floating feeling, and the clouds, and the yellow trains. Only I can't get at it any more.'

'Is he going to call again?' asked the friend.

The girl twitched the curtain; the cars shimmered and flashed. 'Actually, yesterday I wanted things just to stop there. Until I said go on. I wanted to keep it – feeling like that. I wanted to learn what it was like.'

'Looking forward to something,' the friend began, 'is . . .'

'I wasn't really looking forward. Don't you see? It was just being like that. Happy. Now I'm unhappy and it's nothing, it's a no-feeling. It doesn't exist.'

The friend said, 'Mmn – I'm not so sure about that.' After a moment she added, 'I'm sure he'll call again.'

'I expect he's calling now,' said the girl. 'I expect he's desperately trying to get through, dialling and hanging up again and asking the operator if the line's engaged talking or out of order. Dialling and dialling.'

The friend coughed. 'Excuse me. Where does his mother live?'

'In Surrey. Reigate. His sister lives with her. She has red hair and works in the library. What I can't get over is how things push on like they do and take you with them whether you want it or not. Days. They drag you on. One day you're with the yellow trains like daffodils and the next you're sitting here with a knot in your insides. Sometimes I'm not sure if I can go through with life if this is the way it's going to be.'

'Oh, come on now . . .' said the friend. After a moment she went on, 'Hello? Are you still there?'

'I'm here. There's this dog outside that's got its paw muddled up in a bit of plastic. Do you think I should go out and help it?'

The friend said, 'I don't know. Of course he wouldn't have known about you making the pizza.'

'It's all right – the dog's got its paw out of the plastic. I couldn't get the big olives so I had to use the other kind. I had them in my bag when I was walking along the platform at Clapham Junction and now there they are in the fridge. Same bloody olives. Funny, when you come to think about it.'

The friend said sadly, 'I suppose you're in love with him.'

'Is that my trouble? God, how unoriginal. And here was I going on about clouds and yellow trains. Oh, and there was Battersea Power Station. I didn't tell you about Battersea Power Station. It looked like a temple. Egyptian, I think. Do you imagine he's going to see someone else instead?'

'Look, don't think about that kind of thing.'

'I'm not. It's not a question of thinking. I'm not thinking about anything. I just get attacked from time to time.'

'I know,' said the friend, after a moment.

The girl said, 'Do you remember the way when you were a child you always wanted it to be next week? Today was so boring. Next week was always Christmas and birthdays and going to the cinema.'

'He'll ring up,' said the friend. 'You see. Next week. Tomorrow.'

'Ah. Will he? Since when were birthdays always last week? And yellow trains.'

'These trains . . .'

'Sorry about the trains.' The girl saw sparrows float down from a tree and hop among crisp packets and paper bags. 'He said it was a pity and we'd have to fix something another time. He ran out of coins and had to go.'

Miles away, across roads and buses and taxis, the friend said, 'Then that's how it is. Another time. There's always other times.'

'I don't want other times,' said the girl. 'I want yesterday. I want to be so happy like I was yesterday. I want to go back into yesterday and settle down there and live there for ever. I want to spend the rest of my life riding out of Clapham Junction on yellow trains, looking at the smoke against those clouds. I don't want to be here; I want to be there. I want to be sitting on those bright blue seats, watching the houses go by. I don't like now, I want to be then.'

The friend sighed. 'Go and eat that pizza. It won't keep.'

'The Ghost of a Flea'

HE MET her at the opening party for an exhibition of paintings by a friend of his brother's. He stood penned against a wall talking to no one with an empty glass in his hand and suddenly there was this short girl with a soft inexorable voice at his elbow, saying things.

'Sorry?'

'I said, you've got such a kind face, I knew you wouldn't mind my coming across. I mean, I can always tell, just looking at people. Most of them here – well, I just wouldn't . . . You see, the thing is . . .'

He couldn't hear the half of it. He bent over her, frowning with concentration. She had thick long fawn hair that sometimes obscured her face and a physical solidity at curious variance with some kind of manic tension. She alarmed him. She was called Angela. As the party thinned out he learned that they were going to have a curry at a place round the corner and then he would walk her back to her flat.

Over the curry, they exchanged telephone numbers. She said it was so lucky he was working in Holborn because actually her office was only just round the corner. She said she was terribly interested in painting, she'd done an art course once herself but as therapy in fact, it had been good, it had helped. After the meal, as they left, she said she was feeling a bit odd. Hang on a minute, she said, do you mind? She stood on the pavement, her back against some railings, staring, it seemed, at the passing traffic, a small stocky girl with something dogged about her, dogged and enclosed. He wondered nervously if she was drunk, but she had had only a glass of lager with the curry. After a moment she said, 'I'll be all right now, Paul, it's just I get this sort of breathlessness, it goes if I keep still a minute. Shall we go?' He left her outside the house in which she had a flat.

He was at home in the evening, five days later, when the phone rang. She said, 'It's Angela. Look, can I come round? I'm having a bit of a bad spell, it's an awful help to talk.'

He made her coffee. She took off her shoes and padded around his

room with bare feet. She said, it must be marvellous to have so many
books, I've got hardly any books. Is that Battersea? You must be able to
see the river from this window, I never know if I love the river or if it
upsets me.

She sat cross-legged on the rug with the coffee mug cradled in her
hands, the thick dun swatches of her hair falling across her face, her soft
quiet voice going on and on, unstoppable, distressing. 'After Mummy
and Daddy were killed in the car crash I lived with Daddy's aunt in
Guildford until she got this liver disease. Then I got rheumatic fever and I
was in St Thomas's for nine months, because of the complications. They
thought I was going to die and the thing is, it's left me with a sort of funny
heart, but it's not too bad, they're terribly sweet, they see me every six
months . . . Then I got the job with Hatchards and then I did the
secretarial course and I went to Steers two years ago . . . I found this flat
through my boss, he's been awfully kind . . . I'm taking Catholic
instruction, I started with one of the fathers at Gregory Street but now I'm
going to St Damian's . . . I absolutely adore flying kites, I've got this new
kite from Selfridges, I thought, let's go and fly it on Saturday, O.K.?'

He was disturbed, concerned. He said, 'Haven't you got *any* relatives,
Angela, honestly?'

She shook her head. 'There's these people, the Stanleys, in Basing-
stoke, I go to at Christmas. Mrs Stanley was a friend of Mummy's.
They've been terribly kind, I can go there any time, absolutely whenever I
want.'

They flew the kite on Hampstead Heath. It wriggled like a tethered
serpent against the luminous London sky. Angela ran about, calling him.
She wore a furry coat and boots, her face grew pink in the wind, she
became quite pretty. Walking to the tube station, he wondered if she
expected him to take her hand; he strode worriedly beside her, a tall
stringy young man, short-sighted, good-tempered and made despond-
ent by injustice. He did not find her sexually attractive. He told her at
length of his work with a firm of architects in order to conceal and distance
the guilt engendered by this absence of desire. He took her back to his
rooms and made them scrambled eggs and bacon. Angela said, I can't
cook, it's silly, I know, I've never learned, all the girls in my office are
terribly good cooks. Later, she declared herself tired and lay on the sofa
where she fell asleep. He sat in the darkening room, peering at
newspapers, glancing at her from time to time in unease. He suspected
she might be a rather unstable girl.

He met her for lunch in the pub near his office. They flew the kite again.
Sometimes she telephoned him late in the evening and talked lengthily,
fluently, her low regular voice coming to him through the noisy London
night, tense and yet stoical. She made him think, uncomfortably and with
a wrench of pity, of those resigned resilient children who stand at the

edge of school playgrounds, unsought, excluded from games. She made him think also, disturbingly, of cripples. At that party, when first he met her, he had looked down, he now remembered, in instinctive search of something: a surgical boot, a leg caliper. You're being the most enormous help, Paul, she said. It's sweet of you to take so much trouble, you don't mind, do you? The think is, I had this beastly business with someone at the office, I can't sleep, it's made me feel all strange, if I could just talk for a bit . . .

She said, I've never been to the Tate, isn't it silly? I had a thing about the river once, I used to keep going to the Embankment to walk up and down, and look over that bridge, the iron one – you know, which is it? – but I never went into the Tate. So I thought, let's go on Sunday. He said cautiously, Look Angela, there are these people I know with this cottage in Suffolk and I was actually thinking of going down there this weekend . . . She nodded and smiled her damaged smile and he winced and hurried on, but next week – next week would be fine.

She often arrived first at the pub or entrance to the Underground. She would have bought the drinks, the tickets, the sandwiches. No, she'd say, it's my turn, Paul, honestly, otherwise it's simply not fair and you've been so terribly sweet to me anyway, I'm not going to be any more of a nuisance.

He saw her from some way off, on the steps of the Tate, standing with her hands in her pockets and a strand of hair blown horizontally across her face, staring at the Thames. When he arrived she said, 'Don't you think seagulls are the most terribly threatening things? Their eyes. When I was a child I used to have nightmares about birds.'

In the Blake Room she pored over the cases. From time to time he lost her in the murky, crowded room and then would catch sight of her small bundled figure in a group, gazing at a picture, always looking somehow apart from other people, isolated. He joined her in front of a case of drawings at which she intently stared.

'Isn't that ridiculous!' she exclaimed. '*The Ghost of a Flea!* But that's mad – it's absurd. A flea couldn't have a ghost.' She began to laugh, loudly. People turned their heads, peering across the dark, respectful room in which the paintings gleamed from their glass cases like tropical fish.

He tried to move her on. 'Blake is a kind of visionary, isn't he? It's rather a neurotic picture. Isn't he supposed to have been a bit mad?'

'Neurotic!' She continued, mirthlessly, to laugh. 'I hate it!'

'Let's go, then.'

'Just a minute. Oh God, look at it – I'll never forget it, now. That awful grotesque head. It gives me the shivers.'

'Come on, Angela,' he said nervously.

'I'm coming. Can we go home?' She began to walk quickly towards the door.

He caught her up. 'But it's only half past two. I thought we were going to . . .'

'I'm sorry, Paul, I'm not feeling too good.' Her voice was even lower than usual. He loped behind her down the steps, out on to the Embankment. He thought she might be crying. The faint gloom always induced in him by her company was unsettlingly compounded now with both pity and irritation. At this time last week he had been having a convivial lunch in a Suffolk pub with an old friend and his jovial, matey wife. He said, 'What's the matter, Angela?'

She was leaning now over the parapet, looking down at the viscous flow of the river. Seagulls bobbed among scarves of plastic. He peered at her. 'You're not crying, are you?'

'I never cry. I can't remember ever crying. It was just that picture, it made me get this feeling I get.'

'What sort of feeling?'

'I'm afraid it's almost impossible to explain to other people.' She had her eyes closed, he now saw. 'It's like being very scared, but you feel a bit as though you might faint as well. Your legs go funny. And you know it's only you who's like that, and there's nothing anybody else can do about it. I'll be fine in a minute. It's beginning to go now.' She continued to hunch over the parapet.

Paul said, 'You know, Angela, I wonder if perhaps it might be an idea to see a doctor sometime.'

She opened her eyes and turned to look at him. She had brown, rather large eyes. 'I have done.'

'Ah. And . . . ?'

'What do you think?' she said wearily. 'Look, Paul, I think I'm just about all right now, but I'd like to go back. Thank you for being so sweet. I'm sorry to be such a bore.'

In silence they returned to her flat.

A week later she telephoned to ask him to come with her to a party.

'Tonight? Well, I'm not sure, Angela, truth to tell I've had a bit of a tiring day, would you mind awfully if . . .'

'Never mind. It's just it helps awfully having someone with me. And I wanted to talk to you anyway.'

He sighed. 'O.K. But only for a bit, if you don't mind.'

At the party, she was in a state of uncharacteristic animation. She towed him around the room, locking in conversation with strangers, talking quickly and loudly, moving on. She drank rather a lot. Pink crests formed on her cheeks. When eventually they left she said, 'Let's go back and have a cup of coffee at your place.' He asked her what it was she had wanted to talk to him about and she said she couldn't remember, it didn't matter now.

In his room she sat as usual on the floor. She did a lot of yoga at one time, she had told him, and this inclination was a legacy of that period. Similarly, a residual distaste for meat stemmed from having once been a vegetarian. She sat sipping coffee and telling him about Father Michael who was such a help and what he had said yesterday. Paul said, 'When are you actually, er, going to be properly converted or whatever it's called?' She stared at him and replied, 'Oh, I'm not, I've decided not to finish it, didn't I tell you? They've been terribly kind but I've decided to stop at the end of the month.'

Presently she said, 'I had too much to drink at that stupid party. I think I'd better spend the night here.'

He shuffled in alarm. 'But there's only my bed, Angela.'

'I'll sleep on the sofa.'

'I will, then. You have the bed.'

'No. It's my own fault. I shouldn't have let those people keep filling my glass. I'm sorry, Paul. You go to bed. I'll just have a wash.'

He retreated to the bedroom. Presently there was silence. With relief, he turned and slept.

He woke with a jump to see her standing in the doorway. 'I can't sleep, I've got that awful feeling.'

His heart sank. He sat up. 'Look, Angela . . .'

She came over to the bed. 'I'll get in with you. I'll just lie beside you and then I'll be fine. Go to sleep.'

He said wildly, 'Angela, I simply don't . . .'

'Go to sleep,' she said again.

He rolled to the far side of the bed. She climbed in. He wasn't sure if she had any clothes on or not. He thought not. He thought she was stark naked six inches from him. He could feel warmth come across the sheet from her thigh. He cowered against the wall.

Presently he heard her breathe more heavily. She sighed, shifted, was asleep. He lay rigid, hour by hour. Once she sighed again and lurched towards him. He shrank into the crevasse between bed and wall where a cold draught strayed along his back.

In the morning, he wriggled precariously from the bed without touching her, grabbed his clothes and took them to the bathroom. When he was making tea and toast she came in wearing his dressing-gown. She said, 'I feel such a fool. I feel such an awful stupid fool. I want to die.'

He avoided her eye. 'It's O.K., Angela, honestly, we were a bit overtired, that's all. Look, the marmalade's in the cupboard, shall I . . .'

'I wish I were dead.'

He forced a laugh; it sounded even worse than he'd feared. 'Oh come on, Angela, everyone has a bit too much every now and then, it's not . . .'

'Actually,' she said, 'I have tried to kill myself. Twice. I wasn't going to tell you.'

He slopped the tea and did some concentrated diversionary wiping up.

'In fact,' she said, 'I probably would have told you. It's only fair, when you've been so sweet. The first time I took some pills and the second time I tried to jump into the river.'

He dumped the cloth in the sink. 'Tried?'

'There was this man who came along.'

'Well,' he said firmly, 'I'm very glad it didn't work. And please don't talk like that, you'll feel fine later on, just you see. It's silly to get so upset. I'll have to rush now or I'll be late for the office. You'll be all right, won't you?'

She sat at the table, a small teddy-bearish figure in his brown schoolboy dressing-gown. She stared down at the table, her hair swathing her face. She did not answer.

'I'll give you a ring,' he said desperately. 'At lunch-time.'

She looked at him. 'That's very nice of you, Paul. I can't tell you what a help you are.'

Outside, he took great gulps of the London morning. He paused at the shop further down the road outside which shocks of daffodils and tulips stood in buckets and he thought of buying her a bunch and going back and leaving them by the door, and then did not because flowers are no compensation for other unperformed actions, and in any case what he would be doing would be to assuage his own feelings, not make her any happier.

Either you take a shine to a girl or you don't. Unless of course you are the sort of bloke who is simply a sexual opportunist.

He shambled disconsolately to his office. He was twenty-seven. When he was nine he had written an indignant letter to the Prime Minister of the day protesting against stag-hunting, a barbarity which had just come to his attention and which had caused him a night of distress. Nowadays, he was the kind of person who gives up his seat to old ladies and contributes heavily to charities. He shambled to the office and at lunch-time he rang up Angela and the next evening he had a drink with her and at the weekend he went with her to a film.

Three weeks later, when the spring had just touched London, Paul fell in love. He met her in the house of some friends and at the end of another fifteen days they were in bed together. She was called Frances. She had dark curly hair and an exuberant personality. She was competent, generous, lithe and merry and she loved him back. He said, 'Look, I'll have to tell you at some point, there's this girl. Not what you might think, not like that at all. The thing is, you see . . .' And then he cried, 'Oh Christ, that's what she says – the thing is – it must be catching. But the thing is . . .'

He introduced Frances to Angela at the pub in which he had so often plied Angela with sandwiches (she always resisted food – it had struck him as curious that she remained so plump, there was in this also a hint about her of a determined survival against all the odds). Angela said, 'I love your boots. I'd adore to wear ankle boots but my calves are too fat. Paul says you're a super cook. Can you teach me to make pizza? I've got this old schoolfriend coming to stay on Sunday and I want to make pizza for her. I thought, if you and Paul came on Saturday morning we could do it then and I could show you the street market round the corner. O.K.?'

They had planned to go to Greenwich that Saturday. As it was, Frances showed Angela how to make pizza till nearly three. Then Angela was feeling a bit low so they stayed till six or so to cheer her up. They never got to Greenwich. They went to a film in the evening and Frances said, 'Angela's very nice, really, isn't she?' and Paul agreed that she was. Frances said, 'It's the most awful shame,' and Paul again agreed. They went to bed and had a lovely night and both, separately, thought once or twice of Angela and felt a trickle of guilt.

When Paul was not with Frances he conjured her from the pavement or the opposing row of faces in the Underground or from the pearly spring sky and dwelt upon her and told her what he was thinking and doing. He hovered over the telephone because to be about to speak to her was almost better than to be actually speaking to her and when she rang him he sometimes delayed answering because the sound of her voice induced such pleasure that it was really almost impossible to do anything but savour it.

Sometimes the voice was not Frances's but Angela's and then he would be hearty and welcoming and if necessary – and it frequently was – concerned. He advised and sympathised and reassured. Angela said, 'I think it's marvellous about Frances and you, I do like her so much,' and he muttered that Frances liked her too, naturally, of course. Angela said, 'What do you think she wants for her birthday?' and Paul said he didn't know, he'd try to find out. In the end he went with Angela to choose a very expensive iron casserole which he knew she could not afford. Frances also knew this, and thereafter the casserole glimmered at them from Frances's kitchen shelf, inducing discomfort.

Once, they were in Frances's bed when the telephone rang. It was half past midnight. Frances said, 'Oh lor, I hope that's not poor Auntie Liz died, Mum said she'd ring.' She was gone five minutes. When she returned she said, 'It's Angela. She tried you first and then supposed you were here. She sounds in the most awful state, poor thing. Something about a picture. Do talk to her, Paul.'

He stood shifting from one bare foot to the other on a stone floor and Angela told him she was seeing these heads, these monstrous heads and she thought she would go mad. She said her doorbell had rung and she'd gone to answer it and there'd been no one there but she'd seen this silhouette of someone going down the stairs with a head like – like that ghastly picture. The teeth, she said, those teeth. That eye. Picture? he queried, flexing his toes, drawing Frances's cotton dressing-gown round his thighs, what picture? Oh, *The Ghost of a Flea*. But honestly, Angela, that's ridiculous, I mean you must *know*, really and truly, it was a trick of the light. You're having nightmares. And from far away across streets and buildings Angela's quiet and level voice told him of voids and chasms and a world that was only partly comprehensible and when presently she paused and for moments he could not hear her he said sharply, 'Angela? Are you still there?'

When he came back to bed Frances said, 'Do you think she'll be all right? I sort of felt we ought to have gone over there; or one of us anyway.' And for a while they lay in unease until they slept and in the morning they phoned her, early. She said she was a little better now but tired. At the weekend she came to see them, bearing a strange primeval plant which subsequently died in a protracted manner. She said she was sorry she'd been so silly but she sometimes got like that and there was absolutely nothing you could do about it. The time when she'd taken all those pills had been when she'd got like that. She said it made all the difference having them there, knowing that all she had to do was pick up the phone. She said they'd been so sweet.

Paul and Frances had planned to go to Brighton for the day and in the end Angela came with them. They walked between the green sea and the sparkling stucco and Angela talked about the school she'd been at and the friend she'd had there that she'd lost touch with now and the new woman in the office who didn't like her, she knew. She walked with her eyes on the pavement through the air that brushed the face like clouds of feathers, under a sky pegged to the horizon by tiny cut-out ships, past murmurous glistening shingle and piers sending long dainty fingers of white ironwork into the milky surf. She passed through all this inside the dark capsule of her own head. Frances said, honestly, Angela, I should forget about that, I mean it's years ago and as for the woman in the office she sounds an old cow, just don't take any notice of her. And Angela smiled her separate smile, her smile from an unshared world and said, yes, Frances, you're absolutely right, of course, you're so sensible, yes, that's what I must do.

Look at Royal Crescent, said Paul, it's very famous, architecturally, isn't it handsome?

Just a little bit like lavatory tiles, suggests irreverent Frances, skipping aside from the lecture that this provokes. And Angela looks with her shuttered eyes and says yes, isn't it pretty, when did you say it was built, Paul?

They ate a fish tea and rode back to London in a train that stitched its way through the Sussex fields. Gorgeous, said Frances, heavenly, let's live in that house – no, that one. And Angela talked of this man she knew who lived in Burgess Hill, who played the flute, and said she felt better now, quite a bit, she'd sleep tonight, she thought, she'd take a pill and have a good night.

Spring opened into summer. Paul and Frances went again to Brighton, alone, and Frances's skin turned a pale coffee colour and Paul wondered if the day would ever come when he could be with her and stop looking at her. He knew now that he would marry her, if this plan fitted in with her intentions, which he rather thought it would, and he woke every morning in a state of astonishment. He could not imagine why he should have been selected for such incredible happiness, there must be some mistake, he had no right.

They were in Paul's room, late one evening, when the phone went. Frances, sleepily, fondly, watched him press the receiver to his ear, scowling, listened to him saying, 'Yes, hello? Hello? *Hello.*'

Put it down, she said, it's a wrong number. And then he was frowning more. 'Angela? I can hardly hear, can you talk louder. What? Angela, where are you?' There was a pause. Frances sighed and sat up. Paul said urgently. 'Stay there. What's the number – I'll ring you back.' He looked over at Frances. 'She's in a phone box somewhere, she sounds awful, she says there's some man following her. She's talking about killing herself.'

Frances said, 'Oh God.' They stared at each other for a moment. Paul dialled.

Faintly, insistently, Angela's voice whispered into the room. Paul said, 'Yes. Yes. Yes, I see.' And then, 'No, no, Angela, don't – stay where you are.'

Frances stood up. She fetched pencil and paper, handed them to Paul. She watched Paul talk, scribble, talk. As he put the receiver down she was putting on her coat.

They saw the phone box from some way off, a brown figure huddled within it. Behind, the river glittered away to left and right, a carnival of lights and rosy floodlit buildings. When Angela saw them she came out of the phone box and stood in front of them with her hands in her pockets. She said, 'The man came again, the man in the drawing. He followed me and every time I turned round I saw his face, that awful face. I went up on to the bridge and he was still there. I was going to jump in.'

They steered her to a taxi. They took her back to Frances's flat. She went to bed in Frances's bed. Paul went home.

The next day Frances said to him, 'I think this is going to drive me bananas. Quite honestly.' After a moment she went on, 'Do you think she ever would?'

'Kill herself?'

She nodded.

'I don't know,' said Paul. 'You read things in newspapers. About – you know – cries for help and that sort of stuff.'

'Some of them actually do.'

They stared at each other.

Paul said, 'I'm sorry, darling. It's me who landed her on you. On us. But you can't just . . .'

'No. I know you can't. That's the whole point.'

Paul and Frances went to Cornwall for a holiday. They walked for miles on shaggy cliff paths and waded into icy seas and made incessant love and arranged to marry in the autumn. They sent Angela a postcard of lobster pots and a shiny unreal sea. On the day they returned to London they found a note from her at Frances's flat with a basket of fruit and a bottle of wine. A few days later they met her for a drink and she was animated, sprightly, and talked of this girl she'd met whom she might go to Portugal with later on. They told her about the wedding and she said I think that's marvellous, how super, you will invite me, *won't* you? She asked Frances to come shopping with her and help her buy some clothes. Afterwards, Frances said, 'She seems fine, doesn't she? I mean really much better, more together, more . . .'

'More like other people?'

'That, I suppose.'

'The terrible thing,' said Paul after a moment, 'about Angela, the terribly sad thing, is that she is only just one notch away from being, well, perfectly all right. To lots of people most of the time she probably does seem fine.'

'Quite.'

They were silent, with separate and similar visions of Angela's small resolute figure, forging on, alone, possessed, unreachable.

The London summer ripened and the streets flowed with tourists and Paul redecorated Frances's flat as a preliminary to married life therein. He moved, gradually, his few possessions and spent long hours in the meticulous application of paint to walls and ceilings with the windows open to the warm clattering evenings. He had never been prone to religious belief except once briefly in adolescence when he had been smitten by the personality of the new school chaplain. Now, in the tranquillity of his happiness, he looked for someone to whom to offer thanks; it seemed irrational that all this should have come to him from a void. Frances cooked him exquisite meals with the minimum of fuss.

It was in the midst of one such evening that a call came from St Thomas's Hospital. Were they, a voice wanted to know, Miss Frances Bennett and Mr Paul Freeland?

In apprehension and with gathering expectation Frances replied that they were. She knew now what would come next, and Paul, the paintbrush arrested in mid-stroke, looked across the room, met her eyes and experienced for the first time that wordless communication of married people: he read her. When she put the phone down he said, 'Angela.' Frances nodded.

At the entrance to the hospital ward a sister briskly held them. 'Miss Bennett and Mr Freeland? For Angela Holywell? She's in the end bed. She gave you as next of kin. I gather there are no parents or anything. You'll find her fairly comfortable now, a bit dopey still. She was asking just now if you were coming, she specially wants to see you. I shouldn't stay too long.'

'What exactly,' said Paul, 'happened? They just said . . .'

'Sleeping pills. The usual. Not enough, fortunately, and she'd left the door of her flat ajar for some reason and a neighbour came in with a message.'

They sat on either side of the high hospital bed in which Angela lay propped up on pillows. Her hair had been brushed and lay in two neat hanks down each side of her face. She wore a flannelette nightgown sprigged with small blue flowers. She looked rather younger than twenty-seven. She held their hands in her own small, surprisingly powerful grip and said, 'Don't let go for a minute – d'you mind? Just for a minute. It was sweet of you to come. The thing is – I'd been seeing that man again, you know, the picture – for days and days now. I couldn't stand it any longer. You must think I'm an awful fool.'

Paul said, 'The man doesn't exist, Angela. It's just a picture.'

'I know. Oh, I know. There's always been something you see. Voices, sometimes. There always will be. But I think I'll be all right now – they've been terribly nice to me here. There's this doctor – he's coming in to see me again tomorrow. And it makes all the difference just knowing you're there, both of you. You didn't mind me giving them your names, do you? You're not annoyed?'

And Paul and Frances said that no, of course they weren't annoyed and of course they didn't mind. The grip of Angela's small warm hand slackened but her low voice continued to narrate and explain and Paul and Frances looked at each other across the bed, both separated and tethered by her, perplexed and saddened and sharing a spectral, queasy vision of what was yet to come.

The Art of Biography

SHE WAS eighty if she was a day. Which was of course to be expected: Edward Lamprey would be eighty-seven if he were still alive and the daughter had said Miss Rockingham was a contemporary. Miss Lucinda Rockingham. A curiously lavish name for the spare, slightly bent old lady who stood now in her doorway, looking up at him.

He put out a hand, smiled his charming open young man's smile. 'Miss Rockingham? I'm Malcolm Sanders. It's so good of you to let me take up your time like this.'

Twenty-eight interviews, duly recorded and filed. Seventeen card index boxes. Seven hundred and nineteen letters in the British Library and the University of Texas and in God knows how many box files and drawers of desks. Notes and footnotes and references and cross-references; checks and cross-checks and headings and sub-headings. Names and places and times and dates. All sewn up and stashed away, or just about. A man's life reduced to paper and print – or rather, card and tempo pen. The material, the valuable laboriously gathered material for the definitive biography of Edward Lamprey, poet and man of letters, born eighteen-ninety-three, died nineteen-fifty-eight.

He yawned, discreetly, into the back of his hand, turning momentarily aside as though to admire the view of the estuary beyond the wide window of Lucinda Rockingham's sitting-room. A flat, melancholy East Anglian view, all sea and sky and fleeing birds and, far away, cars twinkling along the coast road. Bleak and impersonal, as was the house bleak and impersonal – an Edwardian villa, faintly hostile from without and chilly within, the sofa too hard, the room too neat, the pictures too square upon the walls.

And Lucinda Rockingham an agreeable enough old thing but not of any use, he could tell within the first five minutes, nothing of any significance to say about Lamprey ('He was a great poet, you know, Mr Sanders, yes, I knew him since nineteen-forty, yes, he visited this house . . .'), the trip a waste.

He smiled and jotted the odd note and let his mind drift. He examined his feelings – took them out and prodded them, held them up to the light, took their temperature, and they were the same. He was in love, no two ways about it. Conjure her up, right here on the worn patterned carpet beside the unlit Rayburn Maxistove, and there was that delicious liquefaction of the vitals. He smiled and made another note and held her in his arms, against his cheek, her mouth . . . Better phone as soon as he was through here, before she left the office, there was a phone booth on the sea-front, he'd just catch her if he cut this short . . .

That, actually, was the funny thing about Lamprey. The one odd, unsatisfactory blank. Love. For a man whose passionate nature spun from every line of the poems, the absence of any evidence that he ever experienced intensity of love was curious to say the least of it. Certainly there'd been none in the marriage, probably not even at the very beginning. A haphazard union that drifted into a convenient arrangement for the upbringing of the four cherished daughters. For them, certainly, there had been love, devotion indeed, but not the kind of love to account for the depth of feeling that lurked in the poetry, the pastoral poems in particular that read at times like something quite other, like . . .

'. . . occasionally helped with some of the more tedious clerical tasks,' said the old lady. 'The study of Coleridge, which I daresay you know . . .' She smoothed the cotton print dress across her knees and smiled, a rather sweet smile, a beauty once probably – no, not a beauty, just a very pretty woman (no husband, apparently, odd, that) – and bless her yes one did indeed know the study of Coleridge, every chapter and verse of it, what did she imagine one had spent three years doing, for heaven's sake? The daughters had had some vague idea that she did odd bits of secretarial stuff for Lamprey, that sort of thing – the kind of useful friend a man like that sometimes attracts. But they'd not known much about her, none of them, only as a name that cropped up once or twice, hadn't suggested her until this late point, with everything ready to be written, the first three chapters drafted indeed. And then she had to be looked into, of course, just in case. Another index card, another reference.

He got up. He beamed. He thanked. He took her warm, dry small hand and thanked again. He went out to the car, got in, looked back, waved, started the engine, glanced down at the AA road book open on the seat beside him.

And there she was suddenly at the car window, a little breathless, saying something he could not quite catch.

He switched the engine off.

'Letters?'

'Letters, Miss Rockingham?'

She hadn't known whether to mention, had wondered if it were perhaps better . . . had thought suddenly, seeing him about to go, had decided that no, really, that it would be wrong, that . . .

About two hundred letters, she thought. Upstairs. In two shoeboxes. No, three shoeboxes.

'Letters to whom, Miss Rockingham?'

To her. All of them. Two hundred.

They went back into the house. Upstairs. Into a spare bedroom with a whiff of damp to it and the sense of being for many years unslept in. And out of a cupboard came the boxes.

'If you would like to have a glance,' she said, 'to see if you might wish to make use of them. They are in chronological order.'

He took the first letter from the envelope. '. . . Until I saw you come into the room yesterday,' wrote Lamprey, 'I never understood the meaning of delight. I have never, until now, delighted. I have seen, since then, again and again, the door open and you walk in and my whole being has surged upwards. I cannot endure to wait until . . .'

He put the letter down and looked at her.

'Edward Lamprey and I,' she said, a little stiffly, 'loved each other for many years.'

'Christ,' said the girl. 'How weird. I mean, how absolutely extraordinary. I bet you're thrilled.'

'Hang on – I'll put another ten pence in. Hello? The thing is she won't let them out of the house which is fair enough but she's willing for me to make copies and thank God she's got an old typewriter so I can get going right away. She's extraordinarily helpful – set up a table for me and fussed round with electric fires and whatnot and now she's cooking us some sumptuous meal. Routed out some pyjamas, even.'

'Oh,' she said. 'I see. So you won't . . .'

'No. Not this weekend. And I wanted to see you. I've been thinking about it all day. Hello?'

'Yes. I'm still here. Oh, well . . .'

'Thursday was – just incredible.'

'What?'

'I said Thursday was marvellous.'

'Yes,' she said. 'Wasn't it. I've been thinking too . . . Oh, bother. Never mind. How long do you think it'll take?'

'I don't know. They're long letters. Actually, they're beautiful. The most beautiful letters I've ever read. Love letters. They're – oh God I can't explain. It's going to change the book entirely, finding this. It's changed Lamprey. I feel – oh, really involved for the first time. It's not just work any more, I actually care about him as a person. Oh, Christ, that's the last ten pence – look, I'll ring again tomorrow. O.K.?'

She stood in the doorway with a towel over one arm, and a pair of blue and white striped pyjamas. 'I got these out for you, Malcolm. I think they would be about the right size.'

Lamprey's?

'My brother,' said Lucinda, 'stayed here for several months before his death. Some of his things have not yet been cleared out.' She looked in sudden doubt at the pyjamas. 'But perhaps you would rather not. They have of course been laundered.'

He held out his hand. 'It's very kind of you. In fact the whole thing is extraordinarily kind. I can't tell you how grateful I am.'

'It would be as well,' she said, 'to go to the chemist for the shaving things before they close. I thought we might take some sherry together at about seven, before we eat. There are one or two points I have thought of that may interest you.'

There was sherry, good sherry at that, and whisky and gin and a soda siphon, magicked from heaven knows where in this surprising house. And Lucinda Rockingham wearing now some long velvet dressing-gown-like garment, looked pink and frail and yet, when it came to conversation, animated. And the Rayburn Maxistove had been lit and there was this extraordinarily good smell coming from the kitchen.

It was midnight before he went to bed. She had left him at eleven or so and he had sat on looking through the bundle of letters he would copy out the next day and, finally, reading some of Lamprey's poems. *The Cycle of the Year* sequence, written shortly after he met Lucinda Rockingham and which, knowing what one now knew, took on a new meaning. Overhead, boards delicately creaked, and presently there was silence. Outside, the occasional car rustled through the rain. He put the letters away, went to bed, lay awake for a while consumed with erotic yearnings, and fell asleep to dream of Lucinda Rockingham bicycling once, as she had described, along the waterfront with Edward Lamprey. A dog had run in front of his bike, causing him to fall and sprain an ankle. He had walked back to the house supported by Lucinda's arm. They had known one another, at that point, Lucinda thought, six weeks or so. Malcolm felt, in his dream, the touch of Lucinda's hand upon Lamprey's arm; he walked, with Lamprey, in a blaze of love.

'The amazing thing is,' he said, 'that they only saw each other at most every few months. Usually they met in London and every now and then he came down here. Her mother was alive then, and living with her so they weren't even alone that much if he came to the house. And then all the letters . . . Honestly, I wish I could . . . I'd love to read some of them to you. They're some of the best stuff he ever wrote.'

'You certainly seem very involved in it all.'

There was a pause.

'What are you doing?' he said. 'At this minute. Apart from talking to me. So I can imagine.'

'I'm looking out of the window. There's a white cat walking along the window ledge opposite. It's pouring with rain.'

'It's chucking down here too. What are you wearing?'

'Oh, goodness,' the girl said. 'A sort of blue shirt thing. And jeans. How's it going – I mean apart from being good and all that – how much longer will it take?'

'Another week at least. I can't see any way of getting through before.'

'Oh, gosh,' she said.

He read and typed and the old lady brought him coffee and occasionally aspirin. Twice, they walked down to the sea, he with his hand hovering beside her arm across the roads. Edward Lamprey, she said, had loved to walk along the beach collecting driftwood. Yes, she said, the poem 'Seashapes' was written after such a walk and yes, she supposed the references were more particular than might be supposed. She talked of a concert at the Maltings to which they had been together and of meetings in London, always with some shared activity in mind, visits to art galleries and places of interest and walks in Kew Gardens and Richmond Park. Lucinda Rockingham stayed with a cousin in Putney; Lamprey had a room in a friend's flat in Fulham which he used when in London. Each September they went to a Prom; in the spring they took the steamer to Greenwich.

And the letters, one upon another, a passionate narrative of love and commitment.

No, she said, we never travelled together. It would not have been possible. I had my mother to think of for many years; Edward took his family always to Cornwall. No, I never met his daughters; he talked of them a great deal, they were very close, I have a photograph of them when Marion was twelve and the others of course a little younger.

Year after year; through autumns and winters and springs and summers; moving from one longed-for, hoarded time to another.

She spoke of Lamprey's eclectic tastes, in music and in literature. She took down from the bookshelves the copies annotated in his hand, passages scored in the familiar red ink ('He used the same fountain pen for twelve years'), observations scribbled in the margins ('I have to confess that I never liked Edward's habit of defacing books, albeit with the best of intentions'). She peered into the intestines of the shining mahogany box in the corner, fiddled with slow crooked fingers, tutted and exclaimed, and produced, astonishingly, Duke Ellington and Sydney Bechet.

The rain turned to sunshine and the sunshine fell in wide mossy shafts upon the growing pile of letters on the deal table in the spare bedroom.

Upon gaiety and sadness and delight and regret. Upon eighteen years.

'Soft lights and sweet music!' said the girl. 'New Orleans and Eartha Kitt! Well, I never! What's a radiogram, by the way? I must say, if she wasn't eighty I'd feel I'd been cut out.'

'My head's spinning. I've been at it six hours on the trot. I got so absorbed I didn't even hear her bring me in tea. It got cold. The cucumber sandwiches went soggy.'

'All this vicarious experience. I don't know . . .'

'I had this dream about you last night.'

'What was I doing?'

'I couldn't possibly tell you. It was disgraceful.'

'Now, now,' she said. Winds sighed and whistled across four counties.

'What?'

'I didn't say anything.'

'It's ten days,' he said, 'since Thursday. Ten days and – six and a half hours.'

'Look,' said the girl, 'I *know*. Don't I know.'

'When I see you, I'm just going to . . .'

'I can't hear.'

'It doesn't matter. At least it does. Darling.'

'Listen,' she said. 'Have a break for a day or two. Come to London. You could always go straight back.'

'No,' he said. 'No, I can't. I want to – goodness, I want to – but I can't. I'm right in the middle of it. You see there's something I just can't . . . There's an enormous thing I simply don't . . . Hello? Are you there?'

Miss Rockingham, in the interests of literary history I have to ask you if your relationship with the poet was a physical one?

Miss Rockingham, did you sleep with the man or did you not?

Perhaps, he told himself, it doesn't matter. So far as the book is concerned, it need never be stated. Prurience, after all, is only an arm's length away. The letters matter; the relationship matters; let the rest be silence.

But I need to know. For myself, not for the book. Because. Because I have read the letters and humbly experienced through them the feelings of Edward Lamprey and seen with the eyes of Edward Lamprey the woman he loved. Because I care.

They sat up late, with the radiogram turned low, and Lucinda Rockingham opened a bottle of madeira, a relic of her brother. She poured the madeira into crystal glasses off which the lamplight snapped, and talked of the onset of Lamprey's illness, of an afternoon in London when she had, for the first time, understood that he was dying. An exhibition at the Tate, she said. She turned the glass in her fingers and light flew from it into the corners of the room. Chagall, I remember, and Kandinsky.

'It seems a bit creepy to me,' said the girl.

'You see I honestly do not know. I think it's quite possible they didn't. Which makes it all the more remarkable. The letters. All of it.'

'I don't mean them. I mean you.'

'Sorry?'

'You seem,' she said resentfully, 'to find them more compelling than real life.'

He delved frantically in his pocket; the coin clunked. 'Hello? It's O.K., I've put another one in . . . You sound cross. Please don't sound cross.'

'I'm not,' she said, 'cross.'

'Actually, I love you. What? I said, I *love* you.'

'Oh . . .,' she said at last. 'Oh, Malcolm.'

'And I keep thinking . . .'

'Yes?'

'Oh, just . . . I keep thinking about us.'

'You keep thinking,' the girl said, 'that we haven't been to bed together either?'

The pile of letters diminished. Lucinda Rockingham, standing at his elbow with a proffered cup of coffee said, 'Dear me, I shall soon be losing you. One more day? Two more days?'

'Three, I think. Saturday should finish it. I'm never going to be able to thank you enough for all this.'

'It has been a pleasure,' she said graciously. 'I've enjoyed your company. I lead a solitary life these days. It has done me good to talk. I hope I have not talked too much.'

'Oh, goodness . . . I don't know quite honestly when I've been more fascinated. You've – well, you've just changed everything for me, so far as the book is concerned. I only hope you will be happy with it, eventually. That you won't um . . .'

'Have any regrets?' said Miss Rockingham. 'I think not. I've thought it all over and am certain I made the right decision. It is what Edward would have wished. Now that his wife is no longer alive. So – Saturday will be our last evening together.'

'Thank goodness you rang. I was so terrified you might not. Listen, the most incredible thing. You know that friend of mine – the girl who plays in an orchestra at Snape? Well, she's driving down on Saturday and she said why not come along? Several of them have got this cottage and there's a room I could have for the night.'

'That's amazing,' he said. 'That's wonderful.'

'So what do you think? Shall I . . .'

'Is this room a big room?'
'Actually,' she said, 'I think it is quite a big room.'

There were seventeen letters left. He read them through, in order, one after another, until the last. The final three were written from the nursing home in which Lamprey died.

There was no indication. Nothing to confirm, one way or another. Just as throughout.

'A cup of tea,' said Lucinda Rockingham. 'Earl Grey this morning. Edward had leanings towards Earl Grey. A small point I had forgotten to mention.'

He pulled the typewriter towards him, smoothing out the one-hundred-and-seventy-sixth letter.

'We should hit Aldeburgh,' the girl said, 'at about six. So where shall we meet?'

'I'll ring you at this cottage place. Does it have a number?'
'Yes. Hang on. Here it is . . .'
'O.K. I've got that. Sixish? Wonderful. Twenty-four hours.'
'I know. I can't believe it.'
'I can't either. Yes, I can. I'm about ten years older, incidentally. Since the week before last.'
'Silly . . .' she said. 'How's it going, by the way?'
'Practically gone. All tied up, nearly.'
'Have you found out if . . .'
'No.' He looked through the glass of the phone box at grey sea marshalled beyond the sedate lamp-posts of the esplanade, at the back of a cast-iron bench, at the cold eye of a sea-gull. 'No, I haven't.'
'Does it still matter?'
'Yes,' he said. 'It does.'
'Couldn't you ever so discreetly ask?'
'Christ, no.'

'I have been thinking,' said Lucinda Rockingham, 'that in view of the fact that this is your last evening we might have a little celebration. I have ordered a duck from the butcher and I find that happily there is a bottle of what seems to be quite a nice wine in the storeroom.'

'Oh . . . Oh, that's terribly kind but in fact as it happens a friend of mine . . .'

'You were intending to stay overnight?'
'Well, I had been going to suggest actually that . . .'
'It has occurred to me that now you have read all the letters there may be one question that is bothering you.'

He stared at her – neat, old, bent, her eyes bright amid a soft tissue of wrinkles. 'Well – yes. Yes, there is – there is something I had been wondering about.'

'This evening,' said Miss Rockingham. 'This evening over our little celebration, I think might be a suitable time.'

'Oh,' he said. 'You've come. You're here. Did you have a good drive down?'

'I think so. I hardly noticed. Where are you?'

'In the phone box on the sea-front.'

'Then you can drive over in about ten minutes. Look, I'll tell you how to get here, it's a turning off the coast road just after . . .'

A sea-gull gawped at him again, from the wall, with a metallic eye. 'I tried to ring you in London. You'd gone. You see, the thing is she says . . .' The sea-gull raised its bill to the white sky and shouted; he could hardly hear his own words, his inexplicable inexcusable words '. . . so you see I must, I simply must. Shall I ring you say at eleven or so? She goes to bed then.'

'I'm not sure,' the girl said eventually. 'That I'll be here. I may go over to Snape with Diana.'

'Well, I'll try, shall I, all the same?'

'You can try,' she said.

Miss Rockingham feared the duck was perhaps a little tough but thought the wine adequate. She allowed him to clear the table and moved with her still half-full glass into the sitting-room. She opened the front of the Rayburn Maxistove and stabbed energetically at the coals within. She sat down.

'You have presumably wondered about the nature of my relationship with Edward Lamprey. We were never lovers. In the physical sense.'

'Oh,' he said. 'Yes. Quite. I see. Not that I . . . There would really be no reason to . . . For the purposes of the book.'

'It was agreed between us. On account of his family. And now that that point is out of the way shall we have some music?'

Later, much later, when she was in bed, he walked down to the phone box. Youths with motorbikes revelled on the esplanade, spilling from the pubs; a small white dog trotted purposefully past the darkened shop fronts; the sea slapped against a jetty. He dialled the girl's number. When it had rung a dozen times he put the receiver down and examined his feelings. He felt nothing, nothing at all. Just a faint regret, a pale decreasing sense of loss.

What the Eye Doesn't See

THE MISSES Knight, Joyce and Nora, on the threshold of old age, lived in a large Georgian house in Pershore, Worcestershire. Pershore is one of those medium-sized market towns that give an impression of slight detachment from the present, despite such normalities as supermarkets, petrol stations, and billboards. Something to do with the symmetry of eighteenth-century brick façades, perhaps, and side streets secluded from the thunder of through traffic. The Knights' house, number seven St Joseph's Place, was in just such a side street, or cul-de-sac, rather, and here the detachment achieved was quite remarkable.

There was little to tether the house to year or even decade: no recent electrical appliance or quickly identifiable piece of decor, no contemporary books, no magazines or periodicals. The Misses Knight had achieved a selective repudiation of the society in which they lived; they took what they wanted, such as Bendicks chocolates, Bath Oliver biscuits, main drainage, antibiotics and insecticides, the protection of the law and a constant supply of heat, light and water, and rejected the rest. What the eye doesn't see, the heart doesn't grieve over, they said; Nora and Joyce had trained the eye to see only what it wished to see, and the heart to restrict its concern. We know very little, they would say, about what is going on; we lead our own lives.

They took *The Times*, of course, for the Hatches, Matches and Despatches, as Nora called them. She would run her eye carefully down the columns every day at breakfast, in search of a relevant name. 'Someone called Lucy Symington got married. Do you think that could be anything to do with Molly Symington?' They pondered. 'A daughter couldn't be as young as that,' said Nora. 'Granddaughter if anything.' Molly Symington had been at school with them. The address gave no clue; in any case they had not communicated for forty years. 'A John Chalmers died. Eighty-nine. Weren't those people on holiday at Salcombe called Chalmers? The father, perhaps.' Nobody had been born who could be linked in any way to their own lives. Joyce folded the paper up carefully, for consignment to the fire-lighting pile in the pantry.

The house was called Cader Idris, in fond tribute to that part of Wales in which the sisters had spent the war years, in retreat from such dangers and aggravations as seemed bound to interfere with normal life in Hove, where they were living in 1939. It was a wise decision; in Dolgelly it had been possible – except for nuisances like rationing, black-out and lack of petrol – more or less to ignore what was going on elsewhere. They had had a good war; Nora taught herself petit point and Joyce grew irises with notable success. A photograph of the iris border in May 1943, a blaze of *I. xiphium* and *I. laevigata*, had been printed in *Country Life* – a heady moment. It hung now, framed, over the bureau in the drawing-room. They had done a little warwork with the local WVS, because one really should show willing. And had acquired a taste for King Charles spaniels, the latest in a long line of which lay now in a patch of sunlight on the Turkish rug, flopping his tail around in expectation.

'Let Ben have a bikky,' said Nora. 'And then put him outside.'

French windows opened from the breakfast-room on to the terrace and large walled garden. The garden was remarkable. Although right in the centre of Pershore it was half an acre or so in size; an aerial view would have shown it, like the grounds of Buckingham Palace, as a startling green oasis amid roofs and roads, an unsuspected haven. The walls were so high and thick that although on one side traffic passed within a few yards of the herbaceous border, the lilac walk and the rose garden, one was barely conscious of its presence; the occasional rattle or bump, blast of a horn, jangle of an ambulance, served only to emphasise the island seclusion of number seven. And yet only a few minutes away were the conveniences of the High Street: Boots, W.H. Smith, Sainsbury's. Not, of course, that Joyce and Nora did the household shopping themselves – that was done by the housekeeper. They employed a housekeeper and a lady gardener, both resident in the west portion of the house beyond the kitchens, which was converted into a self-contained unit. Mr Knight had been a textile manufacturer; the firm had boomed in the fifties with the development of artificial fibres. His daughters' capital, cushioned and bolstered almost literally by Dralon, Courtelle, Terylene, Polyester and so forth, had kept up nicely with inflation. They were still quite comfortable, thank goodness. Which makes all the difference, as Joyce said, between being able to lead one's own life as one wants and having to get involved with things one wouldn't care for.

The housekeeper and lady gardener were a couple called Beryl and Sylvia. They had turned out to be an excellent arrangement, being close friends so that, as Joyce was fond of telling people, there was none of that friction so common between two women working together. It was a harmonious household.

Joyce and Nora made certain sorties to the High Street themselves: to the library, Debenhams, and The Cake Shop. They both had a sweet tooth. Tea was the pinnacle of the day. The lingering decisions between cream-topped cherry tarts, macaroons, chocolate fancies, eclairs, meringues and slices of coffee gateau enriched each afternoon. They took it in turns to go out for the cakes. Otherwise they remained for much of the time in St Joseph's Place. Occasionally they attended local functions, but did not take an active part in the life of the town. The complaints of their acquaintances and contemporaries about change and desecration left them unmoved; they did not themselves much notice such things. When they found their route to the park made disagreeable by the building of a housing estate, they simply took Ben round a different way, avoiding the mud and rubble. The new multi-storey car park had been in the process of erection nine months before it caught their eye from the spare room window, blocking the view of the Abbey, which was a pity. Joyce ran up some net curtains, a pretty flounced nylon from Debenhams.

Beryl and Sylvia were efficient, cheerful, and kept themselves to themselves. They did their work and sat over the television of an evening; its muted quacking could be heard from behind their sitting-room door. Nora and Joyce also had a television set, on which they watched nature programmes, serialisations of classic novels, 'Gardeners' World' and the weather forecast. Joyce had made a small art of switching on at precisely the right moment to catch the forecaster's opening words without being subjected to the closing paragraphs of the news. Beryl and Sylvia, on the other hand, watched things like 'Panorama' and 'Man Alive', and sometimes, tiresomely, tried to initiate conversations about politicians and strikes and some bother in the Middle East. Joyce had to be a bit firm about that sort of intrusion, but on the whole they were nice types, and Beryl was an excellent cook. Beryl was the dominant partner, a small dark woman, her wiry black hair suggesting Welsh blood. She sang in the Abbey choir. They had been at St Joseph's Place for three years now.

In view of which, and the generally good relationship, the Misses Knight had felt inclined to go along with Beryl's request, made as she cleared the breakfast things one morning. Even so, they exchanged wary glances.

'How old?' asked Joyce.

The niece was eleven, apparently. Joyce and Nora nodded with relief: a younger child, of course, would have been out of the question. A quiet little thing, Beryl asserted. You'll hardly know she's there, through in our part, she won't touch anything in the garden, Sylvia'll see to that. And it'll give my sister and her husband the chance of a break on their own, ten days in the Italian Lakes, I mean, it's no fun for a child, that sort of trip, they took Tracy to Spain last year and she was bored stiff, had tummy upsets and all that. So I said Sylvia and I'd have her, this once. Well, thank you very much then, Miss Knight, as I say she'll be no bother at all, we'll see she stays put our side of the house.

And indeed when the time came Nora and Joyce were not even aware of the child's arrival for the first three days of her presence at Cader Idris. She came to Joyce's attention, eventually, as a shadowy extension of Beryl on the stairs, gathering up the trailing end of some dirty sheets that her aunt was carrying, so that Beryl, for a moment, looked like a bride with ghostly attendant. Joyce jumped and exclaimed. Beryl said, 'Say how do you do to Miss Knight, Tracy. She's been giving me a hand with the laundry. Right, I'll have those pillowcases now.'

She was a very thin child. Knobs stuck out all over her, accentuated by the clinging material of her jersey and trousers: hip-bones, the swoop of collar-bones, spiky shoulders, furrowing of ribs, small discs of nipples. A bit pasty, too. The kind of child, Joyce thought, that needed fresh country air and cod liver oil. Memories stirred, of evacuees in Wales during the war. But this was no East End waif: Tracy's father, one had been told, was quite high up in a frozen food firm. They had a four-bedroomed house and two cars. Joyce said kindly, 'Hello, Tracy. I hope you're enjoying your holiday.'

The girl was watching her with small, sharp, observant eyes, the narrowed look of a reflective cat, a little disconcerting. She tugged her aunt's arm and whispered something. Beryl laughed. 'Tracy was wondering if she could come and see the china dogs in the drawing-room. She noticed them from the terrace through the window and thought they were really pretty.'

In front of the china cabinet Joyce said instructively, 'They are a kind of china called Staffordshire. They used to belong to my mother.'

'Are they valuable?'

'Yes, I suppose so.'

'My mum's got a glass vase she got in Venice that cost fifteen pounds.' Tracy was standing on one leg now, scratching the back of her knee with the other, an irritating contortion. 'Excuse my saying so, Miss Knight, but you've got a smudge on your cheek.' She watched with detached interest as Joyce, ruffled, scrubbed at her face with a handkerchief. 'What's your dog called?'

'Ben.'

'Come here, Bennie – good dog, come on then, Bennie.' She began to play on the hearth-rug with him. Joyce went to her desk to sort out some bills. After a few minutes she said, 'Ben, not Bennie.'

'He likes being called Bennie, don't you, Bennie?'

'I expect your aunt will be wondering where you are,' said Joyce firmly.

During the next few days Tracy drifted more and more frequently into the main part of the house. Joyce and Nora would become aware suddenly of her presence, swinging on the handle of a door, squatted on the stairs, staring. Or her voice would make them jump. 'Excuse me, Miss Knight, can I ask you something? Why's that clock say the wrong time?' And, thus insinuated into the room with them, she would chatter on. My mum this, my dad that, the teacher in our school says this, when I'm at home I do that. Excuse me, Miss Knight, did you know your cardy has a button missing? Bennie likes me, doesn't he? Bennie likes me coming to see him. Did you see Eric and Ernie on telly last night, wasn't it funny when they dressed up like Arabs, I *love* Eric and Ernie, I really love them. Do you like Eric and Ernie? Excuse me, Miss Knight, shall I open that bottle for you, my mum always puts the lid under hot water, then they shift.

'You don't need to say excuse me all the time, Tracy.'

And the child, silent for a while, would stare with that look of assessment so that after a bit Nora or Joyce would start to feel uncomfortable; she had a knack of putting one at a disadvantage. There was a wizened maturity about her, a precocious worldliness; a most unchildlike child, the Misses Knight agreed, who had never had much to do with children in any case. Oh, they were fond of children, of course, smiled indulgently in the presence of the offspring of friends or neighbours. The local Cubs were allowed to clean the ground-floor windows of Cader Idris in Bob-a-Job week, cheerful robust little boys who said thank you nicely for their money, looking politely upwards at you. Tracy looked upwards too – she was rather small for her age – but gave this disconcerting impression of somehow looking also downwards. And her conversation flew off at alarming tangents, you never knew where it might lead next. One day there was an embarrassing account of some feminine complaint of her mother's full of oblique references – her you-know-where, her down-below.

'Yes,' said Joyce briskly. 'Now I wonder if Sylvia would like you to help her with sweeping up the leaves outside.'

'Shall I take Bennie in the garden?'

The dog lay on his side, deeply asleep, occasionally twitching. His penis jutted pinkly from the long soft fur of his belly. Tracy said with interest. 'He's got his thing out, for making puppies with.'

Nora and Joyce had always felt that that was where a bitch was nicer. Of course, there were other problems with a bitch, but not this visible indecency. Ben was a bother; he did it a lot. 'I think Ben would be better in the garden for a bit, dear,' they would say to each other. Ben, shut out, would sit resentfully on the terrace, his member shrinking against the cold stone.

'Do you see, Miss Knight? Why's he doing that?'

Joyce got up jerkily, slopping the tea-cup in her hand, and opened the french window. I am going to have to have a word with Beryl, she thought, the child is supposed to stay through in their part. She watched

Tracy and Ben run across the lawn together towards Sylvia, who was methodically raking leaves into golden pyramids. Beyond the lilac walk, a bonfire smoked. From the street came the sound of a loudspeaker or something, a tiresome blaring voice. And on the skyline, just above the crimson flare of the garden sumach, was the arm of some enormous crane with a pulley and a man in a glass box; how long had that been there? Joyce could not remember noticing it before. There was a sense of things pressing in, of intrusion; she closed the window again and poured another cup of tea.

It was early evening when Beryl came through to the drawing-room. She was wearing going-out clothes and spoke with some embarrassment. The thing was, she and Sylvia had promised themselves a film with a friend in Birmingham tonight, and they'd reckoned with taking Tracy along, but when it came to the point Tracy didn't want to come – there was something she fancied specially on the telly, and no getting her to budge. So would it be all right if . . . I mean, she'll put herself to bed, and she'll be happy as larry till then with her supper on a tray and the TV to watch, it's just for her to know she's not on her own in the house.

Joyce and Nora exchanged looks. It was the moment, of course, for a firm but tactful word about the Tracy situation in general. But just as Joyce (like Beryl, the dominant partner and customary spokeswoman) was starting to say, 'Well, yes, Beryl, of course just for this once we . . .' the doorbell rang, Ben flew off with a fusillade of shrill barks, and Beryl was saying, 'I'll get it, and thanks very much, Miss Knight, I'll tell her to be sure and not bother you.'

They heard Beryl and Sylvia leave in the Mini soon after seven. Their own supper, cold except for the soup to warm up in the kitchen, had been set out on the sideboard. Joyce, attending to the soup, heard the television on in the adjoining room – quickfire conversation punctuated with outbursts of laughter that swelled and receded like waves pounding a beach. She considered checking that the child was all right, rejected the idea (with a twinge of guilt) and carried the soup back to the dining-room.

They were in the drawing-room, Joyce playing patience and Nora knitting, when all the lights went out. One moment all was tranquil normality; the next they sat in isolation and confusion. 'There must be a fuse gone,' said Joyce. They began to tell one another to be careful, to go slowly, to try to think where the torch was. Neither of them remembered Tracy. When a couple of minutes later, they heard the door open, Nora screamed.

Tracy said, 'Bang in the middle of "The Good Life". Wouldn't you just know it! Pity you haven't got an open fire, Miss Knight, at my friend's they've got this real fire and when the lights went out we all sat round and did part singing, lovely it was.' She seemed to be skipping round the room; her voice came now from here, now from there – Ariel-like, it chattered at them from invisibility. 'Oh, do be careful, dear,' cried Nora. 'The little table with the Sèvres dish . . .' There was a bump and a clatter, but it was Joyce, trying to find her way to the door and stumbling against the sofa. She stood still, the familiar rendered treacherous, stranded in the middle of her own drawing-room. Tracy, her voice dodging now over to the window said, 'Whoops! Can't you see where you are, Miss Knight? Here, shall I hang on to you?' and Joyce felt a moth-like brushing against her sleeve, and then a cold little hand on hers. She twitched. 'Can't you feel where you are? I can – look, the door's over there, mind the desk, isn't it fun!' 'The fuses,' Nora began 'Aren't they in the kitchen drawer, Joyce? Oh dear, I never know how you fit them in, they . . .' But Tracy broke in scornfully, 'It's not a *fuse*, it's a power-cut, they said on the news, West Midlands and parts of the South-East, because of the strike, up to three hours, we'll have to go to bed with candles, where do you keep the candles, Miss Knight?' 'Strike?' said Joyce, 'Power-cut? But it's disgraceful, they haven't got any right to . . .' 'Because of their money, what they earn, they want something per cent and the government says they can't. Ooh, here's Bennie – I nearly stepped on you, didn't I, Bennie?' 'Three hours, but how are we expected to . . .', and now Joyce barked her shin, excruciatingly, against the fender. 'Oh,' cried Nora. 'Are you all right, dear?' and to and fro, in the darkness, went their exclamations of annoyance and distress. The house and its contents crouched around them, turned nasty, waiting to trip or obstruct.

The phone rang, in the hall. Joyce, marooned still somewhere west of the sofa, said, 'Oh, bother it, now of all times', but already Tracy's voice, receding beyond the door, was crying, 'I'll get it, don't worry, Miss Knight, I know where it is.'

'Hello?' they heard her say, and then, 'Oh, Auntie Beryl – guess what, we're having a power cut, bang in the middle of "The Good Life". What? Ooh, goodness, did it really? Yes. Yes, I'll tell them, auntie. No, quite all right. Yes. Not to worry, auntie – will do. 'Bye for now.' And back she came, flitting confidently across the room, her voice important with information and bad news. A breakdown. The gasket. Garages just don't want to know. Stop over the night with Mandy in Solihull and an early bus tomorrow. Terribly sorry. Put meself to bed and not be a nuisance. Candles in the landing cupboard. Ever so sorry.

Nora, too, now was on her feet. 'No, I can manage, dear. Really, isn't it the limit! First the lights and now this. Surely they . . . Oh, well, we must just make the best of it. I'll find the candles' – and to Tracy, firmly – 'No, Tracy, thank you very much, there are some rather fragile things in the landing cupboard and I know whereabouts the candles will be.' She began to grope her way through the door and across the hall: a bump, an exclamation, a yelp. 'Oh, *Ben*, get out of the way . . .' 'Do be careful, Nora.' 'I'm all right now, I've found the banister.' Clump and shuffle up the stairs; creak of boards; another exclamation, distant now; bangs and clatters. 'Here we are! I've got them, Joyce.' Steps on the stairs again, less cautious now, and . . . An awful, slithering crash. Silence. 'Oh, Miss Knight, I think she's fallen down the stairs.'

It seemed hours. The fumble for matches, grope for scattered candles, why doesn't she *say* anything? Tracy vanished and then suddenly re-appeared with a blessed, reassuring beam of light – the torch, however did she find it? Never mind. And thank heavens Nora is trying now to heave herself up, groaning something about her back, saying she feels a bit queasy, don't worry, dear, be fine in a minute.

And collapses again.

It was Tracy, in the end, who dialled 999. 'Excuse me, Miss Knight, you're putting your finger in the wrong hole. I can see, shall I . . .' And appeared from the kitchen, breathless and important with cups of tea. 'My mum's got this friend who's a nurse and she says it's the best thing, when you've had a shock, it steadies people up. I put two sugars in, is that O.K.?' And let the ambulancemen in and skipped from one leg to the other in the now candle-lit hall, a-twitter with interest and involvement.

The reviving sight of uniformed men (on one's own side, there to serve, like policemen and commissionaires), or possibly the tea, put heart into Joyce once more. She was able to adjust her tone of voice, step aside from those awful dithery moments when even Tracy had seemed a support, and behave normally. She told Tracy to shut Ben up in the cloakroom, and exhorted the ambulancemen, shouting slightly, as though the power-cut affected hearing as well as vision. 'O.K., love, take it easy,' they said, shooting powerful beams of torchlight into the gloom. 'She's conscious, is she? Don't worry, it doesn't look like a bad one, you sit back and leave it to us now.' And Joyce, explaining that she was not worried, not unduly, found herself pushed to the fringe of things, screened from Nora by large competent backs, not quite picking up what was said.

They did not think there was anything broken. Concussion, probably, X-rays. Observation. And now there was Nora being carted off, her hair all anyhow, looking white but stoical, strapped up in a nasty red blanket that somehow suppressed personality: she might have been anyone. 'Right,' said the ambulanceman. 'We'll get off then. That's it, you come along too, that's the best thing' – as Joyce groped for her hat and coat.

Again, she forgot Tracy. It was not until she was climbing into the ambulance that she found the child at her side, bright-eyed, tucking herself into an unoccupied corner. 'Oh,' Joyce began, 'I don't really think . . .' But they were off now, rounding the corner into the High Street, and the men were laughing at some remark of Tracy's that Joyce did not catch. 'She's a card, your granddaughter,' said one of them. Joyce opened her mouth to deny relationship, but Tracy was already off on a saga of explanation. Nora turned her head to one side and closed her eyes.

Joyce and Nora, all their lives, had enjoyed good health. The occasional tiresomeness had been attended to by their G.P. – as private patients, naturally. Joyce had seldom set foot inside a hospital, except once to have a nasty boil lanced and otherwise only to visit less fortunate friends (and then with some reluctance – there but for the grace of God, and one did not want to be reminded of that). Now, she was disconcerted by the detachment and dexterity of the nurses who whisked Nora away from her down gleaming corridors. Nobody consulted her or asked her what she would like done. She sat disconsolate in a waiting-room; Tracy, beside her, was immersed in some cheap women's magazine, stuffed with advertisements for sanitary towels and deodorant. There were other people also waiting, an elderly man who shuffled and muttered (possibly drunk, Joyce realised with alarm), a black woman with a small child, an adolescent boy with a radio that emitted vulgar music, turned low but still irritating. Joyce would have told him to turn it off were it not that she herself felt so uneasy in this place as to be quite without the protective armoury of personality. She felt a fish out of water, as though she were abroad (she and Nora had never cared much for abroad), as though she were displaced in time. And yet it was here and now, and she was not half a mile from St Joseph's Place. When at last a young doctor appeared, saying, 'Miss Knight?', she gathered herself with an effort and began, 'Ah, now perhaps you will be so good as to take me to my sister, we must discuss various things and . . .' But the man was already explaining that the X-rays showed a cracked rib, nothing worse, though there was certainly concussion, and Nora was drowsy now, and quite comfortable in Ward C in the main building and would be best left to herself tonight, visiting hours tomorrow were from . . . 'Ward?' said Joyce. 'Oh no, we shall want a private room, there's been some mistake, I'm afraid, my sister and I always . . .' The private wing, the doctor explained, courteous but positive, was full and no amenity beds available tonight. 'Oh, but really,' cried Joyce. 'That won't do. Surely there must be some way of arranging something, Doctor er . . .' 'Tomkins,' chirped Tracy. 'Doctor Kevin Tomkins. Isn't that funny, my dad's called Kevin, too!' And now Joyce saw the little white-lettered metal strip against the doctor's jacket. 'Doctor Tomkins,' she continued, 'I'm afraid I really can't have my sister in . . .' But the young man was beaming at Tracy, saying really, fancy that now, well, well, and what's your name? And the wretched child was off on yet another spiel of my mum this, my auntie that, actually I don't live at, our house is . . . And the man also came from Derbyshire, it appeared, which accounted for the eerie similarity between his speech and Tracy's accent – a diction which, Joyce now realised, had jarred her ear for many days. She felt in even further alienation, tumbled against her will into a discordant and wayward world. It was as though the television could not be switched off, or the front door to number seven St Joseph's Place would not close.

'Don't worry,' said the doctor kindly. 'Your sister will be well taken care of, I promise you. Why don't you get along home now, it's getting late.' He patted Tracy on the head. 'You see your auntie gets herself a nice hot drink and a good night's sleep, eh?' And Tracy, smirking, was saying, 'Yes, 'course I will, actually it's Auntie Beryl's my auntie not . . .' at the same moment as Joyce snapped, 'The little girl is not my niece. Thank you very much, doctor, no doubt I shall see you in the morning.'

They took a taxi home. The power-cut was over; the house blazed with light. Joyce, a little restored as she stepped into the hall, was filled with sudden rage against these unknown people, whose activities had caused the whole thing, but for whom she would be filling Nora's hot water bottle, while Nora put Ben to bed in the downstairs cloakroom. What had they to do with her, what right had they to intrude in her life? She hung up her coat with clumsy, jerky movements, while Tracy and Ben skittered about her in joyful reunion. 'Oops!' said Tracy. 'You've knocked down Miss Knight's hat, Miss Knight – here, I'll get it. Isn't it muddling, you both being called Miss Knight, if I was going to be here a long time I'd have to call you Auntie Joyce, wouldn't I?' She followed Joyce through into the drawing-room, singing to herself. A cheerful little soul, Beryl had said, quiet, I promise you she won't be any bother, you'll hardly know she's here.

It was half past eleven. 'Time to go to bed,' said Joyce firmly. She felt more in control now, braced by the security of the house, the controlled and ordained atmosphere, nothing unchosen, nothing out of place. 'Bed, Tracy. I'll just come through with you and see everything's all right.'

She did not often go into the staff quarters beyond the kitchen; staff, she and Nora had always affirmed, had a right to privacy too. Now, walking into the sitting-room without knocking, she felt awkward. Tracy bounced ahead through the door of the small boxroom that had been turned into a bedroom and then out again, saying, 'Left my nightie in their room – just have to get it.' She opened the door of the other bedroom, and Joyce saw, to her surprise, a double bed. She stood staring; on a bedside table was a photograph of Beryl and Sylvia, arm in arm, in bathing costumes. Joyce said, 'Oh dear, Beryl's had to turn out of her room for you.'

Tracy was rummaging under the bed. She popped out, a garment in her hand. 'Oh no, this is where Auntie Beryl and Auntie Sylvia sleep, in the big bed – always – they had it put in special when they came, didn't you know?' 'When they . . .?' said Joyce faintly, looking round the room now, untidy, the dressing-table a muddle of pots and bottles, a smell of powder and scent. 'Didn't you know? Because of being married to each other, like ladies and men are. My mum told me, she said I'm quite old enough to know about that sort of thing and it's nothing to make a fuss about, quite a lot of people are like that, you get men marrying each other too.' She giggled. 'Catch me marrying another girl when I'm grown-up, I don't see the point, my mum says she wouldn't fancy it either but it's not her business and it takes all sorts to make a world. I like Auntie Sylvia, she's ever so nice – she made drop scones with me yesterday. I'll just go and clean my teeth.'

Joyce stood in the doorway, looking at the bed. From the bathroom came brisk sounds of scrubbing and spitting. She felt physically unsteady. It was as though the house had been shaken up around her, like the glass in a kaleidoscope, and reassembled in an unrecognisable pattern. The place had been violated – by unknown men in some power station, by the association of these women. One had always known the world was not entirely to one's own taste, and had made one's arrangements accordingly. What the eye doesn't see, the heart doesn't grieve over. It was possible, she had thought, to detach oneself, to be selective, to be in the world but not of it; tonight, a spiteful world had disputed this. She was sixty-eight, not as fit as she used to be; if this kind of thing was going to go on, she did not know for how long she could hold out.

Tracy came out of the bathroom, wearing a flowered nightdress; thin, unchildish, and as powerful as a coiled spring. She said, 'Nightie-night', and then coyly, 'Auntie Joyce.'

Joyce went through into the main part of the house. In the hall sat Ben, wagging his tail. As he jumped at her in greeting she saw that he was protruding again beneath. Bitches they had usually had spayed. She and Nora had long ago agreed that Ben was not a complete success, but once you own an animal you are committed to it, there is nothing you can do. She shut him in the cloakroom and went upstairs to bed, slowly, the sound of the High Street traffic suddenly loud beyond the landing window.

The Emasculation of Ted Roper

JEANIE BANKS, rigid with emotion, her cardigan on inside out, muttering rehearsed words, deaf and blind to the bright morning, made her way down the village street. Past the post office, the one, two, three, four cottages, past the pub, Mrs Halliday's, the garage, the one, two, three new bungalows, the Lathams', Cardwell's yard. She stopped outside Roper's, simmering, reached out to open the gate, lost her nerve, plunged on down to the lamp-post where the village ended, yanked up her resolution again, turned, aimed back, fumbled furious with the latch on Roper's gate.

The front garden a disgrace, as always, strewn with empty oil cans, plastic sacks, rusting iron objects, the excretions of Roper's hand-to-mouth odd-jobbing dealing-in-this-and-that existence. Furtive, un-reliable, transacting in dirty pound notes, dodging his taxes without a doubt, down the pub every evening. Dirty beggar, cocky as a robin, sixty if he was a day.

Feeling swelled to a crescendo, and courage with it; she hammered on the door. Then again. And again. No answer. He'd be there all right, he'd be there, nine-thirty in the morning, since when did Roper go out and do a decent day's work? She shoved at the side gate.

He was round the back, fiddling about with a great pile of timber, good timber at that, planks all sizes and shapes and how did he come by it one would like to know? A whole lot of tyres stacked up in one corner, stuff spilling out of the shed, filth everywhere.

'Hello, Jeanie.'

She halted, breathless now. Words fail you, they do really. They leave you huffing and puffing, at a disadvantage, seeing suddenly the run in your tights, seeing yourself reflected in the eyes of others – angry, dumpy, middle-aged widow, just Jeanie Banks. In the beady spicy nasty eyes of Ted Roper, stood there in the middle of his junk like a little farmyard cock. A randy strutting bantam cock.

'What can I do for you, Jeanie?'

She said, 'It's not what you can do it's what's been done, that's what's the trouble.'

'Trouble?' He took out tobacco, a grubby roll of cigarette papers. 'Trouble?' His dirty fingers, rolling, tapping, his tongue flickering over the paper.

'My Elsa's expecting.'

'Expecting?' he said. 'Oh – expecting.' A thin smile now, a thin complacent smile. Grinning away at it, the old bastard, pleased as punch. As if it were something to be proud of, as if it did him credit even, stood there with his thumbs stuck in his trouser pockets like those boys in western films. Some boy – Ted Roper. Boy my foot, sixty if he's anything.

'That's what I said. Expecting.'

He put the cigarette in his mouth; thin smoke fumed into the village sunshine. Not trousers, she saw now. Jeans – jeans just like young men wear, slumped down on his thin hips, the zip sliding a bit, a fullness you couldn't miss below, stuck out too the way he stood, legs apart, thumbs in pockets.

'Well,' he said, 'I s'pose that'd be in the nature of things. She's getting a big girl now.'

Grinning away there, wiry and perky and as blatant as you like. She felt her outrage surge.

'It's rape,' she said. 'That's what it damn well is. A little creature like that, a little young thing. Bloody rape!' The colour rushed to her cheeks; she didn't use language like that, not she, never.

'Now, now, Jeanie. Who's to know who gave who the come on.'

She exploded. She shouted, 'You take that blasted cat to the vet, Ted Roper, and get it seen to, the rest of us have just about had enough, there's kittens from one end of the village to the other and my Elsa was nothing but a kitten herself.' She swung round and stormed to the gate. When she looked back he was still standing there, the cigarette laid on his lower lip, his jeans fraying at the crotch, the grin still on his face. 'Or you'll find it done for you one of these days!'

All the way back to the cottage her heart thumped. It didn't do you any good, getting yourself into a state like that, it took it out of you, she'd be jumpy all day now. Back home in the kitchen, she made herself a cup of tea. The old cat, the mother, was sprawled in the patch of sun on the mat and Elsa was in the armchair. When Jeanie came in she jumped down and shimmied across the floor: pretty, graceful, kittenish and distinctly lumpy, no doubt about it, that unmistakable pear-shape forming at the end of her. And Jeanie, subsiding into the chair, drinking her tea, eyed her and eyed the old cat, not so old come to that, five or was it six, and as she did so a whole further implication leaped into the mind – why hadn't she thought of it before, how disgusting, if it were people you could have them slapped in prison for that.

'Fact is,' said her sister Pauline, that afternoon, 'there's probably hardly a one in the village isn't his. Being the only tom round about, bar him on Lay's farm and he's beyond it if you ask me. So you let Ted Roper have it? Good on you, Jeanie.'

Jeanie, cooler now, calmer, righteous and ever so slightly heroic, went over it all again, word for word: I said, he said, so I said, and him as cocky as you like.

'He's a cocky little so-and-so,' said Pauline. 'Always was. I bet he got the wind up a bit though, Jeanie, with you bawling him out, you're bigger than he is.' She chuckled. 'Hey – d'you remember the time they got him in the girls' playground and Marge ripped the belt off his trousers so he had to hold 'em up all afternoon? God – laugh . . . ! Donkey's years ago . . .'

'Funny, isn't it,' Pauline went on, 'there's four of us in the village still as were at school with Ted. You, me, Nellie Baker, Marge. Randy he was, too. Remember?'

'Funny he's never married,' said Jeanie.

Pauline snorted. 'Out for what he can get, that one. Not that he'd get it that often, is my guess.'

'Can't stand the man. Never could. 'Nother cup? Anyway, what I say is, he ought to be made to have something done about that cat. It's shocking. Shocking.'

In the basket chair the old cat raucously purred; Elsa, in a patch of sunlight, lay flirting with a length of string.

'Sick of drowning kittens, I am,' said Jeanie. 'I'll have to get her seen to after, like I did the old cat. Shame.'

'Shame.'

The two women contemplated the cats.

'I mean, we wouldn't care for it, if it were you or me.'

'Too right.'

'Not,' said Pauline, 'at that time of life. That's a young creature, that is, she's got a right to, well, a right to things.'

'Hysterectomy's the nearest, if it were a person.'

'That's it, Jeanie. And you'd not hear of that if it were a girl. Another matter if it's in middle life.'

'That cat of Roper's,' said Jeanie, 'must be going on twelve or thirteen.'

Later, as she walked to the shop, Roper's pick-up passed her, loaded with slabs of timber, belting too fast down the village street, Roper at the wheel, one arm on the sill, a young lad beside him, one of the several who hung around him. She saw Roper see her, turn to the boy, say something, the two of them roar grinning across the cross-roads. She stood still, seething.

'Cardwell's boy, weren't that?' said Marge Tranter, stopping also. 'With Roper.'

'I daresay. What they see in that old devil . . .'

'Men's talk. Dirty stories, that stuff. Norman says he doesn't half go on in the pub, Roper. He's not a one for that kind of thing, Norman isn't. He says Roper holds out hours on end sometimes, sat there in the corner with his mates. Showing off, you know.'

'Fat lot he's got to show off about,' said Jeanie. 'A little runt, he is. Always was. I was saying to Pauline, remember the time you . . .'

'Pulled his trousers down, wasn't it? Don't remind me of that, Jeanie, I'll die . . .'

'Not pulled them down, it wasn't. Took his belt. Anyway, Marge, I gave him an earful this morning, I'll tell you that. That cat of his has been at my Elsa. I went straight down there and I said look here, Ted Roper. . .'

A quarter of a mile away Ted Roper's pick-up, timber dancing in the back, dodged in and out of the traffic on the A34, overtaking at sixty, cutting in, proving itself. Cardwell's boy and Roper, blank-faced, be-jeaned, the cowboys of the shires, rode the Oxfordshire landscape.

In the village and beyond, Roper's cat – thin, rangy, one-eyed and fray-eared – went about his business

And, according to the scheme of things, the ripe apples dropped from the trees, the *jeunesse dorée* of the area switched their allegiance from the Unicorn to the Hand and Shears taking with them the chattering din of un-muffled exhausts and the reek of high-octane fuel, the road flooded at the railway bridge and Jeanie's Elsa swelled soft and sagging like the bag of a vacuum cleaner.

'Several at least,' said Jeanie. 'Half a dozen, if you ask me. Poor little thing, it's diabolical.'

'There's a side to men,' said Pauline, 'that's to my mind just not like us and that's the only way you can put it. And I don't mean sex, nothing wrong with that when the time and the place are right. I mean . . .'

'It's a kind of men rather, I'd say. Harry's not that way, nor was my Jim. I mean, there's men that are normal men in the proper way but don't go on about it.'

'In Italy,' said Pauline, 'all the men are the other kind. All of them. From the word go. Young boys and all. They wear bathing costumes cut deliberately so you can see everything they've got.'

'Which is something you can take as read, in a normal man. It doesn't need shouting about.'

'Exactly. If I were you, Jeanie, I'd give that cat a drop of cod liver oil in her milk. She's going to need all her strength.'

Perhaps also according to the scheme of things, Ted Roper's pick-up, a while later, was involved in circumstances never clarified in a crash with Nellie Baker's Escort at the village cross-roads. No blood was shed and the pick-up, already so battle-scarred as to be impervious, lived to fight again, but the Escort was crippled and Nellie Baker too shaken and confused to be able to sort out exactly what had happened except for a strong conviction that aggression had been involved. At the Women's Institute committee meeting she held forth.

'He came out of nowhere and was into me before I knew what was happening. I was either stopped or the next best thing, that I'll swear.'

'What does he say?'

'Whatever he's saying's being said to the police. He took off, without a word hardly. It was Mr Latham ran me home and got the garage for me. I've told them my side of it, at the police station. It's up to them now.'

'The police,' said Jeanie Banks, 'have been down at Ted Roper's more than once. Asking about this and that. They could do some asking just now, the stuff he's got there and one wonders where it all comes from.'

'The police,' said Pauline, 'are men. Remember Ted Roper at school, Nellie? Jeanie and I were talking about that only the other day – how we used to take him down a peg or two.'

And, according to a scheme of things or not, no case was brought against Ted Roper for careless driving or dangerous driving or aggression or anything at all. Those who failed to see how that pick-up could have passed its MOT continued to speculate; Ted Roper's insurance company ignored letters from Nellie Baker's insurance company.

Jeanie's Elsa had five kittens, two of them stillborn.

Ted Roper, wiry and self-assured as his cat, continued to cruise the local roads, to make his corner of the pub an area of masculine assertion as impenetrable and complacent as the Athenaeum. From it came gusts of hoarse laughter and anecdotes which were not quite audible, bar certain key words.

It may have been the stillborn kittens that did it, as much as anything, those damp limp little rags of flesh. Or the sight of the emptied Elsa, restored to a former litheness but subtly altered, wise beyond her years. Or months.

Jeanie, tight-lipped, visited Marge to borrow her cat basket.

'You'll take her to be done, then?'

'Have to, won't I? Or it'll be the same thing over again.'

'Shame.'

'Just what Pauline said.'

Marge, lining the cat basket with a piece of old blanket, paused. 'It's like with people. Always taken for granted it must be the woman. Pills, messing about with your insides . . .' She swung the door of the basket shut and tested the catch. 'There's an alternative, Jeanie. Thought of that?'

'What do you think I was down Ted Roper's for, that time?'

'And much joy you got out of it. No, what I'm thinking of is we see to it ourselves.'

The two women stared at each other over the cat basket. Marge, slowly, even rather terribly, smiled. 'I wouldn't mind, I wouldn't half mind, giving Ted Roper his come uppance.'

In a village, people come and go all day. Women, in particular – to and from the school, the shop, the bus stop, each other's houses. The little group of Jeanie, Pauline, Marge and Nellie Baker, moving in a leisurely but somehow intent way around the place that afternoon, glancing over garden walls and up the sides of cottages, was in no way exceptional. Nor, unless the observer were of a peculiarly enquiring turn of mind, was the fact that they carried, between them, a cat basket, a pair of thick leather gardening gloves, and a half a pound of cod wrapped in newspaper.

Presently, the cat basket now evidently heavy and bouncing a little from side to side, they emerged somewhat breathless from the field behind the pub and made their way rather hurriedly to the garage of Nellie Baker's house, where an old Morris replaced the deceased Escort. The Morris drove away in the direction of Chipping Norton passing, incidentally, the very school playground where once, donkey's years ago, four outraged and contemptuous schoolgirls had a go at the arrogance of masculine elitism.

In a village, also, change is more quickly observed than you might think. Even change so apparently insignificant as the girth of a cat. In this case, it was habits as much as girth. A cat that has previously roamed and made the night hideous, and which takes instead to roosting, eyes closed and paws folded, in the sun on the tops of walls, idling away the time, will be noticed.

And the more so when the change eerily extends to the cat's owner.

At first it was just the paunch jutting below the sagging belt of Ted Roper's jeans. Then, balancing the paunch, came a fullness to the face, a thickening of the stubbly cheeks, a definite double chin. 'Put on a bit, haven't you, Ted?' people said. 'Have to cut down on the beer, eh?' And Ted would wryly grin, without the perky come-back that might have been expected. With physical expansion went a curious decline of those charismatic qualities: the entourage of youths dropped off. Some nights, Ted sat alone in the pub, staring into his glass with the ruminative and comfortably washed-up look of his seniors. A series of mishaps befell the pick-up: punctures stranding Ted on remote roads, a catastrophic fuel leak, a shattered windscreen. It was driven, presently, in a more sedate way; it no longer rode or cruised but rattled and pottered.

It was as though the old assertive stringy cocky Ted were devoured and enveloped, week after week, by this flabby amiable lethargic newcomer. The jeans gave way to a pair of baggy brown cords. He began to leave his corner of the public bar and join the central group around the fireplace; there, the talk was of onions, the ills of the nation, weather and fuel prices.

And, in the village or outside his own gate, meeting Nellie Baker, say, or Marge or Pauline or Jeanie Banks, he would pass the time of day, initiate a bit of chat, offer small gifts by way of surplus timber, useful lino offcuts, the odd serviceable tyre.

'Poor old so-and-so,' said Pauline. 'They're easily taken down, aren't they? That's what comes of depending on the one thing. You can almost feel sorry for them.'

A Long Night at Abu Simbel

IN CAIRO they had complained about the traffic and at Saqqara Mrs Marriott-Smith and Lady Hacking had wanted a lavatory and blamed her when eventually they had to retire, bleating, behind a sand-dune. She had lost two of them at Luxor airport and the rest had sat in the coach in a state of gathering mutiny. Some of them were given to exclaiming, within her hearing, 'Where's that wretched girl got to?' At Karnak the guide hadn't shown up when he should and she had had to mollify them for half an hour with the shade temperature at 94°. On the boat, a contingent had complained about having cabins on the lower deck and old Mr Appleton, apparently, was on a milk pudding diet, a detail not passed on to the chef by the London office. She knew now that not only did she not like foreign travel or tour leading but she didn't much care for people either. She continued to smile and repeat that they would be able to cash cheques between five and six and that no, she didn't think there was a chiropodist in Assuan. When several of them succumbed vociferously to stomach upsets she refrained from saying that so had she. They sought her out with their protests and their demands when she was skulking in a far corner of the sun deck and throughout every meal. In the privacy of her cabin she drafted her letter of application to the estate agent in Richmond where there was a nice secretarial job going.

At Edfu the woman magistrate from Knutsford was short-changed by a carpet-seller, to the quiet satisfaction of some of the others. At Esna Miss Crawley lost her travellers' cheques and Julie had to go all the way back to the temple and search, amid the pi-dogs and the vendors of basalt heads and the American party from Minnesota Institute of Art (biddable and co-operative, joshing their ebullient blue-rinsed tour leader). They all called her Julie now, but on a note of querulous requirement, except for the retired bank manager, who had tried to grope her bottom behind a pillar at Kom Ombo, and followed her around suggesting a drink later on when his wife was taking a nap.

None of them had read the itinerary properly. When they discovered that they had an hour and a half to wait at Assuan for the flight to Abu Simbel they rounded on her with their objections. They wanted another plane laid on and they wanted to be assured that they wouldn't be with the French and the Japanese tours and Lady Hacking said over and over again that at least one took it, for goodness sake, that there would be adequate restaurant facilities. She got them, eventually, into the plane and off the plane on to the coach, where the guide, Fuad, promised by the Assuan agency, most conspicuously was not. She went back to the airport building and telephoned; the Assuan office was closed. The man at the EgyptAir desk knew of no Fuad. She returned to the coach and broke the news in her most sprightly manner. The American coach and the French coach and the Japanese coach, smoothly united with their Fuad or their Ashraf, were already descending the long road to the temples in three clouds of dust.

They said their say. The coach driver spat out of the window and closed the door. They bumped across the desert. Lake Nasser lay to their right, bright blue fringed with buff-coloured hills. Those who had sufficiently recovered from their irritation at the non-appearance of Fuad exclaimed. Those who had not continued loudly to reiterate their complaints. The coach driver pulled up at the top of the track down to the temple site. They disembarked. Miss Crawley said she hadn't realised there was going to be even more walking. They straggled off in twos and threes and stood, at last, in front of the blindly gazing immensities of the god-king. Mrs Marriott-Smith said it made you think, despite everything, and Miss Crawley found she had blistered both feet and the chartered surveyor's wife was sorry to tell everyone she couldn't, frankly, see a sign of anywhere to eat. They stood around and took photographs and trailed in the wake of the guided and instructed French and Japanese into the sombre depths of the temple and when they were all out of sight Julie left them.

She walked briskly up the hill to where the American coach, its party already aboard, was revving its engine. She got on and went with them back to the airport, where, with a smile, she deposited an envelope containing twenty-two return halves of Assuan–Abu Simbel–Assuan air tickets with the fellow at the EgyptAir desk. She then boarded the plane, along with the American party. They were shortly joined by the Japanese and the French. The plane left on time; it always did, the stewardess said, truculently, glancing out of the window at the solitary airport building tipping away beneath.

The Magitours party continued to devote themselves to the site. They gathered in front of the stone plaque unveiled by Gamal Abdul Nasser as a memorial of international collaboration for preserving a human heritage. The other tours were now wending their way up the track to the coaches. 'Peace at last!' said Lady Hacking. 'I don't know which drive me dottier – those American women screaming at each other or the French pushing and shoving.' Mr Campion, the senior police inspector, being in possession of an adequate guide-book, assumed the role of the absent Fuad and briefed them on Rameses the Second and on the engineering feat involved in hoisting the temples to their present position. The party, appropriately humbled by the magnitude of both concepts, moved in awe around the towering pillars of the temple and the equally inhuman twentieth-century shoring-up process within the artificial hillside. They all agreed that it was frightfully impressive and well worth coming for. Those still suffering from internal disorders were becoming a little fidgety, and Mrs Marriott-Smith was longing for her dinner, but on the whole the mood was genial. They emerged from the temple and sat around admiring the lake, tinged now with rose-coloured streaks as the late-afternoon sun sank towards the desert. Some of the women put their woollies on; it was extraordinary how quickly it got chilly in the evenings. Mr Campion read out more from the guide-book. None of them paid any attention to the distant hootings of the coach driver, at the top of the hill. Someone said, 'That damn girl's vanished again.'

The coach driver, hired for so long and no longer, hooted for five minutes. Then, in the absence of any instructions, he threw his cigarette out of the window and drove his empty coach back to the depot.

The sun had almost completely set when the first of them reached the airport building. The stragglers, including the grimly stoical Miss Crawley, now hideously blistered, continued to arrive in dribs and drabs for another quarter of an hour. It had been a good two miles. It was Mr Campion who discovered the envelope with the flight tickets, shoved carelessly to one side of the EgyptAir desk. And it was another ten minutes or so, as the party slowly gathered around him, subdued now and in a state of mingled fury and apprehension, before the penny dropped. 'I simply do not believe it,' said the chartered surveyor's wife, over and over again. The EgyptAir official, subjected to a barrage of queries, shrugged, impassive. Those on the edges of the group, who could not quite catch what was going on, pushed closer, and as the enormity of their plight was conveyed from one to another, the murmurs grew louder. Mr Campion, determinedly keeping his cool, concentrated on the EgyptAir fellow. 'When is the next plane, then?' There was not another plane; the last plane left each evening at five-thirty.

'Then,' said Mr Campion with restraint, 'You'll have to call Assuan, won't you, and have them send up another plane.' The EgyptAir official smiled.

'Oh, rubbish,' said Mrs Marriott-Smith. 'Of course they can send another plane. Tell him not to be so silly.' The EgyptAir official shrugged

again and made a phone call with the air of a man prepared, up to a point,
to placate lunatics. The outcome of the call was clear to all before he put
the receiver down.

'All right, then,' said Lady Hacking. 'We shall just have to endure. Ask
him where the local hotel is.'

The police inspector, a man accustomed to matters of life and death, did
not bother to reply. The woman's manner had been getting on his nerves
for days anyway. He simply pointed towards the long windows of the
airport building, overlooking a vista of desert enlivened here and there
with a scrubby tree or a skulking pi-dog and sliced by the single runway.
The sand, now, was lilac, pink and ochre in the sunset. The rest of the
group also followed Mr Campion's pointing finger.

'Heavenly colours,' said the Knutsford magistrate. She had tended to
display artistic sensibilities since the first morning in Cairo Museum.

The dismay, now, was universal. 'I don't *believe* it,' said the chartered
surveyor's wife. 'You'll damn well have to,' snapped her husband. The
group, with appalled mutterings, surveyed the uncompromising reality
of the airport hall. There were half a dozen rows of solid plastic bucket
seats in bright orange, welded to a stone floor with a thick covering of
dust, two or three plastic tables, and a soft-drinks counter attended by a
young boy who, like the EgyptAir official and the several cleaners or
porters, watched them now with mild interest. There was also the
EgyptAir desk, on which the official had placed a grubby sign saying
CLOSED, some tattered posters on the walls of the Taj Mahal and Sri
Lanka, and a great many overflowing rubbish bins. Those who had
already sped into the ladies' lavatory had found it awash at one end with
urine and attended by a woman who handed each client a dirt-spattered
towel and stood expectantly at their sides. Lady Hacking pointed
accusingly at the swilling floor; the woman nodded and indicated one of
the cubicles from which fumed a trail of sodden toilet paper: 'Is no good.'
'Then *do* something,' said Lady Hacking sternly.

It was now six-thirty. The group, with gathering urgency, had
converged on the soft-drinks counter. It was Miss Crawley, a late-comer,
who revealed that all that was left were half a dozen cans of 7-Up and four
packets of crisps. Those in possession of the only three packets of
sandwiches and the single carton of biscuits sat watching, in defiance or
guilt according to temperament. 'There are thirteen of us,' announced
Miss Crawley loudly, 'without anything at all.' The principle of first come
first served was in direct collision now with some reluctant flickerings of
community spirit. The two retired librarians offered a sandwich to Mrs
Marriott-Smith, who accepted it graciously; they did not offer, it was
noted, to anyone else. The temperature had now fallen quite remarkably.
The few who had coats put them on; most people shivered in shirt-sleeves
and light dresses. The architect who had served in Libya in 1942

reminisced, as he had done before – too often – about the desert campaign. The chartered surveyor's wife told everyone that bloody girl would be bound to get the sack, if that was any comfort. Miss Crawley, with a sigh, took a book from her bag and began ostentatiously to read. A clip-eared white cat lay on one of the plastic tables, luxuriantly squirming. The Knutsford magistrate reached out to stroke it; the cat flexed its claws and opened a red mouth in a soundless mew; Miss Crawley observed without comment.

Outside, it became dark. The EgyptAir official was no longer there. Those sufficiently interested – and resentful – pin-pointed a bungalow at a far corner of the airfield in which lights cosily glimmered. The soft-drinks boy continued to slump at his counter and the ladies' lavatory attendant emerged and squatted on the floor outside. The one remaining porter or watchman came to squat beside her, smoking and exchanging the occasional desultory remark. They ignored the Magitours party, who were now dispersed all over the hall in morose clumps, sitting on the upright bucket seats or leaning against the EgyptAir counter. The architect tried, unsuccessfully, to get together a foursome for whist. Those who were unwell sat near the lavatories, grim-faced. The Knutsford magistrate offered the cat a crumpled ball of newspaper; it lashed out a paw and she withdrew her hand with a squeak.

'I hope it's not rabid,' said Miss Crawley with interest. 'You have to expect that, in places like this.' The magistrate examined her hand, on which beads of blood had appeared. 'Oh *dear* . . .' said Miss Crawley. 'I wonder if it's worth putting on some antiseptic.' The magistrate, glaring, applied Kleenex.

It was at around nine-thirty that the feelings of those without provisions of any kind became insupportable. The mutiny was provoked by the revelation that the surveyor's wife was in possession of a cache of oranges, Ryvita and Garibaldi biscuits which she now attempted furtively to distribute among those of her choice. The murmurings of those excluded became impossible to ignore; Mr Campion, eventually, rose to his feet, crossed the hall and had a brief and gruff word with the surveyor's wife, who bridled angrily. He then cleared his throat and announced that given the circumstances some kind of a kitty situation as regards food might be a good idea. This produced a small assorted pile which Mrs Campion, with evident embarrassment, divided up and carried round on a tray borrowed from the soft-drinks counter. The several sick said they didn't want anything, prompting further complex and minute division. These comings and goings caused a considerable diversion, so that it was some while before anyone – including his wife – noticed that there was something wrong with old Mr Appleton. He sat slumped down in his seat, intently muttering and emitting, from time to time, a sort of bark that was neither laughter nor a cry of distress. His wife, with as much embarrassment as concern, leaned over him, murmuring exhortations. Presently one of the librarians bustled across with a bottle of mineral water. Aspirins were also produced, and a variety of throat lozenges.

'Poor old chap,' said the Knutsford magistrate. 'Mind, I've been thinking all week he was ever so slightly gaga. What a shame.' Others declared that they weren't surprised – this was enough to unbalance anyone. 'You know what it makes me think of?' said the Knutsford magistrate. 'That place in Orkney – Maeshowe. Anyone been there?' No one had; those for whom she had already over-done the widely travelled bit returned emphatically to their books or their magazines. 'Oh, it's quite extraordinary – you really should go. BC three thousand or something but the fascinating thing is these Viking inscriptions by some sailors who spent the night there in a storm and one of them went barmy.' There was a silence. The cat, writhing seductively, wrapped itself round the magistrate's calf; she pushed it away with her bag.

'How does your hand feel?' enquired Miss Crawley.

'Perfectly all right,' said the magistrate with irritation. She watched the cat, which sat lashing its tail. Miss Crawley lowered her book and eyed it. 'Of course all the animals out here look unhealthy. What *is* that on its mouth?'

At eleven o'clock the only functioning ladies' lavatory packed up, a circumstance causing a frail-looking and hitherto silent woman to burst into ill-concealed sobs. Someone else's husband admitted some amateur plumbing proficiency, rolled up his sleeves and braved the now softly rippling floor. 'Good chap,' said the police inspector loudly.

The attendant at the soft-drinks counter wrapped himself up in a tartan rug, lay down and was seen to fall instantly into deep and tranquil sleep. 'Lucky sod,' said the architect. 'Mind, we used to be able to do that, back on the Halfaya Ridge.'

'Oh, do shut up about the Halfaya Ridge,' said Mrs Marriott-Smith, her voice inadequately lowered. The architect, a more sensitive man than was superficially apparent, and who had shared a genial lunch-table with her and Lady Hacking only yesterday, sat in bristling silence. 'Ssh, dear,' said Lady Hacking. 'Of course, these people aren't made like us physically. It's something to do with their pelvises. Haven't you noticed how they can squat for hours?'

'What absolute nonsense,' muttered the police inspector's wife. Lady Hacking swung round, but was unable to identify the speaker.

The party, by now, had divided into those determinedly enduring in as much isolation as possible and those seeking – tacitly – the faint comfort of collective suffering. One or two had tried to clean up a section of the floor and lie down upon it, inadequately cushioned by newspapers and the contents of handbags, but soon gave up. A few people, drawn to authority, had settled themselves around Mr Campion, as though in wistful belief that he might yet effect some miracle. Old Mr Appleton continued to mumble and bark; his wife, now a little wild-eyed, plied him with mineral water.

Mrs Marriott-Smith said, 'Oh my goodness, it *can't* only be half past midnight . . .'

'Tell you what,' said the chartered surveyor's wife. 'We should do community singing. Like people stuck on Scottish mountains.' She giggled self-consciously. 'Don't be so damn silly,' muttered her husband. Miss Crawley, lowering her book, stared with contempt: 'A peculiarly inappropriate analogy, if I may say so.' No one else spoke. The chartered surveyor's wife got out a powder compact and dabbed angrily at her nose.

A detached observer, arriving now at Abu Simbel airport, could not have failed to detect something awry. The complex lines of hostility and aversion linking the members of the Magitours group were like some invisible spider-web, grimly pulsing. Apart from the small group of acolytes around Mr and Mrs Campion, the bucket seats, in their uncompromising welded lines, were occupied in as scattered a manner as possible. Married couples were divided from other married couples by an empty seat or two. Solo travellers like Miss Crawley and the Knutsford magistrate sat in isolation. The two retired librarians had fenced themselves off, pointedly, with a barrier of possessions spread over two unoccupied seats. Old Mr Appleton's barking and muttering had cleared a substantial area around him; he appeared, now, to be asleep, his jaw sagging. From time to time someone would cough, shuffle, murmur to spouse or companion. An uneasy peace reigned, its fragility manifest when someone grated a table against the floor. 'Some of us,' said Lady Hacking loudly, 'are trying to get what rest we can.'

It was at one forty-five that Mr Appleton, apparently, died. He sagged forward and then toppled to the ground with a startling thud, like a mattress dropped from a considerable height. His wife, for a moment or two, did nothing whatsoever; then she began, piercingly, to shriek.

Everyone stood up. Some, like the Campions, the Knutsford magistrate and the librarians, hurried over. Others hovered uncertainly. Miss Crawley, moving to a position where she could see what was going on, said loudly that one must assume a stroke, so there probably wasn't a lot to be done but in any case there was no point in crowding round. Those trying to offer assistance had split into two groups, one devoted to Mr Appleton, the other admonishing his wife, who continued, with quite extraordinary vigour, to scream. 'Hysterics,' said Mrs Marriott-Smith. 'Something I know all about. We had a girl for the children who used to do it, years ago. Someone should slap her face – it's the only thing.'

Mrs Campion, her arm round Mrs Appleton's shoulders, was imploring her to be quiet. 'It's all *right*. Everyone's doing what they can. Do please stop making that noise. *Please.*' Mrs Appleton paused for a moment to draw breath, glanced down at the prone body of her husband, and began again. 'Be quiet!' ordered the inspector. 'Stop that noise!' The librarians and the magistrate were arguing about whether or not to turn Mr Appleton over. 'I tell you, I *know* about this sort of thing – he shouldn't be moved.' 'Excuse me but you're wrong, I know what I'm doing. Is he breathing?' 'I don't think so,' said the magistrate, her words unfortunately falling into a momentary respite in Mrs Appleton's screams, and serving to set her off again nicely.

The soft-drinks attendant had unfurled himself from the tartan rug and, along with the lavatory attendant and the porter, stood watching with interest. 'Tell them to get a doctor,' said Lady Hacking. 'I should think that's the best thing to do.'

'Shut up, for Christ's sake, you stupid woman,' said the police inspector. There was a startled silence; even Mrs Appleton, briefly, was distracted. Lady Hacking went brick red and turned her back. The chartered surveyor's wife burst into frenzied laughter. The Knutsford magistrate, kneeling over Mr Appleton, looked up and snapped that she didn't frankly see what there was to laugh about just at the moment. Mrs Appleton had been led to a seat somewhat apart and was being damped down, with some success, by Mrs Campion. Mr Campion, having picked up the receiver of the phone on the EgyptAir desk and listened for a moment, was trying to convey to the porter that the EgyptAir official must be summoned. 'Is sleeping,' said the porter. 'Office closed.' 'Give him some baksheesh,' advised the architect. The police inspector, a big man, ignored this; he leaned forward, seized the porter's jacket in either hand, and violently shook him. The lavatory attendant uttered a shrill cry of outrage.

'Frightfully unwise,' said Mrs Marriott-Smith loudly. 'That simply isn't how to deal with these people.' Interest, now, was diverted from the Appletons to the EgyptAir counter.

The porter, muttering angrily, picked up the phone, and, presently, was heard to speak into it. 'Tell him to bloody well get over here at once,' said Mr Campion, 'and bloody well get on to Assuan for us.'

'The man doesn't understand English,' said Miss Crawley.

'At least some of us are trying to *do* something,' hissed the magistrate. 'Which is more than can be said for others.'

Miss Crawley stared, icily: 'There's no need to be offensive.'

Lady Hacking, tight-lipped, was sitting stiffly while Mrs Marriott-Smith spoke in a mollifying undertone. 'I have no intention,' said Lady Hacking loudly, 'of getting involved. One simply ignores such behaviour, is what one does.' The chartered surveyor's wife gazed at her, beady-eyed.

The porter had put down the phone and was loudly reiterating his grievances. 'All right, all right, old chap,' said the engineer. 'We've got the message. Calm down.' Mrs Appleton continued keening; Mrs Campion, still in attendance, was becoming visibly impatient. The woman who had been reduced to tears by the collapse of the surviving ladies' lavatory was again quietly weeping. 'I just want to be at home,' she kept saying. 'That's all. I want to go home.'

At this point Mr Appleton twitched convulsively and made an attempt to roll on to his back. 'He's coming round,' announced the magistrate. 'Good grief! I thought he'd croaked, between you and me.' The librarians, with cries of encouragement, heaved him into a sitting position.

The porter, shrugging, looked meaningfully at Mr Campion: 'Is O.K. now.' 'Go to hell,' said the police inspector, advancing towards Mr Appleton, who was heard to ask where he was. 'Don't tell him,' advised the engineer. 'It'll be enough to knock the poor fellow out again.'

Mrs Appleton, supported by Mrs Campion, was led across to her husband and began attempting to brush the dust off his trousers and jacket while reproaching him for giving everyone such a nasty shock. The old man, ignoring her, allowed himself to be helped up into a seat; he stared round, wheezing. 'That's the ticket,' said the police inspector, patting him on the shoulder.

The EgyptAir official arrived, tie-less and with one shirt-tail untucked. The porter fell on him in noisy complaint. The police inspector, cutting in, took him aside. 'Spot of baksheesh might save the situation,' said the architect. Mr Campion continued, in quiet but authoritative tones, to explain that a member of the party had been taken ill, and was undoubtedly in need of medical attention, but that fortunately the immediate crisis seemed to have passed. 'Man not dead,' stated the EgyptAir official, aggrievedly. 'No, I'm happy to say,' said Mr Campion.

And when, presently, dawn broke over the desert and a grey light crept into the airport building the scene there was one of, if not peace, at least an exhausted truce. A few of the Magitours party, done for, were in restless sleep; the others, raw-eyed, sat staring out of the windows at the reddening desert or braved the lavatories to attempt whatever might be done by way of physical repairs. The librarians graciously offered cologne-soaked tissues. A few people ventured outside for a breath of air and even wandered a little way along the road to the temples, at the far end of which those stone immensities, in their solitude, were contemplating yet another sunrise.

And when, three hours later, the first flight from Assuan decanted its passengers the arrivals found the place occupied by a party of people grim-faced but composed. Members of a Cook's tour bore down on them: 'I say, is it true you've been here all night? It must have been ghastly!' Those who saw fit to respond were deprecating. 'The odd little contretemps,' said Lady Hacking graciously. 'But on the whole we muddled through quite nicely.' Miss Crawley, in sepulchral tones, warned of the condition of the lavatories. The librarians, gaily, said it had been a bit like an air-raid in the war, if you were old enough to remember. Mrs Appleton, supporting her husband, who was demanding a morning paper, valiantly smiled. The wan appearance of the party was defied by an air of determined solidarity, even perhaps of reticence. 'The thing was,' said the Knutsford magistrate, 'we were all in the same boat, so there was nothing for it but grin and bear it.' The exclamations and queries of the Cook's tour members were parried with understated evasions. Mrs Marriott-Smith assured the new arrivals that the temples were absolutely amazing, unforgettable, no question about that. 'Absolutely,' said the police inspector heartily. 'Extraordinary place.' There was a murmur of agreement and, as the Cook's tour filed towards their coach, the Magitours party, rather closely clumped together, made their way across the sand-strewn tarmac to the waiting plane.

Bus-Stop

THE 73 BUS, plunging from the heights of Islington down Pentonville Road towards King's Cross, put on a burst of speed between the traffic lights. The conductor, collecting fares from the standing passengers, smiled indulgently: a private smile, and hardly detectable in any case below the lush droop of his yellow-white moustache. He was a big man, a shambling figure with a stoop, the London Transport jacket even more ill-fitting than most, hanging lankly on him, the trousers sagging and supported by a broken belt.

'Any more fares then? King's Cross next stop!'

The diction was upper class – Edwardian upper class at that, a whiff of long-retired statesman about it; indeed, his whole head, if you isolated it from the grey uniform jacket and the paraphernalia of the ticket-machine, was that of, say, some city magnate, the kind of face that features in *The Times* above a brief note about an appointment to chairmanship of a bank or building society. Any incongruity, though, attracted no interest; a good many of the bus passengers, indeed, were foreign in any case and perhaps impervious to such subtleties. A Scandinavian couple wanted South Kensington and were redirected on to a 30. The lower deck thinned out at King's Cross and the conductor went to stand for a moment at the end of the aisle, leaning against the driver's window, his very large feet braced against the floor, stooping slightly to keep an eye out of the window and humming to himself. He had an expression of benign detachment, but there was also something faintly *louche*, a suggestion, the merest hint, of afternoon drinking clubs, of the odd flutter on the horses.

At Euston he came loping down the aisle to help a woman with a push chair. As the bus halted at the Park Crescent traffic lights he restrained an elderly man from getting off – 'Not the stop, watch it! Just hang on till we get across the lights.' In Gower Street he remonstrated with a bunch of teenagers pushing their way up the stairs against the descending passengers. He ran an orderly bus, it was apparent. At the Great Russell

Street stop he paused a full minute or so before ringing the bell to direct a party of Japanese to the British Museum; a querulous fist knocked on the panel of the driver's window. 'All right, all right,' he muttered amiably, reaching for the cord. The bus swung round into the seedier wastes of New Oxford Street, leaving behind it the grace of Bloomsbury, its cargo constantly mutating – raincoated map-laden tourists, bright-eyed shoppers, girls with rainbow hair, a West Indian woman with a tiny staring doll-like baby propped over her shoulder.

At the bottom of Tottenham Court Road there was a surge from a waiting queue, sending the conductor racing up the stairs to check empty seats on the upper deck. The lower deck filled up completely. A plump woman in her late sixties, fur-jacketed, forged her way panting to one of the seats up front. The bus proceeded in fits and starts along Oxford Street; the conductor moved down the aisle, collecting fares.

When he reached the fur-jacketed woman she said, 'Barkers, please', delving in her purse. Then she looked up, met the conductor's gaze fair and square, and gave a gasp that caused heads to turn.

'Hello, Milly,' said the conductor. 'Fancy seeing you. Barkers – forty, that'll be.'

The woman found, at last, speech. 'George!' She clutched a pound note in a gloved fist, staring transfixed.

The conductor glanced back at the platform, rang the bell for the request stop. 'How's Philip, then?'

'George . . .' whispered the woman. 'I don't believe it. Oh my God, how could you . . .'

'Come on, Milly,' said the conductor with a trace of impatience. 'How could I what? Forty, please.'

The woman closed her eyes for a moment and hugged the jacket about her. She turned to the conductor, spoke in shocked hushed complicity; 'Oh my God, George, what would Shirley say . . .'

'Look, turn it down would you, Milly.' The bus lurched, stopped. 'Oxford Circus! Anyone for Oxford Circus?' Passengers jostled on and off. 'I'll come back, Milly. Forty, to Barkers.' He made for the platform, gave an arm to a woman with a stick, stowed another pushchair for a mother, swung up the stairs.

When he was on the top deck, sorting out two English-less Spaniards wanting Harrods, the bell urgently rang. Someone shouted up, 'Oy – there's a lady been took ill down here.' The conductor, with a sigh, hurrying but unfussed, made his way down. The bus had come to rest alongside a jeans shop; music gushed into the street. There was an atmosphere of unrest on the lower deck. People craned and stared; at the front two women had stood up. The conductor pushed his way through.

'What's up, Milly?'

She was leaning forward, her head in her hands. Her voice rose faintly from beneath her hat, from amid her furs. 'The shock, George . . .'

'Oh, come off it,' said the conductor briskly. 'It's a job, that's all. What d'you expect? Can't pick and choose at sixty-one. I'm fine.'

'It's not you I was thinking of.' Querulously. 'You were always difficult, George. Poor Shirley . . .'

The passengers rustled and peered. A singer screeched from the jeans shop. 'Look,' said the conductor, 'you'd better get off, Milly, if you're feeling under the weather. I'll stop a taxi.'

She raised her head. 'She'd turn in her grave, I tell you.'

A girl now pushed her way up the aisle; a girl in her mid-twenties, blonde neat hair to her shoulders, also in London Transport grey. 'What's the matter, George?'

'Nothing. Small problem, that's all. Leave it to me, there's a good girl.'

'What's up, luv?' said the girl.

Milly transferred, now, her attention. She stared suspiciously. 'What's she doing? What does she want? She's never the . . .'

'She's the driver. Now d'you want to get off or don't you, Milly? We can't stay here.'

She closed her eyes again. 'I simply do not believe it. The *driver*. A girl that age.'

'What's wrong with that?' said the girl angrily. 'I'm qualified. Who is she, anyway?'

'My sister-in-law. Take no notice.' The conductor gave her a pat, headed her back down the aisle. 'Come on, let's push off. I'll sort things out.' Voices, now, were wanting to know what was going on. People were crowding on to the stationary bus. The conductor fought his way back to the platform. 'Full up! Sorry – full up on this one. Another behind.' The bus leapt forward, dislodging one or two of those standing. 'Watch it! Hang on there. Anyone for Selfridges? Selfridges next stop!'

Marble Arch and Park Lane siphoned off at least half the passengers. The conductor unfurled a pushchair for the West Indian woman and chucked the baby under the chin. He directed two Arabs to Grosvenor Square. He allowed himself, as the bus entered the long haul down Park Lane, a brief glance over into the park. Then he vanished to the upper deck. 'Any more fares, then, please . . .'

When he came down the bus had stopped at the lights. He reached, at last, Milly. 'All right, Milly, forty please.'

She held out a pound note between finger and thumb. 'What Philip will say, I dare not think. I simply dare not think.'

'Don't tell him then,' said the conductor amiably. 'But you won't be able to resist, will you, Milly? Make your day.' He tore off the ticket, held it out. The lights changed. The bus, a broad unoccupied stretch of road ahead, rushed forward.

Milly clasped the rail in front of her with both hands and drew in her breath sharply. 'Does she want to kill us all, that girl?'

'Oh, stuff it,' said the conductor. 'The girl's perfectly competent.'

'What's a girl want to do a job like that for, I'd like to know.'

'Rubbish, Milly. Plenty of women driving buses in the war.'

'That was different.'

He shrugged.

She took out a powder compact, bravely. 'You've got me shaking all over, George. When I saw you I thought I was dreaming. I said to myself, it's impossible, it can't be.'

'Oh, put a sock in it.' He turned back down the aisle. 'Hyde Park Corner! Next stop Hyde Park Corner!'

The clientele of the bus, Knightsbridge now within sniffing distance, had undergone a sea-change, shifted up-market, blossomed with leather and fur. 'Knightsbridge for Harrods!' called the conductor. 'Hold tight now!' He propped himself on the platform as the bus swung round the maelstrom of traffic and up Grosvenor Place, ran a huge hand round his shirt collar, curbed a woman trying to jump off at the lights. He contemplated, pensively, the green spread of the park as the bus halted throbbing on the corner; he marshalled passengers on and off at the next stop. The bus was now polyglot; it chattered in French, Italian, Arabic, unidentifiable tongues.

The next time he reached Milly she was waiting. A lengthy transaction over a five-pound note for which he had to find change gave her her moment. 'To set off on a simple ordinary little expedition to Barkers' sale for sheets and pillowcases – I'm staying with Mary Hamilton for a couple of days, not that you ever had a civil word for her, I remember – just any ordinary shopping excursion, and find your own brother-in-law handing you your bus ticket, it's beyond belief, simply beyond belief. And the bus driven by a chit of a girl, the sort of girl that should be doing a decent job behind a counter, not risking all our lives . . .'

'Leave the girl out of it, Milly,' said the conductor. He showered silver into an outstretched palm. 'Fifty, sixty, eighty, one pound. Thank you, madam.'

'And that frightful grey jacket thing . . . With a *number* on you. Shirley would *weep*.'

'Leave Shirley out too, d'you mind, Milly. Any more fares then? Albert Hall next stop!'

'And when I think of that gorgeous little house in Sunningdale, and Shirley's lovely drawing-room with the chintz three-piece . . .'

'I shouldn't,' he advised.

'Well, at least *she's* spared this.'

'That's right, Milly.'

'I'll never get over it. Never. I'll not sleep a wink tonight, I can tell you that now.'

'Get old Philip to give you a nice shot of whisky. Does marvels.'

The bus, cruising alongside the park, was relaxed now, easy, down to a dozen passengers, taking time off. Albert brooded in his Memorial; the Broad Walk swept grandly upwards; tulips stood in ranks. A woman heading for Oxford Street discovered she was going in the wrong direction; 'Oh, what rotten luck,' said the conductor, pulling the cord for the request stop. He stood on the platform, tugging at his moustache, watching a posse of shrieking French schoolchildren on the pavement. He turned to the interior of the bus; 'High Street Ken! Barkers next stop!' The French schoolchildren invaded at the traffic lights; 'Watch it, there! Only the lights – hold on, please.' The park was left behind; traffic gripped the bus; the pavements bloomed with racks of clothes, a field of Agincourt in crimson, puce, lilac and blue denim. He thumped upstairs to sort out the schoolchildren, rampaging overhead.

When he got down again the lower deck had filled. He arrived at Milly.

'And *how* old is that girl?'

'Milly, you've missed your stop.'

'A chit of a creature! One feels like writing to the papers.'

'I thought you wanted Barkers, Milly.'

She stared ahead, in transports of outrage.

'All right, then,' he said. 'That'll be another twenty pence, if you're stopping on the bus. And twenty more at Earls Court Road.'

She surfaced, glared, gathered herself into her coat, rose. 'I'm getting off. And there's no need to smile like that, George. I don't find anything amusing about this, nothing amusing at all.'

He agreed that it was not amusing. He escorted her down the aisle, handed her on to the pavement. She stood for a moment, stumpy, upright, befurred, affronted; 'I'm shattered, George. I simply do not know what to say.'

He inclined his head. 'Sorry about that, Milly. You've done your best, I'd have thought.'

'I'll never bring myself to use this route again.'

'Come, now, no need to go to those lengths.'

A blonde head appeared from the window of the driver's cab. 'What's up, George?'

'Nothing,' he called. 'Let's go.' The blonde head vanished; the bus quivered and moved. 'Cheero, then, Milly. All the best to Philip.' A hand, a small hand, stuck now from the driver's window, thumb up. Milly, on the pavement, gave one hard, dismissive stare and turned away to the consoling certainties of Barkers' sale. The conductor stood braced on his platform, the bus plunging ahead for Hammersmith and the terminus.

Clara's Day

When Clara Tilling was fifteen and a half she took off all her clothes one morning in school assembly. She walked naked through the lines of girls, past the headmistress at her lectern and the other staff ranged behind her, and out into the entrance lobby. She had left off her bra and pants already, so that all she had to do was unbutton her blouse, remove it and drop it to the floor, and then undo the zipper of her skirt and let that fall. She slipped her feet out of her shoes at the same time and so walked barefoot as well as naked. It all happened very quickly. One or two people giggled and a sort of rustling noise ran through the assembly hall, like a sudden wind among trees. The Head hesitated for a moment – she was reading out the tennis team list – and then went on again, firmly. Clara opened the big glass doors and let herself out.

The entrance lobby was empty. The floor was highly polished and she could see her own reflection, a foreshortened pink blur. There was a big bright modern painting on one wall and several comfortable chairs for waiting parents, arranged round an enormous rubber plant and ashtrays on chrome stalks. Clara had sat there herself once, with her mother, waiting for an interview with the Head.

She walked along the corridor to her form-room, which was also quite empty, with thick gold bars of sunlight falling on the desks and a peaceful feeling, as though no one had been here for a long time nor ever would come. Clara opened the cupboard in the corner, took out one of the science overalls and put it on, and then sat down at her desk. After about a minute Mrs Mayhew came in carrying her clothes and her shoes. She said, 'I should put these on now, Clara,' and stood beside her while she did so. 'Would you like to go home?' she asked, and when Clara said that she wouldn't, thank you, Mrs Mayhew went on briskly. 'Right you are, then, Clara. You'd better get on with some prep, then, till the first period.'

All morning people kept coming up to her to say, 'Well done!' or just to pat her on the back. She was a celebrity right up till dinner-time but after that it tailed off a bit. Half-way through the morning one of the prefects came in and told her the Head wanted to see her straight after school.

The Head's study was more like a sitting-room, except for the big paper-strewn desk that she sat behind. There were squashy chairs and nice pictures on the walls and photos of the Head's husband and her children on the mantelpiece and a Marks & Spencer carrier bag dumped down in one corner. The window was open on to the playing-fields from which came the cheerful incomprehensible noise, like birds singing, of people calling to each other. Except for the distant rumble of traffic you wouldn't think you were in London.

The Head was busy writing when Clara came in; she just looked up to say, 'Hello, Clara. Sit down. Do you mind if I just finish these reports off? I won't be a minute.' She went on writing and Clara sat and looked at the photo of her husband, who had square sensible-looking glasses and her three boys who were all the same but different sizes. Then the Head slapped the pile of reports together and pushed her chair back. 'There . . . Well now . . . So what was all that about, this morning?'

'I don't know,' said Clara.

The Head looked at her, thoughtfully, and Clara looked back. Just before the silence became really embarrassing the Head pushed a hand through her short untidy fair hair, making it even untidier, and said, 'I daresay you don't. Were you trying to attract attention?'

Clara considered. 'Well, I would, wouldn't I? Doing a thing like that. I mean – you'd be bound to.'

The Head nodded. 'Quite. Silly question.'

'Oh no,' said Clara hastily. 'I meant you'd be bound to attract attention, Not be bound to be trying to.'

The Head, a linguist, also considered. 'Well . . . That's a fine point, I think. How do you feel about it now?'

Clara tried to examine her feelings, which slithered away like fish. In the end she said, 'I don't really feel anything,' which was, in a way, truthful.

The Head nodded again. She looked at her husband on the mantelpiece, almost as though asking for advice. 'Everything all right at home?'

'Oh fine,' Clara assured her. 'Absolutely fine.'

'Good,' said the Head. 'Of course . . . I was just thinking, there are quite a lot of people in Four B with separated parents, aren't there? Bryony and Susie Tallance and Rachel.'

'And Midge,' said Clara. 'And Lucy Potter.'

'Yes. Five. Six, with you.'

'Twenty-five per cent,' said Clara. 'Just about.'

'Quite. As a matter of fact that's the national average, did you know? One marriage in four.'

'No, I didn't actually,' said Clara.

'Well, it is, I'm afraid. Anyway . . .' She looked over at her husband again. 'You're not fussing about O-levels, are you?'

'Not really,' said Clara. 'I mean, I don't *like* exams, but I don't mind as much as some people.'

'Your mocks were fine,' said the Head 'Physics and chemistry could have been a bit better. But there shouldn't be any great problems there. So . . . Are you still going around with Liz Raymond?'

'Mostly,' said Clara. 'And Stephanie.'

'I want people to come and talk to me if there's anything they're worried about,' said the Head. 'Even things that may seem silly. You know. It doesn't have to be large obvious things. Exams and stuff. Anything.'

'Yes,' said Clara.

The phone rang. The Head picked it up and said no, she hadn't, and yes, she'd be along as soon as she could and tell them to wait. She put the receiver down and said, 'It wasn't like you, Clara, was it? I mean – there are a few people one wouldn't be *all* that surprised, if they suddenly did something idiotic or unexpected. But you aren't really like that, are you?'

Clara agreed that she wasn't, really.

'I'll be writing a note to your mother. And if you have an urge to do something like that again come and have a talk to me first, right?' The Head smiled and Clara smiled back. That was all, evidently. Clara got up and left. As she was closing the door she saw the Head looking after her, not smiling now, her expression rather bleak.

Most of the school had gone home but all those in Clara's form who had boyfriends at St Benet's, which was practically everyone, were hanging around the bus station deliberately not catching buses because St Benet's came out half an hour later. Clara hung around for a bit too, just to be sociable, and then got on her bus. She sat on the top deck by herself and looked down on to the pavements. It was very hot; everyone young had bare legs, roadmenders were stripped to the waist, everywhere there was flesh – brown backs and white knees and glimpses of the hair under people's arms and the clefts between breasts and buttocks. In the park, the grass was strewn with sunbathers; there were girls in bikinis sprawled like starfish face down with a rag of material between their legs and the strings of the top half undone. Clara, with no bra or pants on, could feel warm air washing around between her skin and her clothes. Coming down the stairs as the bus approached her stop she had to hold her skirt in case it blew up.

Her mother was already home. She worked part-time as a dentist's receptionist and had what were called flexible hours, which meant more or less that she worked when it suited her. Afternoons, nowadays, often didn't suit because Stan, her friend, who was an actor, was only free in the afternoons.

Stan wasn't there today, though. Clara came into the kitchen where her mother was drinking tea and looking at a magazine. 'Hi!' she said. 'Any news?' which was what she said most days. Clara said that there was no news and her mother went on reading an article in the magazine called, Clara could see upside down across the table, 'Orgasm – Fact or Fantasy?' Presently she yawned, pushed the magazine over to Clara and went upstairs to have a bath. Clara had another cup of tea and leafed through the magazine, which was mostly advertisements for tampons and deodorants, and then began to do her prep.

The Head's letter came a couple of days later. Clara heard the post flop on to the doormat and when she looked over the banister she knew at once what the typed envelope must be. At the same moment Stan, who had stayed the night, came out of her mother's room on his way to the bathroom. He wore underpants and had a towel slung round his neck like a football scarf, and was humming to himself. When he saw her he said, 'Wotcha! How's tricks, then?' and Clara pulled her dressing-gown more closely round her and said, 'Fine, thanks.'

'That's the stuff,' said Stan vaguely. 'Hey – I got you a couple of tickets for the show. Bring a friend, O.K.?' He was a stocky muscular man with a lot of black hair on his chest. The smell of him, across the landing, was powerful – a huge inescapable wave of man smell: sweat and aftershave and something you could not put your finger on. Clara always knew when he was in the house before she opened the sitting-room door because whiffs of him gushed about the place. She said, 'Thanks very much. That would be super,' and edged into her room.

When she came down they were both having breakfast. Her mother was just opening the post. She said, 'Coffee on the stove, lovey. Oh goody – my tax rebate's come.' She opened the Head's letter and began to read. First she stared at it with a puzzled look and then she began to laugh. She clapped her hand over her mouth, spluttering. 'I don't *believe* it!' she cried. 'Clara, I simply do not believe it! Stan, just listen to this . . . Isn't she the most incredible girl! Guess what she did! She took off all her clothes in school assembly and walked out starkers!' She handed the letter to Stan and went on laughing.

Stan read the letter. Grinning hugely, he looked up at Clara. 'She'll have done it for a dare, I bet. Good on yer, Clara. Terrific! God – I wish I'd been there!' He patted Clara's arm and Clara froze. She went completely rigid, as though she had turned to cement, and when eventually she moved a leg it seemed as though it should make a cracking noise.

Her mother had stopped laughing and was talking again. '. . . the last thing anyone would have expected of you, lovey. You've always been such a prude. Ever since you were a toddler. Talk about modest! Honestly, Stan, she was hilarious, as a little kid – I can see her now, sitting on the beach at Camber clutching a towel around her in case anyone got a glimpse of her bum when she was changing. Aged ten. And when her bust grew she used to sit hunched over like a spoon so no one would notice it, and if she had to strip off for the doctor you'd have thought he'd been about to rape her, from her expression. Even now I can't get her out of that Victorian one-piece school regulation bathing costume – and it's not as though she's not got a nice shape . . .' – 'Smashing!' said Stan, slurping coffee – '. . . spot of puppy fat still but that's going, good hips, my legs if I may say so. Which is what makes this such an absolute scream. Honestly, sweetie, I wouldn't have thought you had it in you. I mean, I've not been allowed to see her in the buff myself since she was twelve. Honestly, I've wondered once or twice if there was something *wrong* with the girl.' Her mother beamed across the breakfast table. 'Anyway, old Mrs Whatsit doesn't seem to be making a fuss. She just thinks I ought to know. More coffee, anyone? God – look at the time! And I said I'd be in early today . . . I'm off. Leave the breakfast things, lovey – we'll do them later. Coming, Stan?'

Clara went on sitting at the table. She ate a piece of toast and drank her coffee. Her mother and Stan bustled about collecting her purse and his jacket and banged out of the house, shouting goodbye. The front gate clicked, the car door slammed, and then Clara began to cry, the tears dripping from her chin on to her folded arms and her face screwed up like a small child's.

The French Exchange

THERE WOULD be the Kramers, Tony and Sue, in their Volvo and the Brands, Kevin and Lisa, in Lisa's new Sprite. And Dad had decided to take the Renault not the Cortina because the hatchback would be better with the picnic things. And the forecast was good. They would go to this prehistoric fort or whatever, anyway it was a hill with a view, Tony Kramer said it was a gorgeous spot. Sue was bringing some new quiche thing she was frightfully proud of and Lisa of course, inevitably, would be stacked to the eyeballs with her precious home-made sorbets. And Kevin was doing some sort of wine cup.

And oh, her mother went on, voice a notch higher, shouting up the stairs, isn't it a shame, Nick Kramer isn't coming after all. He's in France. On an exchange. The Kramers have got the Exchange so they're bringing him instead. He's your and Nick's age and he's called Jean something. Oh well, we'll just have to be nice.

She stood in front of her mirror. She heard her mother clatter back to the kitchen. It didn't matter about Nick Kramer; he was duff anyway. What did matter was that the new jeans quite definitely made her look fat. She took them off and put on the blue skirt instead but then the stripy T-shirt was wrong so she substituted the pink embroidered top with the low neck and suddenly her collar-bones looked enormous. Deformed. She'd always known there was something wrong with her collar-bones, it didn't matter how much people she confidentially asked swore there wasn't. So the pink top was hopeless. That left the yellow shirt that made her look pasty, which was definitely out, so there was nothing for it but to start all over again with the jeans and the loose cream top that hid her bulge but made her bosom non-existent. And then her mother was shouting that they were here so in despair she had to stay like that and go down, bulging and bosom-less and discontented, and say hello to them all – Sue Kramer with tight white pants and one of those great baggy shirts and Lisa Brand in a short pink linen jacket and skirt thing and her hair done with silver highlights.

Hello, hello, they were all saying, and her mother was wondering if the barbecue stuff should go in the Volvo not the Renault and her father was showing Kevin Brand the new ice-bucket. Hi there, Anna, Sue Kramer cried, Jean-Paul here's Mary and Clive Becket, and Anna, and the Brands you've already met, I say Kevin we were pursuing you all the way down the dual carriageway . . .

He wasn't very tall and he wore glasses and had spots. Copious spots. Not even remotely good-looking. Oh well. He inclined his head neatly, five times, and said *'Bonjour'*. 'English, Jean-Paul,' scolded Sue. 'You must *try*.' And Jean-Paul said 'Good day' and inclined again. But everyone was busy now arguing about who should go in which car and her father was looking at Kevin's this year's *AA Book of the Road* with a new bypass on it.

Eventually it was all sorted out. Jean–Paul would come in the Renault with them and the Kramers would take the barbecue stuff and follow and Kevin and Lisa would go on ahead because Lisa would want to go like the clappers once they were out of the speed limit.

He didn't say much. He got in the back beside her and said *'Pardon'* when their knees bumped and when her mother asked where he lived in France he told her and when her father asked if he was keen on sport he said no, perfectly politely. She took a look at him, sideways, without turning her head. Poor boy – it must be awful being so spotty. She could see half her own face in the driving-mirror; the new eye shadow was good, really good. Her mother was talking about Lisa and how she'd put on weight, did you notice, Anna? And then she remembered Jean-Paul and asked if he had any brothers and sisters and Jean-Paul said yes, he had one sister younger and one brother older, Solange and Stéphan, and that rather finished that off so her mother went back to Lisa and wondered if she'd like a copy of the *F-Plan Diet*.

South London thinned out and became Surrey towns all joined on each other and presently bits of country appeared and villages. Jean-Paul gazed out of the window. Once they passed a church and he turned, watching it recede. He said, *'C'est beau, ça.* It is of when?' 'That's a church,' said Anna's mother. 'Yes,' said Jean-Paul. 'Of what time, I ask.' 'Oh goodness,' said Anna's mother. 'I'm no good on that sort of thing.' *'Pardon,'* said Jean-Paul. He must be Catholic, Anna thought. She looked down and saw that he had awful shoes on, not the sort of thing people wear at all, but presumably they were French. She felt a bit sorry for him. The next time he looked her way she smiled brightly, to make up for the spots and the awful shoes, and he smiled back. His smile didn't somehow go with the rest of him; it was somehow detached, as though perhaps he didn't realise about the spots, or the shoes, or the peculiar way his hair grew at the back. Oh well.

Another village. A stretch of more open country. Jean-Paul leaned forward and said, 'Excuse. I wish the toilet please.'

Anna went crimson. How ghastly. Poor thing. Having to ask. If it had been her she'd have died rather, in someone else's car, people you didn't know. Actually Jean-Paul should have died rather, in fact. Waves of embarrassment and irritation came from the back of her parents' heads. Her father said, 'Oh . . . Yes . . . Sure thing. Soon as there's a likely spot, right?' And after another minute he pulled in at a lay-by beside a wood and the Kramers' Volvo pulled in behind and Jean-Paul got out and plunged off into the bushes.

Anna's mother sighed. 'I ask you! I mean, you can't tell a sixteen-year-old he should have been before we started.'

Sue Kramer appeared at the window. 'Sorry. But there it is – if Nick doesn't get his French O-level he'll have to take it again next year. Jean-Paul's been awfully little trouble, actually.' And she began to talk to Anna's mother about the holiday the Kramers were going to have in Portugal and presently Jean-Paul came out of the wood and got into the car and Sue went back to the Volvo and they all set off again.

Anna's cheeks still flamed. She slid a glance at Jean-Paul. He didn't, actually, seem embarrassed at all. He was looking out of the window and when they went through a place with a market square with old-looking houses he opened his mouth as though about to say something and then shut it again and smiled slightly, but to himself. Anna's cheeks went back to normal and she thought about their own holiday which would be in Greece and the awful problem was would she or would she not have lost five pounds by then and be able to feel absolutely all right in a bikini or would she have to spend all of every day on the beach holding her tummy in. None of the barbecue today, definitely none, and only a sliver of Sue Kramer's quiche.

Jean-Paul was saying something. She abandoned the bikini problem. 'Sorry?'

'I say, you should wear a hat of fur. Pretty – with black hair.' He gestured, circling her head, an odd, rather stylish gesture.

'A hat?' She stared, perplexed. Actually, her hair was very dark brown, not black.

'Karenina. Anna. For your name.'

'Oh.' She saw now; there was some Russian novel, the film had been on the telly once. 'Well . . .' She laughed, awkwardly. 'It would be a bit hot, on a day like this.'

Jean-Paul looked at her attentively, and then shrugged. 'Tant pis.' He gazed once more out of the window.

And now they were turning off on to the B-road that would take them to this hill and her mother was saying let's pray the charcoal lights properly, I felt such a fool last time with the Kramers, and oh God did I put the avocado dip in? Down lanes and through a village and round a corner and there was the red Sprite parked on the verge and the Brands sitting beside it on folding chairs like film directors use with Lisa and Kevin stencilled on the backs in big black letters.

There was a lot of shunting of cars to and fro to get them off the road and then a lot of unpacking and arranging of who would carry what and in the middle of it Anna's mother suddenly shrieked and pointed at the front of the Kramers' car.

'Tony! You got it! And we never even noticed!'

So everyone looked and now Anna too saw the number-plate: AJK 45.

'Oh, neat!' said Lisa. 'Your age too. I'm green with envy.'

'How much did that set you back?' asked Anna's father, and Tony Kramer grinned and said he wasn't telling. Jean-Paul was looking at Tony in a most odd way; he wasn't smiling but you felt he was somehow laughing. Everyone began to fuss round the picnic things and the folding chairs and the barbecue again and Jean-Paul said to Anna, 'Why?'

'Why what?'

He pointed at the number-plate.

He must be a bit slow on the uptake, she thought. 'It's his initials. And his age.'

'I know,' said Jean-Paul. 'But why?'

She couldn't think, when it came down to it. 'Well, it's a thing people do. There are lists in newspapers. Some of them are terribly expensive.' Actually her parents had been looking for ages for MRB or CTB but for some reason she decided not to say so. Jean-Paul gazed thoughtfully at Tony Kramer and said, '*Curieux.*'

'You're supposed to talk English,' said Anna sternly. He was four months younger than her, it had emerged.

'*D'accord,*' said Jean-Paul, and grinned. Really, his spots were the worst she'd ever seen.

There was a fuss going on now because Lisa had discovered she'd forgotten her sun-tan lotion and although Sue and Anna's mother had some they were the wrong kinds apparently, Lisa had to use this special one, but eventually she decided she might be able to manage with a hat, and they set off, through the gate and up the hill along a rough track.

Everyone was carrying something: the men quite loaded with chairs and loungers and barbecue equipment, the women more lightly burdened with picnic hampers and coolers and ice-buckets. Anna and Jean-Paul were at the back of the procession. Anna had her mother's basket with paper napkins and plastic cutlery and garlic bread in foil, Jean-Paul bore the bag of barbecue charcoal and Kevin Brand's wicker wine-bottle carrier with four bottles wrapped in tissue paper. He padded along a couple of paces behind her; the rest of them snaked ahead, calling out to each other, Lisa slipping and sliding on high-heeled sandals.

Jean-Paul said, 'Very serious – *le pique-nique.*'

She turned to look at him. Was he laughing? No, his expression was perfectly solemn. But something about his voice . . . Anna stared ahead at her laden parents, and their laden friends, at the glitter of chrome and the bright glow of plastic. She said – attack and defence together – 'Don't your parents do this kind of thing?'

'Ah yes. Absolutely. Also very serious.'

She felt, now, faintly uncomfortable. It was as though you were playing a game with someone you knew was much worse at it than you and suddenly they started doing things they shouldn't be able to.

'You enjoy yourself?' enquired Jean–Paul.

'Of course,' said Anna firmly. After a moment she added, 'Aren't you?'

'*Bien sûr*,' said Jean-Paul. He was, she saw, grinning hugely. He waved a hand at the landscape – 'It is beautiful day. The sun. shines. All is agreeable.'

The track had petered out and they were walking on close-cropped turf up the hillside, which rose ahead of them in a series of bumpy terraces on which sheep grazed and small bright flowers grew. The leading group – Kevin and Lisa and Anna's father – had come to a halt and as the others caught up with them an argument arose about the appropriate point at which to pitch camp. Anna's mother wanted further on, at that flat place; Lisa wanted to be near a tree in case she needed some shade. Everyone disputed. Lisa said, 'Oh never mind me, I'll manage somehow, at a pinch I can go back to the car,' and Tony Kramer said, 'Oh no, we're not having that, love. Right then, the tree has it.' Kevin gave him a look that was sort of not quite as friendly as it might be and Anna's parents were telling each other that they needn't be so bossy in that joke-tone that, Anna knew, could topple over into not joking at all. And Sue Kramer wasn't joining in but gazed into the distance and tapped one toe on the grass.

Jean-Paul said to Anna, 'They enjoy themself too, do you think?' Anna, ruffled, pretended to be doing up her sandal. She was sweating after the climb and suddenly had the most ghastly feeling she might have forgotten to use any deodorant.

A decision, eventually, was made. Chairs, loungers, barbecue were disposed upon the bright grass. Lisa had loosened the heel of her shoe and Tony Kramer was trying to fix it with his natty miniature pliers on a key-chain and Sue Kramer was wishing loudly he'd get on with the fruit cup – everyone must be parched. Kevin was setting up the barbecue, in silence. Anna's mother was speaking to Anna's father in that bright, high voice that meant trouble.

The barbecue was lit. The fruit cup was made. Kebabs sizzled. Sue Kramer arranged herself on a lounger, gazed skywards and said, 'Bliss!' Glasses were filled. Birds sang. The spare ribs and the chicken joined the kebabs. Glasses were refilled. Anna's mother uttered an awful cry – 'Oh Christ, I've left the second barbecue sauce at home in the fridge!'

'Oh, for heaven's sake . . .' said Anna's father.

There was a silence. 'But there's this delicious-looking one over here,' said Sue Kramer.

'But just the one!' cried Anna's mother. 'There should be a choice!'

'We'll manage,' said Kevin Brand. 'Forget it.'

'*Quelle horreur* . . .' said Jean-Paul, to the grass, shaking his head.

And now the kebabs were handed round on the gay paper plates, and the spare ribs and the chicken and the one sauce and the bright serviettes, two apiece – for lips and lap. And everyone was saying how brilliant of Tony to know about this gorgeous place.

'We are in the middle of a . . . what is it? . . . a field of battle?' asked Jean-Paul.

They all stared at him. 'Some sort of camp, I think,' said Tony. 'Prehistoric.'

'Or thereabouts,' said Lisa. There was general laughter. 'Now, now,' said Tony. 'It's not nice to make fun of other people's ignorance.' Lisa pulled a face at him and he aimed a spare rib at her, threateningly. 'Don't you dare!' cried Lisa. 'These pants are sheer hell to wash, I'll have you know.'

Jean-Paul watched, without expression. He turned to Anna and remarked, quietly, 'There is a tradition, then, of picnic here.'

'I suppose so,' muttered Anna. She had this feeling that everything was getting out of control – not least, in some odd way, Jean-Paul. There he was, with his spots and his awful shoes, and four months younger than her and yet you had this peculiar sense of him being somehow much older and floating above and beyond the spots and the shoes. She stroked her armpits, surreptitiously; she was sure there were visible sweat-marks on the cream top.

The quiche was being handed round now, and the salad, and the garlic bread, and more wine cup. Everyone was talking at once and Lisa Brand was shouting rather and Kevin was having an argument with Tony Kramer about something to do with the insides of cars, whether Tony's Volvo had a this or a that. Jean-Paul said to Anna, 'You interest in cars?'

'Not really,' said Anna, after a moment's hesitation.

'*Moi non plus*,' said Jean-Paul.

And now they were moving on to the dessert: the mousse and the sorbet and the little biscuity things Sue Kramer had brought. A different lot of gay paper plates; more bright plastic cutlery. There was debris all around now: heaps of plastic and paper and left-over food and bottles and glasses. A little way off a small posse of sheep stood gazing and chewing. 'Don't look now,' said Lisa, 'but we're being watched.' Tony Kramer laughed uproariously.

Anna glanced at Jean-Paul, but not so that he would notice. He was looking at some little orange butterflies that danced above the turf, and then his attention switched to a bird that hung in the sky just above the brow of the hill, its wings quivering. And then, as Kevin circulated again with the wine cup and a few drops got spilled on Lisa's white pants, causing distress, he observed that, in just the same grave and attentive way as he watched the butterflies and the bird.

The chatter decreased. Lisa was still dabbing at her pants, scowling. Kevin had wandered off a little distance and was lying on his back on the grass. Anna's mother was saying that of course it was heavenly here but what would be nice now would be a swim.

Jean-Paul rose, stowed his dirty plate, cutlery and napkin neatly in Anna's mother's basket and strolled away over the grass. He squatted down beside a clump of flowers.

Sue Kramer said to Anna, 'You are being so frightfully good with him. I'm afraid he's rather a dull boy, but there it is. Anyway, you're sweet.'

Anna smiled, embarrassed. Actually she'd never been entirely sure she liked Sue Kramer. Nick Kramer she'd known since he was about three, and he was absolutely hopeless.

'And the acne . . .' said Lisa. 'One wants to simply pick them up and plunge them in some enormous vat of disinfectant, boys of that age.'

Anna looked towards Jean-Paul who, at that moment, glanced over his shoulder, caught her eye and waved. 'Look . . .' he called.

'Be nice, darling,' said Anna's mother.

There was a glinting coppery butterfly sitting on a plant, opening and closing its wings. Jean-Paul pointed, without speaking. Anna was at a loss; it was a bit odd, to put it bluntly, for a boy to be going on about a butterfly.

'A butterfly,' she said, with slight desperation.

'Yes,' said Jean-Paul. 'Of what kind?'

'I've no idea.'

'You are not interest in nature, either?'

'Well, quite,' said Anna (blushing now, curse it).

'I am interest,' said Jean-Paul, 'in astronomy, philosophy and the music of Mozart.'

Anna went rigid. Thank heavens at least the others hadn't heard him; they'd have died laughing. He was perfectly serious, that was the awful thing. What on earth could one say? He was gazing at her, reflectively.

'Tell me,' he went on. 'Why did your parents embarrass? About I need to go to the toilet from the car.'

She didn't know where to look. 'I don't know,' she muttered.

Jean-Paul laughed. 'Perhaps they are people who do not need to go to the toilet, never. *Formidable!*'

She looked back to the picnic group. Kevin Brand was still lying on the grass. Her parents were tidying up. Sue Kramer was sitting a little apart, reading a magazine. Lisa Brand and Tony Kramer were walking up the hill together; you could hear them laughing.

'I'm sorry,' said Jean-Paul. 'Now I make you embarrass too. I am not very nice. Shall we go for a walk?'

'All right,' said Anna. In the car, she remembered, she had smiled brilliantly at him to make up for his spots and his shoes.

They went round the flank of the hill, along the crest of one of the great ridges that lapped it. And Jean-Paul, incredibly, began to sing. She was afraid the others might hear. He sang this cheerful little song, the words of which she could not quite catch, and when they got to a point from which you could see great blue distances of landscape all around he stopped and waved at it and said, *'Pas mal, alors?'* He was, she saw, perfectly happy.

She stared at him in surprise. There he was, this not at all nice-looking boy who wasn't tall enough, spending the day with lots of people he didn't know, most of whom hadn't spoken a word to him, and he was happy. It was ridiculous, really.

She said, 'Do you like staying with the Kramers?'

Jean-Paul shrugged. *'Ça va.* They are very kind. I must learn English for my examination.'

'Like Nick's got to get his French O-level.'

He grinned. 'So everybody inconveniences themself a little.'

They had reached the brow of the hill. Below them on one side was the picnic site, with Anna's parents and Kevin and Sue Kramer just as they had left them and on the other, sitting on the grass, were Tony Kramer and Lisa. Lisa's laugh floated up to them. And then suddenly she was flapping her hands around her head and there was a shriek and Tony was flapping his hands too and bending over her.

'La pauvre dame,' said Jean-Paul. 'She is bit, I think. A – how do you say it – *une guêpe.'*

'Wasp,' said Anna. She didn't feel all that sorry for Lisa Brand. Actually she thought Lisa had been going on rather, with her precious white pants and her jokes. Lisa and Tony were starting back up the hill now, Lisa with her hand clasped to her shoulder

'Do you believe in God?' said Jean-Paul.

She looked at him in horror. 'I don't know.'

'Moi – non. Not since I am twelve years old. Because of he makes everything beautiful and then puts in the middle a wasp. Everything is nice and then – pouff! – a bus come and run over your mother.'

'Honestly?' said Anna, shocked.

'Pas actuellement. But it is what happen. *La souffrance.* So I do not think there can be anyone who make a world like that, or if there is he is bad and he is not God, because God is good. *Pas vrai?'*

Quite frankly, she'd never heard anyone talk like that in her life. You didn't know whether to laugh, or what. I mean, sitting on a hill talking about God. But there he was, doing it as though it were the most normal thing in the world.

Lisa and Tony passed them. Lisa was leaning on Tony's arm still clutching her shoulder. Tony waved and Lisa smiled bravely. Jean-Paul said, 'Perhaps that lady does not suffer so terrible. In the Middle Age people are roasting each other on fires and putting in hot oil.'

'Don't,' said Anna. She was hopeless at history, anyway; it was her worst subject, except maths. And this conversation was quite beyond her, out of control like everything on this stupid picnic. For two pins she'd have gone back to the others, except that in some peculiar way it had now become Jean-Paul who made decisions, not her. Just as, eerily, it was Jean-Paul who seemed at ease in this place, on this hillside in a foreign country, rather than the rest of them.

He said, 'When I will be president of the Republic – no, when I will be king – king is more amusing, *tant pis pour la Révolution* – when I will be king there will be no earthquakes and no bad weather and I will give to everyone discs of the music of Mozart.' He looked at Anna. 'And what will you make, when you are queen?'

It was silly, this, really – I mean, if any of one's friends could hear . . . 'No more maths.'

'Ah. That is difficult for the banks and the shops and the men of business. Never mind, we arrange.'

She didn't know if she liked him or not. But more disconcerting was the fact that, so far as he was concerned, it quite evidently didn't matter. He wasn't bothered, one way or the other. And, maddeningly, it began to matter what he thought of her. Which was absurd . . . a boy like that. She tried to think of something to say that would be funny, or clever; nothing came.

'So that's where you've got to.' Her mother appeared suddenly behind them. 'Lisa's been stung by a wasp. The most unnecessary commotion, frankly. Tony's gone off to that village we came through to get some antihistamine. And someone left the top off the ice-bucket – wouldn't you know – so I can't do the iced tea.' She looked round irritably. 'I said all along we should have gone to the beach.'

'Where's Dad?'

'He's got one of his headaches, rather predictably. So Sue and I have been clearing up entirely on our own. Kevin's gone off in a huff.' She remembered Jean-Paul and said brightly, 'I'm so glad Anna's been looking after you.' She gave Anna a conspiratorial glance of sympathy. 'Anyway, I thought I'd better start rounding people up.'

They walked down the hill. Anna's mother told Jean-Paul that this was a frightfully pretty part of the country and Jean-Paul nodded politely and Anna's mother glanced at his shoes and his haircut and Anna knew what she was thinking. She wished she was somewhere else. She wished, particularly, that Jean-Paul was somewhere else but for her own sake rather than for his.

They reached the picnic place, where Anna's father, Lisa Brand, Kevin Brand and Sue Kramer were all sitting a little apart from each other and not saying anything. Lisa was holding a handkerchief to her neck and Anna's father had his eyes closed. And then Tony Kramer came panting up the hill waving a tube and Lisa cried, 'Oh, Tony, bless you – you really are an angel.' Kevin Brand picked up a newspaper and began to read it and Sue Kramer said, 'Sir Lancelot to the rescue,' and laughed in a not particularly amused way.

Anna's mother had just discovered she had trodden in a pile of sheep-muck and was hopping about with one of her new Russell & Bromley sandals off, trying to clean it.

Jean-Paul looked around at them all. He smiled benignly. He said, 'I wish to thank for you bring me to this charming place.' They all gazed at him in astonishment and he continued to smile benignly and sat down on the grass. 'I enjoy myself very much,' he said.

For a moment there was silence. Then Tony Kramer exclaimed heartily, 'And that goes for everyone, I imagine. Terrific outing. Sort of day that should go on for ever.'

'Absolutely,' murmured Lisa.

'Quite,' said Anna's father. 'Though alas we, I'm afraid, will have to push off shortly.' He gave Anna's mother one of those looks that was not a look but an instruction and she scowled back and continued to rearrange picnic baskets and barbecue stuff.

They walked in procession down the hill. This time Jean-Paul led the way and was the most heavily burdened, having insisted on carrying the two loungers. Even so, he walked faster than anyone else; he was, Anna could hear, singing that little song again. No one else was saying much except Lisa who was telling Tony Kramer her neck felt heaps better now, entirely thanks to him.

The right possessions were stowed into the right cars. They told each other what a marvellous day it had been. Anna's mother kissed everyone and Sue Kramer kissed everyone except Lisa Brand, and Jean-Paul went round shaking hands. When he got to Anna he said, 'When I am king I make you minister of finance, O.K.?' and Anna went scarlet. Jean-Paul got in with the Kramers and Kevin and Lisa got into their Sprite and Anna got into the Renault with her parents. Engines started. Everyone waved.

Anna's mother said, 'What on earth was that boy saying?'

'Nothing.'

'Did you manage to find something to talk to him about?'

'Sort of,' said Anna distantly.

There was a grass-stain on her new jeans and she had eaten not one small slice of quiche but two helpings of everything so she would have put on about three pounds. But all that was the least of it.

They travelled back along the same roads but she did not feel the same at all. Ahead of them was the Kramers' car and through the rear window she could see Jean-Paul's head, and that too was different, uncomfortably different; it spoke now not of spots and a ghastly haircut but of small coppery butterflies and conversation that embarrassed, that left you uncertain, as though you had peered through strange windows. Jean-Paul did not turn round and presently the Volvo was lost in traffic.

The Dream Merchant

THERE WAS once a merchant of dreams. He sold dreams every day except Sunday, to young people and to old people, cheap dreams and costly dreams, short dreams and dreams that would last many days and weeks. The window of his shop was bright with the stuff of his dreams; it offered moonlit nights of love, it offered the spoils of the Orient and the treasure of kings, it promised happiness and mystery and romance. His customers saw themselves transfigured; they saw themselves as they really were – glad and healthy and beautiful, always laughing, feeding on pomegranites and ambrosia, bare-bodied and clean-limbed, having sexual intercourse fifteen times a week. Those of the dream merchant's customers who were of a different caste of mind also saw themselves as they really were – walking tall in an antique land, communing with gods, possessors of all knowledge and all wisdom, superior in all things and especially to their neighbours, who would be made to feel this in the fullness of time. There were dreams to suit everyone, wonderful in their variety and their ingenuity, a world unto themselves, and at prices to suit every pocket.

Sometimes people came back and complained about the dreams. They said, 'This was not a good dream. This dream was not the dream you said it would be. The journey was not a flight into paradise and our bedroom in the hotel was already occupied and the sea was not where the dream promised it would be and the swimming-pool was not built and there were not pomegranites or ambrosia.' And the dream merchant would be very sorry and explain that he did not manufacture the dreams, he only bought the dreams and made them available to others, sometimes at cut rates and amazing reductions, and he could not be held responsible for the quality of the dreams. His regret was genuine, because he was a good merchant of dreams and he genuinely wanted his customers to enjoy their purchases. He passed on their complaints to the manufacturers of dreams, and sometimes he even told a manufacturer sternly that he would not sell his product any more, he would buy dreams elsewhere, proven dreams that gave satisfaction, dreams to be relied on. For he felt sorry for his customers, often – the bright-eyed girls who came in with their savings, wanting to buy handsome young princes, and the tired people and the sad people and the old people, bargaining for peace of mind and adventure and eternal life. Sometimes, he tried gently to explain that his dreams could only be guaranteed in certain respects, but very few of his customers listened to this. Where else, after all, could they buy dreams?

The dream merchant, who lived in South Harrow between the Amoco garage and the Co-op, had never bought one of his own dreams. His wife, an unusual woman, said she was quite happy as she was and did not need dreams. And indeed the dream merchant did not covet his own wares; he respected them and he was interested in them, he unfurled the bales of silk and velvet and ran his hand over the fabric and scrutinised the marvellous designs but he did not yearn to dress himself in them. He knew everything that there was to know about gold and silver and lapis lazuli and turquoise and jade and he knew how to tell real pearls from counterfeit pearls and where to find the Holy Grail and the Land of Prester John and the North-West Passage and Shangri-La, but he did not particularly want any of these things for himself. He was Vice-Chairman of the Rotary Club and a member of the Automobile Association and South Harrow Conservative Party and what he most desired in life was to win first prize for cactus dahlias at the Horticultural Society's annual show.

But he was also a man of conscience, and as the years went by he began to feel more and more strongly that he ought to experience one of his own dreams. His assistant in the dream shop, a girl called Sandra, had tried out many dreams, indeed the main reason she worked in the dream shop was to get a discount on dreams – she could almost have been called a professional dreamer, so obsessive was her need for dreams. But this very obsession made the merchant of dreams doubtful of the accuracy of her accounts; he suspected that she had ceased to be able to distinguish between dreams and real life. She was very good at typing and filing and remembering the price of a high-season return ticket to Samarkand or the names of three-star castles in Spain but when it came to describing her own dreams she became evasive and muttered that it had been smashing, thanks, which the dream merchant did not consider a dispassionate assessment. And so, in his fiftieth year, without enthusiasm but with a certain sense of virtue, he told his wife that he would select a dream for them.

He made his selection carefully. He knew that neither he nor his wife would want to indulge in pomegranites, ambrosia or more sex than they were accustomed to. He rejected cloth of gold and mother-of-pearl and Nirvana and the Hanging Gardens of Babylon. He pored over the offerings of those dream manufacturers he considered most honest, and eventually he settled for a dream to which he thought his wife would not object too much, in a land of eternal sunshine but possessed of a reasonable climate, a dream offering what he considered modest promises by way of castles in the air, miracles, transfigurations and nectar. In any case he did not want to be transfigured and he was not a drinking man. He took out an insurance policy that guaranteed to despatch his body (and his wife's) back to South Harrow by air in the event of his death, had himself (and his wife) vaccinated against typhoid, beriberi, green monkey disease and Lassa fever, and presented himself (and his wife) at the British Airways check-in desk at Heathrow on the appropriate day.

In the aeroplane the dream merchant read the newspaper and his wife did her knitting. From time to time they looked out of the window and the dream merchant pointed out the rosy snow-capped peaks of the Mountains of the Moon beneath, or the silvery glint of a river, perhaps the far-distant Oxus, or even Abana or Pharphar, the rivers of Damascus. They were served a meal charmingly laid out in dolls'-house portions – and indeed it turned out to be made of painted plaster. The girl who served it to them, whose face was the wanton and alluring face that promised so many pleasures on the picture in the dream shop, offered the dream merchant a choice of coffee or tea; if she had more esoteric wares no mention was made, nor, to be frank, would the dream merchant have been especially receptive, being a happily married man, but we must remember that he was dreaming for purposes of detached investigation and not just for fun. He made a note in his new king-size notebook.

When they reached their destination, in the land that was distant but not excessively distant, whose climate was reasonable and whose inhabitants were given neither to revolution nor to unpredictable acts of war, the dream merchant and his wife collected their baggage and were transported by coach to the hotel of their choice. They passed by glittering lakes and craggy mountains, they saw rushing streams and brilliant grassy glades and the dream merchant's wife, who enjoyed scenery, said this wasn't a bad dream at all so far. The dream merchant looked at her warily.

For the dream merchant's intention was to examine not so much the content of the dream as its effect on those taking part. It had long seemed to him that the success of dream manufacturers – and indeed of dream merchants – lay in the response of their customers quite as much as in the quality of their goods. And so he had decided to study the effect of dreaming on his wife, who after all he knew inside out in what you might call her right mind, and also on himself. So far he could detect no effect on himself, except a certain fatigue.

The hotel did not have silken sheets nor did doe-eyed Circassian slave-girls offer the dream merchant and his wife sweetmeats on silver platters, but the bathroom was perfumed and the water was hot. The dream merchant's wife behaved quite normally. She did not peel off her clothes and fling herself upon the dream merchant in paroxysms of lust but read the instructions about what to do in the event of fire (in four languages), did her unpacking and proposed that they should go for a walk before dinner.

The dream merchant observed the other occupants of the hotel, who spoke in many tongues. They were old and young and fat and thin. He watched them eat and drink and depart in buses for the never-never land beyond the mountains and return in the evening, looking much the same. He watched them swim in the hotel swimming-pool and their skins turn many colours as though they were chameleons. The dream merchant's wife put on a swimsuit for the first time in many years and became a delicate shrimp-pink, which the dream merchant found rather appealing. He made love to her before dinner, which startled her and indeed somewhat startled the dream merchant, for whom this was not customary. In fairness to the record, he made a note of this in the king-size notebook.

The dream merchant observed his surroundings – the glittering lake and the craggy mountain and the benevolent blue sky – and conceded that it was more agreeable than the stretch of South Harrow between the Amoco garage and the Co-op. He asked his wife if she would like to stay amid this scenery for ever and she said no, politely but firmly; very nice in its place, she said, but enough's enough. The dream merchant asked several people in the hotel the same question; they looked at him in embarrassment and talked of something else. But they were prepared to give their opinion of the dream; they were happy to compare it with other dreams, criticise it, praise it or discuss alternative dreams. Dreaming, he noted, is a matter of recollection and anticipation almost more than it is a matter of participation. Sometimes he almost wondered if the dream were actually taking place, if he were actually walking among these mountains, eating in these marble halls, sleeping every night in his bed that was not his bed, alongside his shrimp-pink wife who wore now a robe of many hues and of strange fabric, purchased locally. The dream merchant did not much care for the robe, but was too tactful to say so.

The dream merchant was diligent in his investigations. He went for excursions and exposed himself to the *son et lumière* and the display of national dances and he ate everything that was set before him. He had paid good money for his dream, after all, just like his customers (only rather less than they did on account of a special arrangement advantageous to dream merchants). He took careful note of his feelings, and found them to be identical to the feelings he had in South Harrow or in the dream shop itself; irritation, boredom, impatience and compunction, mixed with occasional bouts of guilt, contentment, exhilaration and gloom. He continued to observe his wife; aside from her skin colour and the robe of many hues (which she now considered unlikely to wash well) she was much as she had always been. She had not become younger or thinner or better-informed or wittier or more exuberant. The dream merchant felt disappointed in them both. Since he could not in fairness find fault with the dream, he found fault with himself (and his wife). They must, he decided, be bad dreamers – quite exceptionally bad dreamers. He asked his wife if she would like another dream next year and after careful reflection she replied that on the whole she would prefer a greenhouse, or possibly a new brand of cooker in which she had been interested for some time.

The dream merchant and his wife went home to South Harrow. The dream merchant's wife put her swimsuit away in the cupboard and reverted to her normal colour. The robe of many hues shrank definitively when it was washed and was given to a jumble sale. At night the dream merchant would lie in bed and force himself to think of the glittering lake and the craggy mountains, of the benevolent blue sky and the caressing touch of the sun. He could summon up neither nostalgia nor yearning; in fact he felt precisely nothing. When occasionally he read of that distant country in the newspapers he found himself doubting its existence. Perhaps such places were indeed a fabrication of newspaper reports and television cameramen. 'That's where we went,' his wife would say doubtfully. 'Isn't it, dear?' And the dream merchant would mutter that he believed it was.

The dream merchant continued to sell dreams, from nine to five-thirty every day except Sunday. He continued to advise his customers about the availability of houris in far Cathay and the mean temperature in the Garden of Eden during August. He knew now that his wares were even more miraculous than he had suspected, that they were quicksilver things that blended with the aspirations of their purchasers. He envied, indeed, his customers. He became more intolerant of those who came complaining of the dreams, suspecting them of being incompetent dreamers like himself. His business expanded and he moved to larger premises and increased his turnover by thirty per cent. The sumptuous promises of his window drew crowds; he was considered one of the best dream merchants in the city. He gave an address at the conference of the National Association of Dream Merchants; younger colleagues admired him for his competence and his experience. No one ever knew that the dream merchant himself had only ever dreamed once, and that he had found himself unable to believe in his dream. And perhaps, when you come to think about it, that was the secret of his success.

Pack of Cards

SHE CAUSED him sleepless nights. He lay awake lusting after her, aflame for her, the darkened room full of her voice and her face and her round full limbs. He would get up and open the window in the hope that cooling night air might do something for him; he would put on the light and reach for a book. Books were definitely therapeutic, certain books; it was a new insight into the function of literature. You needed something familiar, but with abiding power. The Russians were best. Turgenev. Chekhov. He stilled the flesh with *Home of the Gentry* and *Spring Torrents*. Which she of course would not have read; most certainly would not have read

She worked as receptionist at a firm of management consultants. She sat amid rubber plants and deep leather chairs answering the phone in her clear confident tone; she processed visitors from the leather chairs to the offices of the consultants, varnished young men with the same sort of voice. He knew those voices; he had heard them in his childhood, in the shops of Suffolk market towns, at point-to-points and later, of course, at Oxford. Five-pound note voices, his mother used to call them. Voices that survived wars and revolutions, ringing down the years; you could not but feel a certain admiration.

How he came to be in thrall to such a voice he could not think; considered dispassionately, it set his teeth on edge. If he closed his eyes sanity returned – almost. But then, opening them, he saw her round flawless face, her ashy silken hair, her flesh . . . ah, her flesh, into which he longed to sink his teeth as though into a peach – no, a nectarine, a golden pink-stained juice-rich nectarine . . . And to hell with the voice. And with what it said.

'Honestly, I don't know *what* I see in you . . .' Accompanied by a peck on the cheek, a pat, some propitiatory gesture. In bed, it told him he was dreadful, awful, really she must be mad, she couldn't think what she was doing. And when he informed her (she was twenty-five, after all, it was time she put a name to these things, called a spade a spade) she would put her hand over his mouth and bury her face in his neck, giggling. 'Stop it!'

she would say. 'Nick, I absolutely forbid . . . I'm not listening, right?'

She was always busy, about to dash off somewhere – for the weekend, or to meet this old old friend, or to get her hair seen to. And when she wasn't she was far too expensive for him: Ronnie Scott's, cocktail bars, theatres. She told him he absolutely must get a car, just something second-hand, a silly little Renault or something, and when he said he couldn't afford one she stared at him and laughed uncertainly. When, occasionally, she introduced him to her friends, she stressed his eccentricity. 'Nick's so *clever*,' she said. 'He's got this extraordinary job on some magazine that sells about ten copies because it's too brilliant for anyone to understand.' And the friends rolled their eyes and murmured. 'He's your original intellectual, he simply does not care about *things*. He can live absolutely anyhow, isn't he marvellous!'; and the friends smiled indulgently, or not. He was a pet, he saw – an intriguing, amusing, faintly disturbing *divertissement*. Sometimes she hinted at inadequacies of dress or behaviour. She gave him an expensive sweater, which he lost. She wished he'd get out of that grotty bed-sitter and find a proper flat – it would be easy to fix up a mortgage, her godfather was head of a building society. When she met his friends she was bright and gracious and said afterwards that she couldn't think *quite* why he hung around with people like that, of course they were interesting in a way but.

He assumed, in calmer moments, that it would pass. In the meantime there was nothing for it but to burn.

She said, 'You've got to meet Granny. You'll adore her. Now she really is absolutely your cup of tea. She's a real book lady. She's the literary person in our family. *Her* mother, you see, Great-Granny – not that I ever knew her she died before I was born – anyway she was part of a sort of set, famous writers and people, she knew absolutely everyone. She's got letters from Galsworthy and Tennyson and people. Granny has, I mean.'

'Tennyson?' he said.

'I think so. Anyway, that sort of person. Granny's got an amazing library. You'll be frightfully impressed. She's a terrific character. Anyway, we're all going down there for lunch on Sunday – we go once a month, everyone – and it's O.K. for you to come.'

'Where?' he said.

'Henley, of course. Daddy'll drive us.'

Her father was a director of one of those companies whose function is so abstruse that they appear to exist only in order to manage money, unassociated with anything so mundane as a specific product – oil or bricks or shoes or soapflakes. There would also be, she explained, her uncle Dickie who was in banking, and his wife, and Mummy of course, and another uncle who was with Cluttons, and *his* wife. And some cousins.

'Cluttons? The estate agents?'

'Well – property people, really. Anyway, you'll come with us and they'll all be going separately. Oh, and it's usually tidyish sort of clothes, for Granny. I don't mean a suit. Just sort of casual tidy, see?'

He saw, arriving at her house: her father in well-creased trousers and crisp open-neck shirt straight from the window of Simpsons. Mummy in something trim and silky. He had met them once before; they greeted him this time with just a shade too much fervour. Her father had the bonnet of the car open; 'Sorry, Nick – can't shake you by the hand, oil everywhere. Good to see you. Excellent. Couple of minutes and we'll be off. Why don't you and Charlotte go in the back together?' The car bonnet dropped with the clunk of expensive engineering. 'Ever been in one of these?'

Nick said he hadn't.

'Ah. Well, I think you'll find it rather fun. This is the new model, of course. Fuel injection, power-assisted steering, hydraulic engine mounting – the works. Great fun to drive. You keen on driving?'

Nick said he wasn't.

'Ah. Well. When I was your age I had an old Lancia. Did about ten to the gallon – absurd motorcar for a penniless young man. Great fun, though. Right – all here, are we? Let's go, then – there'll be hell to pay if we keep mother waiting.'

In the car Charlotte patted the knee of his trousers with what he recognised as an admonitory gesture. The trousers were not clean. He had intended to wash them but had left it too late. His shirt was clean but unironed. He shifted his knee slightly and gazed at the back of Charlotte's mother's head, of which each hair appeared to have been separately arranged. Charlotte removed her hand from his knee, slid it into his and tickled his palm. London slid soundlessly past; white stucco, black railings and polished doorknockers gave way to hoardings advertising whisky and airlines. From time to time Charlotte's father pressed switches; windows moved up or down, water sprayed on to the windscreen, air discreetly blew.

'Let's see now, Nick – what's your line? Can't quite remember. Journalism – that right?'

Nick explained.

'Interesting, I should imagine,' said Charlotte's father after a moment. 'And where d'you go from there, then?'

Nick said he hadn't thought much about that.

They reached the motorway. Charlotte leaned forward. 'Do a hundred, Daddy, go on!'

'Don't be silly, darling,' said her mother.

'Not with the sort of idiots there are around. Besides, too early won't do either. You know your grandmother.' The father raised his voice slightly, for Nick's benefit, as though he might be slightly deaf. 'My mother's something of a grand old lady – I daresay Charlotte's told you.

Remarkable woman. Keeps up her own mother's tradition. The literary connection.'

'She knew all sorts of famous writers,' said Charlotte's mother, 'Galsworthy and um . . . Kipling, was it? And . . .'

'Tennyson?' said Nick.

'Oh, I'm sure,' said the mother.

'Amazing library,' said Charlotte's father. 'I daresay you'll get a look round.'

'Ah . . .'

'You'll be interested. More up your street than some of Charlotte's friends.'

'Oh, shut up, Daddy,' said Charlotte.

'Keep your hair on, sweetie. No one's criticising. Tell the truth, Nick, I'm not a great reader myself. The odd Len Deighton, that sort of thing. Mother's in a different league. Wonderful collection of books. Extremely valuable, of course.'

'That house is just stuffed,' said the mother. 'What's to be done eventually one hates to think.'

'I'm *starving*,' cried Charlotte. 'I hope it's not going to be sherry for hours before we eat.' She rubbed the back of her hand against Nick's thigh. He wondered why he was not getting an erection; perhaps speed inhibited the libido in some curious way.

They arrived, turning sharply off the road into a concealed entrance, down a driveway and out on to a precise circle of creamy gravel bordered by a ring of mown grass and high, scrupulously clipped hedges. Tubs of geraniums stood around. A flight of steps led up to the front door. The house was large, architecturally undistinguished and of the inter-war years. Very clean cars in unusual colours were parked on the gravel, as though displayed for advertising purposes. Charlotte's mother, getting out, said, 'Oh lor – we're the last.'

They went through to a large drawing-room overlooking the garden, in which a dozen or so people stood holding glasses. There were cries and embraces. Charlotte led him round: 'This is Nick . . . Hello, Aunt Frances – oh, fantastic – Jamie's here!' They were all sleek and glowing, like animals fed and groomed to show condition; the older men shook him by the hand, the women smiled, the young said, 'Oh, hello . . .'

On a sofa sat the old woman – small, with a dowager's hump. Charlotte said, 'Granny, here's Nick who we told you about.' He held out his hand and she took it and then dropped it at once. She stared at him for a moment and turned to Charlotte's father: 'You're late, Rupert.'

'Ten minutes, mother. Traffic the London end. Sorry.'

'Well, we'll go in and eat. Tell them in the kitchen.' She began to heave herself up; sons sprang forward. 'No, leave me alone, I can manage. Get the rest of them through to the dining-room. I want Dickie next to me, and

Clarissa. Put Charlotte's young man somewhere near – I'll talk to him. Is he the one who's something to do with some magazine?'

A huge oblong mahogany table, glinting with silver and cut glass; dark oil paintings on the walls (dead pheasants, bowls of sheeny fruit, Stubbs-looking animals); thick carpets and a smell of roast meat. They were disposed around the table by one of the women – 'You there, Charlotte, and um, Nick beside you, and I'll go here and what about Jamie and Sue over the other side . . .' Girls in aprons whisked in and out carrying dishes; Charlotte's father stood at a sideboard sharpening a carving-knife.

The old woman sat hunched at the head of the table, unfurling a white napkin, talking loudly to a daughter-in-law half-way down. Charlotte shouted to a cousin at the far end about a party she'd been to. An uncle – the estate agent or the banker? – was talking about something he'd bought (house? factory? set of golf clubs?). Caught in the crossfire of several conversations, Nick pondered the warring snatches; everything was referential, named names, specified: 'Those last catering people were no good so I've sacked them. These girls are from Binneys in Maiden-head. What's that meat like, Rupert?' . . . 'Lucy and Camilla were there, and both the Warrington boys, and the band was fantastic' . . . 'So I got them down from frankly a silly price to something worth talking about and if Handley okays it I think we may well be in business.' One of the aunts, a clone it seemed to him of Charlotte's mother, leaned across the table and said, 'Do you know this part of the world at all, Nick?' Did she take him for a foreigner? But no, the reference was purely local, it seemed – she was talking about Henley; 'Mother thinks it's quite ruined, of course, since her day, but actually it's really very civilised still.'

Each time the old woman made some remark at large they all quietened in deference, smiled indulgently at her pronouncements.

'What's that peculiar outfit Charlotte's wearing? The colours swear appallingly.'

'Granny! It cost the earth!'

'I daresay. The latest thing, I suppose. I never went chasing after fashion when I was your age. I had good clothes and they lasted me for years. Of course mother had such marvellous taste.'

'There's a portrait of Great-Granny in the library,' murmured Charlotte. 'I'll show you later. She was gorgeous when she was young.'

'What are you talking about, Charlotte?'

'I was telling Nick I'll show him Great-Granny's portrait after lunch.'

Mrs Lavington fixed him with her small, black, glittery eyes. 'What is it you do?'

'I work as editorial assistant on a journal.'

'What sort of journal?'

'An academic journal. It's called the *English Language Critical Quarterly*. The editor was my tutor at Oxford.'

The table had fallen silent.

'What college?' demanded Mrs Lavington.

'St Edmund Hall.'

'My husband was at Magdalen. Apparently Oxford isn't up to much nowadays.'

'Really?' said Nick.

'No. It's gone to pot completely. My sons didn't go there.'

'Not intellectual types like you and father,' said Rupert Lavington. 'Anyone want another slice off the joint? Second helps?'

Mrs Lavington was still fixed on Nick. 'What do they pay you?'

'Sorry?'

'At this magazine. What do they pay you?'

'Granny!' said Charlotte.

'Six thousand a year.'

A ripple of embarrassment ran round the table. 'I think I *will* have some more,' said Charlotte's mother. 'Come on, Clarissa, keep me company.'

'God!' said the youngest male cousin. 'I don't know how you manage. I'm on eight and a half and I'm always skint.'

Nick considered Mrs Lavington. She made him think of the tortoise he had had when he was ten: the wrinkled neck, the small head on the end of it turning slowly this way and that. He watched her eat and remembered the tortoise (whose name was Fred) – lettuce leaves withdrawn half inch by half inch with each deliberate crunch of horny jaws, occasional glimpses of a grey tongue. He had liked Fred; he did not care for Mrs Lavington at all.

'Nick's like you, Granny,' said Charlotte. 'He's a terrific reader. He's got hundreds of books. All over the floor mostly in his crazy room. Paperbacks, of course.'

The old woman stared down the table at him. 'I can't stand a paperback. I've got to have a properly bound book. I can't bear to go into a bookshop nowadays, all those garish covers screaming at you. I always ordered everything from Bumpus. I don't expect you've ever heard of Bumpus?'

'No.'

'It's gone now. When my mother went there they used to put out the red carpet. Old Mr Bumpus always served her himself.'

'Aren't books a price nowadays!' said one of the daughters-in-law. 'Proper books. I got that David Attenborough wild life thing the other day for Timmie. Fifteen pounds!'

Mrs Lavington's reptilean head swung round. 'I was talking about my mother, Clarissa.'

The daughter-in-law, rebuked, patted her mouth with her napkin.

'Galsworthy once told my mother that her collection was one of the finest he'd seen. There is a Nonsuch Shakespeare. I don't imagine you've ever seen a Nonsuch Shakespeare?'

'No,' said Nick. 'I haven't.'

'And of course a large number of first editions. My mother was interested in modern writing also. Arnold Bennett always asked her to read his work before publication.'

'And Tennyson?' enquired Nick.

Mrs Lavington, who had just put a forkful of food into her mouth, chewed, eyeing him. Around the table, there were rustlings; people cleared their throats, applied themselves to food, embarked on new conversations. Mrs Lavington, her mouth finally empty, said, 'Growing up in a house with an outstanding collection makes all the difference. Books are one's world.'

'Are your people frightfully bookish, Nick?' asked Charlotte's mother.

He reflected. Mrs Lavington's cold eye was still on him. He said, 'They don't have all that many books. We always used the public library a lot.'

Mrs Lavington glittered; she almost smiled. 'I have never been into a public library.'

Plates were cleared. An apple tart with cream was served. The conversation turned to choice of holiday destinations, the wedding of a relative, the price of stereo equipment. The format appeared to be not so much an exchange of views and information, or a process whereby someone said something which prompted an addition or comment from someone else, but everyone saying whatever came into their head. The dog-leg effect was peculiarly disorienting. From time to time Mrs Lavington would slice into the middle of someone's statement with a pronouncement, not relevant. Nick sat silent; he could see no point in adding to all this. When, at last, everyone had finished eating, Mrs Lavington said, 'Tell those girls to serve coffee in the library,' and began to grind her chair backwards; sons, again, leapt to her aid and were waved away.

Out in the hall, the women trooped upstairs, chatting. The men stood about, lighting cigars. They were all large and extremely clean; Nick had been noticing, during the meal, the manicured hands around him, nails cut level and scrubbed. Charlotte often picked his hands up and made a little face.

She was waiting now at the foot of the stairs. 'Just going up to powder our noses. The men's loo is that door there. What do you think of Granny – isn't she a character!' The others had gone through the open double doors at the end of the hall. Charlotte leaned up against him and nuzzled his neck. 'Mmn . . . Enjoying yourself?'

'Yes,' he said, 'I rather think I might be.' She was still nuzzling; interestingly, he found himself once more inert.

She peered at him. 'Well, that's a funny way of putting it.'

He moved away. 'I think I'll have a pee.'

He came out of the lavatory and washed his hands in a washroom liberally equipped with fluffy towels and new pieces of soap. Charlotte's father came in. 'Ah, Nick . . . Excellent. Coffee on offer in the library when you're ready. Chance for you to take a look at the famous collection.'

The library was as large as the drawing-room; the walls were panelled, and lined with glass-fronted bookcases. They were all there, sitting about on leather sofas or perched on the arms of the chairs. As he came in Charlotte's mother was saying to one of the other women, 'Oh no, not serious we hope. You know Charlotte – always prone to passing fancies . . .' She looked up, broke off and flashed a smile: 'Coffee on the side, Nick, we just help ourselves.'

He poured a cup of coffee and began to move along in front of the bookcases. Everything in sets – leather-bound, gold-tooled. Complete works of everyone. The Nonsuch Shakespeare. Nothing antiquarian. Everything circa 1910, by the look of it. He tried to open a glass door; it was locked. One of the uncles came forward; 'Having a look at the books? Quite an impressive sight.'

'I was trying to open the case,' said Nick. 'It seems to be locked.'

'Oh, I imagine it would be, yes. Mother'll know where the keys are. Mother! Nick here wanted to have a squint at some of the books.'

Mrs Lavington, sunk into the depths of an armchair, glared across the room. 'Why?'

'I wondered if the Dickens was Phiz or Cruikshank.'

'I can't look out the keys just at this moment. Those cases over there are open.'

He crossed the room. Here, the glass was of the lift-up kind – raise the panel and slide it back into the groove above the shelf; a cumbersome process not conducive to easy browsing. He put his coffee down and began to investigate. Kipling, red morocco edition, 1920. He took out *Plain Tales from the Hills*; the spine had the stiffness of a new book, the flimsy India paper pages clung together. He put it back and tried *Kim*; again, the creaking spine and tacky edges of an unopened book. He moved from shelf to shelf, sampled Trollope, Hardy, Meredith, Tennyson (aha! Tennyson . . . stout brown calf gilt Gothic-lettered definitely virgin Tennyson); an invoice for ten shillings and sixpence (Bumpus, Booksellers, Oxford Street) fell out of *A Passage to India*. The books, in their undisturbed, airless ranks, were arranged according to size; there were no unseemly gaps, no volume slumped against another.

He heard Mrs Lavington say, 'Mind you put things back in the right places.'

He took out *The Seven Pillars of Wisdom*, sat down on the arm of a leather chair and began to read. He became aware that the room was falling silent around him. He felt Charlotte standing over him; 'Nick! You can't just sit there *reading* the books!'

He looked up. 'Why not? It's about time someone did.'

She flung a glance towards the old woman. 'Nick . . . Honestly!'

Mrs Lavington said, 'What did he say?'

Nick closed *The Seven Pillars* and returned it to the shelf. 'I said it's high time someone read these books. But I don't think it's going to be me. Thanks for the lunch – it was very good. Lots of it, too.'

He walked out of the room. None of them spoke. He caught, for an instant, the old woman's stare, stupid with disbelief; he could feel all those other incredulous eyes upon him, coffee cups halted half-way to lips, cigar smoke trembling in shafts of sunlight. It was as though he had snapped his fingers and frozen them all to a tableau. He knew at once what it made him think of and as he went out through the front door he said it aloud, and began to laugh: 'You're nothing but a pack of cards!'

He walked across the gravel and into the drive. He heard Charlotte shouting something. He looked back and waved. She was standing at the top of the flight of steps, as bright and glossy as some handsome animal, an antelope, perhaps, and she aroused, he noted with satisfaction, just about as much lust as would an antelope. He waved again and walked on, down the drive, on and on – he didn't recall it being so long – past an open five-barred white gate that said PRIVATE, NO ENTRY and out on to the road. He went along the verge for twenty yards or so and then settled himself comfortably at an angle to the traffic, with his thumb stuck out high into the spring wind.

The Crimean Hotel

CAROLINE OAKLEY had taken to foreign travel after the death of her husband, who preferred to spend holidays on the Cornish coast or in the western Highlands.

Caroline had had no complaints at the time, but after the first two or three searing years of widowhood she began to feel that she must take herself in hand and make a determined effort to live more positively. Travel was one of the tasks she set herself. She visited Italy and Greece, on group excursions with friends, and then became more ambitious. She joined the local Literary and Philosophical Society not for intellectual reasons but because she learned that it organised annual foreign tours; the trip for this year was to Yalta, on the Black Sea, to visit Chekhov's house. Caroline had seen *The Cherry Orchard* several years ago and had once had a collection of the short stories out of the library. One of them, she remembered, was set in Yalta – something about a lady and a dog; at the time she had been baffled and faintly irritated by it, the dog seeming in the event irrelevant.

But Chekhov, in a way, was neither here nor there. The interesting thing would be to go to the Black Sea, a place that had almost fabulous overtones, like Shangri-La or the Hanging Gardens of Babylon. And it was in Russia, which was of course intriguing and then there were other associations – Florence Nightingale, the Charge of the Light Brigade. It would be well worth the subscription to the Lit. and Phil. and the enforced company of some of its members. In any case Caroline was by temperament a passive traveller, preferring to have arrangements made for her and thus be able to sit back and experience without the bother of decision and negotiation.

It was early September when the eighteen-strong group from Middleton Lit. and Phil. arrived at Simferapol airport in an Aeroflot Ilyushin. The inside of the Ilyushin had been exactly the same as the inside of any other large jet aircraft, down to the piped Muzak and the nets on the backs of seats for advertising material (though these were empty). The air hostesses had been dumpier than usual. Nothing felt, yet, at all alien. The group stood around on the tarmac commenting on the balmy sunshine and were processed through immigration and customs and eventually into an Intourist coach, carefully counted and recounted by the Intourist girl. Caroline, tired after the flight and disinclined for conversation, found herself a seat alone at the back and watched the landscape roll past: enormous harvested fields which presently gave way to mountainous country with vineyards and plots of sweetcorn. She felt melancholy and a little bleak and thought continuously of her husband. The first days of a holiday usually had this effect on her; Florence or Athens were overlaid by St Ives or Glenelg and she would move around within a capsule of recollection, staring out through the glass at the unreal world beyond.

The rest of the party were somewhat dismayed, upon arrival in Yalta, to find that their hotel was an immense cliff-like structure, commanding impressive views of the sea and the coast but fourteen storeys high and with a thousand rooms. The entrance lobby was a vast shiny-floored concourse in which scores of people milled about talking German and the languages of eastern Europe and looking like the holiday crowds of any other resort. The Middleton party gathered around their luggage while the Intourist girl went to claim the room keys; the county librarian, the only member of the Lit. and Phil. to have read carefully the information on the brochures they had been given, kept pointing out that they had in fact been told about the hotel. Most people, though, distracted by photographs of palms and bougainvillaea and nineteenth-century villas, had skipped the less evocative stuff about modern touristic facilities and formed a picture of some pleasant local *pension* with bosky courtyard. Still, as they kept saying to each other, there's a lot to be said for mod. cons. and reliable food.

Caroline Oakley, before she went to bed, stood on her balcony (a rather sickening drop below, at which she was careful not to look) and watched the light fade from the sky above the dark shapes of the mountains that rose so sharply from the sea. One of these mountains, seen from the coach, had had a bare rock surface towards its summit on which was a just-visible inscription in red paint; this had been translated by the guide – it said, apparently, 'Glory to the Party'. The Lit. and Phil. had joked about this; 'Catch me climbing Snowdon to write "Vote for Thatcher!"' said someone. The county librarian observed tartly that that was hardly an appropriate parallel. Caroline, in her capsule, had paid little attention; now, in the soft warm night air, she was filled for the first time with the sense of being in another country. On the next balcony, a deckchair scraped and someone said something in a tongue she did not recognise; music seeped up from far beneath; lights twinkled along the coast. The sea was quite flat and still, a shade darker than the sky, and split by a wide shimmering belt of reflected light from a huge yellow moon.

She tried to remember exactly when the Crimean War had been and what it had been about. Who was against whom, and who won? All she could recall was Florence Nightingale and the Light Brigade. She had read a book on Florence Nightingale fairly recently. Written from a feminist position, it had left Caroline rather more affected by the unenviable situation of men at that time. The descriptions of the sufferings of the soldiers were something you could not forget – typhus, cholera, gangrene, those hideous suppurating wounds. The mud and the cold; the sick and wounded laid out in rows like corpses; the operations without anaesthetic. As you read of all that, it was no wonder that you ended up paying little attention to what it had been all about or who won. Now, that seemed irrelevant – like the dog in Chekhov's story.

She looked down, gingerly, at the forecourt of the hotel, where Intourist buses roosted under a floodlight. Sevastopol, she supposed, must be somewhere further along the coast. Perhaps they would be taken there.

They were not to be, as it turned out. The Intourist girl said it would not be interesting. They would visit, on various days, the Livadia Palace where the famous conference took place, a vineyard, the Botanical Gardens and, of course, Chekhov's house. They were urged to take full advantage of the hotel's facilities – the saunas and massage rooms, the theatre in which there would be concerts of Ukrainian folk music, and the private beach accessible by lift.

Caroline went to the beach with other members of the party on the first morning. The lift, plunging precipitately down through the cliff, disgorged them into a tunnel just like the approach to a tube station – a curious way in which to go bathing. Once outside, the prospect was uninviting: narrow concrete promenades with rows of changing cubicles and shower-rooms, from which steps led down to a strip of shingle beach on which many people sat or lay upon wooden boards. The Lit. and Phil. party changed into swimming costumes and descended to the shingle, where they equipped themselves with boards and sat in the sunshine.

The sea, flat and motionless, was studded with heads and torsos. People swam round in circles or simply stood, chest deep. Beyond them the smooth grey expanse reached away to the horizon, quite empty – no white sails, no power boats. The Intourist girl, now wearing a flowered bikini, reiterated facts and figures about the development of the coast as a place of rest and recreation for the Soviet people. Caroline, gazing at that bare inactive sea, said, 'People don't go sailing?' The Intourist girl replied that Russian people were not very interested in boats.

'How odd,' said Caroline.

'No. Not odd. Just they are not interested.'

Caroline got up and made her way down to the water. The function of

the wooden boards became apparent; the pebbles were quite excruciatingly painful to the feet, like walking on blunt knives. Lurching from
side to side she achieved the water, which was tepid and full of very small
inoffensive jellyfish that brushed against her thighs as she waded out.
The sea slopped around her, lethargically; she sank into it, swam for a
little and then trod water. All around her other heads stuck up. She
turned away from the beach and stared out across the empty sea, the
horizon now seeming very close, as though you could reach out and
touch it. She wondered how far away Turkey was.

The afternoon was devoted to Yalta itself – a tour of the town on foot to
be followed by the visit to Chekhov's villa. Shepherded by the Intourist
girl, they walked slowly along the front amid decorous crowds, noting
the absence of transistor radios, litter and hooliganism. People patiently
queued at a funfair for dodgems and the big wheel; rows of teenagers sat
on a wall, looking at the sea. They seemed to walk for a long time; the
sea-front was more extensive than anyone had realised.

Caroline, falling behind the others at one point, and separated from
them by the crowd – there really were a great many people – found a man
alongside and was startled to realise that he was speaking to her:
'American?'

'English.'

There was a pause. 'I like very much England,' he said.

'Really?' said Caroline with interest. 'You've been there, then?'

He was a big burly man, balding, tanned, neatly dressed in clean white
shirt and drill trousers. A large chrome watch glittered on a hairy arm; he
evoked, for some indefinable reason, the sea. And indeed it emerged that
he had worked as engineer on a refrigerator container ship plying the
North Sea and frequently calling in at Hull, which accounted for his
knowledge of England. He was recently retired and lived near Gorky. Still
walking side by side, jostled by the thickening crowd (they were
approaching the central square) they talked of Hull ('Very nice people –
very kind – I am visiting in many houses of friends'), of the circumstances
of Caroline's visit to the Crimea, of the man's situation, which perturbed
her a little – an inadequate pension, food shortages, problems about
accommodation which he had to share with a sister ('We are not always
liking each other very much, I am afraid'). His openness surprised her.

They had caught up, now, with the rest of the group. Caroline
explained her companion's familiarity with England; the conversation
became more general; the Intourist guide said, 'And now we are making
our visit to Chekhov's villa.' To Caroline she added, 'I think this is a very
boring man, we must get rid of him.' 'No,' said Caroline. 'He's rather
nice.' 'I do not think so,' said the girl. 'Good, here is our bus. Get on,
please.'

The man, when Caroline looked out of the coach window, had

vanished into the crowd. The woman beside her, wife of a prominent Middleton headmaster, said, 'How interesting – someone turning up like that and talking English. Hull, of all places!' Her husband leaned across the aisle: 'Mind you, their language teaching is a sight better than ours, it seems to me. But that chap had learned his on the job, one gathered. You had quite a chat, Mrs Oakley?' 'Yes,' said Caroline. 'We did.' The coach was squeezing through narrow streets; large Edwardian houses sheltered behind high walls and foliage; people clutching plastic carrier bags were queueing beside a lorry that had tipped a heap of potatoes on to the pavement.

The Chekhov villa was reached by way of a museum displaying memorabilia and photographs. Letters in glass cases; early editions of the works; a very long black coat, a pair of gloves, a handkerchief. A photograph showed the writer wearing what appeared to be that very coat, standing with two dogs beside a large watering-can. The dogs, prick-eared curly-tailed creatures, stared alertly at the camera; Chekhov looked sad. Caroline examined it for a couple of minutes, wondering if the dogs related at all to the dog in the story. She found their beady, interested eyes, gazing at one from eighty years ago, curiously moving. So, in some humdrum way, was the watering-can. The Intourist girl was recounting, in an uninterruptible monotone, the story of the last years of Chekhov's life: the tuberculosis, the exile to Yalta's beneficial climate, his loneliness separated from Olga Knipper and his Moscow friends. The Middleton party moved repectfully through the villa, fenced off by velvet ropes from the desk, the dining-table, the favourite chair. Caroline, alone for a moment in a small room overlooking a tree-filled garden with which little winding paths disappeared into greenery, could hear nothing but the creak of a floorboard and a clock ticking. She thought of long aching afternoons in an empty house.

That evening in the hotel a vocal group appeared in the immense dining-room; conversation was blotted out by the crash of amplified music. The Lit. and Phil., grimacing, ate without speaking, while rainbow shafts of strobe lighting swept across them. Caroline went to bed early with a headache and lay awake for a long time. She felt as though she had been sleeping in this room for many weeks. Its landscape was infinitely familiar: the matching orange-patterned curtains and bed-spread, the cheap veneer dressing-table, the glass-topped chest, the squat fifties-style armchair. Above, below and on all sides were a thousand similar rooms, like the cells of a honeycomb, each with its embedded occupant or occupants, lying there dreaming in assorted languages. Eventually she got up, put the light on and fetched a book from her suitcase. Before getting back into bed with it she stood for a while looking at the map of the Soviet Union thoughtfully supplied by the hotel in a folder along with the list of charges for laundry, hire of a refrigerator, use of the sauna, etc. She saw a great shapeless mass cementing Europe to China; there were the familiar almost cosy outlines of Scandinavia, the Germanies, Austria, Hungary, Yugoslavia, neat and small, and then this immense sprawl of space – emptier and emptier of place-names – reaching across the top of the world with India and the Malaysian archipelago dangling from it. She put her finger on the Crimea and thought: there am I.

They visited the Botanical Gardens. They tasted Crimean wines at a vineyard. They walked or plunged in the lift down to the beach and swam in that tepid sea. People kept saying Russia somehow wasn't at all as one had imagined. On the fourth day they climbed once again into the coach to be taken to the Livadia Palace, scene of the conference. The Intourist girl recited recent history to them, doggedly, through the megaphone. Harold Innis, the headmaster, became irritated, interrupting *sotto voce*: 'Yes, yes, my love . . . we're not complete ignoramuses.' Inside the palace the party stood before glass cases and inspected the signatures of Roosevelt, Stalin and Churchill; the conference table, at the far end of an expanse of parquet, looked deceptively homely, like something you might have breakfast at. 'There is now exhibition of photographs,' announced the girl. 'This way, please.' 'Well, I don't know . . .' said Rosemary Innis. 'I'm not that mad about photography. I may just slip out and enjoy the gardens a bit.' 'Everyone comes, please,' said the girl sternly. 'It is very interesting. You will wish to see.'

They were war photographs. Caroline, absorbed, moved from one grey scene to another: a towering mound of German helmets, a man sitting head in hands beside the shot bodies of his wife and daughter, people digging in the rubble of Berlin, an aircraft embedded in the façade of an eighteenth-century Belgrade house, the lunar landscape of destroyed cities. A great bleakness crept over her; when someone spoke she could not reply but moved away to the window. Outside, some small children ran round and round on the gravelled paths of the palace gardens. One of the photographs had shown people sunbathing amid the ruins of Sevastopol. Caroline thought again of an illustration in that book about Florence Nightingale; soldiers laid out on stretchers, row upon row of them, mummy-like with bandaged arms, legs, heads.

They came out into the sunshine. 'We walk a little, I think,' said the Intourist girl. 'It is very nice to walk in these gardens.'

It was indeed. Caroline, though, still chilled by the photographs and feeling tired, sat down on a bench, saying to the guide that she would wait there until the rest of the party finished their tour. 'I think you will not like to be alone,' said the girl. 'It is better you come also.' 'I'll be fine,' said Caroline firmly. 'Please . . .' The group moved away among the trees.

It was hot. She lay back, her head against a tree, and closed her eyes.

After a few moments, though, the sense of a presence made her open them. A man was standing over her – sprung, apparently, from behind the tree for there had been no one near when she sat down. He wore only a pair of bathing-shorts and glistened with sweat. It was, she realised with amazement, the man from the promenade at Yalta – the English-speaking engineer. He was smiling broadly.

'Good morning.'

'Good morning,' said Caroline.

'I am very pleased to be seeing you again.'

She continued to stare at him, quite nonplussed. He carried a rolled bathing-towel under one arm which he shook out and applied vigorously to his shining bronzed torso.

'I am very hot. I have done much walking. I may sit down?'

'Yes – of course.'

He sat beside her on the bench. 'You have enjoyed your visit to the Livadia Palace?'

'Well . . . I'm not sure that enjoy would be quite the right word. It's certainly very interesting. Those war photographs are rather . . . disturbing.'

'Ah . . .' He appeared to ponder. 'I too have seen.'

There was a silence. 'Where were you in the war?' Caroline asked. Wondering, at once, if this was tactless.

It was not, apparently. He began to talk with animation about his service on a destroyer in the Barents Sea off Murmansk. Caroline sat listening in the sunshine; around her carefully tended trees and shrubs shifted in the breeze and a squirrel ran across the grass. Images flickered before her eyes – figures in oilskins battling along tipping decks, bearded faces iced with spray – derived, she realised, from old Pinewood Studios films. When he stopped speaking she said, 'I'm afraid I find it almost impossible to . . .' – not to imagine, that was wrong, imagining was what one did, so ineptly – '. . . to have any idea of,' she ended lamely.

'You are child in the war, I think?'

'Well . . . adolescent. I was at a boarding school in Devon.'

'Please tell me how that was. You were happy?'

'It's hard to say. I missed my parents a lot. I was only eleven when I went there. I suppose it was like many adolescences – happy some of the time, rather wretched at others.' The school re-created itself and hung invisible around them in the Crimean park: expanses of shiny linoleum, Spam, powdered egg, the smell of metal polish, the thin high cries of girls playing hockey. The man was gazing at her with kindly, puzzled brown eyes: 'Wretched?' 'Miserable. Unhappy.' He nodded, 'I am like so too. I am very difficult as boy, my mother say. I think perhaps boy is more difficult than girl, always? Yes?' 'I've never had children, so it's something I'm a bit ignorant about.' 'I too have not children – not wife either. I would like wife, several times, but it is not good life for woman, husband always going away on ships. So I am not marry.' 'Married,' said Caroline. 'You did not marry or you were not married'; really! she thought, how pompous! And blushed. 'I am sorry – I speak English very badly.' 'No you don't,' Caroline exclaimed. 'You speak it very well – extremely well. And I don't speak a word of Russian.'

The man lit a cigarette. 'We are coming from very different countries.'

She glanced at him, wondering.

He waved the cigarette – at distant mountains, at the hammer and sickle rippling above the wedding-cake palace. Sparks of sunlight snapped from his chrome watch-strap. 'You are not seeing young sailor on a destroyer. I am not seeing this school in . . . where it is?'

'Devon. Yes – I understand what you mean. But in a way isn't it a more general difficulty. I mean . . .' – she groped, surprised at herself – '. . . in fact even where people one knows well are concerned, my husband even, you see he used to go to an office every day – he was a solicitor – and after he died I realised I had very little idea of what it was *like* for him. Really like. He wasn't a person who talked a lot about himself. It upsets me sometimes, now – feeling that I had so little idea.' She couldn't think what had come over her – talking like this to a complete stranger.

'Russian people are talking more about themselves, I think.'

'Are they? Well, I should imagine that's a good thing.'

'I am not talking so much because there is my sister only to listen and she has heard much already. Here now are your friends coming again.'

'Yes,' said Caroline. 'So they are.' The Lit. and Phil., herded by the Intourist girl, straggled from the woodland path.

'I am going now.' He stood up. 'Perhaps we meet again on the beach. I am swimming there tomorrow early. Before breakfast. Do you like to swim before breakfast?'

Caroline did not look at him. 'I do quite like swimming before breakfast,' she said. He walked away. She picked up her bag and rejoined the group. 'Miles of trees with little labels,' said Rosemary Innis. 'You were wise to stay behind.' 'I say!' exclaimed her husband. 'Wasn't that the same chap we talked to in Yalta?' 'Yes,' Caroline replied. 'It was.' 'What an extraordinary coincidence! I suppose it *was* a coincidence?' 'I don't know,' said Caroline. 'Do you think it was?' The Intourist girl, restive, was trying to head them towards the coach.

Caroline sat at the front, a position that gave you the best view. Within the coach's shell of tinted glass you moved between sea and mountains, gazing dispassionately down at people, houses, cars, knowing that you would never see them again: the place passed by like a film, unreachable and impinging only on the vision. You saw it but did not feel it. Indeed, since the coach was air-conditioned you forgot even that it was hot outside.

There were only two more days to go. The Lit. and Phil. had fallen by now into small interior groupings; Caroline found herself frequently with the Innises. 'I've enjoyed it,' declared Rosemary, at dinner that evening. 'But I don't think I'd want to come back. Once is enough. It's another country all right – I mean in a way that others aren't.' Her husband turned to Caroline, 'I've been thinking about that chap again. Very odd – him turning up like that. I mean – things may not always be quite what they seem. You don't know what he may be after. It's probably innocent enough – spot of hard currency, that sort of thing. Or it may be more complicated. I'd steer clear, if I were you, if he shows up again.'

'But how could he possibly have known we'd be at the Livadia Palace at that moment?' said his wife. 'Surely it was coincidence?'

Harold Innis shrugged. 'I daresay.'

After the meal they wandered for a while in the warm darkness of the hotel grounds, amid polyglot crowds. Moonlight glittered on the sea, as it had on the first evening; the hotel, a white cliff packed with light, rose against the black mountainside; music thumped from one of its several discos. It had been built, apparently, ten years ago but its positive occupancy of the night seemed immutable, solid and confident in a different way to the Tsarist palaces along the coast. It was as though complacent nights like this, moonlit and stormless, reached away forwards and backwards in an uninterrupted succession, giving the lie to those photographs and to the Sevastopol soldiers on their stretchers.

Caroline got up at half past six. There was no one waiting for the lifts; she descended alone to the vast entrance hall, where cleaning women operated huge polishers. She walked down the winding cliff path to the beach; a few swimmers bobbed in the water and joggers pounded up and down the promenade. She sat on the beach and presently, when she looked up, there he was coming down the stone steps, a bathrobe over his swimming costume.

They went together into the sea and swam out. He was a strong swimmer, forging through the water with a purposeful breast-stroke, holding back from time to time to allow Caroline to keep up. Turning, she saw the beach now disconcertingly distant and felt slight panic: 'I think this is as far as I'd better go – I've not done much swimming lately.' He said, 'It is quiet, this sea, it has not strong . . . how do you call it? Forces?' 'Currents,' said Caroline. 'But even so . . .'

Back on the beach they dried themselves off. 'I am finding at last a map of England,' he said. 'It is not easy but at last I am finding a person who has. So I see Devon where is this school is at one end . . . so' – he drew in the air a shape, and stabbed – 'there . . .'

The sea was almost empty, and the beach: a couple of lazily bobbing heads, someone a few hundred yards away doing press-ups on the shingle. They were alone. 'I looked at a map too,' said Caroline. 'To find

Murmansk. I hadn't realised how very far north it is. Almost in the Arctic
Circle.' She turned to him; he had nothing with him except for his towel
and the bathrobe. She had only her towel and the dress she had now
slipped on over her damp bathing costume. If either of us could be
thought to have something to give to the other or something to receive,
she thought, then it is clear by now that we haven't got it. We neither of us
have anything but towels, bathing costumes and whatever is in our
minds.

He said, 'I think you are going back to your home tomorrow?'

'Yes.'

He too now turned and faced her. 'I am,' he stated, 'a man who is very
much lone.'

'Lonely,' she said. 'We say lonely, not lone.' She got to her feet and
stood looking down at him. 'I am lonely too. Quite a lot of the time. So I do
understand. And now I think I had better go.' She held out her hand. He
rose, took it, and they stood there thus until Caroline took a step
backwards, turned away and began to climb the stairs to the promenade.

When she was half-way up she looked back. He was still there, sitting
on his board and gazing at the sea. The sun was up now, and the heat of
the day beginning to concentrate. Caroline climbed on towards the hotel
which now, at nearly half past eight, was spilling scantily clad people on
to the concrete concourses which surrounded it.

A Dream of Fair Women

RICHARD SWINTON listened to the chairman's introduction, which was satisfyingly eulogistic. He allowed the applause to die down, went to the lectern and arranged his papers in front of him. A full house, he observed, an audience of eighty to a hundred or so filling the panelled carpeted upholstered interior of one of the most agreeable public rooms in London. Naturally, for the Brent-Caxton lecture. And for himself. More women than men; his glance swept over the rows of faces – spiky-haired art students, female academics, the smarter coterie from galleries and museums. Provocative black leather, colour-supplement chic, the careful neutrality of tweed and muted patterns. Ah, women were so endearingly self-revealing, clothed or unclothed.

He looked quickly at the screen and then at the girl in charge of the slides. The lights were dimmed. He began to speak. This was his 'The Nude in Nineteenth-Century French Painting' talk, touched up a little for the occasion, but as familiar as an old coat. As he slipped into the opening paragraph he allowed himself to inspect the audience more closely, his eye roving over the faces of strangers and alighting, almost at once, bang in the second row, on that of his third mistress.

There she sat, her hands folded in her lap, gazing at him impassively. Well, no; not at him but at a point about eighteen inches behind his left ear. She wore a lilac-coloured suit, white silky shirt and a rope of pearls; she looked very nice – healthy, complacent, older naturally – though not perhaps all of . . . let's see now . . . fifty-one – no fifty-three more like.

He faltered, lost his way for a moment, picked it up again before anyone could have noticed and tapped his pointer for the first slide. Valerie. Well, well. Once upon a time, time out of mind ago, he and she had sunbathed naked on the deserted beach of a Greek island. He could see her now, a delicate prawn pink against the white sand, demanding applications of Ambre Solaire. He still possessed, expediently buried among some old papers that his wife wouldn't be interested in, a photo of her sitting on a rock wearing a yellow bathing costume, nicely tanned by then. And one of himself of which he was rather fond in which the blue of his shirt exactly matched the blue of the cluster of morning glory flowers behind his head; his eyes, in a bronzed face, were becomingly crinkled against the sun – one was, at thirty, a good-looking chap, not to put too fine a point on it.

And wearing pretty well at fifty-five. Bit of a paunch (reminded, he drew it in), a few grey hairs, but (compared to some one could name) extremely presentable. He turned to the screen, talking of outlines and skin tones, his pointer wandering across the ivory flank of Ingrès's *La Grande Odalisque*. It occurred to him – the thought had a certain irony – that in fact he knew the bodies of the great female nudes of European art with greater intimacy than those of any real women. For instance, he could not for the life of him now recall much about Valerie's thighs or buttocks, but he could give a perfect account of the form of the Ingrès lady – or of Velázquez's *Venus* or Rubens's *Three Graces* or of a score of others. Faces, though, were another matter. He could have conjured up Valerie's face, a trifle blurred perhaps but accurate in essentials, at any point over the years. To glimpse her just now for but a fraction of a second had been enough to recognise her; whereas had it been merely a limb, a torso, a breast that he had seen he would presumably have passed it by without a tremor.

He had not run across her at all in the last twenty years. She had married a wine importer, he remembered hearing at some point, had a child or two, did a bit of up-market cookery journalism – he had found himself reading a piece by her once, in a dentist's waiting-room.

How – interesting, touching in a way – that Valerie should attend his Brent-Caxton lecture.

He reached the bottom of another page, paused, put his elbows on the lectern and began to extemporise – the sort of off-the-cuff light discursion with a joke that often came off rather well. Looking down at the upturned faces – less distinct now in the dimmer lighting – he saw the audience respond: smiles here and there, the engaged expressions of people who feel themselves addressed personally. He always enjoyed that feeling of command – indulgent command. It must be akin to the feeling stage actors get on a good night. He had always been a good lecturer; it wasn't something he'd ever had to work at. Of course presumably either you were or you weren't, it was one of those God-given things, like so much in life.

He looked quickly at Valerie – attentive but gazing at the screen, not at him. His gaze passed beyond her towards the centre of the hall and there sitting by the aisle was his first love, Susan.

He dried up completely. Words failed him. He floundered, coughed, retrieved some lame conclusion and fled back to the safety of his text. Christ! What a bizarre really rather entertaining coincidence!

Susan – she of the long flaxen hair with whom he had first known complete unabashed consummation. In cold stuffy college bedrooms and subsequently in third-class *pensions* in Paris and Avignon. How closely one's early erotic experience had been interwoven with exploration of Europe. France still evoked Susan. And there she was, the flaxen hair no longer flaxen nor long but a rather attractive corn-colour, cropped short with a wispy fringe. He looked at her again – caught her eye, he thought, and looked hastily at the screen, where his pointer had summoned up *Le Bain Turc*. Oh yes, it was Susan all right – different as she was now. He began to talk about the painting; that ferment of female flesh, suspended there for inspection, seemed suddenly quite pornographic – he found himself almost embarrassed, indicating a breast here, an armpit there. He cut short his disquisition on the ambiguities of the picture and moved on to the next page.

Susan was wearing some smock-like garment. She looked wholesome, just as she had at nineteen, more ripely wholesome but still with that wholemeal-loaf-and-cream-cheese aura that had attracted him then, an intriguing antidote to the glossy lipstick and pencilled eyes of the day. A wonderfully compliant girl, one had often regretted her since, up against more difficult women. An adorable creature. And here she was! She painted still, of course, had had the odd exhibition from time to time in small provincial galleries. He had seen her once fifteen years or so ago at a Burlington House exhibition, and had introduced her to his wife, who asked rather a lot of questions that evening. Susan's presence today was not, when one came to think about it, all that startling. She was, after all, a painter. Still, she hadn't *had* to come. Touching, again. He felt rather glad, now, that Elizabeth had elected to stay at home on the grounds that she had heard the lecture several times before and she got awfully bored at those receptions afterwards full of milling strangers. There could have been more questions asked; Elizabeth's memory for faces was infallible.

His confidence regained, Richard ventured another departure from the script, inviting the audience at rather greater length than usual to consider the cool gaze of Manet's *Olympia* – 'Isn't it somehow at odds with the rest of her? That calculating stare, a bourgeois stare – you expect to see black bombazine below it, not nudity. Her body invites; her face rejects.' He thought he saw Susan's head tilt to one side a fraction, in consideration; he almost smiled. Thus had she listened to his youthful perceptions in the Louvre and the Jeu de Paume.

She would have observed his progress – the appointments, the publications, the chairmanships of this and that, the CBE. As would Valerie and . . . quite a few others. Benign observation, he imagined – there had not been bitter endings, merely movings on, though perhaps it was he who had usually moved first. One really couldn't quite remember now. It was beginnings you remembered – that moment of ripening interest in another woman. When had one first had that heady realisation that there was no end to them, that it was as though you had been let loose in a strawberry bed? It had seemed thus at twenty, and truth to tell one had never really lost that intoxicating sense of possibility. To walk down a crowded street, or to enter a room like this, was still to find oneself scanning with appreciation the wonderful variety of women, in an almost detached way, not necessarily sexual, marvelling simply at that abundance of faces and shapes. Of people. I like women, he thought. I get on with women. And they like me. Sex aside. Of course in the fullness of time one had begun to feel a need for stability, and Elizabeth had come along, but even then . . .

Valerie shifted, crossed her legs, smoothed her skirt. Susan was looking down so that he could no longer see her face. What were *they* thinking? He felt indulgent and a touch sentimental. And amused. What an absurd situation! And how tiresome that one could share it with no one.

He had arrived at Renoir; the screen was filled with the glowing fruity flesh of *baigneuses*, the whole room seemed suffused in reflected colour. He summoned them up one after another – the sloe-eyed biddable girls with their pouting nipples. He himself had reservations, he told the audience, one admired the sensuality, the flow of line, but felt ultimately drenched. All the same, look at them . . . and his pointer flicked at a rump here, a bosom there. They showed themselves off one after another – a play of luscious impervious light upon a sheet of canvas. 'In some ways,' said Richard, 'these women seem to me unreal – idealised creatures, manifestations of the painter's imagination. To utter a heresy – they are a nudge or two away from *Playboy*.' He tapped the pointer to dismiss the Renoir houris, turned back to the audience, and saw Elaine, the mistress of his maturity, sitting in the back row.

No. Impossible. He stared, leaning forward a little. But yes, it was she all right. No mistaking her, even at that distance. The shock struck home and he dropped the pointer. The chairman leapt to pick it up; so did Richard. In the ensuing scramble he had time to cleanse his face of the expression of pure horror. Thank God Elizabeth hadn't come; she and Elaine had overlapped for a time, causing problems. But no sooner had horror given way to a flicker of relief than that was replaced by a surge of awful stomach-shrinking doubt. Just what was going on here? Valerie. Susan. And now Elaine. Elaine sitting there large as life looking young and pretty with her hair done differently and large fashionable specs.

He was finding it difficult to continue. He lost his place, mumbled, improvised, picked up the sense again. The audience rustled, embarrassment transmitting itself. This was more than coincidence. It had to be more than coincidence. But how could it be? They don't know each other. How could they know each other? Of course they know vaguely *of* each other . . . Naturally one had let drop this and that to the current girl about others, women find that slightly titillating and anyway it's natural enough to talk of one's past in all its manifestations, and besides one could hardly appear to be a eunuch, it would be neither truthful nor appealing. Of course one had chatted a bit, probably rather specifically on occasion.

But surely it was inconceivable that they had . . . It was too absurd to think that they . . . Or was it?

He struggled on with the lecture. Words, somehow, came forth. And the thoughts boiled around in his head. They had set this up, somehow, got together and schemed, laughing at him. What a typically, *feminine* thing to do. Like plotting schoolgirls. Let's give Richard the shock of his life. Let's have ourselves a ball. It was so . . . childish . . . that it should just be ignored, except that he couldn't ignore it, stuck up here with them down there goggling at him. And supposing . . . God! – were there any more of them? For a hysterical moment he thought that he was going to discover he had been to bed with every woman in the audience. He stopped talking and took a drink of water. He allowed himself a long pause; he scrutinised the faces in front of him – the distinct and the indistinct. Please God, no more.

There were no more. That was it. And quite enough. He was now in a cold sweat. He had to find a handkerchief and wipe his forehead. He felt the chairman's anxious eye on him. Grimly, he made himself go on with the lecture, turn from text to screen, talk of tonal values and composition, address himself to body after body, an eternity it began to seem of displayed flesh, woman after woman with their curves and dimples and shadows, their strategic wisps of material or concealing hand, their carefully arranged limbs and inscrutable faces.

He did not look again at Valerie. Or at Susan. Or Elaine. He could feel their gaze on him like . . . well, like a bunch of harpies, to put it bluntly. What they were going to do, of course, was descend on him afterwards, at this blasted reception which he could not possibly escape. To which he would be led by the chairman, at which a glass would be put in his hand and the audience, eager to get the rest of its money's worth by way of liquor and conversation, let loose upon him. At which point Valerie, Susan and Elaine would converge upon him, grinning hugely, to feast upon his exposure, the target set up and brought down, the fall guy. What a treat for them. What fun to ring each other up later and have a laugh about it.

He seriously thought, for a few moments, of feigning illness – dropping his papers, putting hand to head, allowing himself to be escorted from the platform and into a taxi. Going home to a loving and solicitous Elizabeth, who would fuss over him and put him to bed with aspirins and hot-water bottles, where he could fall immediately asleep and forget the whole unsettling occasion.

No. Impossible. He hadn't the nerve. Besides . . . He tried to pull himself together – what could they do to him? No one else had any idea of the connection, after all – only he and they knew. No, this was ridiculous, he was playing into their hands getting into a state like this. All he had to do was brave it out, feign imperviousness, appear surprised and friendly if they – if any of them – accosted him.

He delivered the final paragraph of his lecture; the rosy voluptuous girl sprawled on a couch behind his head was extinguished; the lights came on; he acknowledged the applause and was ushered by the chairman down the steps from the platform, out of the door and into the refectory, where waitresses stood about with trays of drinks. The audience surged after them; the room filled up; his attention was required – 'Red or white wine, sir?' 'May I introduce our Provost?' 'Professor Swinton, you don't know me but I just had to say how much I enjoyed . . .'

He looked furtively around. No sign. And then he saw Valerie, ten feet away, talking animatedly. Oh God! Elizabeth should be here, he thought petulantly, I shouldn't have to cope with this sort of thing on my own, Elizabeth should be here to back me up, to help me make discreet apologies and leave. His panic gave way for a few moments to resentment – Elizabeth was not always as supportive as she ought to be – sitting at home with a book or the telly when one was being harassed like this. It was really too bad of her.

Some woman was chuntering on at him about his Watteau book. He kept looking through the crowd at Valerie; all of a sudden she looked back, raised a hand in greeting and went on with her conversation. What was she up to? Planning some sort of shock assault in her own time? He said 'Excuse me' to the Watteau woman and pushed his way to Valerie.

'Hello, Richard. You were awfully rough on poor old Renoir. Do you know John Hailey?'

Her companion began to speak. Richard interrupted, 'I saw you in there. Why did you come?'

Valerie laughed. 'Really! John brought me. I'm afraid I didn't realise who was lecturing till just now.' She was as cool as you like. Laughing at him, no doubt about it. The man must be in it too, whoever he was.

Richard said, 'Susan's here.'

'Susan?'

'Susan Marwood.'

'I'm sorry,' said Valerie. 'Is this someone I should know?'

'Apropos of what you were saying about the Ingrès restoration,' said the man, 'I've always felt myself that . . .'

Richard caught sight of Elaine – a glimpse of that unmistakable profile on the far side of the room. He knew now that the thing was to move first.

Stand around like a dummy while they worked up to whatever it was they had in mind and he was done for. Get in first – that was the thing – wrong-foot them. He turned his back on Valerie and the man, shouldered his way towards Elaine. Someone seized his arm and said, 'Professor Swinton, I've been dying to ask you if . . .' He shooed them off. Elaine had her back to him now, talking to a man he vaguely knew – Walters, that was who, that art critic – and a woman in red. He pushed himself into their group and said, 'Well, Elaine . . .' In a strong, let's-have-no-nonsense voice. And the Elaine-figure turned to him the face of a stranger.

'Ah, Richard,' said Walters. 'We were just rubbishing the Hayward exhibition. Have you seen it?' The not-Elaine person stared at him. The woman in red said, 'Oh, Professor Swinton, you know my brother, I think, Tim Rogers, he was saying only the other day that you . . .'

Richard backed off. He stepped on someone's foot, felt someone's drink slop on his arm. He mumbled something, scattered irritable apologies. Stupid woman. He could have sworn. Spitting image of Elaine, seen from thirty feet off.

The room was packed. He tried to shove his way through, landed up against a colleague who started to introduce someone, sidled this way and that in an attempt to escape, looked at last at the woman who was being offered to him, started to say, 'Yes, how do you do, I'm frightfully sorry but I'm afraid I've got to rush now . . .' – and the woman was Susan.

Except that she was not. She was wearing Susan's smock dress and had Susan's cropped corn-coloured hair but a bland never-seen-before face and irritating affected voice that was now saying how much she'd always wanted to meet and how thrilled she was and she wondered if.

'I'm sorry,' he said, 'I've got to go.' He waved as though acknowledging some summons, turned, got past another group, found himself blocked again. The noise was frightful, the frenzied amplified insect buzz of a party, women's voices predominating and giving it that upper edge that jarred the ear. Everywhere he looked there were mouths opening and shutting showing teeth and tongues, while elbows and backsides and swinging shoulder bags knocked against him as he tried to head for the exit. He edged his way past emphatic thighs, found his arm up against a squashy bosom, smelt the bathroom smell of bodies, that compound of sweat and perfume, thought he would go mad if he was stuck here another minute. And emerged at last into a sparser area. Where there was Valerie again, alone now, sipping her drink, quite at ease, observing him.

She said, 'You look as though you're in the most awful tizz about something.'

'I'm perfectly all right.'

'Well, good,' said Valerie. She put her hand to her mouth, deftly smothering a yawn. 'I must be off. I've lost John. Funny meeting up like this. I got quite a shock when I saw who was giving this lecture.' She grinned. 'Anyway, I enjoyed it. I say, are you sure you're all right? You look knackered.'

'I'm fine,' he snapped. 'You're well yourself, I take it?'

She looked attentively at him. 'Extremely well, thank you, Richard.'

'Good night, then.'

'Good night.'

He plunged into the street. Ten yards along the pavement he realised he had forgotten his raincoat. He turned back. A woman was hurrying away in the opposite direction, the shape of her instantly emotive. He stood on the pavement in the rain staring uncertainly at what seemed to be the retreating figure of his wife.

Black Dog

JOHN CASE came home one summer evening to find his wife huddled in the corner of the sofa with the sitting-room curtains drawn. She said there was a black dog in the garden, looking at her through the window. Her husband put his briefcase in the hall and went outside. There was no dog; a blackbird fled shrieking across the lawn and next door someone was using a mower. He did not see how any dog could get into the garden: the fences at either side were five feet high and there was a wall at the far end. He returned to the house and pointed this out to his wife, who shrugged and continued to sit hunched in the corner of the sofa. He found her there again the next evening and at the weekend she refused to go outside and sat for much of the time watching the window.

The daughters came, big girls with jobs in insurance companies, wardrobes full of bright clothes and twenty-thousand-pound mortgages. They stood over Brenda Case and said she should get out more. She should go to evening classes, they said, join a health club, do a language course, learn upholstery, go jogging, take driving lessons. And Brenda Case sat at the kitchen table and nodded. She quite agreed, it would be a good thing to find a new interest – jogging, upholstery, French; yes, she said, she must pull herself together, and it was indeed up to her in the last resort, they were quite right. When they had gone she drew the sitting-room curtains again and sat on the sofa staring at a magazine they had brought. The magazine was full of recipes the daughters had said she must try; there were huge bright glossy photographs of puddings crested with alpine peaks of cream, of dark glistening casseroles and salads like an artist's palette. The magazine costed each recipe; a four-course dinner for six worked out at £3.89 a head. It also had articles advising her on life insurance, treatment for breast cancer and how to improve her love-making.

John Case became concerned about his wife. She had always been a good housekeeper; now, they began to run out of things. When one evening there was nothing but cold meat and cheese for supper he protested. She said she had not been able to shop because it had rained all day; on rainy days the dog was always outside, waiting for her.

The daughters came again and spoke severely to their mother. They talked to their father separately, in different tones, proposing an autumn holiday in Portugal or the Canaries, a new three-piece for the sitting-room, a musquash coat.

John Case discussed the whole thing with his wife, reasonably. He did this one evening after he had driven the Toyota into the garage, walked over to the front door and found it locked from within. Brenda, opening it, apologised; the dog had been round at the front today, she said, sitting in the middle of the path.

He began by saying lightly that dogs have not been known to stand up on their hind legs and open doors. And in any case, he continued, there is no dog. No dog at all. The dog is something you are imagining. I have asked all the neighbours; nobody has seen a big black dog. Nobody round here owns a big black dog. There is no evidence of a dog. So you must stop going on about this dog because it does not exist. 'What is the matter?' he asked, gently. 'Something must be the matter. Would you like to go away for a holiday? Shall we have the house redecorated?'

Brenda Case listened to him. He was sitting on the sofa, with his back to the window. She sat listening carefully to him and from time to time her eyes strayed from his face to the lawn beyond, in the middle of which the dog sat, its tongue hanging out and its yellow eyes glinting. She said she would go away for a holiday if he wished, and she would be perfectly willing for the house to be redecorated. Her husband talked about travel agents and decorating firms and once he got up and walked over to the window to inspect the condition of the paintwork; the dog, Brenda saw, continued to sit there, its eyes always on her.

They went to Marrakesh for ten days. Men came and turned the kitchen from primrose to eau-de-nil and the hallway from magnolia to parchment. September became October and Brenda Case fetched from the attic a big gnarled walking stick that was a relic of a trip to the Tyrol many years ago; she took this with her every time she went out of the house which nowadays was not often. Inside the house, it was always somewhere near her – its end protruding from under the sofa, or hooked over the arm of her chair.

The daughters shook their tousled heads at their mother, towering over her in their baggy fashionable trousers and their big gay jackets. It's not fair on Dad, they said, can't you see that? You've only got one life, they said sternly, and Brenda Case replied that she realised that, she did indeed. Well then . . . said the daughters, one on each side of her, bigger than her, brighter, louder, always saying what they meant, going straight to the point and no nonsense, competent with income-tax returns and contemptuous of muddle.

When she was alone, Brenda Case kept doors and windows closed at all times. Occasionally, when the dog was not there, she would open the upstairs windows to air the bedrooms and the bathroom; she would stand with the curtains blowing, taking in great gulps and draughts. Downstairs, of course, she could not risk this, because the dog was quite unpredictable; it would be absent all day, and then suddenly there it would be squatting by the fence, or leaning hard up against the patio doors, sprung from nowhere. She would draw the curtains, resigned, or move to another room and endure the knowledge of its presence on the other side of the wall, a few yards away. When it was there she would sit doing nothing, staring straight ahead of her; silent and patient. When it was gone she moved around the house, prepared meals, listened a little to the radio, and sometimes took the old photograph albums from the bottom drawer of the bureau in the sitting-room. In these albums the daughters slowly mutated from swaddled bundles topped with monkey faces and spiky hair to chunky toddlers and then to spindly-limbed little girls in matching pinafores. They played on Cornish beaches or posed on the lawn, holding her hand (that same lawn on which the dog now sat on its hunkers). In the photographs, she looked down at them, smiling, and they gazed up at her or held out objects for her inspection – a flower, a sea-shell. Her husband was also in the photographs; a smaller man than now, it seemed, with a curiously vulnerable look, as though surprised in a moment of privacy. Looking at herself, Brenda saw a pretty young woman who seemed vaguely familiar, like some relative not encountered for many years.

John Case realised that nothing had been changed by Marrakesh and redecorating. He tried putting the walking stick back up in the attic; his wife brought it down again. If he opened the patio doors she would simply close them as soon as he had left the room. Sometimes he saw her looking over his shoulder into the garden with an expression on her face that chilled him. He asked her, one day, what she thought the dog would do if it got into the house; she was silent for a moment and then said quietly she supposed it would eat her.

He said he could not understand, he simply did not understand, what could be wrong. It was not, he said, as though they had a thing to worry about. He gently pointed out that she wanted for nothing. It's not that we have to count the pennies any more, he said, not like in the old days.

'When we were young,' said Brenda Case. 'When the girls were babies.'

'Right. It's not like that now, is it?' He indicated the 24-inch colour TV set, the video, the stereo, the microwave oven, the English Rose fitted kitchen, the bathroom with separate shower. He reminded her of the BUPA membership, the index-linked pension, the shares and dividends. Brenda agreed that it was not, it most certainly was not.

The daughters came with their boyfriends, nicely spoken confident young men in very clean shirts, who talked to Brenda of their work in firms selling computers and Japanese cameras while the girls took John into the garden and discussed their mother.

'The thing is, she's becoming agoraphobic,'

'She thinks she sees this black dog,' said John Case.

'We know,' said the eldest daughter. 'But that, frankly, is neither here nor there. It's a mechanism, simply. A ploy. Like children do. One has to get to the root of it, that's the thing.'

'It's her age,' said the youngest.

'Of course it's her age,' snorted the eldest. 'But it's also her. She was always inclined to be negative, but this is ridiculous.'

'Negative?' said John Case. He tried to remember his wife – his wives – who – one of whom – he could see inside the house, beyond the glass of the patio window, looking out at him from between two young men he barely knew. The reflections of his daughters, his strapping prosperous daughters, were superimposed upon their mother, so that she looked at him through the cerise and orange and yellow of their clothes.

'Negative. A worrier. Look on the bright side, I say, but that's not Mum, is it?'

'I wouldn't have said . . .' he began.

'She's unmotivated,' said the youngest. 'That's the real trouble. No job, no nothing. It's a generation problem, too.'

'I'm trying . . .' their father began.

'We know, Dad, we know. But the thing is, she needs help. This isn't something you can handle all on your own. She'll have to see someone.'

'No way,' said the youngest, 'will we get Mum into therapy.'

'Dad can take her to the surgery,' said the eldest. 'For starters.'

The doctor – the new doctor, there was always a new doctor – was about the same age as her daughters, Brenda Case saw. Once upon a time doctors had been older men, fatherly and reliable. This one was good-looking, in the manner of men in knitting-pattern photographs. He sat looking at her, quite kindly, and she told him how she was feeling. In so far as this was possible.

When she had finished he tapped a pencil on his desk. 'Yes,' he said. 'Yes, I see.' And then he went on, 'There doesn't seem to be any very specific trouble, does there, Mrs Case?'

She agreed.

'How do you think you would define it yourself?'

She thought. At last she said that she supposed there was nothing wrong with her that wasn't wrong with – well, everyone.

'Quite,' said the doctor busily, writing now on his pad. 'That's the sensible way to look at things. So I'm giving you this . . . Three a day . . . Come back and see me in two weeks.'

When she had come out John Case asked to see the doctor for a moment. He explained that he was worried about his wife. The doctor nodded sympathetically. John told the doctor about the black dog, apologetically, and the doctor looked reflective for a moment and then said, 'Your wife is fifty-four.'

John Case agreed. She was indeed fifty-four.

'Exactly,' said the doctor. 'So I think we can take it that with some care and understanding these difficulties will . . . disappear. I've given her something,' he said, confidently; John Case smiled back. That was that.

'It will go away,' said John Case to his wife, firmly. He was not entirely sure what he meant, but it did not do, he felt sure, to be irresolute. She looked at him without expression.

Brenda Case swallowed each day the pills that the doctor had given her. She believed in medicines and doctors, had always found that aspirin cured a headache and used to frequent the surgery with the girls when they were small. She was prepared for a miracle. For the first few days it did seem to her just possible that the dog was growing a little smaller but after a week she realised that it was not. She continued to take the pills and when at the end of a fortnight she told the doctor that there was no change he said that these things took time, one had to be patient. She looked at him, this young man in his swivel chair on the other side of a cluttered desk, and knew that whatever was to be done would not be done by him, or by cheerful yellow pills like children's sweets.

The daughters came, to inspect and admonish. She said that yes, she had seen the doctor again, and yes, she was feeling rather more . . . herself. She showed them the new sewing-machine with many extra attachments that she had not used and when they left she watched them go down the front path to their cars, swinging their bags and shouting at each other, and saw the dog step aside for them, wagging its tail. When they had gone she opened the door again and stood there for a few minutes, looking at it, and the dog, five yards away, looked back, not moving.

The next day she took the shopping trolley and set off for the shops. As she opened the front gate she saw the dog come out from the shadow of the fence but she did not turn back. She continued down the street, although she could feel it behind her, keeping its distance. She spoke in a friendly way to a couple of neighbours, did her shopping and returned to the house, and all the while the dog was there, twenty paces off. As she walked to the front door she could hear the click of its claws on the pavement and had to steel herself so hard not to turn round that when she got inside she was bathed in sweat and shaking all over. When her husband came home that evening he thought her in a funny mood; she asked for a glass of sherry and later she suggested they put a record on instead of watching TV – *West Side Story* or another of those shows they went to years ago.

He was surprised at the change in her. She began to go out daily, and although in the evenings she often appeared to be exhausted, as though she had been climbing mountains instead of walking suburban streets, she was curiously calm. Admittedly, she had not appeared agitated before, but her stillness had not been natural; now, he sensed a difference. When the daughters telephoned he reported their mother's condition and listened to their complacent comments; that stuff usually did the trick, they said, all the medics were using it nowadays, they'd always known Mum would be O.K. soon. But when he put the telephone down and returned to his wife in the sitting-room he found himself looking at her uncomfortably. There was an alertness about her that worried him; later, he thought he heard something outside and went to look. He could see nothing at either the front or the back and his wife continued to read a magazine. When he sat down again she looked across at him with a faint smile.

She had started by meeting its eyes, its yellow eyes. And thus she had learned that she could stop it, halt its patient shadowing of her, leave it sitting on the pavement or the garden path. She began to leave the front door ajar, to open the patio window. She could not say what would happen next, knew only that this was inevitable. She no longer sweated or shook; she did not glance behind her when she was outside, and within she hummed to herself as she moved from room to room.

John Case, returning home on an autumn evening, stepped out of the car and saw light streaming through the open front door. He thought he heard his wife speaking to someone in the house. When he came into the kitchen, though, she was alone. He said, 'The front door was open,' and she replied that she must have left it so by mistake. She was busy with a saucepan at the stove and in the corner of the room, her husband saw, was a large dog basket towards which her glance occasionally strayed.

He made no comment. He went back into the hall, hung up his coat and was startled suddenly by his own face, caught unawares in the mirror by the hatstand and seeming like someone else's – that of a man both older and more burdened than he knew himself to be. He stood staring at it for a few moments and then took a step back towards the kitchen. He could hear the gentle chunking sound of his wife's wooden spoon stirring something in the saucepan and then, he thought, the creak of wicker-work.

He turned sharply and went into the sitting-room. He crossed to the window and looked out. He saw the lawn, blackish in the dusk, disappearing into darkness. He switched on the outside lights and flooded it all with an artificial glow – the grass, the little flight of steps up to the patio and the flower-bed at the top of them, from which he had

tidied away the spent summer annuals at the weekend. The bare earth
was marked all over, he now saw, with what appeared to be animal
footprints, and as he stood gazing it seemed to him that he heard the pad
of paws on the carpet behind him. He stood for a long while before at last
he turned round.